A KILLING RESURRECTED

Also by Frank Smith

The Chief Inspector Paget Mysteries

ACTS OF VENGEANCE
THREAD OF EVIDENCE
CANDLES FOR THE DEAD
STONE DEAD
FATAL FLAW
BREAKING POINT
THE COLD HAND OF MALICE
A KILLING RESURRECTED

Other Novels

DRAGON'S BREATH
THE TRAITOR MASK
DEFECTORS ARE DEAD MEN
CORPSE IN HANDCUFFS
SOUND THE SILENT TRUMPETS

A KILLING RESURRECTED

A DCI Neil Paget Mystery

Frank Smith

This first world edition published 2010
in Great Britain and in the USA by
SEVERN HOUSE PUBLISHERS LTD of
9–15 High Street, Sutton, Surrey, England, SM1 1DF.

British Library Cataloguing in Publication Data

Smith, Frank, 1927–
    A Killing Resurrected. – (A DCI Neil Paget mystery)
    1. Paget, Neil (Fictitious character) – Fiction.
    2. Police – Great Britain – Fiction. 3. Detective and
    mystery stories.
    I. Title II Series
    823.9'14-dc22

ISBN-13: 978-0-7278-6878-7   (cased)

All Severn House titles are printed on acid-free paper.

Severn House Publishers support The Forest Stewardship Council [FSC],
the leading international forest certification organisation. All our titles that
are printed on Greenpeace-approved FSC-certified paper carry the FSC logo.

 **Mixed Sources**
Product group from well-managed
forests and other controlled sources
www.fsc.org Cert no. SA-COC-1565
© 1996 Forest Stewardship Council

Typeset by Palimpsest Book Production Ltd.,
Grangemouth, Stirlingshire, Scotland.
Printed and bound in Great Britain by
MPG Books Ltd., Bodmin, Cornwall.

ONE

Detective Superintendent Thomas Alcott ran a finger around the inside of his collar, but it stuck back to his skin the moment he released it. It had been four days since the stifling heat had settled into the valley, and there was no sign of it shifting. Barely ten o'clock in the morning, but it felt more like high noon in Saudi Arabia. He eyed the open file on his desk with distaste, then pushed it away and sat back in his chair as if trying to distance himself from it.

He should never have agreed to meet with the Hammond woman, he thought irritably. The last thing he needed was some old woman rattling on about a thirteen-year-old case when they could barely keep up with the current ones. He glanced at the time. He'd give her a few minutes, then find an excuse to leave the room and let Paget take over. He was toying with the idea of having Fiona ring him with an urgent message, when Paget appeared in the doorway.

'Morning, Paget,' he said tersely. 'I hope this woman isn't going to be late. God knows we have enough on our plate without digging up old cases. You've read the file, I take it?'

'Enough to get the general picture,' Paget told him. 'But I would like to . . .'

He stopped as Fiona popped her head around the door to say, 'Miss Hammond is here, sir. Shall I show her in?'

Alcott gave a grudging nod and rose to his feet as Fiona opened the door wider and ushered the visitor into the office.

Claire Hammond was younger than Alcott had pictured her when they'd spoken on the phone. Much younger. Thirtyish or thereabouts, he guessed, and *very* attractive. Tall, slim, dark shoulder-length hair, luminous eyes, generous mouth. Smartly dressed and looking remarkably cool, considering they were in the middle of a heat wave. Plain white blouse beneath a pale-blue linen jacket that followed the curve of the waistline; a flowing A-line calf-length skirt in a summery print, and white ankle-strap sandals. Ankle-strap wedges, if he was not mistaken. The Superintendent was by no means an expert when it came to women's clothes, but he had two daughters who were, so, like it or not, he was kept abreast of what was 'in' and what was not, and Claire Hammond was definitely 'in'.

His hand went to his tie to straighten it, and suddenly felt as if he were only half dressed, with his jacket off and his sleeves rolled halfway up his arms.

'I asked Detective Chief Inspector Paget to join us,' he explained as introductions were made and he guided Miss Hammond to a seat, 'because if there is to be any follow-up on what you have to tell us, it will be his responsibility.' He moved back around his desk and sat down. 'Now, you say you have information that appears to connect the suicide of a young man by the name of Barry Grant with the death of two people who were killed during the course of a robbery thirteen years ago. Is that right, Miss Hammond?'

'That's right, Superintendent.'

'And how, exactly, did this information come into your possession?'

Claire opened her handbag and drew out a folded brown envelope, but it remained in her hand while she asked a question of her own. 'Do you remember Jane Grant, Super-intendent?'

'The boy's grandmother? Yes, I do. As a matter of fact, I was thinking about her after I spoke to you on the phone. Poor woman. She took her grandson's death very hard, as I recall.'

'Yes, she did,' Claire agreed, 'and she remembered you from that time, which is why I asked for you when I rang the other day. But she wasn't his grandmother; she was his great aunt. Barry was her sister's grandson. The Grant's adopted him when his mother died in rather tragic circumstances when he was six years old. But the reason I asked was because Jane Grant died last week, and it is because of her that I am here, and if you'll bear with me for a moment, I'll try to make my own position clear.

'You see, we moved into the house next door to the Grants when I was about five years old, and Barry and I more or less grew up together. As you will remember, the Grants had an orchard at the back of their house, and Barry and I used to play there. I became very fond of Aunt Jane – we're not related, but I've always called her that because that was what Barry called her – and despite the difference in our ages, Aunt Jane and I became very close friends over the years. In fact, she treated me more like a daughter than a friend. Even so, I was stunned when I learned last week that she had left everything to me: the house, the orchard, everything, including a letter to me, and these, the letters Barry tried to write before he died.' Claire slid the envelope across the desk towards Alcott.

The Superintendent opened a drawer, took out a pair of latex gloves and pulled them on before touching the envelope. 'You've read the letters, I take it?' he said as he picked up the envelope.

'Of course.'

Alcott nodded absently. There was nothing remarkable about it: plain, brown and unmarked except for the handwritten inscription that simply said: *Claire Hammond*, and creases where it had been folded twice. Inside was a single sheet of A4 paper that smelt faintly of lavender, and a smaller envelope containing several sheets of paper torn from a notebook. Originally crumpled, they had been smoothed out and folded carefully. Alcott held the scented page by the corners, and began to read.

My Dear Claire,

I know it was wrong of me not to tell the police about the letters Barry tried to write to me, but I just couldn't bring myself to do it at the time. I found them all screwed up in the corner beside his bed when I went in to make it that morning, and found it hadn't been slept in. If only he'd talked to me instead of trying to write it down, he might still be with us. I knew something was wrong, but I thought he'd come round in his own good time, so I let him be, but he never did. Just went inside himself the way he used to do when he was little. Barry wasn't a bad boy, not really, you must

know that, Claire. He just wanted everyone to like him,
but he fell in with the wrong crowd and they took advantage. It wasn't all his fault, so I couldn't bear the thought
of having people thinking the worst of him after he
died. I believe him when he says he didn't know what
was happening inside that shop. Oh, Claire, I'm sorry
to burden you with this, but keeping these letters secret
has been on my conscience these past few years, so I
want you to take them to Superintendent Alcott. He
was an inspector when he came to see me when Barry
died, and he was very nice. I don't think he remembered me, but I knew him when he was just a small
boy. His mother and I sang in the same choir for a
number of years, and we were good friends until they
moved away and we lost touch. Please tell him I'm
sorry for what I did, and I hope it's not too late to find
the people who committed that terrible crime and drove
Barry to take his own life.

All my love, and God bless you, Claire,

It was signed, *Aunt Jane.*

Alcott passed a pair of gloves to Paget along with the letter
before turning to the pages in the smaller envelope. They were
undated and unsigned, but as he scanned through them, he
was left with the impression that an attempt had been made
to put them in some sort of order. He returned to what appeared
to be the first one and began to read.

I know I've let you down, Auntie, and I'm sorry, but I
have to tell someone because I don't know what to do.
I was the one who drove the van when Bergman's was
robbed, same as I did for the other robberies at the pub
and that lawyer's house, but I swear on the Bible I didn't
know anyone would get killed. I wasn't even in the shop
when they did it.

I can't face David. Not after what happened. It was
horrible. I feel sick inside all the time, and I know by
the way you keep looking at me you know something is
wrong. If I'd known what they were going to . . .

The next few words had been scratched out, but Alcott felt confident that Forensic would be able to bring them up.

> All I did was get the van for them and keep watch in the lane behind the shop while they went in. I never . . .

More words were crossed out.

> I didn't see David's dad come out of the bakery and go into the back of Bergman's shop until it was too late to warn them. I thought they'd just tie him up like they said they were going to do with Mrs Bergman, but they told me he struggled and pulled one of the masks off, so one of them hit him with the bar and killed him. They said Mrs Bergman started to scream, so they killed her too. But you have to believe me, Auntie, I knew nothing about it until it was all over.
>
> Nobody was supposed to get hurt. It should have been easy like the others, because we knew . . .

More words crossed out . . .

> It started out as a bit of fun, a sort of exercise to prove that it . . .

The letter ended there with the last two lines crossed out and completely illegible – if indeed it was intended to be a letter and not something the boy was rehearsing to tell his aunt. The Superintendent passed the letter over to Paget, and turned to the next page. It repeated much of what had been said before, except this time it seemed to Alcott there was an undercurrent of hysteria as Barry Grant tried to explain to his aunt how he wanted nothing more to do with the others, but wanted to go to the police and try to explain what had happened.

Give me a name, *for God's sake!* Alcott scanned the page, searching for a name, a nickname, anything that might point to an individual, but there was nothing.

> When they came out, they said it was all my fault that it went wrong, because I should have warned them and didn't, so I'd better keep my mouth shut or they would

all swear I was inside with them and I was the one who
panicked and hit David's dad, and I don't know what
to do . . .

The rest was a jumble of words crossed out, ending in three
heavy lines across the bottom of the page, and the word *SHIT!*
scored into the paper with such ferocity that the page was
torn.

The third page was shorter and even less coherent. Whole
sentences were crossed out, and Alcott sensed a rising desperation rather than mere frustration at being unable to find the
right words. The boy was trapped and saw no way out.

'Who else knows about these letters?' he asked Claire.

'To my knowledge, no one. The envelope was sealed when
it was given to me by Aunt Jane's solicitor. He told me she
had given it to him a couple of years ago, with instructions
to hold it until after her death, then give it to me when the
will was read. Aunt Jane didn't tell him what was in it, and
he said he didn't ask.'

Alcott opened the bottom drawer of his desk, took out
several clear plastic bags, and gave them and the remaining
letters to Paget, saying, 'I doubt if Forensic will be able to
find anything of value after all this time, but you never know.'

He turned back to Claire. 'This David he refers to?' he said.
'That would be David Taylor, the son of George Taylor, the
baker who was killed?' Alcott had had Records dig out the
file, now archived, after his conversation with Claire Hammond
on the phone.

Claire nodded. 'That's right, Superintendent,' she said. 'I
wasn't in the country at the time, but I heard about it later,
and I could never understand why they killed Mr Taylor and
Mrs Bergman, but after reading those notes from Barry, it
makes more sense.'

'It does,' Alcott agreed. 'It was a sensational case at the
time, but I wasn't directly involved. The case was handled by
Detective Inspector Rogers, who's retired now. But I was
directly involved with Barry Grant's suicide, and there was
never the slightest reason to connect the death of the Grant
boy to the robberies. They were two completely separate events
as far as we were concerned. You say you grew up with Barry,
and you were a close friend of Mrs Grant, but I don't recall

talking to you at the time. Did any of our people speak to you?'

'No. As I said, I was out of the country, attending a summer arts course in Spain when Barry died. I came back for his funeral, but returned to Madrid the following day. No one so much as mentioned the death of David's father at that time, in fact I didn't hear about it until I returned a month later. But even if they had, there would have been no reason to connect it with Barry's death.'

'Mrs Grant didn't mention it, knowing what she did?'

Claire shook her head. 'She was in shock. Uncle Arnold had died the year before, and she was only just beginning to come to grips with that when Barry killed himself. Now, having read the letters Barry tried to write to her, I realize she must have been absolutely devastated. I could see she was suffering, and I offered to cut my course and stay with her for a while, but she wouldn't hear of it.'

Alcott still looked puzzled. 'But surely some of Barry's friends and yours were at the funeral? Yet you say no one so much as mentioned the burglary?'

Claire shook her head. 'I think that was the saddest part of it all,' she said softly. 'Aunt Jane and I were the only ones there.'

'And she said *nothing* about why she thought Barry had killed himself?'

'No. Except she blamed herself.'

Alcott frowned. 'Why would she do that, when she knew the reason?'

'Aunt Jane felt she'd failed him. She felt it was her fault that he'd turned out the way he did, although God knows she had done everything she possibly could to give Barry a good home. But Barry was a strange boy. He . . .' Claire shrugged and fell silent, seemingly unable to find the words to express her thoughts.

Paget looked up from the letters he held in his hand. 'You say he was a strange boy, Miss Hammond. Would you mind telling us in what way? Because if what Barry Grant is saying in these letters is true, and we reopen the investigation into the deaths of the two people who died during that robbery, the more we know about him and his friends, the better.'

Claire didn't respond immediately, but sat looking down at

her hands, lips pursed, her brow furrowed. 'I find it hard to describe Barry,' she said at last. 'You see, I prefer to remember him as he was when we first came to live next door. He was a year older than me, and I suppose you could say he sort of adopted me.'

Claire smiled as she saw the questioning look on Paget's face. 'It isn't obvious now,' she explained, 'but I was born with a deformed leg, and I had to wear a metal leg brace for several years. It was an ugly thing and, as children will, they picked on me, called me names, and made fun of me. But Barry never did. He was only a year older than me, but he literally took me under his wing when I started school, and he would always walk with me. It was funny, because he was no bigger than I was when I first met him, although he soon filled out with Aunt Jane's cooking, but he was ready to take on the world if necessary.

'And that,' she ended wistfully, 'is the way I prefer to remember Barry, because he changed so much over the years that almost everyone he'd grown up with avoided him – including me, I'm afraid. So when you ask about his friends, all I can tell you is that he knew a lot of people, and I'm sure he regarded many of them as his friends, but I can't think of anyone who would claim Barry as *their* friend.'

'Changed in what way, Miss Hammond?'

'In trying too hard to be liked,' said Claire. 'He couldn't stop acting: acting the fool; putting on a show; doing almost anything to draw attention to himself. He simply *had* to be the centre of attention, and that put people off. He couldn't bear to be excluded from anything. He would attach himself to people, insist on being part of the group even when it was clear to everyone except Barry that he wasn't wanted. He was his own worst enemy in that regard, and I felt sorry for Aunt Jane and Uncle Arnold, because they did everything they could to make him feel loved and wanted in their home, but it still wasn't enough for Barry.'

'You told us earlier that his mother died in tragic circumstances,' Paget said. 'How did he come to live with the Grants? Was there no father? No other relatives?'

Claire became aware of Alcott moving restlessly in his seat as if impatient to be off somewhere. 'It's a long story, and not a very pleasant one,' she said quickly, 'but to give you an idea, I can tell you that Barry's mother, Aunt Jane's niece, was a prostitute who died of an overdose of drugs, and Barry, by all accounts, had a pretty miserable upbringing. There were no other relatives, at least not in England, so the Grants adopted him.'

'Which was very good of them, I'm sure,' Alcott said brusquely, 'but the lad must have had *some* friends, surely? I mean according to what he's written here, he claims to be part of a gang.'

'What about David Taylor?' Paget broke in quickly before Claire could reply. 'Barry speaks of David in these letters as if he were a friend. Was that true?'

Claire smiled wryly as she said, 'When David was about sixteen, his uncle gave him an old broken-down Hillman Minx, and said he could have it if he could get it going and make it roadworthy. There was nowhere near David's home where he could work on it, so he asked Uncle Arnold if he could use the space beside the old shed at the back of the orchard. There was a bench and a vice and all sorts of tools in the shed, and Uncle Arnold let David have the run of the place. David likes to work on his own, he always has, but Barry kept pestering him so much to let him help that finally David gave in, and that was a mistake, because Barry wasn't content with that; he expected David to include him in everything he did. No matter where David went, no matter what he did, Barry would be there, and he kept it up until David went off to Slade. David thought that would be the end of it, but it wasn't. When he came back to work in the bakery during the summer break, there was Barry once again, cocky as ever, ready to pick up where he thought they'd left off.'

'I remember David Taylor,' Alcott said. 'He was one of the boys I spoke to at the time of Barry's suicide. He worked for his father, I believe. Did he stay with the business after his father died?'

Claire shook her head. 'No. He stayed on until the end of summer, then left to continue his studies in art at Slade. But he still lives here. He owns the Brush and Palette art shop in Sheep Lane. We work together occasionally.'

'Your work being . . .?'

'I'm a designer and interior decorator. Small businesses, mainly, banks, shops, offices and private homes. David is an

excellent artist, and he's been a great help to me on some of
the bigger jobs. I did the overall design and interior decor-
ating, but he did that big mural in the town hall last year.'

Alcott was impressed, and was about to say so when Paget
asked a question. 'Do you believe Barry when he says in his
letter that he had no hand in the killing of those two people,
Miss Hammond?'

'Yes, I do,' she said firmly.

'Why?'

'Barry was great on bravado, but it was all show. I could
be wrong, but I think Barry was scared to death most of the
time.'

'Scared? Of what?'

'Of not being accepted. Not belonging. Of failure.'

'But why kill himself if he was innocent?'

'That, I don't know,' said Claire. 'Perhaps he felt he'd been
backed into a corner and couldn't see a way out. I've read
those letters over and over again, and I think Barry had come
to the end of the line. He was in over his head, running with
a bunch of people who were quite obviously prepared to go
to any lengths to protect themselves. They used him. People
did that to him all the time. They took advantage of the fact
that he was prepared to do almost anything to be liked and
accepted, which may be how he came to be involved in the
robberies in the first place. He loved cars, so I believe him
when he says he was just the driver. The others probably
wouldn't trust him with anything else, and when they said
they'd swear it was he who did the killings if he didn't keep
his mouth shut, he must have felt trapped.'

Paget looked perplexed. 'I don't understand,' he said. 'If,
as he says, they were prepared to swear that he was directly
involved in the killings, why doesn't he give their names?
From what you've told us, it sounds as if you knew Barry as
well or better than most, so while these people may not have
been friends in the strictest sense of the word, surely you must
have known who some of them were?'

But Claire was shaking her head. 'Once Barry left Gordon
Street and went on to Westonleigh Secondary, I saw very little
of him,' she said.

'Even though you were living next door to the Grants?'
Paget persisted.

A flicker of irritation crossed Claire's face. 'I think it was simply time for both of us to move on,' she said. 'I suppose it was the end of our childhood in a sense. Barry became so involved with impressing his new-found friends at Westonleigh, that he spent very little time at home from then on. From there, he went on to Leeds University to take Mechanical Engineering, while I went to York on a scholarship, so we only ran into each other again on rare occasions.'

'I'd like to go back to David Taylor,' Paget said. 'Barry says in one of the letters that David's father pulled a mask off one of the thieves, and that was why he was killed. He goes on to say he couldn't face David after what happened, but that is something that can be taken two ways. Is it possible that the reason Barry Grant stopped short of naming names was because he couldn't bring himself to turn on someone he considered to be his friend?'

Claire stared at Paget. 'You're accusing *David*?' she said. Her voice rose. 'Of killing his own *father*?'

'I'm not accusing anyone of anything,' he said. 'I'm simply looking at possibilities. You know these people better than I do. All I'm asking is, do you think that's possible?'

'Absolutely not!' Claire said icily. 'I think I know David pretty well, and there is no way he would have been involved in such a terrible crime.'

Claire Hammond had gone. Alcott, who had risen to usher her out, returned to his seat. 'So what do you think?' he asked. 'Was young Grant telling the truth about those murders? Or did he actually kill those people, then try to put together a story to tell his aunt?'

'Judging by the writing, I'd say he was telling the truth or at least trying to,' Paget told him. 'But whether he was or not, we can't ignore this new evidence, although to be honest I don't relish the idea of opening up a thirteen-year-old case. Memories fade, witnesses move. It won't be easy.'

'What about Miss Hammond herself?' Alcott said. 'She seems to be a no-nonsense sort of woman, but I'm not convinced she was telling the truth when she said she didn't know who Barry's friends were?'

'I don't know about that,' said Paget, 'but she did react quite strongly when I asked if she thought it possible that

David Taylor was involved in the robbery, which makes me
wonder about their relationship.'

'She did seem a bit touchy on the subject,' Alcott agreed,
'but perhaps she's been asking herself that same question after
reading young Grant's letters. At least it could be a place to
start – with Taylor, I mean. If nothing else, he might know
who Grant's friends were back then.' He nudged the file in
Paget's direction.

But Paget made no move to pick it up. 'I think I'm going
to need more than that,' he said, 'and since you were person-
ally involved at the time, I might as well begin right here with
you. What can you tell me about Barry Grant's death? Was
there any doubt in your mind that it *was* suicide?'

'None whatsoever,' Alcott said. 'As far as I was concerned,
sad as it was, young Grant was just another unhappy teenager
who topped himself, and although we found no note, there
was nothing suspicious about the death. Nor was there any
suggestion that the lad was involved in any way with these
robberies, or in any criminal activities for that matter.

'As for the robberies themselves, the two earlier ones Barry
refers to were done by the same gang of four masked men
wearing loose-fitting black clothing, and they did all their
communicating by using flash cards. They never spoke the
whole time the robberies took place. They struck late at night
and got away clean.

'The Bergman robbery was completely different. It took
place in broad daylight, and if it hadn't been for a couple of
flash cards they left behind in their hurry to get away, we
might never have connected it to the two earlier jobs. They
got clean away with something like thirty or forty thousand
in cash, gold, and jewellery – I don't remember the figure
exactly, but, to my knowledge, none of it ever turned up –
and they were never heard of again. All three robberies were
investigated, as I said, by Jack Rogers, so if you need more,
I suggest you talk to him.'

'And the suicide?' Paget prompted.

'As I told you, I investigated that myself,' said Alcott. 'Barry
Grant, nineteen years old, killed himself with a sawn-off
shotgun in the packing shed at the back of the house. There
was no note, and no one seemed to know why he did it, but
neither was there any reason to suspect foul play. The thing

I remember most vividly is the trouble the boy took to kill himself. He used an old shotgun that belonged to his uncle, but found it too long to reach the trigger when he turned it on himself, so he used a hacksaw to cut it down. The sawn-off barrels were there on the bench, along with the hacksaw. Stuck the gun under his chin and pulled both triggers. Took most of his head off.'

Alcott's mouth drew down in a hard line. 'It was not a pleasant sight, I can tell you, and what made it all the worse was it was Mrs Grant who found him. Poor woman was beside herself.'

'After she discovered his bed hadn't been slept in, according to her letter to Claire Hammond,' Paget said. 'So when did Barry actually die?'

'The pathologist put it at somewhere between one and two o'clock in the morning, as I recall.'

'Didn't anyone hear the shot? If he used both barrels, it must have been pretty loud. Surely someone would have heard it?'

Alcott shook his head. 'He was inside the shed with the doors and windows closed, and it was some distance from the house and the nearest neighbours. Just about everyone within hearing range would be asleep. In any case, no one admitted to hearing anything that sounded like a shot.'

'And this happened just a few days after Bergman's was robbed, and two people were killed?'

Alcott sat forward, palms flat on his desk, preparing to rise. 'Bergman's was hit on the Saturday morning,' he said tersely, 'and Barry Grant killed himself on the following Monday. But as I said, there was absolutely nothing to connect the two events.' He rose to his feet. 'Read the files, then go and talk to Rogers himself. He retired to somewhere near Manchester. Pensions will have his address, so—'

He was interrupted by the familiar rap of Fiona's knuckles on the door as she opened it and entered the room. 'Sorry to interrupt, Mr Alcott,' she said, 'but it's Dr Miller. He's on the phone, and he says he needs to speak to you right away. I told him you were in a meeting, but he insists on talking to you.'

'Miller?' Alcott's brow furrowed as he peered at Paget as if expecting him to explain why his doctor wanted to talk to him so urgently, then shrugged and picked up the phone.

'I'll be outside,' said Paget quietly as he rose and followed
Fiona from the room. The secretary flicked a worried glance
in Paget's direction. She looked as if she wanted to say something, but she remained silent as she took her seat behind the
desk.

'It's probably none of my business,' said Paget, 'but is something wrong, Fiona?' He nodded towards the door.

Fiona frowned. 'Not that I know of,' she said, 'but I've
spoken to Dr Miller before, and I've never heard him sound
quite like that. He's usually very polite.'

'But not this time?'

'Well, he wasn't rude,' Fiona conceded, 'but he was certainly
brusque, and he was very insistent on talking to Mr Alcott
immediately! He made that very clear. It's just . . .'

Her words were cut off as Alcott's door swung back and
he came out of the office, one arm in the air as he struggled
into his jacket. 'It's Marion,' he said. 'I knew she had a doctor's
appointment this morning, but she said it was just to get some
more tablets for her cough. But Miller tells me he's put her
in the hospital. Sent her over in an ambulance.'

'Oh, I am sorry,' Fiona said. 'Did he say what was wrong?'

Alcott looked puzzled. 'Can't think what's come over the
man,' he said. 'All he would say was that Marion wasn't in
any immediate danger, but he refused to say more on the phone.
Simply told me to meet him at the hospital, and hung up.'

He turned to Paget. 'I have to go,' he said, 'but I want you
to get started on this case immediately. Go and see Rogers. I
know he'll be glad to help if he can. He'll want to see these
killers caught and punished.' Alcott fished a packet of cigarettes
from his pocket, stuck one in his mouth and lit it. 'No need to
look at me like that,' he told Fiona sharply. 'I'll be out of the
building in thirty seconds, so there's not much point in calling
the anti-smoking police, is there?'

'Has his wife been ill?' asked Paget as Alcott strode away.

'Not that I know of, and I'm sure I would have heard.'
Fiona's motherly features showed concern. 'But it doesn't
sound good if Dr Miller sent her to hospital in an ambulance.'

TWO

Detective Sergeant John Tregalles checked the reference number of the files once more to make sure he had them all before settling himself in his seat. This was not the way he had intended to spend the afternoon, stuck here in the office, with the temperature hovering close to thirty-three degrees, sorting through ancient files, when he could have been out there at the Westhill Golf and Country Club, talking to members about the petty thievery going on out there. He'd been looking forward to that, but Paget had sent Molly Forsythe out there instead, and he was stuck with this lot.

He opened the first file.

Jack Rogers had led the investigation. A bit rough around the edges, was Jack – a bit *too* rough at times for some of the top brass, which may have had something to do with the inspector's early retirement – but he got results. Usually, that was, but not in this case. Without evidence, without witnesses, and without so much as a whisper from the usually reliable sources on the street, even Rogers had found himself stumped.

Paget seemed to think that this new information might lead to some sort of breakthrough, but Tregalles had his doubts. Thirteen years was a long time, and judging by his own recollection of events compared to what he had just read, it showed just how unreliable one's memory could be.

The first robbery had taken place on Tuesday, January 2nd, when four men, wearing dark clothing and ski masks, burst into the living quarters of the Rose and Crown in Beggars Lane, one of the oldest and certainly one of the most popular pubs in Broadminster. The landlord, a man named Thomas Grady, and his eighteen-year-old daughter, Sharon, were in the kitchen at the rear of the premises, counting and recording the takings from the previous evening, when the men entered by the unlocked back door. Grady, sitting with his back to the door, had told Rogers that the men were inside before he'd had a chance to turn round. In fact, he said, it was the sound of crockery, swept from the Welsh dresser beside the door, smashing on the tiled floor that first alerted him. He said he'd started to his feet, but they slammed him back into his chair and slapped tape over his mouth, while a third man pulled Sharon out of her chair and taped her mouth, then continued to hold her.

And it had all taken place without a word being uttered.

Grady said one of the men behind him had slid a metal bar beneath his chin and gripped it on both sides, forcing his head back against the top of his chair, half choking him, and he had the bruises to prove it. The man who appeared to be the leader took a white card from his pocket and held it up for Grady to see. The words on it were printed in bold capitals. They read:

DO AS YOU ARE TOLD AND NO ONE WILL BE HURT
OPEN THE SAFE

When Grady had shaken his head, his statement said, the man behind him shoved his head down on the table, then slammed the bar down so hard beside it that he'd felt it brush his hair. 'Then they all started doing it,' he said, 'smashing those bars down like they was beating a drum. They hit the table so hard that the tray from the till flew off the table, and coins and notes were scattered all over the floor. You only have to look at what they did to the table to see what I mean. I don't mind telling you, I was so shit scared I gave them the combination. God knows I didn't want to. We had the takings right from the Friday night through New Year's Eve and New Year's Day, and I'm sure those bastards knew that.'

'You say you gave them the combination. Who opened the safe?'

'I did. He made me do it.'

'Did he *tell* you to do it?'

'I *told* you, they never spoke, not once,' Grady said, and went on to say that one of the men had hauled him out of his chair and led him to the safe. 'They had gloves on, leather ones, and the bloke beside me kept smacking the iron bar in the palm of his hand like he was beating a drum. He didn't say anything. He didn't have to, because I had a bloody good idea about what would happen if I refused to cooperate.'

Using hand signals, the leader had made Grady take the cash from the safe and put it in a cloth bag, then he'd held the bag open and pointed to the money on the table and on the floor.

'The one who had hold of Sharon made it very clear that she would be hurt if I didn't do what they wanted,' Grady continued, 'so I got down on my hands and knees and scooped that money into the bag as fast as I could. I'm not easily scared, but those bastards had me going, and with Sharon there I wasn't going to take any chances. All I wanted by that time was for the two of us to come out alive.'

When asked for descriptions, neither Grady nor his daughter could come up with anything worth circulating. 'It was hard to tell with them all dressed in black and the clothes being so baggy and all,' Grady told Rogers.

The inspector had tried another tack. 'You're a fairly big man,' he said, 'yet you say you were hauled out of your chair by the man behind you. Was he bigger than you? Was he particularly strong? Did you notice any smell? Tobacco? After-shave? Body odour? Anything at all?'

'The way he was using that iron bar, the bugger didn't need to be strong,' the landlord growled. 'One tug on my collar, and I got the message. Sorry, but I can't tell you more than that – except they had a car waiting.'

'Colour? Make? Registration?' Rogers had asked, and was told that neither Grady nor his daughter had actually *seen* the car; they were too shaken to go to the door until they were sure the men had gone.

Sharon had said it had sounded more like a van to her. 'Heavier motor, more like my boyfriend's van.'

Rogers had taken the reference literally and checked on the boyfriend, but he'd been working that night, and had an airtight alibi. Several days later, the burnt-out remains of a van, reported missing the night before the robbery, was found in a gully on a piece of wasteland on the Welsh border. Forensic had it for a week, but found nothing to connect it to the robbery.

Nothing more had been heard of the gang in the months that followed, and the general feeling by midsummer was that the robbery had been a one-off, probably prompted by someone learning that the money taken over the holiday weekend wouldn't be banked until the following Tuesday. So, with no further activity and with no new evidence to go on, the case was quietly shelved and more or less forgotten.

Until shortly after one o'clock on a Saturday morning in July, when four men, dressed in black, baggy clothes, wearing ski masks, and each carrying a short iron bar, burst into the home of a local solicitor, where he and a small group of business friends were enjoying their weekly poker game. The stakes weren't large by some standards, but there could be chips worth several hundred pounds on the table at any given time, and the rule of the house was that all bets had to be settled in cash at the end of the evening.

Four men and one woman were at the table: Walter Roach, the host of the weekly card game; Paul Preston, owner of a leasing company dealing in heavy earth-moving equipment; Roy Appleyard, who owned a plumbing business; Alice Nelson, owner-manager of the Broadminster Volvo dealership; and Dr Gerald Warden one of the partners in the Broadminster Medical Clinic.

As before, the gang moved in fast, demonstrating with one swift blow to the front of an antique bookcase that they meant business. Two of them hauled Alice from her seat, slapped tape over her mouth, then sat her down again, while the other two laid their weapons against the neck of Roach and Appleyard as a warning. Once again, not a word was spoken.

Directed by flash cards, the players were told that no one would be hurt if they did as they were told. If they resisted, the woman would be the first to be hurt. To demonstrate, one of the men forced Alice's hand on to the table, then slammed his weapon down within inches of her fingers. 'And then,' Roach told Rogers, 'they all joined in, slamming their weapons on the table with such force that chips were flying everywhere.

'It was unnerving,' he said. 'Utterly and completely unnerving, which was the intent, of course, because I don't think any of us doubted that they would carry out their threat if we tried to resist.'

Again by using cards, the players were told to empty their wallets of cash – nothing else – and to drop the money into a cloth bag that was being passed around. Then they were told to turn their pockets inside out, and Alice's handbag was emptied. The amount alleged to have been taken that night was just short of five thousand pounds.

The phone in the room was ripped from the wall. Mobile phones were taken from Roach and Warden, to be found later by the police in the shrubbery part way down the drive.

'Still using the cards,' Roach said, 'they told us to lie on our faces under the table, and that was the way they left us. I got to the door as fast as I could when I heard a car leave, but they were gone by the time I got there.

'They were very deliberate in the way they went about things,' Roach continued. 'Clearly they knew there was no one else in the house and they wouldn't be disturbed, and the fact that one of the cards referred to "the woman", referring to Alice Nelson, tells me they knew exactly who would be there that night.'

It came as no surprise to Rogers, when he asked each player for a description of the thieves, they all said the same thing: the men were all roughly the same height and size, but it was hard to tell because they all wore dark, loose-fitting clothing, and their faces were covered by black ski masks. 'They even wore black trainers,' one of the players told him. Under 'Description', Rogers had dutifully recorded their statements, but had scrawled TBU in the margin, translated by those who knew him as Totally Bloody Useless.

There could be little doubt that the two robberies had been done by the same gang, but the question was: why now? And why were the robberies more than six months apart?

Other than taking part in the initial door-to-door enquiries, Tregalles, a uniformed Constable at that time, hadn't been involved in the investigation itself, but reading through the transcripts now it became clear that Rogers suspected an inside job. The fact that the gang had known ahead of time that a woman would be at the table was enough to make the inspector wonder if the robbery had been arranged by one of the players – perhaps someone who had lost a great deal of money and wanted to get it back. But an exhaustive check into their backgrounds failed to show that any of the players were in financial difficulty.

A van, stolen the night before the robbery, and assumed to be the one used by the thieves, was found abandoned in a quiet country lane in the early hours of the following morning.

It had been doused in petrol and set on fire. Once again, Forensic had hauled in the charred remains, examined them and issued a report but it, too, in Rogers' words, was TBU.

Tregalles picked up the Bergman file.

The call to the police by a barely coherent Sam Bergman had come in at 10.09 on a Saturday morning. He told them that his wife, Emily, and George Taylor, a baker from the shop next door, had been killed in his shop.

The first policeman on the scene arrived at 10.18, and he had called immediately for assistance.

Bergman, a jeweller and goldsmith, told police that he and his wife, Emily, always arrived at their shop in Bridge Street at eight thirty each morning except Sunday, in order to vacuum the carpets, clean and polish the display cases, and enter the previous day's sales in the books. They would also take particularly valuable pieces from the safe for display, and generally get ready for the opening of business at ten o'clock.

At nine thirty, it was Bergman's habit to leave the shop by the back door, which, he said, his wife always bolted after him, and walk down the lane to the café on the corner, where he would join a number of other businessmen for their morning chat before starting business for the day. At ten o'clock, he would return to the shop, entering by the back door. When asked how he would do that if the door was bolted on the inside, he said he always gave a coded knock so his wife would know it was him, and she would let him in. It was a simple system that had worked for years, he said. As for the burglar alarm, he'd told the inspector that he always switched it off when he and his wife arrived each morning, and he didn't switch the CCTV camera on until opening time at ten.

Idiot! Rogers had pencilled in beside this statement.

Sam Bergman told Rogers that he had seen nothing untoward in the lane when he had left the shop, and knew nothing about what had taken place until he returned at ten o'clock and saw his wife and George Taylor lying on the floor in a pool of blood. One of the display cases had been smashed, the safe was open, someone had been sick on the floor, and there was a scattering of rings and other items of jewellery trodden into the carpet.

In answer to Rogers' question as to why George Taylor would have been in the shop, Bergman told him that

Taylor sometimes called in and they would walk down to the café on the corner together. He said no one was particularly concerned when Taylor failed to appear for coffee that morning; they simply assumed that the demands of his business wouldn't allow him to get away, which was sometimes the case.

It was at that point, according to Rogers' notes, that Bergman had collapsed. Fearing delayed shock, Rogers had called an ambulance and had the jeweller taken to hospital. But Bergman had refused to go until he'd made sure that Loretta Thompson, his part-time assistant, could be contacted and brought in to help determine exactly what had been taken by the thieves. 'She keeps the records, so she'll know,' he told Rogers.

Tregalles flipped through the pages to the formal interview that had taken place in Charter Lane the following Tuesday.

Loretta Thompson and her husband, both chartered accountants, had run a small but successful business from their home for a number of years, but when her husband was killed in a road accident, business had fallen off to the point where Loretta had been forced to look for work to supplement her income.

'It seems that some of our clients were quite happy with my work while Ted was there,' she explained, 'but they weren't willing to trust a mere woman on her own. My father was a jeweller, so I had some knowledge of the business, and when Emily mentioned that they were spending far too much time on paperwork and keeping track of inventory, I offered my services on a part-time basis, and I've been working for the Bergmans now for five years.'

She'd estimated the loss to be about £42,000. About £12,000 of that was in cash, but both Bergman and his wife were goldsmiths by trade, and the rest was made up of sheet gold, gold wire, wafers, and settings, as well as silver bars, rings, bracelets, earrings, pendants, and miscellan-eous precious stones.

'It is only an estimate,' she told Rogers, 'but I've been over it carefully, and I don't think it will be far out. I can give you a more accurate figure when I do a complete inventory, which will have to be done for insurance purposes anyway. It's a lot of money, but it could have been worse, because they missed some very valuable pieces.'

The gold and silver, Loretta explained, were used by Bergman and his wife in repair and custom work. 'Mr Bergman does most of the custom-made rings, although he'll do special orders such as crosses and settings for pendants and brooches from scratch – he's very good on design – while Mrs Bergman did mostly bracelets and repair work. In fact we are rather low on gold at the moment, but it still amounts to quite a lot of money at today's prices.'

The crime scene, both in the shop and outside in the alley, were subjected to the closest forensic examination, but there was little to go on in the way of physical evidence: a few black threads caught on the door latch; a partial bloodstained footprint made by someone wearing trainers; and a patch of regurgitated breakfast on the carpet.

Three days later, a dark blue van, reported stolen two days before the robbery, was found, still smouldering, in Collier's Wood, a reforested area on the site of a strip mine abandoned in the early 1900s.

It was clear from DI Rogers' notes that he'd been convinced that all three jobs had been done by the same gang of four despite the obvious differences. While others cited the differences, Rogers concentrated on the similarities, such as the vans stolen just before the robberies, and destroyed by fire in remote locations afterwards. And, of course, there were the flash cards, dropped apparently in their hurry to leave after the killings. When shown to those involved in the earlier robberies, they all agreed they were identical to the ones they'd seen. But the clincher, as far as Rogers was concerned, was that the indentations left behind on the tables in the first two robberies, and those on the counter in the jewellery shop, were also identical according to Forensic.

Rogers had been right, Tregalles thought as he closed the file, and now the notes Barry Grant had left behind confirmed it. But if evidence had been hard to find thirteen years ago, what were the chances of finding anything now?

'Well, what do you make of it, Tregalles?' Paget asked. 'It seems to me that DI Rogers was right in linking the three robberies, and the letters left behind by Barry Grant confirms it. As to what actually happened inside the jewellery shop, Grant only knows what he was told, unless, of course, he was lying, and he *was* inside the shop. On the other hand, it seems unlikely to me that he would lie about that when he was contemplating suicide.' He frowned. 'Unless the motive wasn't robbery at all, but murder.'

'You're thinking Mrs Bergman could have been the intended victim?' Tregalles said. 'And Taylor just happened to blunder in at the wrong time? Come to that, we don't know for certain who died first, do we? I mean, Mrs Bergman could have been dead before Taylor came on the scene.' He shook his head. 'No, I can't buy that,' he said, answering his own question. 'I can't see a gang like that doing a contract killing. Not four or five of them, when one man could do the same job and still make it look like a robbery gone wrong.'

'Well, at least one thing is certain,' said Paget briskly. 'We're not going to resolve anything sitting around here. So, I want you to get things started here first thing tomorrow morning, while I take a run up to Manchester to have a chat with Rogers.'

'What's the matter with Marion Alcott?' Grace asked when they were sitting down to dinner later that evening. 'Have you heard any more since I talked to you at lunchtime?'

Paget shook his head. 'Haven't heard a thing,' he told her, 'but I thought I'd give Alcott a ring later on this evening after visiting hours.'

'Have you ever met his wife?'

'Just once, and then only briefly.'

'What's she like?'

'Hard to say. I don't think we exchanged more than half-a-dozen words at the time. She's small and quite a dainty sort of woman. Not quite what I'd expected Alcott's wife to be.'

'Dainty?' Grace eyed Paget quizzically.

'Well, small features, small hands. Head came up to my shoulder. I suppose you'd call her petite. She struck me as a quiet, retiring sort of woman.'

'And you were expecting someone more like the super-intendent himself, I suppose?'

'No, not exactly. I'm not sure what I thought,' he admitted, 'but I know I was surprised when I met her.' He took a sip of wine. 'Gentle,' he said quietly. 'She struck me as a gentle person. I hope she's going to be all right.'

THREE

David Taylor had his hands in soapy water, trying to scrape away a layer of burnt cheese in the bottom of a saucepan, when the bell rang. He ignored it and continued to scrub. He wasn't expecting anyone, so it was probably kids. A small gang of them roamed the neighbourhood at night, none of them above the age of eleven or twelve, and they did that sort of thing for fun. The bell rang again insistently. Not kids, then. He dried his hands and went to the top of the stairs. The bell rang again.

'Coming,' he shouted as he clattered down the narrow stairway and opened the door. 'Claire?' he said, surprised, then frowned. 'Have I forgotten something?' He searched his memory. 'Should I be expecting you?'

Claire smiled and shook her head. David could be a little vague about appointments, but not this time. 'No, but perhaps I should have telephoned before descending on you,' she said apologetically as she eyed his rolled-up sleeves. 'Are you in the middle of something?'

'Yes, I am as a matter of fact. You any good at scraping burnt cheese off pots?'

'Is that what I can smell?'

He nodded. 'Left it on the stove too long. I was playing around with some sketches and completely forgot about it. Anyway, come on up. I've opened the windows, so it doesn't smell too bad up there.'

Claire followed him up the stairs and to the flat above the shop, a ten-by-ten foot living room, galley kitchen, minuscule bathroom, and a bedroom that was little more than an over-sized closet.

'At least I was able to keep the shop,' he'd told her not long after the divorce. 'And it's not as if I spend much time up here. Lucille got the house, which was what she wanted, then sold it when she and Ray decided to move out to Grandview. But it worked out all right, because she split the proceeds with me and we're still friends.'

David lifted his head and sniffed. 'It *is* a bit strong, isn't it?' he said hesitantly. 'Would you rather go down into the shop?'

'No, this is fine,' Claire told him. 'I can stand it if you can, and I shan't be staying long.'

'Well, at least take off your coat and sit down. I'm sure you have time for a cup of tea. I could use one myself. Throat's as dry as a bone.' He went to the sink and began to fill the electric kettle.

'Thank you.' Claire shrugged out of her coat and draped it across the back of a chair before sitting down at the table.

David plugged the kettle in. 'So, what brings you here?' he asked as he, too, sat down. 'Another job?'

Claire shook her head. 'Sorry, David, although I think I might have a sale for that evening seascape if all goes well. I know the perfect place for it in a home I'm doing in Uplands, and money wouldn't be a problem. I should be able to let you know by the end of next week.'

'But that's not what you came to tell me?'

'No.' Claire fell silent, brow furrowed as she searched for a way to begin.

'So, what's the problem?'

'It's not a problem – at least, I hope it doesn't turn into one, but I came to warn you that you might be getting a visit from the police in the near future.'

'The police? Are you serious? What on earth would the police want with me? My MOT is up to date, at least I think it is, and I haven't parked on any double lines lately, so what am I supposed to have done?'

'Nothing that I know of, David, but I am serious, and I suppose the best way to explain how you come into it is to start at the beginning. You know, of course, about Aunt Jane leaving me the house and everything, but what you don't know is that she left me something else as well. Some letters Barry Grant wrote before he committed suicide.'

Taylor frowned but remained silent, waiting for her to go on.

'You see, it seems that Barry was involved in the robbery in Bergman's shop when your father was killed. Not that he was actually *in* the shop when it happened,' she hastened to explain, 'but he was outside in the back lane. He drove the getaway van.'

Taylor's expression hardened as Claire went on to tell him in some detail about Jane Grant's letter to her, and the letter Barry had tried to write to Jane Grant before taking his own life. 'The police have the letters, now,' she concluded, 'and they've assured me that the case will be reopened. The trouble is –' Claire grimaced guiltily – 'I'm not at all sure that Chief Inspector Paget got hold of the right end of the stick.'

'In what way?'

'He'd been asking me about Barry's background, and I happened to mention that you and he had worked together on that old Hillman one summer. I was trying to point out that you had been a good influence on him, keeping him occupied and out of trouble, but Chief Inspector Paget seized on that and sort of turned it around.'

Taylor's eyes were steady on her face as he said, 'Go on.'

'Well, Barry said in one of his letters, that he couldn't face you after what happened to your father, and the next thing I knew, I was being asked how close you and Barry were, and if I thought it possible that you could have been involved in the robbery, and you were the person your father unmasked.'

Taylor stared at her. 'Are you telling me that this policeman is suggesting that *I* was the one who killed my own *father*?' he demanded hoarsely. 'Based on some letters Barry Grant wrote before he killed himself? You know as well as I do that Barry was a nutter, and you never could believe anything he told you. For God's sake, Claire . . .' Words failed him.

The kettle began to bubble, but he ignored it.

Claire shook her head. 'That is *not* what I said,' she told him firmly. 'What I said was, Barry mentioned you in the letter in such a way that it could have been taken more than one way. I'm sure he didn't mean it that way, but it is a bit ambiguous, and all the Chief Inspector was asking was whether I thought it *possible* that it could have been you your father unmasked, and I told him absolutely not.'

'Well, thanks a lot for that much,' Taylor said ungraciously as he shoved his chair back and left the table to unplug the kettle and make the tea. His face was grim when he returned. He placed both hands on the table and looked down at her. 'You say Barry admitted to being involved in the robbery, but insists he wasn't inside with the others when Dad was killed.

But how do we know that's true? Barry never took the blame for anything in his life. Nothing was ever his fault. You should know, Claire; you grew up with him. What if it was *Barry* my father recognized, and Barry panicked? Isn't that more likely to be the reason why he said he couldn't face me?'

Claire rose to her feet. 'Look, David,' she said quietly, 'I'm only telling you my impression of what the Chief Inspector *might* be thinking, and to be fair, I suppose he has to look at every possibility. No doubt they'll come round to talk to you, but when they find out that they're wrong, they'll look for others who were Barry's friends at the time. I came to let you know what's happening, that's all, so please don't blame me for the way the police think or go about their work.'

But Taylor wasn't listening as he began to pace within the narrow confines of the room. 'The thing is, we weren't even friends when all this happened,' he said. 'In fact we never were what you could call *friends*. I only let him work on the car with me because his uncle was letting me work there and use his tools for nothing. But to put it bluntly, he was a pain in the arse, always wanting to take the shortcuts, impatient to get the car on the road no matter what condition it was in.'

He stopped in front of Claire. 'Barry and I parted company long before Dad was killed,' he said. 'In fact I rarely saw him after that summer, and when I did see him coming, I did my best to avoid him. He seemed to think that because I'd let him work on the car when we were kids, it made us friends for life. He was like a damned leech, always wanting to attach himself to me.'

'Now that is unfair, David. Barry looked up to you; he respected you, and he loved working with you on that old car. I remember how he dragged me over there one day to show me the car, and he introduced you as his best friend.'

Taylor grimaced and shook his head. 'I remember,' he said grimly, 'and he may have thought that, but I certainly didn't. As I said, the only reason I let him anywhere near that car was because I felt I owed his uncle that much for letting me use the shed and tools, but to be brutally honest, I was glad to see the back of Barry Grant when he went back to school. Even then, he kept coming back almost every weekend, and I had to put up with him until the car was finished. After that, as I said, I rarely saw him. I was away at school myself that winter, and when I did come back I did my best to avoid him. The trouble was, Claire, Barry always came on too strong, and he drove people away. You know what he was like, and if it comes to that, you were closer to Barry than I was. After your parents moved away, you used to stay with your Aunt Jane when you were in town, so you must have seen more of Barry than I did. You must know who his friends were.'

But Claire shook her head. 'We were seldom there at the same time,' she said, 'and as for who his friends were then, I have no idea. I hate to admit this, because he was good to me when we were younger, but, like you, I avoided him. I even made excuses to Aunt Jane to avoid staying there when I knew Barry would be at home.

'Anyway, I really must be going,' she said, picking up her coat. 'I'm sorry if I've upset you, but I really don't see that you have anything to worry about if the police do come round, because—'

'Apart from being accused of killing my own father, you mean?' he said truculently. 'What else did you tell this Chief Inspector of yours?'

Annoyed by his belligerent tone, Claire came back at him. 'He's not *my* Chief Inspector, David, and I think you're over-reacting. I came here tonight as a friend to warn you about what may happen, and to let you know that they've reopened the case. I did not suggest they talk to you, and I will not be held responsible for whatever line the police choose to take. My only reason for taking those letters to them in the first place was because I thought what I had to tell them might help them find out who killed your father.'

David Taylor spread his hands in a gesture of apology. 'I'm sorry, Claire,' he said. 'I know it's not your fault, and I would like to see these people caught, but it's my impression that once the police get an idea into their heads, it's damned hard to shift it.'

He followed her as she made her way to the door. 'You're still welcome to stay for tea,' he said, but Claire shook her head.

'Perhaps another time, David,' she said as she went down the stairs ahead of him and opened the door to the street. 'I'll be in touch about that seascape.'

'Right,' he said uncertainly. 'Good night, then, Claire.' He closed the door behind her, but instead of going back upstairs, he sat down on the steps, elbows on his knees, chin cupped in his hands.

Barry Grant! The guilt had come rushing back the moment Claire mentioned the name, and he could hear the kid's voice inside his head as clearly as he had that night thirteen years ago. David groaned aloud. Just as he'd been in life; just when you thought you were rid of him, there was Barry, like an overeager puppy trying to nudge his way into your life. Always there even when you'd made it clear that you didn't want him there, and you could only put up with that for so long before you became really annoyed. David closed his eyes, but there was no way he could shut out the sound of Barry's pleading voice inside his head.

Claire slid the key into the ignition, but she didn't start the car. She was puzzled by David's reaction. She'd thought he'd be pleased to hear that the police were reopening the investigation into his father's death. As for the Chief Inspector's questions, from what she had learned from watching crime shows on TV, the police always started out suspecting everyone, and they had to start somewhere, so it wasn't as if David had anything to fear. All she had meant to do was let him know that the police would be coming round to talk to him about the things Barry had said in the letters to Aunt Jane.

But it had come out all wrong.

Claire had known David since she was about fourteen years old. He was a quiet boy, a couple of years older than she was, and she'd had quite a crush on him back then. But that had passed and she thought of him more as a brother now than just a friend.

Their studies had taken them along different paths, but they would meet whenever they were in town together, and Claire had made a special trip back home to be at David's wedding to Lucille Edgeworth, a girl he'd met on one of his field trips. She liked Lucille, who was outgoing, spontaneous, and full of fun, and a good match for David, who was inclined to take himself a bit too seriously. And yet, she remembered now the almost overwhelming sense of loss she'd felt as she'd watched the two of them join hands before the altar.

Claire had left for Paris shortly afterwards, where she spent two years studying interior design and working six and sometimes seven days a week in a variety of part-time jobs to support herself and pay for her tuition. She'd heard nothing from David in all that time, but that was hardly unusual, since neither of them were great letter-writers, so it came as something of a shock to learn that he was no longer married when she returned to start her own consulting business in Broadminster.

'We're still good friends, Lucille and I,' David told her. 'We just couldn't live together. Turns out our lifestyles simply didn't mix, so we thought it best to go our separate ways, and I must say we've been getting on famously ever since. Lucille is marrying a very nice chap by the name of Ray Fisher. He owns several travel agencies. Pots of money, which is a good thing, because one of our problems was there never seemed to be enough money to go round, and Lucille does love to shop and buy nice things. Me, I just like to be left alone to paint.'

Claire sighed as she started the car. She and David had been good friends for a long time, and she hoped she hadn't jeopardized that friendship tonight. Odd the way he'd reacted, though . . .

FOUR

Wednesday, July 8th

Jack Rogers, Paget discovered, lived in Wilmslow, not far from Manchester's airport.

'But there's no need to come all the way in to Wilmslow,' he told Paget on the phone. 'Best meet me at the Three Bells. You'll be on expenses, so you can buy lunch. Cut over to Congleton and come up on the A34. It's about five minutes north of Congleton on the left-hand side. You can't miss it. Make it half twelve. It gets a bit crowded if you leave it any later. Tell me what you're driving and I'll keep an eye out for you.'

Rogers was a big, ruddy-faced man, running to fat. 'I'd have had you come to the house, but the wife's away to her mother's while I do some painting and wallpapering, and the place is in a bit of a mess,' he explained when they met at the pub. 'Besides, if it's information you want, and it's worth your while to come all the way up here, I reckon the least the old firm can do is buy me lunch. Still, fair's fair, so I'll buy the first round. Boddingtons bitter do you, will it?'

'Make mine a half,' Paget told him. 'I'll be driving straight back after lunch.'

'Suit yourself,' said Rogers, 'but I'm having a pint.' He nodded in the direction of the chalkboard above the bar. 'I'd stay away from the scampi if I were you; all batter and no prawns. Hotpot's always good, though. I'm having mine with chips. What about you?'

It had been a long, hot, tiring drive, but, thankfully, it was cool inside the pub, and once he'd had a chance to cool off, Paget realized he was famished. He took out his wallet. 'In that case,' he said, 'I'll have the hotpot as well, but without the chips.'

Now, seated at a scarred wooden table, Paget tucked in while Rogers drew deeply on his beer before setting the glass down and picking up his knife and fork. 'So, what brought this on?' he asked. 'I'd have thought you had enough to do without digging up thirteen-year-old crimes. New evidence, you said on the phone?'

'Letters that have only recently come to light, from a nineteen-year-old boy who committed suicide shortly after the robberies took place,' Paget explained. 'Claims he was the driver of the getaway van, and was outside in the lane when Emily Bergman and George Taylor were killed. According to his story, Taylor pulled the mask off one of the men and recognized him, so they killed Taylor, then killed Emily Bergman as well when she started to scream. At least that was the reason they gave for killing Mrs Bergman.'

'So *that's* why they killed them,' Rogers said softly. 'I always wondered about that. But what do you mean about the reason for killing Mrs Bergman?'

'I'll come to that later,' Paget promised, 'but right now—'

'Who was this lad – the one who killed himself?' Rogers broke in.

'Barry Grant.'

Rogers thought for a moment, then shook his head. 'Doesn't ring a bell, but then, it's been a while. Did he give you names?'

'Unfortunately, no. He was more concerned with explaining his own role in the robberies, and distancing himself from the killings.'

Rogers grunted. 'So what do you want from me?' he asked.

'I've read the statements taken at the time, and I've listened to the tapes,' Paget told him, 'but what I would like from you is anything that is *not* on record: your impressions of various witnesses; suspicions you may have had, but were unable to back up with evidence. It seems to me that the strongest bits of evidence tying the three crimes together were the flash cards they left behind on the last job, but I couldn't help wondering if that was deliberate.'

Rogers jabbed his fork into a couple of chips, added a sizeable chunk of meat, and popped them into his mouth. 'Don't think you're the first one to ask me *that* question,' he said as he chewed. 'And I'll tell you the same as I told them. It wasn't just the cards or the burnt-out van, it was the timing of the jobs, the planning – and the gut feeling that it was the same mob. Not that you can put *that* in a report.

'See, these blokes were different,' he went on. 'You know what it's like. Ninety-nine times out of a hundred, robberies, break-ins, assaults, are run of the mill done by amateurs. Even killings are usually pretty simple when it comes down to it: family members, a fight over a girlfriend or boyfriend, pub brawls. But it was different with this lot. Professional, they had everything worked out – except of course for the unexpected, like the baker walking in on them and putting up a fight. Otherwise, they knew exactly who would be there when they went in, and they knew how to use those iron bars to scare the shit out of their victims, making noise, smashing them down so hard they gouged chunks out of the tables so everyone could see what could happen to them if they failed to cooperate.'

Rogers swallowed and scooped up another forkful. 'And all this without so much as uttering a sound themselves. That was a nice touch.' There was just a hint of admiration in his voice. He popped the food into his mouth.

'Did you ever establish a connection between the people who were robbed?'

Rogers paused to pry a piece of meat out of his teeth with a fingernail. 'Oh, we looked into that angle all right,' he said, 'but you have to remember the victims were mostly local businessmen, so they all knew one another. Besides, almost anyone could have found out when that poker game was on, or when the take was counted at the pub. And Sam Bergman had been leaving the shop by the back door at nine thirty every morning for years, so almost anyone could have known that.'

'Considering how well organized they were, it seemed odd to me that they hadn't hit more profitable targets before hitting Bergman's,' said Paget. 'Which made me wonder if they had another objective, and one of the possibilities that occurred to me was that the first two robberies were intended to make us believe that robbery was the motive in all three cases, but the real objective was the killing of Emily Bergman. I may be completely wrong, but we had such a case earlier this year, which is why the thought crossed my mind.'

Rogers set his fork aside, picked up his drink, and nodded slowly. 'Funny you should say that,' he said, 'because much the same thought crossed my mind back then, but there wasn't a shred of evidence pointing in that direction. But I think you're right in a way about the first two jobs. I think they were practice runs to make sure they had the technique down pat before going on to bigger things. But when the robbery turned to rat shit, and they realized they'd be facing a murder charge if they were caught, I think it scared them off and broke up the gang, because we never heard of them again, nor did anyone else as far as I know.'

The pub was becoming crowded. The doors were wide open as more people pushed their way in, bringing with them the midday heat from outside, and suddenly, the hotpot no longer appealed to Paget. He pushed his plate away.

Rogers picked up his glass, then pushed it across the table and said, 'It's your shout and I'll have the same again.'

When Paget returned from the bar with the drink, Rogers was mopping up the gravy with the last of the chips. 'What was your impression of Sam Bergman?' Paget asked as he sat

down. 'Any problems with the business at the time? Any problems at home that you knew of?'

Instead of answering the question, Rogers picked up his
beer and drank almost half of it before setting it down and
wiping his mouth with the back of his hand. 'Look,' he said,
'Sam might have been a bit on the sharp side when it came
to business, but murder? No. Poor devil was devastated that
day, and it was no act, believe me. Imagine, married nigh on
thirty years, and you walk in and see that lot. It's no wonder
the poor sod went to pieces. And if you are suggesting that
we didn't do our job, back then, you're dead wrong. We investigated every possibility, and I'm telling you, it was a robbery
that went wrong, and that's all it was.'

Paget shook his head. 'I'm not suggesting anything of the
kind,' he said, 'but you must remember that the only information I've had to go on till now comes from the files, and
these are some of the questions that came to mind. So I'm
not looking to pick holes in your investigation; I'm looking
to you to put me right about some of those questions.'

'Well . . .' Rogers eyed Paget suspiciously. 'So what else
do you want to know?' he asked.

Paget hesitated. 'I hate to keep going on about this,' he said,
'but what about Taylor himself? Were there ever any doubts
about *why* Taylor was in the shop at that time?'

Rogers scowled. 'What do you mean by "any doubts"?'

Paget avoided a direct answer. 'How old was Taylor at that
time?'

Rogers thought for a moment. 'Don't know, exactly. Mid
to late forties; something like that. Why?'

'And Emily Bergman?'

'About the same. Maybe a couple of years younger.'

'Attractive?'

Rogers shrugged. 'Not particularly,' he said. 'She was . . .'
He broke off sharply. 'You're not listening, are you?' he said,
now visibly annoyed. 'I keep telling you, it was a robbery
that went wrong. Taylor looked in to see if Sam was still there.
That's it. He'd done it many times before. I don't know what
you think you have to gain by making out it was more complicated than it was.'

Undaunted, Paget asked another question. 'Bergman had a
part-time shop assistant, a woman by the name of Loretta

Thompson, but she wasn't there that morning. Do you recall why that was?'

Rogers frowned. 'As you say, she only worked part-time. They only called her in when things got busy.'

'Quite a bit younger than Sam Bergman, wasn't she?'

Rogers sighed. 'So what are you suggesting now?' he asked with exaggerated weariness. 'That there was something going on between Sam and Loretta?'

'I have no idea,' said Paget, 'but I made a few enquiries before I came up here. Did you know that Sam Bergman had married again?'

Rogers eyed him warily. 'I know he sold his shop and moved away a few months after his wife died. Said he couldn't bear to be in the place after that. Went somewhere south, I believe; don't recall where, exactly, but if he's married again, good luck to him, I say. Happen recently, did it?'

Paget shook his head. 'Christmas Eve that same year to Loretta Thompson. Less than four months after his wife died. And they didn't go south; they opened another shop in Cambridge.'

'I have the results of the tests, and they confirm my own diagnosis, Tom. Marion has COPD, Chronic Obstructive Pulmonary Disease. Emphysema in this case, and it is well advanced. I'm afraid there's no other way to put it, Tom. Marion is in serious trouble.'

Dr Joseph Miller took off his glasses and began to polish them. He was a tall, stoop-shouldered man, whose grey hair and craggy face made him look older than he really was. He had been the Alcotts' family doctor for more than twenty years, and they had become friends, at least to the extent where they could talk freely to one another.

The two men were standing at the window at the end of the hospital corridor, looking out across Abbey Road to where the weathered stones of the minster ruins shimmered in the searing rays of the midday sun. A busload of tourists took pictures of one another against the backdrop of the ancient walls, while the driver, clearly bored, leaned against the bus, smoking a cigarette.

It was a pleasant summer scene, but it was wasted on Alcott, preoccupied as he was with what Miller had just told him.

'And what I would like to know,' the doctor continued, 'is why Marion let it go so long before coming to see me? She must have been having trouble for a long time; emphysema isn't something that comes on suddenly; it takes time to develop, and she must have known something was seriously wrong long before now. The coughing, the wheezing, the shortage of breath. To be brutally honest, Tom, I would have been far less surprised if it had been you with that condition, and from the way you're going on, that could still happen. God knows I've been trying to get you to stop smoking for years, but you wouldn't listen, and now it seems it's your wife who is suffering the consequences.'

Alcott bristled. 'Are you saying it's *my* fault she has emphysema?'

Miller shrugged. 'I've been in your house, remember? Who else in your house is a chain smoker? You must have seen what it was doing to her.'

'I know she's had this cough she couldn't seem to get rid of,' Alcott admitted, 'but we thought it was probably the after effects of the flu she had last winter.'

'Oh, for God's sake, Tom, it's July! Or is that something else you didn't notice?'

Colour rose in Alcott's face. 'What about you?' he demanded. 'You're her doctor. You've seen her. We have check-ups every year. Surely *you* would have noticed if there was—?'

'Marion hasn't been in to see me for more than two years,' Miller cut in sharply. 'She missed last year altogether, and she's cancelled two appointments so far this year, so don't try to blame me for Marion's condition.'

'It hasn't affected me,' Alcott shot back, 'so why would it affect Marion. She could be allergic to—'

'Now you *are* being wilfully blind!' Miller said scornfully. 'This has nothing to do with allergies, but it does have every-thing to do with second-hand smoke, and I wouldn't be too confident about it not affecting you. Of course it's affecting you; you know it and I know it, and quite frankly, Tom, I'm getting sick and tired of telling people to stop smoking, have them ignore everything I tell them, then expect some sort of miracle cure when they fall prey to COPD.'

Alcott took a deep breath. 'So what can be done for Marion?' he asked. 'What sort of treatment will she have to take?'

Miller eyed Alcott bleakly. 'I said it was serious, Tom, and I meant it. The damage to Marion's lungs is permanent. Lungs don't recover from something like this; they don't mend themselves. All we can do is try to alleviate the condition. The muscle spasms may respond to bronchodilators, and there are one or two other things we can do, but she will never be able to breathe properly again, and she must stay away from anyone who has the flu or any other infection.'

'How long do you think she will be in hospital?'

'That will be up to Dr Nichols – the consultant who spoke to you yesterday – and how well Marion responds to treatment, but I strongly advise you to find somewhere for her to go other than back to your house. I'm deadly serious about second-hand smoke, Tom. As I said, I've been in your house and you may be used to it, but I came out of there with my eyes stinging. The curtains, the carpets, the walls, everything is riddled with it. You must not take Marion back into that kind of environment. It could kill her.'

'I'm not even going to ask how your day went,' Grace said when Paget finally arrived home shortly after six o'clock that evening. 'I'm glad you phoned when you did, because after listening to the reports of a serious accident on the other side of Shrewsbury, I was beginning to worry. Did you see it?'

'No, but I was one of several hundred people stuck in a mile-long tailback because of it,' he said wearily, 'and it was like an oven in the car. Anyway, it's good to be home.'

Grace kissed him, then wrinkled her nose. 'You're right,' she said. 'It *was* hot out there, and I think the sooner you get out of those clothes and have a nice cool shower, the better. You said not to bother about dinner, but I held off just in case.'

But Paget was shaking his head. 'I had a big lunch,' he told her, 'so I'm not very hungry, but a cold beer and a sandwich would go down well. Why don't you go ahead and have your dinner while I have a shower and change?'

'To tell you the truth, I'm not very hungry either,' Grace said, 'so I think I'll wait and join you. A cold beer and a sandwich sounds just about right. I'll have them ready when you come down.

'Oh, I almost forgot,' she said as he started up the stairs. 'Mr

Alcott phoned. He wants you to call him back on his mobile phone. I have the number. He's at the hospital. He didn't say exactly what the problem was, but I gather Marion is quite ill. I told him you might be late in, but he said any time this evening would do.'

When Paget came down again, Grace had prepared a plateful of beef, lettuce and Swiss cheese sandwiches. 'I thought we might take these outside and sit on the back steps,' she said as she took two bottles of beer from the fridge. 'I could be mistaken but I believe I saw a leaf move out there, and I think it's cooling off a bit.'

'Good idea,' Paget agreed, 'but perhaps I should call Alcott first.'

He came out of the house a few minutes later and sat down beside Grace. 'Marion Alcott has emphysema,' he said quietly, 'and it sounds serious. Alcott sounded pretty worried and said he wants to be with her as much as possible while she's taking a series of tests, so it may be a while before he comes back to work on a regular basis. In the meantime, he'd like me to keep an eye on things for him. He says he's cleared it with Chief Superintendent Brock.'

'Can you do that?' Grace asked. 'Aren't you stretched to the limit as it is?'

A wry smile touched Paget's lips as he said, 'No problem, according to Alcott. He said, "Don't worry, you won't have much to do. Fiona knows more about that job than either one of us. Just sign your name when she tells you to, and you won't go far wrong." And I think he was serious.'

FIVE

Thursday, July 9th

Sheep Lane was a crooked little street of black and white half-timbered houses, one of the oldest streets in Broadminster, and the Brush and Palette was halfway down on the left-hand side. It was sandwiched between a betting shop on one side and a dry cleaner's on the other.

The front step was worn, the door frame was crooked, and Paget had to nudge the door with his shoulder before it would give way. An old-fashioned bell on a spiral spring above the door clattered rather than rang as he entered, and clattered even more when he tried to push the door shut.

'Needs a bit taking off,' a man said as he came forward from the back of the shop. 'I keep meaning to take a chisel to it, but I never seem to have time. Now, what can I do for you, sir?'

Paget introduced himself. 'We spoke on the phone earlier this morning,' he said. 'You are Mr Taylor, I take it?'

The welcoming smile disappeared. 'That's right,' the man said neutrally.

David Taylor was shorter than Paget by an inch or two. His broad shoulders, short neck, and well-muscled arms made him look more like a rugby player than Paget's idea of an artist. Paget glanced around the empty shop. 'Can we talk here or . . .?'

'As I told you on the phone, I'm here alone, so if customers come in I shall have to attend to them.'

'In that case, I'll try not to take up too much of your time.'

'Good. So let's get to the point, shall we? Claire said she told you that Barry Grant and I were friends, but I'll tell you what I told her.' Taylor repeated what he had told Claire, concluding with: 'I hardly ever saw Barry after I went off to Slade, but I heard about him from my brother, Kevin, who said he'd run into Barry at university in Leeds. Barry had always been crazy about cars, so the Grants packed him off to Leeds to take Mechanical Engineering. Kevin was three or four years older than Barry, but Barry sought him out and said he was a friend of mine and that I had told him to look Kevin up when he got to Leeds.'

'And you hadn't?'

'Lord, no. That's the last thing I would have done.'

'Your brother is Kevin Taylor? A solicitor? Is he with Bradshaw, Lewis and Mortimer, by any chance?'

'That's right. You know him, then?'

'I haven't dealt with him directly, no, but I met him briefly when my father died. Mr Bradshaw was the one who dealt with my father's will.'

'Who is also Kevin's father-in-law.'

'Sorry?'

'Ed Bradshaw is Kevin's wife's father. Kevin met Stephanie Bradshaw at university, and they were married at the end of their third year there. Kev was taking Law, and Steph was taking Business Administration. When Kevin got his degree, Ed offered him a job with the firm. Kevin is a pretty bright lad, and I expect he'll become a full partner in the firm when Mortimer retires at the end of the year.'

'So, if I understand you correctly, you're saying that while your brother Kevin, Stephanie Bradshaw, and Barry Grant were all at university together, they weren't close friends?'

'Far from it,' David said emphatically. 'In fact I'm sure they went out of their way to avoid him, so there's no need to go pestering Kevin and Steph with your questions about Barry.'

Paget raised an eyebrow. 'Pestering?' he said mildly. 'I would have thought that, now we have been given a second chance to find out who killed your father, you and your brother would be only too happy to help us with our enquiries. Until Miss Hammond came to us with new information, the case was as good as dead, and the killers had nothing to fear. But now we know that Barry Grant and friends of his were involved – although "friends" might be too strong a word, considering the way he claims he was treated by them. Miss Hammond couldn't tell us who his friends were, but she thought you might know. So tell me, why are you so reluctant to talk to me?'

Colour darkened David's face. 'Perhaps it's because I don't take kindly to being suspected of having killed my own father,' he said tightly. 'According to Claire—'

'Ah! So that's it, is it?' Paget broke in. 'She told you that I had asked if she thought you might have been involved. Did she also tell you why I asked that? Did she tell you the reason Barry gave for the killing of your father?'

'She said Dad recognized one of the robbers.'

'And did she tell you that Barry said he couldn't face you after that?'

'Yes, but . . .' David looked puzzled.

'So I asked myself why he couldn't face you, and there were at least two possible explanations. One was that he couldn't face you because he was consumed with guilt for having been involved in the killing of the father of someone he regarded as a friend, but another possibility was that it was *you* your father unmasked. So, assuming for the moment that you were *not* involved, will you at least help me by telling me everything you know about Barry, and who his friends might have been back then?'

David shook his head. 'It's not a matter of not *wanting* to help find out who killed Dad,' he said. 'As I told you, I don't *know* who Barry's friends were at that time. Barry was still at school when I went off to Slade to study art, so, apart from seeing him on the street the odd time when I was home during the summer break, I had no contact with him. I'm sorry, but I really can't help you. But there is one thing I *can* tell you. If you'd done your homework before coming here with your suspicions, you'd know that I was out doing deliveries when Dad was killed. Kev and I did that when we were home during the holidays. It helped Dad out and sort of paid for our free board and lodgings throughout the summer, and we were usually finished by ten o'clock, which allowed us to take on another job for the rest of the day and make a bit of money towards our tuition.'

Paget frowned. 'If I remember correctly, what you said in the statement you made to Inspector Rogers at the time was that you didn't return from your rounds until shortly after eleven that morning,' he said. 'Some sort of delay in getting started, I believe you said? It wasn't altogether clear in your statement.'

'There was an accident in the bakery that morning,' David said carefully. 'I explained that to Rogers at the time, and if he didn't put it down, that's not my fault. As I said, I don't know exactly what happened, but an entire batch of bread was left in the oven too long. The loaves were burnt and we had to wait for the next lot to be done before we could go out.'

'Had this sort of thing happened before?'

'I wouldn't know. I wasn't there for a good part of the year.'

'Was your father particularly upset or distracted that morning?'

'No more than usual.'

'You say, "no more than usual", Mr Taylor. Was your father easily upset?'

David eyed Paget narrowly as if trying to decide where the questions about his father were leading. 'Look,' he said, 'my father was a hard worker and he worried about everything, and if things went wrong he would become very upset, and that's all I meant by what I said. It was not unusual for him to be worried or upset about something. That was Dad. We were used to it, and I don't see what this has to do with your investigation.'

'Frankly, neither do I at the moment,' Paget told him, 'but what I am trying to do is put together the sequence of events as they occurred that day, and I would appreciate your co-operation. Tell me, how well did you and your brother get along with your father?'

David sucked in his breath, then let out a long sigh as he shook his head slowly from side to side. 'So *that's* what you've been leading up to, is it?' he said. 'So what else did Claire just happen to mention?'

He glanced at the door as if expecting it to open, perhaps hoping that someone would come in, but the door remained firmly closed. 'Very well, then,' he said, 'let's get that out of the way. It was no secret back then that Dad and I were barely on speaking terms. He was so set on my following in Kevin's footsteps to university, and I was just as determined to become an artist; it was inevitable that we would clash over it. I've always thought of my father as a stubborn man, but I suppose I must have inherited some of those genes, because I can be pretty stubborn, too, especially when it comes to the way I want to lead my life. So, does that make me a suspect?'

'To be honest, Mr Taylor, everyone is a suspect until proven otherwise in a case such as this,' said Paget, 'so the sooner I know the whole story, the sooner I can make a rational judgement about who should remain on the list and who shouldn't. What I don't understand is why, if things were that strained between you and your father, you were there working for him in the bakery?'

Taylor looked down at the floor, and it was clear by the set of his mouth that he was in two minds about whether to answer the question or not. Finally, looking up, he said, 'What you have to understand is that the one thing had nothing to do with the other. The argument about what I should be doing at university was one thing; work was another. And it was always made clear to me that, regardless of our differences, I always had a home and a job to come back to. But, when it came to my future, he expected me to be more like Kevin; he wanted me to become a solicitor or doctor or engineer – "something worthwhile" was the way he put it. He tried reasoning with me at first, then told me he would see me right financially, as he had with Kevin, if I would just buckle down and do something useful with my life. But when I said my mind was made up, and I wasn't going to be bribed into changing it, he told me I was a fool, and I could forget about any help from him, financial or otherwise in the future.

'So, we both came back and worked for him whenever we could. We didn't get paid, but we did have free board and lodging, and that was a big help to both of us. Kev and I did the early morning deliveries, then went off to our other jobs the rest of the day. Me, I worked afternoons at the Midland garage on the Ludlow road, and I cleaned offices at night. It was a hard slog, but I made it through without his help.'

'Although I imagine it must have been somewhat easier after your father died,' Paget suggested mildly. 'With the money from your father's estate and the sale of the bakery.'

'You can imagine whatever you like –' David walked to the door and opened it – 'but you can do it somewhere else, because you'll get nothing more from me.'

'There is just one thing I should mention before I go,' said Paget as he made his way to the door. 'Miss Hammond told us nothing about you or your relations with your father. I merely asked the question as a matter of routine, so please don't blame her for that. But it was enlightening. Thank you for your time.'

On his return to Charter Lane, Paget stopped at Len Ormside's desk. The grizzled Sergeant, shirt clinging damply to his chest, waved Paget to a seat and held up a single finger to indicate that he was almost finished on the phone. Paget slipped his jacket off and sat down. A small fan on the floor beside the desk made rattling sounds as it laboured ineffectually against the heat. The room seemed unusually quiet, and no wonder, Paget thought as he looked at the empty desks. Apart from

Ormside and himself, there were only two others in the room, and both were busy answering phones.

Ormside made a face as he hung up the phone. 'The fire in Whitchurch Street last night was definitely arson,' he said, 'so that's going to tie up more of my people, and what with holidays and Johnson off with a broken ankle, I don't know how I'm going to cover everything.'

He sat back in his chair, eyeing Paget suspiciously as he lifted the front of his shirt away from his chest and flapped it in an attempt to allow air to circulate behind it. 'And I don't like the look in your eye, either,' he growled. 'It would be nice if you've come to tell me we're getting air conditioning in here next week, but that's not it, is it?'

Paget shook his head. 'Air conditioning isn't the answer, Len. Not in these days of global warming. As Darwin said, we have to adapt if the species is to survive; the alternative is extinction.'

Ormside sighed. 'Ask a silly question,' he said glumly. 'So what is it, then? Not this Barry Grant thing, I hope? I took a quick look at the files Tregalles dumped on my desk yesterday, but the last thing I need right now is a thirteen-year-old cold case.'

'Afraid it is,' Paget said, not without sympathy. 'I've just come from talking to David Taylor. He's the son of George Taylor, the baker who was killed in the Bergman raid, but he insists that he doesn't know any more about who Grant's friends were back then than Claire Hammond does.

'So, I want you to start digging. Since the robberies all took place here in Broadminster, let's assume that his friends were from here as well, so start with a list of Grant's class-mates during his last year at Westonleigh, and his first and only year at Leeds. You might also find out if any of his old teachers are still around. Someone has to know more about this kid than we're being told.'

Ormside cocked a baleful eye at Paget. 'Take a look around,' he said. 'That's what's left of my staff, and they're up to their eyeballs as it is, so I hope you're not in a hurry for this stuff. I mean it's waited this long, so a few more days shouldn't make much difference.'

'Believe me, Len, I'm well aware of the problems,' Paget told him. 'I don't want to be unreasonable, but I do need that information, so let's do it this way: concentrate on the names of his classmates here at Westonleigh, and have those who are still around come in to be interviewed. Tregalles and Forsythe can do some of them, and they will be responsible for any follow-up, which should ease the burden on the rest of your people. As for those who live farther afield, we'll take a look at them if we need to after we've had the locals in.'

'That'll help,' Ormside conceded, 'but I still can't promise anything until at least the beginning of next week. Unless, of course, now that you're sitting in the super's chair, you're prepared to authorize overtime?'

Paget shook his head. 'You know that's out of the question,' he said as he rose to leave. 'But if you could make a start on it tomorrow . . .?' He saw the look on Ormside's face, and raised his hands in a sign of surrender. 'OK, OK,' he conceded, 'the beginning of the week it is, then, and I'll let Tregalles know.'

SIX

Friday, July 10th

I t was a far different looking Claire Hammond who greeted Paget and Superintendent Alcott the following morning when they entered the house Claire still thought of as Aunt Jane's home. Today, she was wearing a headscarf, a pair of rumpled slacks, trainers, and a T-shirt bearing the words: *Save a tree – eat a beaver*; a gift, she explained, from a cousin in Canada.

'I'm afraid the place is in a bit of a mess,' she said apologetically as they stood in the narrow entrance hall. 'When you phoned and asked me to meet you here, I decided to come early and start sorting through some of the cupboards and drawers, but it's hard to know what to do with so many things. Aunt Jane hated to throw anything away, so you can imagine what it's like.'

'I can indeed,' Paget told her, having gone through a similar process himself when his father died. In fact, there were still things in the house for which he had no use at all, but he'd kept them because they'd had meaning for his father. 'Will you be moving in yourself, or will the house be sold?'

Claire ran a hand through her hair. 'I really haven't made up my mind. I'd like to move in, more for Aunt Jane's sake than anything else, but it's really far too big for one person. I'll have to give it more serious thought when I've had time to sort things out. Anyway, I'm sure you didn't come here to listen to my problems, so what was it you wanted to see, exactly?'

Alcott had asked Paget the same question when the Chief Inspector had persuaded the Superintendent to accompany him to the house, and he gave Claire the same answer. 'To be honest, I'm not quite sure myself. But after hearing what you had to say the other day, and reading the old reports, it seemed to me that it might be useful to learn more about Barry himself.' He glanced at Alcott. 'And, since Superintendent Alcott was directly involved at the time of Barry's death, I'm hoping that revisiting the scene might stir a helpful memory or two.'

Alcott had balked at the suggestion that he accompany Paget to examine the place where Barry Grant had died. His first reaction had been to say he couldn't spare the time. Marion was undergoing more tests today and he should be with her at the hospital. But he'd changed his mind, not because he wanted to revisit the scene of a young lad's suicide he still remembered vividly, but because it would be a welcome distraction from his personal situation.

'So, Miss Hammond,' Paget said, 'if you would lead the way, perhaps we could begin by taking a look at what used to be Barry's bedroom.'

'Of course.' Claire started towards the stairs, but Alcott stopped to examine a picture on the wall.

'That's him,' he said, tapping the glass. 'That's a better picture of him than we have on file.'

'Yes, that's Barry,' Claire agreed. She stepped back to allow Paget to see the picture.

Barry Grant was sitting in the driver's seat of an old Vauxhall. The window was down and he was leaning out, grinning and waving at the camera. Long fair hair that fell below the shoulders framed a narrow face.

'He looks pretty proud of himself there,' Paget observed. He looked at Claire, but she remained silent. 'How old would he have been when that was taken?'

'Seventeen, maybe eighteen. I don't know exactly.'

'Any idea whose car that was?'

'Not the slightest.'

'Do you mind if we take this picture with us when we leave? I'd like to see if Forensic can tell us anything about the car. It might have belonged to one of his friends.'

'Of, course, if you think it will help.'

'Thanks. Do you know if there are any group pictures of Barry and his friends?'

Claire frowned in thought. 'Not that I can think of,' she said at last. 'I don't think Aunt Jane owned a camera, but if I come across any pictures, you're welcome to them.'

'Thank you.'

Alcott, who had moved on to study other pictures on the wall, said, 'Do your parents still live next door, Miss Hammond?'

'No. They moved to Southampton about ten years ago. My father's in insurance. He's general manager there.'

'But they were still living next door when Barry died?'

'That's right.'

'Did they ever talk about what happened?'

Claire shook her head. 'Not really. I think as far as my dad was concerned, the less said the better when it came to Barry.' She cast a furtive glance at her watch.

Alcott took the hint. 'Right,' he said briskly, 'best get on, then.' He stood back to allow Claire to lead the way. 'It was the back bedroom, if memory serves,' he said as they reached the landing at the top of the stairs. He pointed to a closed door.

'That's right,' said Claire. 'Aunt Jane would never let anyone else use it after Barry died, so you'll find it virtually the same as it was then. She cleaned and vacuumed in there as she did throughout the rest of the house, and she took the sheets and pillows off the bed, but otherwise it's pretty much the way Barry left it.'

'Are you saying she kept it as some sort of shrine?'

'Oh, no, it wasn't like that,' Claire assured him. 'She simply had no reason to change it, so it's remained as it was.'

Alcott opened the door and stood there for a moment before moving inside. Paget followed, while Claire hovered uncertainly in the doorway. The room smelt musty, suggesting that neither the door nor the window had been opened for some time.

It was as Claire had said: the room looked as if Barry Grant might return to it at any time. There were clothes in the wardrobe; there were books and papers on his desk, and magazines stacked neatly on the floor. Yellowing posters featuring cars and scantily clad girls were still pinned to the walls, and a guitar with broken strings stood in the corner.

The temperature outside was already climbing rapidly, but Claire shivered and wrapped her arms around herself. 'I don't know why,' she said, 'but this room always gives me a funny feeling.'

'You searched this room yourself, did you, sir?' asked Paget.

Alcott nodded. 'Looking for a note,' he said, 'or anything at all that might explain why the boy felt compelled to end his life in such a violent way, but there was nothing. Now we know why: Mrs Grant had taken the notes away.'

Paget turned to Claire. 'I doubt if we will find anything in this room after all this time,' he said, 'but I would like to have someone come in to search the house for anything that might tell us who Barry's friends were – old photographs, letters from university, perhaps, things that Mrs Grant may have kept locked away. With your permission, of course.'

Claire hesitated. 'It's not that I mind,' she told him, 'but I have quite a lot on at the moment. Do I need to be here?'

'I think you should be,' Paget told her. 'And the sooner we do it the better. Do you think you could be here Monday morning? Say about nine? It shouldn't take too long.'

Claire frowned as she mentally rearranged the plans she'd had for Monday, then nodded. 'I can do that,' she told him. 'In fact it will give me a chance to sort a few things out myself.'

'Then that's settled,' Paget said, 'and thank you.'

Alcott was shaking his head as he moved towards the door. 'It's uncanny,' he muttered as much to himself as to the others. 'Nothing's changed. After all these years, it looks exactly as I remember it.'

'Does it trigger any memories that might prove useful to us in this new enquiry?' asked Paget hopefully.

'Memories? Oh, yes,' said Alcott soberly. 'But useful . . .?' He shook his head.

'I believe you wanted to see the packing shed as well,' Claire said as she led the way to the head of the stairs, then started down without waiting for an answer. At the bottom, they followed her down and along the hall towards the back of the house. 'The key to the shed is in here,' she said, pausing beside an open door leading to the conservatory. 'You go ahead and I'll catch up with you.'

Alcott continued on his way to the back door, but Paget followed Claire inside. 'Now this *is* a surprise,' he said as he looked around. Over twenty feet long and perhaps twelve or thirteen feet wide, and all windows down one side, the conservatory looked out on a narrow strip of lawn and a vegetable garden, both woefully overgrown and in desperate need of water, and beyond that was the orchard where Claire had told them she'd played as a child. 'Very nice indeed,' he said. 'I've often thought I'd like something like this on my house. Is it a recent addition?'

'Compared to the rest of the house, I suppose you could say that,' she said. 'Uncle Arnold had it done a couple of years before he died, which would be about fifteen or sixteen years ago. He designed it and helped build it, but it was Aunt Jane who chose the colour scheme, the rattan furniture and the colourful cushions. But, as you can see, she was rather over fond of ornaments.'

Paget couldn't help but agree as he looked around the room. There were ornaments of every description on almost every flat surface in the room. There were a few nice pieces, but they were all but lost amid the clutter of small, glass animals, paperweights, crystals, odd-shaped stones, and seashells.

'And these aren't the only ones,' Claire told him as she took a key from the drawer of a small desk near the door. 'There has to be at least another fifty tucked away in drawers and cupboards. If it shone or sparkled, chances were Aunt Jane would buy it. Uncle Arnold used to say she must have been a magpie in a previous life.'

'And coins as well?' Paget said, indicating a large jam jar almost full of pennies.

Claire laughed. 'No, that was Uncle Arnold's,' she said. 'He used to throw all his pennies in the jar until it was full, then take them down to a little shop off the market place where they collect them for some charity or other. I remember several

years ago asking Aunt Jane if she'd like me to take the money
down there for her, but she said to leave it because it wasn't
full yet.'

'She never added to it herself?'

'Oh, no. That was Uncle Arnold's jar. In a strange sort of
way, I think it was as if he wasn't really gone as long as the
jar still needed pennies to fill it up.'

Paget caught sight of Alcott through the window. 'Better
be going,' he said with a nod towards the window. He held
out his hand out for the key, but Claire closed her own hand
over it.

'I'll come with you, if you don't mind,' she said. 'I haven't
had a chance to go out there myself since Aunt Jane died, so
I'd like to see what sort of state the shed is in. It's been years
since I was inside it; in fact, I think the last time I was in
there was while I was still at school.'

The orchard was long and narrow, bordered on either side
by high wooden fences that showed signs of neglect. The grass
was brown and dry in the summer heat, crackling beneath
their feet as they made their way between the trees towards
the shed at the far end of the orchard. The trees themselves
were old and gnarled, and long overdue for pruning. But it
would take more than pruning to save these trees, thought
Paget, with leaves already brown and curling, and apples the
size of walnuts withering on the stem.

'I'm afraid it's not much of an orchard now,' Claire said as
if reading his thoughts. 'It was far too much work for Aunt
Jane after Uncle Arnold died, and the man she hired to help
her didn't know much about orchards. It's a good job she
didn't have to depend on it for an income. These trees should
have been replaced years ago, but I doubt there would be any
point in doing so now. Too much competition for small
growers, to say nothing of EU rules and regulations that have
to be met these days.'

She ducked beneath a low branch as they emerged from
the trees. 'This is the packing shed,' she said unnecessarily.
'It used to be a busy place in the late summer when I was
small. It was a packing house, garage and workshop all rolled
into one back then, but I doubt if anyone's been inside now
for years.'

'What's on the other side of the back fence?' asked Paget.

'Pettigrew Estates,' Claire told him. 'Here, I'll show you.' She led the way to a high wooden gate. 'I don't think *this* has been opened for years, either,' she said, tugging at a rusty bolt. The hinges screeched in protest as she pulled the gate open. 'The carriers used to come down the lane to pick up the fruit from here and from other orchards farther along,' she explained when Paget followed her outside, 'but the orchards are all gone now. Too much work and not enough money in it to make it worthwhile. This was all open fields when I was growing up, just a mass of buttercups and daisies in the summer, but then the builders moved in so now we have Pettigrew Estates instead.

'But that's not what you came here to see, is it?' she said as she caught Alcott's impatient glance. She closed and bolted the gate, then moved to the shed. 'Mind the sill,' she warned as she unlocked the door.

They followed her in, pausing for a moment for their eyes to adjust to the gloom. The sun was shining outside, but inside the cavernous shed the light lay flat and lifeless against the windows above the bench, barely able to penetrate the layers of grime and tangled cobwebs that filled the corners.

Claire tried several switches before a strip of fluorescent lights above a long wooden bench flickered into life.

The shed was huge. Cobwebs were everywhere, and there was a musty smell in the lifeless air. As Claire had said, it hadn't been used for years.

A rusting, chain-driven lawn mower stood in one corner beside a pile of old tyres, and large wooden crates with faded lettering were stacked against the walls. There were ladders, long-handled pruning shears, baskets, buckets, a bundle of sacks, and on the floor at the far end of the bench, lay what looked like spraying equipment. The bench itself was cluttered with empty boxes, rusting tools and more cobwebs.

There were dark patches on the floor, where oil had stained the concrete, and tracks made by countless vehicles leading to the two large doors at the far end of the shed were still clearly visible.

This, Paget reminded himself, was where Barry Grant had worked with David Taylor on a clapped out Hillman Minx all those years ago – and where Barry Grant had died.

Alcott walked over to the bench and stood looking down at the vice.

'I should be getting back to the house,' Claire said tentatively, 'so unless you need me for anything, I'll leave you to look around.' She handed the key to Paget. 'You will lock up when you're finished here, and bring me the key?'

'Of course, and thanks again, Miss Hammond.'

When Claire had gone, Paget walked over to stand beside Alcott. 'Something interesting about the vice, is there, sir?' he enquired.

'Gun barrels,' Alcott said cryptically. 'This is where he sawed about a foot-and-a-half off the shotgun before he used it on himself. Stuck the gun under his chin, pulled both triggers and blew his head off. Couldn't have reached the triggers otherwise. The sawn-off pieces were still in the vice when I arrived, and the hacksaw was beside it on the bench.'

'I've always thought it would be extremely hard to saw through the barrel of a gun,' said Paget. 'Don't you need a special blade?'

Alcott shook his head. 'The steel isn't all that hard,' he said. 'It's a matter of the tensile strength of the metal rather than hardness. A decent hacksaw blade will go through both barrels in fifteen or twenty minutes. At least, that's what Forensic told me at the time, because I thought the same thing.' He moved along the bench to a tall cupboard at the end. 'The gun was kept in here,' he explained, 'together with the shells. No lock on the door, of course. Mrs Grant told me her husband used the gun to shoot the odd rabbit now and again, and to scare off the birds when they became too much of a nuisance in the orchard. I asked her why it wasn't locked up, and she said she'd simply forgotten it was there after her husband died.'

'I know this can't be very pleasant for you, sir,' Paget said, 'but I would like to get the picture straight in my head. Where, exactly, was Barry when he pulled the trigger?'

Alcott closed the cupboard. 'Over here,' he said, walking to the nearest corner, where a pair of overalls hung on one of a row of wooden pegs. Beneath the pegs were two metal folding chairs and a pair of heavy boots, cracked and broken. 'This was where the workers hung their gear,' he explained. 'There was a lot more hanging on these pegs back then, which may be why no one heard the gun go off. Tucked himself in

the corner among the clothes before he pulled the triggers.'
The Superintendent looked up. 'You can still see where some
of the shot hit the wall up there.'

'Was he standing or sitting down?'

'The chairs were pushed aside, and as far as I could tell,
he was standing in the corner among the clothes.'

Paget stood looking at the corner, 'Curious,' he said. 'I
wonder why he came here to end his life?'

Alcott shrugged. 'Who knows?' he said. He lit a cigarette
and inhaled deeply, then suddenly realized what he was doing
and pinched it out.

'It's just that it strikes me as odd,' Paget persisted, 'that a
boy who, by all accounts, went to great lengths to be noticed,
would come in here in the dead of night, spend fifteen minutes
or more cutting the shotgun down to size, then go and stand
in a corner among the clothes to shoot himself. It doesn't
seem to be in character.'

Alcott snorted. 'I doubt if staying in character is a consid-
eration when you're about to kill yourself,' he said, 'and to
be honest, Paget, I don't see the point of this exercise of yours.
I told you everything I know about what happened, and there's
nothing inside this old shed that is going to help you solve
this case.'

Nothing, thought Paget as he followed the Superintendent
out of the door, except, perhaps, the ghost of a boy who had
blown his head to pieces thirteen years ago.

SEVEN

Saturday, July 11th

The homes on Falcon Ridge, perched high above the river,
faced westward. One could look out across the valley
and the rooftops of the town to the forested hills of
Radnor rising in the distance, shimmering like a mirage in
the heat of the afternoon. It was a gorgeous view, thought
Claire as she drove along the ridge. Kevin must be doing very
well indeed to afford to move up here. She glanced at the

piece of paper on the seat beside her. Number 1035.

'Fifth house from the end,' Stephanie had told her on the phone. 'Right-hand side. Driveway's a bit steep, so make sure you set your brake.'

And there it was. Stone pillars on either side of the gate, and a low stone wall and iron railings along the front of the property. Claire glanced in her rear-view mirror, then swung across the road and entered the driveway. There were cars parked all the way down the drive, but she managed to squeeze in behind a Ford Fiesta hatchback she recognized as David's.

The house wasn't large compared to some of the adjoining properties, but all things are relative, and some of the older homes were very large indeed. But it looked solid and comfortably settled into the hillside as if it belonged there. Brick, two storeys, gable-ended roof, and large bay windows on the ground floor to make the most of the panoramic view, and the rhododendron hedges shielding the house from its neighbours looked as if they had been there forever.

'*Very* nice,' Claire murmured to herself as she made her way up the steps and rang the bell. Kevin *and* Stephanie must be doing well. But then, Stephanie did have her own business, which she ran from home, and they had no children, but even so . . . Claire turned to look at the view once more, and wondered about the size of the mortgage. Probably Stephanie's father had . . .

'Claire! So glad you could come.' The door had opened silently, and Stephanie Taylor stood there, arms spread wide in a welcoming gesture. 'Come in, come in and join the others.' Trim and tanned, Stephanie literally radiated energy. Her short, blonde hair, styled in what she liked to call her wash-and-wear cut, gleamed like a halo above wide-set blue eyes, short nose, and radiant smile. In her open-necked shirt and summer shorts, she wouldn't have looked out of place on a magazine cover. Claire, in blouse and calf-length skirt, suddenly felt overdressed.

Claire paused in the doorway to look back. 'Gorgeous view you have from here, Steph,' she said, 'and a lovely setting.'

'It is nice, isn't it?' said Stephanie perfunctorily as she closed the door. 'But then, Dad always did have a good eye for property, and with the market the way it is, and the previous owner anxious to sell, Dad says it will be a good investment.'

Good investment. Was that all it meant to Steph, Claire wondered? On the other hand, it hardly came as a surprise to find that Steph's father had had a hand in the move. Claire wondered how Kevin felt about it. She knew how much he'd liked the house on Oak Street. It was an old house, but it had a certain charm, and it was close to everything. Best of all, it was paid for. But hardly the right neighbourhood for an up-and-coming young lawyer. At least, that's the way Steph's father, Ed Bradshaw, would look at it.

'Yes, I suppose that's true,' she said as she handed a gift-wrapped box to Stephanie. 'Just a little something for the new home,' she said. 'I hope you like it.'

'Oh, Claire, really, there was no need, but thank you very much. I'm sure I'll love it. But would you mind very much if I wait till later to open it when I have time to enjoy it? I'm a bit rushed at the moment.'

'Of course not,' Claire told her, 'but it's not very much, really.' In fact it *was* very much, but one didn't buy cheap gifts for Stephanie.

'I'm sure I shall be delighted,' Stephanie said firmly. 'Now, I know you're dying to see the rest of the house – you must see the indoor pool – but I thought we'd do the grand tour later when everyone is here. I think you know everybody, well, perhaps not some of our new neighbours, but I'm sure someone will introduce you. So I'll take you along to join them, then pop back to the kitchen to check on a few things. Dad insisted on having the caterers in, and I'm sure they know what they're doing, but I do like to check on that sort of thing myself.'

With a gentle but firm grip on Claire's arm, Stephanie propelled her down a hallway towards an open door. 'Go on in,' she said, 'and do remind Kevin to mingle. You'll prob-ably find Dad's got him stuck in a corner talking shop. And tell him I'll be back in a couple of minutes.'

Claire paused in the doorway before going in. She enjoyed meeting people on a one-on-one basis, or even in small groups, but she had never been comfortable meeting new people *en masse,* so she was pleased to see that Steph had been right; and there were a fair number of familiar faces in the crowd.

She didn't see Kevin, but she spotted Ed Bradshaw working

his way through the crowded room. He paused to speak to a woman Claire didn't recognize, then disappeared through a doorway into another room. Lucille, David's ex-wife, looking as chic and elegant as ever, was there with her new husband, Ray Fisher, while John Chadwell and his wife, Amy, stood at the window, drinks in hand, apparently admiring the view. Claire liked Amy, although she didn't know her well, but she wasn't too keen on John, one of Broadminster's town planners. Heavy-set and somewhat overbearing, he'd always struck Claire as a bit of a bully, and she'd never understood how Amy, a rather gentle soul, had come to marry him.

Roger Corbett, portly and only slightly less rumpled than usual, was talking earnestly to Irene Sinclair. Irene and Claire had been at school together, but they had lost touch with each other as children do when the family moved to Inverness. So Claire had barely recognized Irene when they had bumped into each other on the street some years ago.

She'd come back, Irene told Claire, because she had always thought of Broadminster as her true home, despite the fact that she had been born in Hong Kong, and had spent the first five years of her life there. Her father was a Scot, her mother was Chinese, and the mix was reflected in Irene's features. She was a striking woman, with her rich auburn hair framing an oval face with a distinctly oriental cast. But what Claire had found strangest of all, was that Irene had picked up a Scottish accent during her stay north of the border. Irene was an actress – or *actor* as one was supposed to say these days, Claire reminded herself – and director at the local theatre. She also had a small business designing web pages, and was doing quite well with it.

As for Roger, Claire wondered what he was doing for a living now; the man had changed jobs so many times in the last few years, that she'd lost count. Estate agent was the last she'd heard, but you never knew with Roger.

Claire looked around for Lisa, Roger's wife. Lisa was one of Claire's favourite people. Small, dark and vivacious, Lisa Corbett was a ballroom dancing instructor, and full of life. There was another odd couple, thought Claire. How the two of them had ever got together was one of life's deeper mysteries. But Lisa didn't seem to be there.

Roger turned and saw her. He waved, then said something

to Irene, who also waved, but remained where she was as Roger came over to talk to Claire. 'Good to see you, Claire,' he said, perfunctorily, then leaned closer and lowered his voice. 'As a matter of fact I was going to come round to see you next week, because someone told me that you've inherited the old Grant house, and I was wondering if you were thinking of selling?'

'Why? Were you thinking of buying it, Roger?' Claire asked mischievously. 'That's a beautiful house you have now, and I can't see Lisa giving that up.'

'No, no, I didn't mean for us,' he said, taking her seriously. 'It's just that, being in the business, I thought . . . well, you know, if you *were* thinking of selling, I'd be happy to handle it for you.'

'I'm sure you would, Roger,' Claire said with a smile, 'but I have no idea what I'm going to do with it yet, and I expect it will take me a while to sort things out, but I'll keep you in mind.' Even as she said it, she knew it was a lie. Roger was probably the last person she would go to if she did decide to sell. 'And speaking of Lisa, where is she today?' Claire asked, anxious to change the subject.

'Oh, she's gone off to Scarborough with her Brazilian gigolo to some competition or other,' he replied airily. 'Won't be back until Tuesday. They're probably doing the light fantastic or some such thing right now. In fact Lisa said it would be on telly sometime this afternoon.'

'And you're not going to watch it? Shame on you, Roger; Lisa is a beautiful dancer; you should be proud of her.'

Roger made a face and shrugged. 'She'll be bringing back a DVD to study every move they made, as well as those of the other couples in the competition,' he said, 'so I'll get to watch it whether I like it or not. I wouldn't mind so much if it was only Lisa, but I can't take much more of that partner of hers, Ramon, as he calls himself. Real name's Ray Short, if you please, and I doubt if he could find Brazil on a map. She thinks he's bloody marvellous, and all I'll hear for weeks is, "See that, Roger?" he mimicked. "See how smooth that was? See what Ramon did there? It was like floating on air; it was wonderful". Makes you sick! You watch any of that stuff, do you, Claire? Have you seen him?'

'The last time I saw Lisa was last winter, when she and her partner came in fourth. Was that him? Tall, slim, and quite dark, and a beautiful dancer.'

Roger groaned. 'God! You women are all the same,' he said. 'That's him, and you sound just like Lisa. Anyway, that's enough of that. I need a drink! Give me a bell if you decide to put the house up.'

The last thing Roger needed was another drink, thought Claire as she watched him weave his way across the room to speak to Irene before they both moved off into another room.

Someone waved. It was Peter Anderson, an old school chum of Kevin's. She didn't know him well, so she was surprised by the wave, until she realized that a middle-aged woman she had never seen before had him backed into a corner and he was seeking help.

Claire was about to go and rescue him when she saw Kevin. He was talking to Graham Williams, an old classmate of hers. Thin and gangly, Graham had been a 'brain' at school, and had been more or less ostracized because of it. As a result, he'd fought back, literally, by taking boxing lessons, and had done quite well as an amateur while in his teens. Now, a successful accountant, he worked from home, and rarely came out to social functions, so she was a little surprised to see him there.

Kevin saw her at the same time. He lifted a hand, then broke off his conversation with Williams and pushed his way through the crowd. 'Claire!' he greeted her. 'So glad you could come. Welcome to our new home. Come in and join the party.'

Unlike his brother, who was more than a little casual when it came to dress, Kevin was always smartly turned out. Even now, in the relaxed setting of his own home and in what for him was casual attire – open-neck shirt, cream-coloured slacks with socks to match, and trendy sandals – he looked more like an actor dressed for the part. Not fair, Claire chided herself silently. It wasn't as if Kevin did it deliberately; that was just the way he was, and he looked very smart. And not just smart in appearance, she reminded herself. According to David, Kevin would become a full partner in the firm at the end of the year. Claire didn't doubt it. With Stephanie behind him, and her father head of the firm, Kevin was definitely on his way.

'I was about to,' she replied to his question. 'And thank you for asking me.'

'Our pleasure,' he said, 'but I should warn you, Steph will want to pick your brains for ideas about the decor. Promise me you won't suggest anything too expensive.' He frowned as he glanced into the hall behind her. 'Where is Steph, anyway?'

'She's gone to check up on things in the kitchen. She said she would only be a few minutes, and I was to remind you to mingle with your guests.'

Kevin's eyes flicked towards heaven as he shook his head. 'Probably out there counting the spoons to make sure no one's run off with them,' he muttered, then grinned to show he didn't really mean it. 'Come on in and let me get you a drink. What will you have?'

'Whatever it is, I'm afraid it will have to be non-alcoholic,' Claire told him. 'Sorry, Kevin, but I have to leave in an hour to see a client. He's leaving for South Africa first thing in the morning, and wants to have everything sorted out before he goes. I really am sorry I can't stay longer, but perhaps you could give me a quick private tour of the house before I go. From what I've seen so far, I think it's lovely. And the view from up here is magnificent.'

He grimaced. 'God knows it should be for the price.' The words were spoken lightly, but Claire thought she detected a hint of bitterness in his voice, and wondered once again how he and Stephanie had managed to make the leap from Oak Street in the Old Town to Falcon Ridge.

It was as if he sensed her thoughts. 'Of course, we couldn't possibly have done it without the help of Steph's father,' he said. 'He made it possible.'

Claire said, 'I'm sure you'll both enjoy it, but I thought you both liked where you were living before. It had a lot of character, and I remember you telling me about the plans you had to renovate, so I was surprised when David said you were moving up here.'

'Oh, we did like it,' Kevin agreed. 'At least, *I* liked it, and to tell you the truth I was looking forward to the challenge of whipping it into shape, but Steph wasn't quite as keen. She thought it was all right while we were getting on our feet, but she was always on the lookout for something more . . . upmarket, if you know what I mean. So, when this place came up for sale, and Ed said he was prepared to help us buy it, Steph jumped at the chance.'

Kevin went on to explain that there had always been a strong bond between Steph and her father. 'You probably know that her mother died when she was quite young,' he went on, 'and Ed brought her up on his own. He lives just down the road, so when this house came up for sale, and Ed broached the idea of us moving up here close to him, it was like a gift from the gods as far as Steph was concerned.'

He made a face and lowered his voice. 'A damned expensive gift, nevertheless,' he confided quietly, then smiled to show once again that he wasn't really serious. 'Not that I *really* mind, of course,' he went on. 'It's just that it takes a bit of getting used to, that's all, and I'm sure we will be very happy here once we're settled in. Anyway, that's quite enough of that. Come with me and we'll see about that drink.

'The bar's in the next room,' he explained as he led the way. 'And if my father-in-law tells you he's been called to the bar, pretend you haven't heard it a dozen times before, and smile. It's his favourite pun.'

'As a matter of fact, I haven't heard it before,' Claire told him, 'but I will smile.'

The two of them made their way across the room, pausing every now and then to say 'hello' or exchange a few words before they reached the bar. It was, Kevin explained, a self-contained bar on wheels, complete with a miniature sink, refrigerator, and its own supply of water. 'Belongs to Ed,' he said, sotto voce, as they approached. 'I'd intended to simply have a drinks table, but he insisted on bringing it over and setting it up last night. You have *met* Ed, haven't you, Claire?'

'No, not really,' she confessed. 'I mean I know who he is, and I saw him at your wedding, of course, but I've never actually met him.'

'In that case, let me introduce you.' He waited until the man behind the bar had finished serving the wife of one of the lawyers in his firm before bringing Claire forward.

'Claire Hammond?' Ed Bradshaw repeated slowly. 'I believe I knew your father. Not well, but I met him a few times. Insurance, wasn't it? Moved south somewhere?'

'That's right, Mr Bradshaw. Southampton.'

'Call me Ed. Everyone else does. Now, as you can see, I've been called to the bar, so what will you have?'

Claire smiled dutifully, and asked for an orange juice.

Ed Bradshaw was a small, energetic man who seemed to be on springs. He was never still. Fit and trim, much like his daughter, Ed played squash three times a week, jogged virtually every day, walked almost everywhere, and made sure everyone knew it.

'No orange juice, I'm afraid,' he said, 'but I do have lemonade. Brought it along in case someone was foolish enough to bring a youngster. It's either that or soda water.'

'Lemonade will do very well, thank you,' Claire told him.

'Chock full of sugar, of course,' he couldn't resist saying as he poured the drink, 'but I don't suppose one glass will hurt you.'

'Hello, Claire,' said a familiar voice behind her.

She turned to face the speaker and said, 'Hello, David. I saw your car outside, and I was wondering where you'd got to.'

'Been hiding out in the kitchen until Steph chased me out,' he told her. 'Got tired of listening to a bunch of lawyers talking shop, so I went out there. At least I could understand what they were talking about.'

'He's just being boorish, as usual,' said Stephanie, who had followed him in. 'Give him a drink, Dad. Perhaps that will loosen him up a bit. And give me one as well.'

David drew Claire to one side as more people drifted in to refresh their drinks. 'I could have picked you up if you'd told me you were coming here today,' he said. 'You didn't mention it the other night.'

'As I recall, I didn't have much chance,' she said more sharply than she'd intended.

'Yes, well, I've been meaning to call you about that,' he said. 'I suppose I was a bit short with you, and I'm sorry. Your policeman friend came round to see me yesterday, and I can see now how he could take a perfectly innocent remark and make something out of it that was never intended.'

'I wish you'd stop referring to him as "my policeman friend",' Claire said irritably. 'Why? What did he say?'

'It wasn't so much what he actually *said*, but he left me with the impression that he thought I wasn't being quite straight with him, and I wouldn't be at all surprised to see him back again with more questions.'

Claire grimaced sympathetically. 'As a matter of fact, I had a visit from Chief Inspector Paget and Superintendent Alcott yesterday afternoon. They wanted to look at Barry's room and the shed where Barry died.'

Although he seemed to be absorbed in what he was doing behind the bar, Ed Bradshaw pricked up his ears. 'Alcott?' he asked sharply. 'Superintendent Alcott? What have you been up to, young lady?' He smiled to soften his words. 'Must be something serious to attract the attention of the Superintendent. If you need a solicitor . . .?'

'*Is* there a problem, Claire?' asked Stephanie.

'Good Lord, no! It's just . . .' Claire stopped, not quite knowing what to say.

'It's nothing to do with Claire, really,' David said. 'It's just that when Jane Grant died, she left a letter saying that young Barry Grant – you remember him, don't you, Kevin? – was one of the people involved in the robbery when Dad was killed.'

The murmur of conversation around the bar died.

Stephanie drew in her breath and looked at Kevin. 'Oh, my God!' she whispered. 'Your father, Kevin. After all this time.' She looked at Claire. 'Are you saying it was Barry Grant who killed Kevin's father?'

'No, that's not what I'm saying, Steph,' Claire said. 'It was—'

'It's a bit more complicated than that,' David broke in. 'It seems that Barry left some notes behind when he died. He admitted to being one of the people involved in the robberies. He said he drove the van they used, but he wasn't inside the shop when . . . when it happened.'

Kevin was staring hard at his brother. 'He claims he was one of the people involved?' he echoed, his voice rising, 'and you didn't bother to *tell* me?'

David Taylor made a calming motion with his hands. 'I was going to tell you, Kevin, but I didn't want to spoil your party.' Conscious of the people listening, he lowered his voice. 'I'll tell you all about it later on. The police have it in hand. They've reopened the inves—'

'I don't want to wait till later on,' Kevin cut in angrily. 'I want to know now!'

'Kevin . . .' Stephanie laid a hand on his arm, but he shook it off.

'He was my father, too,' David reminded him, 'and I'm just as anxious to know who killed him as you are. But all I know at the moment is what I've told you. The police came round to ask me what I could tell them about Barry, which wasn't much, and Claire tells me they went to Jane Grant's house to look at his old room and the shed where he killed himself. That's it. That's all we know.'

Everyone turned their attention to Claire.

'I don't know any more,' she said. 'Really.'

Ed came out from behind the bar. 'Looking at his room?' he scoffed. 'That's a bit feeble, even for the police, isn't it? What did they expect to find after all these years?'

Claire shook her head. 'I'm not sure they expected to find anything,' she told him, 'but they're coming back again on Monday to look for anything in the house that might tell them who Barry's friends were back then, some of whom may have been members of the gang. Photographs, letters, things like that.'

Bradshaw seemed suddenly to realize that others were listening, and turned to face them. 'Sorry if we're holding you up,' he said with false heartiness. 'Let's get those glasses filled, shall we? Give me a hand, Kevin; we have a bunch of thirsty people here.' He moved back behind the bar. 'Now then, Roger,' he said to the first man in line, 'what's it going to be?'

EIGHT

Sunday, July 12th

Valerie Alcott sat staring down at her plate, fists clenched beneath the table. She wished she had gone straight home after leaving the hospital instead of agreeing to come back to the house with her father. But she'd felt sorry for him after that ugly scene in the hospital, with Celeste going on and on until a senior nurse had asked them to leave.

'I think that is quite enough for today,' she'd said firmly. 'Mrs Alcott needs her rest and I must ask you to lower your voices and leave. Not only is it bad for Mrs Alcott, but you are disturbing the other patients.'

Her mother, propped up on pillows, looked old, and Valerie remembered thinking that no one should look that old at fifty-two. Her face was grey and her breathing was laboured. She had tried to put on a bold face; tried to pretend she was pleased to see them, but Valerie had caught the grateful look she'd given the nurse when their eyes had met.

But Celeste just wouldn't shut up.

'I've come all the way up here from Bristol,' she said waspishly, 'and I don't intend to be told when I can and cannot visit my mother during visiting hours.'

'Your mother needs to rest,' her father had said, rising to his feet. 'She—'

'So, *now* you're concerned, are you, Dad?' Celeste snapped. 'If it hadn't been for you, she wouldn't be in here in the first place, you and your smoking! I'm not a little girl anymore, so I won't have you telling me what is best for my mother.'

Valerie had taken her sister's arm. 'Come on, Celeste,' she had coaxed. 'Mum is very tired; she does need her rest, so let's go. We can come back tomorrow, and perhaps it would be best if we came one at a time and just sat quietly with Mum.'

'You're as bad as Dad,' Celeste accused, pulling away. 'You keep saying you've stopped smoking, but I know you haven't. I can smell it on you. And just look at what that's done to my mother!'

'For God's sake, Celeste, drop it!' her father hissed. 'If you want to have a go at me, then do it outside. Now, are you coming or do I have to drag you out? Because I will if you keep this up.'

Celeste turned on him. 'There! See? Now look what you've done. You've made Mum cry. It's all right, Mum,' she said, bending over to stroke her mother's hair, 'we love you. Don't cry.'

The nurse had moved in, a sturdy nurse, expertly nudging Celeste away from the bed as she straightened their mother's pillows. Celeste attempted to push back, but the nurse stood her ground. 'You can leave voluntarily, or I can have Security escort you out,' she said in a low voice. Her hand hovered inches away from the emergency call-button on the in-house communications unit.

'You'll be hearing more about this,' Celeste snapped as she moved away. 'I will not be treated like this when it could very well be the last time I see my mother—'

'Celeste! For God's sake!'

Never had Valerie seen such a thunderous look on her father's face as he came round the end of the bed to seize his daughter by the arm and literally drag her away, and for once in her adult life, Celeste looked frightened.

Now, sitting there at the table in the house where she'd grown up, Valerie cringed at her own cowardice. She'd done nothing, absolutely *nothing* back there at the hospital. She'd just stood there, speechless and totally useless while her father marched Celeste out of the ward, down the hall and into the lift, and then outside. Valerie had followed them down, feeling more like a six-year-old than a grown woman.

It had been like that since childhood. Celeste, three years older, had carried on a secret campaign of intimidation as far back as Valerie could remember, and no matter how hard she'd tried, she'd never been able to fight back successfully.

'So, what *are* you going to do when Mum comes out?' Celeste demanded, only slightly more subdued than she'd been at the hospital. She wrinkled her nose as she looked around the room. 'She certainly can't come back here. The place reeks of smoke, so where will she go?' She looked pointedly at Valerie. 'Your flat is too small and there are too many stairs anyway, so that's no good, but you could get a bigger place.'

'And how am I supposed to do that?' Valerie said. 'I'm at work all day and I can barely afford the rent on the place I have now.'

'You might be earning a better wage if you'd paid more attention to your education and gone to university instead of buzzing off to Europe and God knows where else when you finished school,' Celeste snapped. 'Now what are you? Typist in some little office with no prospects. If I were you, I'd—'

'But you're *not* me!' Valerie flared, 'and I thank God for that. It's all very well for you to talk; yes, you went to university, but your main objective was to snag a rich husband, and you succeeded, so don't preach to me about the difference university makes. At least I work for a living. You don't! And I'm sick and tired of—'

'Stop it!'

Celeste gasped and Valerie jumped back so hard her chair almost went over backwards as her father's fist hit the table with such force that the teacups slopped tea into the saucers and on to the tablecloth. 'Just shut it, both of you! Can't you see she's baiting you, Val?' He turned to Celeste. 'And if you are trying to make me feel bad about what's happened to your mother, you are wasting your breath, because nothing you say or do can make me feel any worse than I do now. I *know* it's my fault; I *know* I'm responsible for your mother's condition, and I don't need you or anyone else to tell me that. So either shut up or leave, and I don't much care which one you choose.'

Grim-faced, Celeste threw her napkin down and pushed her chair back. 'In that case, I'll leave and let you two get on with it,' she said thinly. She stood up and moved to the door, then paused. 'With me out of the way, you can both light up and discuss what to do about Mother, when she comes out of hospital – *if* she ever does.'

Claire Hammond shivered and stirred in her sleep. Cramped and cold, she slowly came awake and reached for the coverlet to cover her shoulders. But there was no coverlet, and this was not her bed.

She opened her eyes and looked around. Slowly, the outlines of the room took shape. The conservatory, of course! After spending the whole day and most of the evening cleaning and sorting things out, she'd flopped into one of the over-stuffed chairs for a brief rest before going home. That had been around ten o'clock. So what time was it now? Claire peered at her watch, but the light was too faint for her to see the time.

She wrinkled her nose. Whatever was that smell?

Claire sat up straight, suddenly alert and wide awake. Petrol? She was sure it was petrol she could smell, but where could it be coming from? The windows weren't open, and even if they were, the conservatory was at the back of the house, and there would be no reason for . . .

A sound! She caught her breath; stopped breathing, straining to hear. There it was again! Someone was in the house; someone with petrol . . .

Claire shot out of the chair to move swiftly across the room. Silently, she eased the door open, put her eyes to the crack . . . then froze! Not six feet away in the hall, a dark figure, intent upon the job in hand, was backing slowly down the hall. Guided by the light of a pencil torch gripped between the teeth, he was sloshing petrol on the floor. The smell was overpowering. Claire's eyes watered and her throat convulsed as she choked back a terrible urge to cough.

Panic gripped her. She could feel her heart pounding hard against her ribs as she closed the door and leaned against it, fighting hard to overcome her fear. The whole house was filled with fumes. One tiny spark and the whole place would go up in flames, and she'd be lucky if she got out alive.

She heard a sound; a sound she recognized. The hinges on the back door had been making that sound for as long as she could remember, and that meant . . .

Oh, God! The intruder had opened the back door, and that meant he only had to step outside, light a match, toss it in . . .

Suddenly, Claire was angry, so angry it banished fear. A weapon. She searched frantically for a weapon. Something . . . *Anything!* No time . . . She grabbed the first thing that came to hand, hefted it and grunted in satisfaction as she slipped into the hall. She felt the cool night air on her face. The back door was open. The light from the torch wavering as the last few drops of petrol were shaken from the can.

From somewhere deep within her came an angry, visceral sound, rising to a howl of rage as she charged headlong down the hall to hurl the jam jar full of pennies at the figure in the doorway . . .

'She has some nasty bruises and her clothes were soaked in petrol,' the lead fireman told Paget. 'I don't think the bruises are all that serious, but we had to get her out of those clothes, so we wrapped her up and sent her off to hospital in an ambulance. She didn't want to go; insisted she wanted to stay until you got here, but we finally persuaded her it was for the best. I tell you, that is one plucky lady, and if she hadn't done what

she did, she wouldn't be alive now. That house was so full of
fumes that one spark would have blown the place apart. We've
been here over an hour, now, and we've only just taken off
our masks.'

'Did she tell you what happened?'

'She said she'd spent the day cleaning, sat down for a rest
and fell asleep in the conservatory at the back of the house.
Woke up to hear someone in the house, looked out and saw
this person backing down the hall pouring petrol on the floor
as he went. Of course, it was dark, so she couldn't see much,
and she daren't switch on the light, so she grabbed the first
thing that came to hand, charged down the hall and flung it
at him.

'Bloody great jar full of pennies,' the man continued with a
shake of the head. 'Probably would have killed the bastard if
it had hit him, not that he didn't deserve it. Hit the doorpost;
took a chunk right out of it. Glass and pennies everywhere.
Must have scared the shit out of him because he took off. Lucky
for her he did, because with all that petrol on the tiles in the
kitchen she slipped and fell when she threw the jar, and banged
herself about a bit. She wouldn't have stood a chance if he'd
stayed long enough to set the place alight.'

They found Claire Hammond in Casualty. Wrapped in a
blanket, and with a towel wound round her head, she was
curled up in a chair in a curtained-off cubicle.

'No bones broken, just a few bruises,' she told Paget when
he asked after introducing Tregalles. 'There was no need to
admit me, so technically I'm an outpatient and I'm free to
go. The only reason I'm still here is because I'm waiting for
some fresh clothes.' Claire grimaced. 'Fortunately I was able
to have a shower, hence the towel,' she continued, pointing
to her head, 'but they told me it will probably take at least
half-a-dozen rinses before the smell will be completely gone
from my hair.'

'Have you arranged for someone to bring your clothes?'
Paget asked.

'Not yet,' she said, 'but I have a friend who will. It's just
that I don't want to get her out of bed in the middle of the
night, so I'm going to wait and call her about eight.'

'Oh, I think we may be able to get you home before that,'

Paget told her. 'But before we do, I would like to ask you a few questions if you feel up to it?'

Claire gave a perfunctory nod and said, 'I'm fine, really, but what's happening at the house? The way that man was sloshing petrol about . . .' She shuddered.

It was Tregalles who answered. 'It's certainly not as bad as it could have been,' he said, 'but I'm afraid the carpets in the two downstairs rooms have to go. The fireman I spoke to said you would never get the smell out, so it would be pointless to try to save them. The same goes for the carpet at the bottom of the stairs, and the two big armchairs and sofa in the front room were soaked as well. As for the rest, he told me there are professional cleaners who specialize in this sort of thing.'

Claire nodded slowly as she absorbed the news, and said, 'Thank you, Sergeant,' as if what he'd told her pretty much confirmed her own mental assessment of the damage. 'And as you say, it could have been worse – a lot worse if he'd ever struck a match. On the bright side, the carpets *were* old and threadbare, so I would have had to replace them at some point. As for the rest, we'll just have to wait and see what the cleaners can do.' She turned to face Paget. 'Now, what is it you want to know, Chief Inspector?'

Paget told her what they had learned from the firemen on the scene. 'And what I would like from you is anything you can add to that,' he said. 'I know it was dark, but were you able to see anything of this person at all that might help us?'

Claire shook her head. 'The only time I saw a clear outline of him was when he was standing in the open doorway shaking the last of the petrol out of the can,' she said, 'but that's all it was, an outline.

'But speaking of the can, I think he dropped it when I threw the jar at him. Did he leave it behind? Can you do anything with it? Like fingerprints, perhaps?' she ended hopefully.

'It was left behind, and it will be subjected to a thorough forensic examination,' Paget told her, 'but I rather think he would be wearing gloves. Could you see his hands at all?'

Once again, Claire shook her head. 'I just wish to God I'd hit him,' she said with feeling, 'but my feet went out from under me just as I threw the jar, and the next thing I knew I was skidding across the floor on my backside. It was my own fault. I should have realized the floor would be slippery with all that petrol on it, but I was so angry . . .' Her face clouded at the memory, but Paget didn't allow her time to dwell on that.

'Do you think he knew you were in the house?' he asked.

'I'm pretty sure he didn't,' she said. 'There was no reason why he should. My car wasn't out front because I rode over on my bike that morning and left it at the side of the house, and it was still light when I went to sleep, so there were no lights on. Oh, no, I don't think he was after me. I think it was the house he wanted to destroy before you had a chance to search it.'

'Which makes me wonder,' Paget said, 'how could he have known we were about to search the house again?'

Claire shifted uncomfortably in her chair. 'I'm afraid that is probably my fault,' she confessed. 'At least it's the only explanation I can think of, and I've been sitting here for the past hour going over everything in my head. It's not that I meant to, of course,' she went on hastily as she saw Paget and Tregalles exchange glances, 'it's just that I was at Kevin and Stephanie Taylor's house-warming party on Saturday, when I happened to mention that the police were coming in today to look for clues to Barry's friends. I find it very hard to believe that any one of them could possibly do such a thing, but on the other hand I don't know how else anyone would have known. Unless you told someone . . .?' She looked hopefully from one to the other, then sighed when Paget shook his head.

'In that case it looks as though I brought this on myself,' she said, 'except most of the people there were friends I've known for years, and I can't believe that any of them could be involved in something like this.'

Tregalles took out his notebook. 'In that case, miss,' he said, 'I'm going to need to know where and when this party took place, and the names of everyone there.'

NINE

The offices of Bradshaw, Lewis and Mortimer were on the first floor of what was still known as the Corn Exchange on the corner of Bridge Street and King George Way. The receptionist, an attractive young woman with three gold rings in one ear, greeted Paget and Tregalles with a professional smile and said yes, Mr Taylor was expecting them, and led them down a corridor to Taylor's office.

Kevin Taylor looked every inch the lawyer: white shirt, striped tie, navy two-piece suit, and highly polished shoes. Acknowledging the introduction of Tregalles with a perfunctory nod as he came out from behind his desk, he turned his attention to Paget. 'Have we met before?' he asked, extending his hand.

'Briefly, a few years ago when my father died,' Paget told him. 'Mr Bradshaw handled the estate.'

'Ah, yes, I remember, now.' Taylor returned to stand behind the desk. 'I thought the name was familiar when my brother, David, mentioned it the other day. Please have a seat.' He waited for the two men to sit down before settling into his own chair. 'He told me you are reopening the file on our father's death, and that Barry Grant was involved in some way. He said you were trying to find out who Barry's friends were at the time, but I don't see how I can help you. I barely knew Barry – he was several years younger than me, and I have no idea who his friends were.'

Everyone, it seemed, was distancing themselves from Barry Grant.

'But you were at university together, were you not?'

Taylor smiled. 'It's a big place,' he said. 'Barry was taking Engineering, and I was reading Law. Our paths might never have crossed if it weren't for the fact that he seemed to think, because he knew my brother, he had a right to attach himself to me and *my* friends. I felt sorry for him at first – it was his first year at uni, and he didn't seem to have any friends – so I told him to give me a shout if he needed any help settling in. That proved to be a *big* mistake, because from then on he was like a limpet. No matter where I went, he was always there. I put up with it for a while, thinking the novelty would wear off, but it didn't, and when he made a play for Steph, my fiancé at the time, and started following *her* about, I was forced to warn him off. Fortunately, he packed it in after the first year, and I never did see him again after that.'

'Not even here in Broadminster, say during the summer months?'

'If I did I don't recall it,' Kevin told him. 'I don't know how he spent his summer holidays, but I spent mine at home, helping my father in the bakery. So did David. We worked in the bakery and did rounds in the morning, and both of us had other jobs in the afternoon. We worked long hours, so there wasn't much time for socializing.'

'Do you know if it was usual for your father to go into Sam Bergman's shop on his way down to the coffee shop at the end of the street?'

Kevin shook his head. 'I really couldn't say. All I can tell you is that it was a sort of ritual for several of the local businessmen to meet for coffee most mornings. But how is this relevant, Chief Inspector? We made statements at the time, so surely they're still on file?'

'They are,' Paget agreed, 'but since I wasn't here thirteen years ago, I would like to meet the people involved in order to get a better feel for how things were back then, and perhaps to jog people's memories.

'However,' he continued, 'let's talk about more recent events. I'm told you had a house-warming party on Saturday, and it was there that Claire Hammond told you about the case being reopened.'

Taylor pursed his lips and frowned into the distance. 'As I recall, I believe it was David who told us,' he said with some precision. 'Claire made a remark about talking to the police, and Ed, my father-in-law, made a sort of joke about it and asked if she was in trouble and needed a good solicitor. It was David who explained what it was all about.'

'And that was the first time you'd heard about our enquiries?'

'Yes. And to tell you the truth, I was more than a little

annoyed with my brother for not telling me before. I thought he should have told me when he first found out himself.'

'According to Miss Hammond, there were a number of people gathered around the bar when she mentioned that we would be returning to the house today. Do you remember that, Mr Taylor?'

'I do,' he said cautiously. 'But why . . .?'

'Do you remember who they were? Their names?'

'I might if you can give me a good reason why you're asking these questions, Chief Inspector, because I don't see what that has to do with your investigation.'

'Oh, I believe there is a connection,' Paget told him. 'I suspect that someone at that party overheard what was said, and as a consequence Miss Hammond came within a whisker of being killed earlier this morning when someone tried to burn the Grant house down.'

'*Claire?*' Taylor's jaw dropped. 'Oh, my God!' he whispered. 'Is she all right? Was she hurt? I didn't know she was living there?'

It was an assumption and a question at the same time, but Paget didn't bother to explain. Instead, he said, 'Fortunately, due to quick thinking on her part, Miss Hammond escaped with just a few bruises, but she is lucky to be alive.'

'Thank God for that!' Kevin breathed. 'And the house . . .?'

'There is a small amount of damage, but nothing of importance was destroyed.'

'And you think that someone at the *party* was responsible?'

Paget sat back and let Tregalles answer the question. 'Miss Hammond is quite sure she said nothing to anyone else about the search,' he said.

Taylor tilted back in his chair. 'On the other hand,' he said, 'considering the number of break-ins we've been experiencing lately, isn't it also possible that it had nothing to do with your investigation? Almost anyone could have learned that the house was not being lived in, and taken advantage of the situation.'

'As you say, sir, that is a possibility, but I think it's far more likely that they would have looted the place rather than burn it down. Miss Hammond has given us the names of people she knows, but there were some at the party she didn't know. Perhaps you can help us there?'

Taylor looked sceptical. 'It's not that I don't want to help,' he said, 'but you must realize that we're talking about some of my closest friends, many of whom my wife and I have known since we were at school. And the idea that any one of them could be involved either in this incident or, by extension, in the original crime when my father died, is extremely hard to believe.'

'But a possibility nevertheless,' Tregalles persisted, 'and one we can't ignore. I don't know if your brother told you what Barry Grant said about the reason for your father being killed, but Barry claimed it was because your father recognized one of the men. If that is true, then the killer could well be someone you know.'

'David did tell me that,' Taylor acknowledged, 'but it never occurred to me that the person might be someone in our own age group. I suppose, if I thought about it at all, I assumed it was someone my father knew, rather than someone David and I might know. In fact, from what you've told me, that could still be the case.'

Paget sat forward. 'Except for three things,' he said. 'First, it seems unlikely that Barry Grant would be driving for a group of older men. From what we've learned, he was always trying to ingratiate himself with his contemporaries, as in fact you said yourself he did with you. Secondly, we have reason to believe that these robberies began more as a prank than a serious attempt to gain wealth, which again suggests young people. And thirdly, as far as we know, the only place anyone could have learned that we intended to search the Grant house was at your party on Saturday, where most of your guests were contemporaries of yours. Which is why we would like the list of those who were there that day.'

Before Taylor could respond, there was a perfunctory tap on the door and Ed Bradshaw came in, head down, eyes on the sheaf of papers in his hand. 'I'd like you to take a look at these, Kevin,' he began, then stopped when he saw the two detectives. 'Oh! I do beg your pardon,' he said. 'I didn't realize that Kevin had someone with him. I do apologize.' He began to turn away, then stopped. 'It's Inspector Paget, isn't it? We handled your father's estate some years back, as I recall.' He turned to Kevin before Paget had a chance to reply. 'Is this by any chance to do with what you and David were talking about on Saturday? About your father?'

'As a matter of fact, it is,' Taylor told him. 'And it's *Chief* Inspector Paget.'

'Ah, yes, of course. Sorry, Chief Inspector. As I said, I'm sorry for the interruption, but now that I am here, may I ask how the investigation is going? It's amazing that something new has turned up after all these years. Making progress, are you?'

'It seems that Claire had a narrow escape when someone tried to set fire to the Grant house this morning,' Taylor broke in before Paget had a chance to answer, 'and the Chief Inspector thinks it could have been someone who overheard our conversation at the party.' Swiftly and succinctly, he brought Bradshaw up to date.

Ed Bradshaw looked thoughtful as he pulled up a chair and sat down facing Paget. 'I suppose it is a possibility,' he conceded without conviction, 'but it doesn't seem very likely to me. I mean we've known many of them for years. Are you quite sure that Claire didn't tell someone else?'

'She assures me she did not,' Paget told him, 'and I have no reason to doubt her.'

'In that case, of course we will be only too pleased to assist you in any way we can,' Bradshaw said.

Paget nodded his thanks. 'Did either of you happen to notice anyone taking a particular interest in what Miss Hammond and David had to say on Saturday?'

Bradshaw shrugged. 'I'd say *everyone* was *more* than interested in what was being said. I remember it became very quiet when the police were mentioned.' A quick smile flickered across his face. 'But then, I'm sure you know that's not an unusual reaction.'

He pushed himself out of the chair. 'I can talk to you about this later,' he told Kevin, waving the sheaf of papers in his hand.

'Just one question before you go,' said Paget. 'Would you mind telling me where you were between midnight last night and three o'clock this morning?'

Bradshaw chuckled. 'That's usually my line in court,' he said, 'but it's the first time it's been asked of me. Better have your alibi ready as well, Kevin,' he warned, 'because you'll be next. As for myself, I was home in bed, Chief Inspector, and I live alone, so I'm afraid you'll have to take my word for it. Sorry.' He paused at the door. 'But if there is any other way you think I can help, please don't hesitate to call me.'

'And you, Mr Taylor?' asked Paget as the door closed behind his father-in-law.

'I'm afraid I find myself in much the same situation,' Taylor said. 'Ordinarily, I would have had my wife to back me up, but the fact is I spent last night alone in our old house down on Oak Street. You see, we have this very large antique wardrobe – it belonged to Steph's grandmother, who brought it over from Holland originally, and it's huge – so we decided at the last minute not to have it moved with the rest of the furniture, but to have it done by Whetheralls, who specialize in moving antique furniture. The trouble was they were booked solid, and they are the only ones who do that sort of thing around here. To make a long story short, they finally agreed to squeeze us in at seven o'clock this morning if I would agree to pay the overtime.

'Anyway, I still had a bit of cleaning up to do, so I took the sleeping bag and our folding camp cot down to the house last night about eight o'clock, finished the cleaning up about one this morning, then slept there to be ready for Whetheralls at seven.' Taylor sat back in his chair and spread his hands. 'So, like my father-in-law, I'm afraid I don't have an alibi either,' he ended.

'Your wife would have been in the house alone, then?' said Paget.

'Yes. We have a good security system in the house, so . . .' Taylor stopped dead as he realized the implication of the question. 'Are you seriously suggesting that *Steph* needs an alibi?' he demanded.

'I'm not suggesting anything, Mr Taylor. I'm simply trying to find out where everyone was during the time frame I mentioned. You, your father-in-law, and your wife were just three of the people who were there when Miss Hammond mentioned that we would be searching the house, so we will be putting the same question to everyone who was there. Which brings me back to the same question I asked Mr Bradshaw: did you notice if anyone there seemed to be paying particular attention to what Miss Hammond said?'

Taylor shook his head. 'As Ed said, *everybody* stopped talking to listen. Partly my fault, I suppose. In fact it was a bit embarrassing, really.'

'I see. And the list of names . . .? And addresses would help if you know them?'

'Of course,' Taylor said tersely, 'I remember who some of them were, but as for the rest, I shall have to talk to my wife. She is the one who organized everything, so I'll have to get the list from her. In fact, it might be simpler all round if she could fax them to you.'

'I'd appreciate that,' Paget told him as he rose to leave. He took a card from his wallet and handed it to Taylor. 'The fax number is on there, as is my telephone number. And if you should happen to think of anything that might prove helpful to the investigation, please don't hesitate to call.'

'Funny, that,' Tregalles commented as they descended the stairs a few minutes later. 'We passed right by the open door of Bradshaw's office when we came in, and I know he saw us, yet he pretended he didn't know we were there when he came into Taylor's office later. Do you think he was just being nosy?'

'Either that or he came in to make sure that his son-in-law wasn't in any trouble,' Paget said.

'Wouldn't trust either one of them,' Tregalles declared. 'And that story of his about the wardrobe . . . Even if it's true, it doesn't give him an alibi.'

'On the other hand,' said Paget, 'he'd hardly make up something like that, because he'd know we'd check. But you're right, neither he nor Ed Bradshaw have alibis, and I suspect we'll hear much the same thing from everyone else. After all, most people *are* in bed at one o'clock in the morning, and it's very hard to prove otherwise.'

Apart from a couple of young boys squirting each other with water pistols, and clearly enjoying the soaking, the tree-lined street was deserted when Paget parked the car outside the Grant house. It was noticeably cooler here, and a welcome change from the oppressive heat in the centre of town. Even so, both Paget and Tregalles left their jackets in the car when they went up to the house.

They could hear the deep-throated thrum of a powerful fan as they approached the open front door, and they were met by a strong rush of air as they stepped inside. Air that smelt strongly of petrol.

'Mind the cables, sir,' Detective Constable Molly Forsythe

called from the far end of the hall. She waited until they had eased their way past the large fan in the narrow hallway before directing them into the conservatory. 'Not nearly as much smell in here, sir,' she told Paget, 'and since the firemen left fans in each of the downstairs rooms, except this one, we've been doing the sorting in here. Not that we've found much, have we, Phil?' she ended with a gesture towards the only other person in the room, a young Constable by the name of Wheeler they'd borrowed from Uniforms for the task.

The young man lifted his arms above his head and stretched. His shirt clung to his body, and there were patches of sweat beneath the arms. 'Couple of postcards from when he was in Leeds, and a few pictures of him when he was a kid, but not much else,' he said wearily.

Compared to Wheeler, Molly Forsythe looked remarkably fresh and cool in her crisp white shirt and navy skirt, Tregalles thought, and wondered how she managed it in this heat. Good-looking gal, too, with her short dark hair framing an ever so slightly plump face. And clever, he reminded himself. Commended for her marks being up there in the top twenty-five in the first phase of the Sergeants' exams last March, Tregalles didn't doubt for an instant that she would make Sergeant before the end of the year. Not that she didn't deserve it, but he couldn't help wondering if his own position would be in jeopardy when that happened. He still remembered how well she and Paget had worked together on the Holbrook case last spring, and he'd wondered then if there wasn't some sort of chemistry between them.

Audrey had scoffed at the suggestion when he'd said he wondered if Paget and Molly were 'well, you know, attracted to one another', and she'd been proved right. Not that he'd *really* thought there was anything going on between the two of them, but things like that weren't unknown in the workplace.

Still, he should have known better, he told himself. He'd felt more than a little foolish when he'd found that the reason Paget had insisted on Molly accompanying him was because he was evaluating her performance in the field prior to her taking the Sergeants' exam. On the other hand, Paget *had* talked about the value of a woman's point of view in an investigation, so perhaps he *was* thinking of making a change.

'You all right, Tregalles?'

The words cut in sharply on the Sergeant's thoughts. He drew a deep breath. 'Sorry, boss,' he said, shaking his head. 'Came over a bit faint for a minute, there. Must be the heat and the smell.'

Paget pushed a chair towards him. 'Beginning to feel a bit that way myself,' he said as he sat down. 'Probably dehydrated. We could both do with some water.' He cast a meaningful look at Wheeler.

'Right, sir.' The young Constable heaved himself out of the chair and headed towards the door.

'The only picture I've found of Barry with a group of friends,' said Molly as she shuffled through the papers on the table, 'is this one.' She handed the picture to Paget. 'At least that's who Barry says they are – you'll see what he wrote on the back – but the more I look at the picture, the more I wonder if that was literally true. See what I mean, sir? He's the one on the end; leaning in, big grin on his face, and yet none of the others are smiling. Maybe I'm reading too much into it, but it almost looks as if he pushed his way into the picture.'

Paget studied the picture closely, then turned it over. '*Some of my good friends on campus,*' he read. 'It would certainly fit the profile we've been getting on the boy,' he said, turning the picture over again to study it. 'Attaching himself to people in an attempt to be accepted. Isn't that Kevin Taylor in the middle?' he asked, handing the picture to Tregalles.

'That's him,' Tregalles agreed, 'and the blonde girl hanging on his arm is his wife, or probably his fiancé back then. Remember the picture on Taylor's desk? Same woman only older, not that she hasn't worn well. In fact I'd say she's improved with age. Good figure, and—'

'Yes, well, I'm sure she would be delighted to hear you say that, Sergeant,' Paget observed drily. 'Anything else of interest?' he asked Molly.

'Not really, sir. SOCO finished up here shortly after lunch, but I don't think they found very much. Other than that, there's not much to report. Miss Hammond was here around lunchtime. She was anxious to see the damage for herself, and I think she was quite relieved to find it wasn't as bad as she'd imagined. She told me she's thinking seriously about moving in here once it's cleaned up.'

'How did she seem? Physically, I mean?'

'A bit stiff with the bruises, but otherwise she appeared to be fine.'

Paget nodded. 'Glad to hear it,' he said, 'because I think I may have to talk to her again.'

Wheeler reappeared bearing four glasses of water on a tray. He set it down and handed each of them a glass. Tregalles held his glass up to the light and made a face. 'You didn't happen to see any beer out there in the fridge, did you?' he asked hopefully.

The Constable picked up his own glass. 'Sorry, Sarge,' he said straight-faced, 'there was, but we drank it all at lunchtime?'

TEN

Tuesday, July 14th

The list of names of those who had been at the house-warming party on Saturday was on Paget's desk when he arrived the following morning. Faxed over the previous evening, there was a note on the bottom explaining that the three names crossed out belonged to people who'd been invited but had not turned up for one reason or another, and those with crosses by their names were people who were relative newcomers to the area, and would not have known Barry Grant.

As he went through the list, putting a mark against the names of those Claire Hammond had identified as being close enough to have heard what was said at the bar, it occurred to him that it might save some time if they could go over the list together.

He looked up her number and reached for the phone.

When Claire answered, he explained what it was he wanted to do. 'I have a list of the people who were at the party last Saturday,' he said, 'and what I would like to do is to go over it with you, and have you give me a sort of thumbnail sketch of these people as you remember them. Do you think you could do that, Miss Hammond?'

Claire hesitated. It wasn't so much a matter of not wanting to help, but she felt guilty about talking to someone like Paget about her friends. Not that she could call some of them *close* friends, but she had known them for a long time, and she hadn't made up her mind about Paget. He seemed straightforward enough, but he was a hard man to read, and after what had happened when she had mentioned David having been a friend of Barry's, she felt she should be very careful about what she told the Chief Inspector in the future.

It was almost as if he could read her thoughts. 'I can appreciate that you might have some reservations about talking to me about people who may be friends of yours,' he said, 'but on the other hand, it would help me decide on what approach to take when I talk to them myself, rather than going in blind.'

'I wouldn't want them to think . . .' she began, only to have Paget anticipate her concern once again.

'Of course, anything you tell me would be held in the strictest confidence, Miss Hammond.'

'When would you want me to come in?' she asked cautiously.

'Would it help if I came to you?' he suggested. 'Perhaps later on today?'

He could hear the long, drawn out breath as she gave in. 'I do have some time after eleven this morning,' she said.

'That would work well for me,' he told her. 'And thank you. I really do appreciate it.' He hung up before Claire could have second thoughts and change her mind.

Paget was five minutes early. Claire's flat-cum-studio was on the second floor of a three-storey house that had been converted into flats in Horsefair Street. It was outside what was considered the high-rent district, but close enough and pricey enough to suggest that Claire Hammond's business must be flourishing.

'All the floors are the same,' she told Paget. 'They call them workshop flats, a good-sized work area at the front, and living quarters at the back. Ideal for someone with a small business like mine.'

The work area was quite large. The windows overlooking the street faced south. 'A boon in winter,' Claire told him, 'but it can get pretty hot and sticky in here by mid-afternoon in the summer. Still, it suits me well enough. Would you care for a cup of coffee, Chief Inspector? I made it just before you came, so it's quite fresh.'

'Thank you, Miss Hammond. Yes, I would. Just sugar, no milk.'

'Good. If you'd like to sit down, it will only take a minute.'

While Claire was out of the room, he looked around. Like the woman herself, the room appeared to be well organized and efficient. A large desk held a computer and all its wireless peripherals; a drafting table stood at an angle to the window to make the most of the light, and a large, round table, surrounded by comfortable chairs, occupied a corner of the room. Floor-to-ceiling egg-crate shelving on the wall dividing the workroom from the living quarters contained everything from swatches of material ranging from the finest tulle through drapery and upholstery material, to leather. Colour charts, and large metal rings containing colour chips were there as well, together with a variety of objects he couldn't begin to identify.

Claire returned and set a tray containing two full mugs of coffee and a bowl of sugar on the round table. 'Do sit down,' she said, 'and help yourself to sugar.'

Before sitting down herself, Claire went over to the desk and returned with a notepad. 'I thought it might help if I jotted down a few things about the people I mentioned to you earlier,' she said. 'But if I could see your list, there may be someone on it I've forgotten.'

Paget took several sheets of paper from his briefcase, along with a tape recorder. 'I don't have to use this,' he said, 'but with your permission, I would like to. It saves time and keeps the record straight.'

Claire nodded her agreement. She had done the same with clients for much the same reason.

'Right, then. I brought two copies of the list of people who attended the party,' he said, 'one for you and one for me. Perhaps we could begin by eliminating those who wouldn't have known Barry Grant in the past.'

They sat on opposite sides of the table, marking each name as they went down the list. Thirty-two people had been invited to the party, and only three had not turned up.

'Which means,' said Paget as they came to the end of the list, 'that as well as Kevin Taylor, his wife, his brother, and his father-in-law, we're left with five other people who could have overheard what was said at the bar. Unfortunately, we can't leave it there. I think it's safe to assume that they would have repeated what they'd heard to the other people at the party who may have known Barry Grant.' He picked up his cup and was surprised to find it empty.

'More coffee?' Claire asked.

Paget hesitated. Claire had been very cooperative up till now, but he sensed that she was not entirely comfortable talking about her friends. So, the more he could get her to relax, the better. 'If it's no trouble,' he said. 'You make good coffee.'

'It's no trouble,' she assured him. 'I could use a refill myself. Just be a minute.'

When Claire returned with the coffee, Paget asked about her work and what she was working on at present, and Claire found herself warming to the man. She'd thought him a rather cold fish when they'd first met in the Superintendent's office; the way he'd looked at her then had made her feel as if he were questioning everything she said. But now, facing him across the table, she could see the faint trace of a scar that had left one eyebrow higher than the other, giving him a perpetual quizzical look. Probably an asset in his profession, she thought as she covertly studied his face.

He had good features. Claire had discovered long ago that her interest in shape and form and structure was something that could be applied to virtually everything, not the least of which were faces. And Chief Inspector Paget had good, well-balanced features – apart from the raised eyebrow – but even that worked to his advantage, because it made his face more interesting. She wouldn't call him handsome, exactly, but he was attractive in a rugged sort of way, and not nearly as intimidating as she'd first thought.

Paget smiled. 'Miss Hammond?' he prompted.

Claire felt the colour rising in her face. 'Sorry,' she said hastily. 'I'm afraid my mind was wandering. Now, where were we?'

Paget pursed his lips as he looked at the list. 'I've met Kevin Taylor,' he said, 'but not his wife. What can you tell me about her?'

'Stephanie?' she said, frowning slightly. 'I don't know what I can tell you about her,' she said slowly. 'I didn't know her at school. She's a couple of years older than me, and I didn't meet her until a few days before she and Kevin were married. David told me they met at university. I think he said she was taking Business Administration, or something like that. Her father is Ed Bradshaw, but I wasn't formally introduced to him until last Saturday. David tells me that he is something of a fitness nut, which may be where Steph gets her energy from. She's a very dynamic person. She plays golf, tennis, swims, works out at the gym, that sort of thing, and still finds time to run a consulting business from home.'

'Impressive,' Paget commented. 'Would that be Grey's gym over by St Anne's?' He asked the question thinking that Grace might know Stephanie Taylor.

'Oh, dear, no,' Claire said with a grin. 'She and Kevin belong to Fairwinds. Steph goes out there at least three times a week. I go to Grey's. But I have played tennis with her a few times. She's very good.' Claire grimaced. 'Beats me every time, for what that's worth.'

'Would she have known Barry Grant?'

Claire nodded. 'They were both at Leeds at the same time. In fact I'm told he had quite a crush on her for a while until Kevin warned him off.'

'How did Barry take that?'

'I don't know. You would have to ask Kevin or Steph about that.'

Paget nodded and looked down at his list. 'Right,' he said. 'So let's move on. What can you tell me about this chap, Roger Corbett?'

The Rose and Crown had undergone a number of changes since the time of the robbery, the biggest one being an expansion into the premises next door to make room for a dining area, and it was to a table in there that the landlord, Thomas Grady, led Tregalles and Molly Forsythe.

'No,' Grady said in answer to a question from Tregalles about the kitchen, 'that's been changed as well. Had to move with the times and put in ovens, metal tables, refrigerators – two of them – and don't think they were cheap! Then there was the dishwasher, all new water pipes, ventilation and electrics. I tell you, there were days when I gave serious thought to packing it in, but we were well into it by then, so there wasn't much choice. It was a case of carrying on or losing everything we'd worked for. Used to be you could go into a pub for a quiet pint and a game of darts, but now it's all food and fancy drinks. Hell of a lot more work and damned little to show for it.'

Grady was a big, red-faced man, jowly and running to fat. His breathing was laboured, and he wheezed when he talked. 'Don't know what you expect to find after all this time,' he said truculently. 'If your lot couldn't find the bastards who robbed me thirteen years ago, I don't know how you expect to find them now.' He shot a meaningful glance at a clock on the wall. 'So whatever it is you want to know, best be quick about it, because I've got a lot to do before opening time.'

'I shouldn't think we'll be very long,' Tregalles told him, 'but that depends to some extent on how good your memory is. I've read the statement you gave us back then, but sometimes people remember little details that were missed at the time, and I'm wondering if anything like that has occurred to you?'

Grady shook his head. 'Not that I haven't thought about it a good many times over the years. Those bastards took every last penny of the New Year's weekend's takings, to say nothing of smashing all that crockery, including the wife's fancy plate collection. She'd've gone spare if she'd still been alive to see it. Worth a bit, some of them pieces were, but the insurance wouldn't have it. Believe me, if I'd remembered anything, I'd have let you know.

'Look,' he said, 'we could sit here all day and I'd still have nothing more to tell you, so unless you have something new for me, and like I said, I've got better things to do. I'd help you if I could, but I can't tell you any more than you already know.'

Molly slid her notebook into the pocket of her coat, and rose along with Tregalles. 'Your daughter, Sharon, was there that night, wasn't she, Mr Grady?' she said.

'Aye, she was,' he said in a softer tone. He pointed to a picture on the wall of a bright-eyed girl smiling into the camera. 'That's her, there.'

'Pretty girl,' Molly observed. 'Lovely smile.'

'That's why I keep it there,' Grady said grimly, 'because she's had little enough to smile about since. Not that I didn't warn her, but she wouldn't listen, would she?'

'We would like to talk to her,' Molly said. 'Can you tell us where we might find her?'

'She'll not be able to tell you any more than I can,' Grady said. 'She was scared stiff at the time, but she soon got over it. In fact I think she enjoyed being the centre of attention with her friends, talking about it all the time. But then, she was only eighteen at the time, and they don't take anything seriously at that age, do they?'

'We'd still like to talk to her,' Molly persisted.

Grady shrugged. 'Don't see as it can do any harm,' he said. 'Married name's Jessop. Husband's a lorry driver, at least he was last week, but you never know with that one. She never knows where he is, either, or when he'll be home, except on pay days – hers, of course. Leaves her to bring up two kids, working full time, then expects her to keep him supplied with beer money. I keep telling her to pack it in. Get a divorce, I tell her, but she doesn't listen to me. Never has for that matter since her mum died.'

He sighed, and for a moment looked genuinely sad. 'She lives not ten minutes from here in Peel Street,' he said. 'Number 12, but she'll not be home now. She works on the till at Fairways Foods. Doesn't get off till six this week. Now, I don't mean to be rude, miss, but I do have to get on.'

'Perhaps we could go out through the kitchen,' Tregalles suggested. 'I'd like to take a look for myself, even if things have changed, and I want to take a look at the back lane as well.'

With Grady leading the way, they went through the kitchen to the back door. The smell of fresh-baked pies permeated the air, and Tregalles lingered beside a tray containing something like three dozen meat pies in the vain hope that Grady would suggest he try one.

The room itself hadn't changed; it matched the photographs taken of the scene at the time of the robbery, but the old wooden kitchen table had been replaced by a stainless steel work-table; the fireplace had disappeared, and in its place were two large ovens. Stainless steel sinks, a dishwasher, and commercial-sized microwave stood against another wall, and the space where the Welsh dresser had been was now occupied by the two refrigerators Grady had mentioned.

A young oriental lad stood at the centre table wrapping sandwiches in cling-wrap, and stacking them on a long wooden tray, while a small, dark-haired woman stood at the sink, washing lettuce. Neither of them looked up as Molly and Tregalles passed through, in fact the woman bent even lower over the sink and kept her face averted as they went by.

Illegal immigrants? Possibly, Molly couldn't help wondering, but she wasn't about to ask.

'Just one more question before we go,' Tregalles said as they reached the door. 'Does the name Barry Grant ring any bells from back then? Young lad, bit of a show-off by all accounts. About the same age as your daughter.'

Grady frowned in thought, then shook his head. 'Doesn't mean anything to me,' he said, 'but if he was the same age as Sharon, she might have known him. You'd have to ask her. Why? Does he have something to do with the robbery? Was he one of the bastards who robbed us?'

'Still working on it,' Tregalles said evasively.

'Have you talked to him?'

'Can't, I'm afraid. He's dead.'

'Just as well if he was one of them,' Grady growled. 'Saves me the trouble of strangling the bastard myself.'

Little had changed behind the pub. A van parked there would have blocked the narrow lane completely, but no one else was likely to be using the lane at the time of night the robbery had taken place.

'Fat lot of good that did us,' Tregalles grumbled as they made their way back to the car. 'I told the boss it would be a waste of time, but he wouldn't have it. And I doubt we'll do any better by talking to Grady's daughter.'

'Still, it's worth a try, isn't it?' said Molly. 'She'll be at work now, but we could go round this evening.'

'Can't go tonight,' Tregalles told her as they got into the car. 'I have an ESSA meeting tonight.'

'I've heard of ESL, but what's an ESSA when it's at home?'

'English Schools Swimming Association. I'm on the committee, and we're preparing for a competition at the end of August, and I have to be there.'

'I could go to see Sharon myself,' Molly offered. 'Unless you'd rather . . .?'

'No, no,' Tregalles assured her hastily. 'As a matter of fact, it might be better if you did go on your own; she might talk to you more than she would to me. Now, what was the name of the next one on the list? The one who organized the poker games back then.'

'Walter Roach was the solicitor who organized the games,' Molly reminded him, 'but he left Broadminster several years ago, so the name I have at the top of my list is Appleyard. Roy Appleyard. He's the man who tried to resist when they demanded money. He owns that big plumbing supplies business in Glendower Road, but his office is in the back of the Bathroom Boutique, which he owns as well. When I phoned him this morning, he said he'll be in the office all day, but he also said he wasn't interested in talking to us unless we were coming to tell him we'd recovered his money.'

ELEVEN

'**M**r Corbett?'

The man lowered the newspaper and peered at Paget over the top of his glasses. 'Yes,' he said cautiously. 'Mr . . .?'

'Paget. Detective Chief Inspector Paget. Sorry to just walk in on you like this, but there is no one at the desk out front, so . . .'

'Ah, yes, of course.' Corbett swung his feet off the open filing drawer, closed it, and folded the newspaper. 'Joanie's probably in the back doing some copying or making tea,' he said. 'I wasn't expecting you to get round to me so quickly.' He took off his glasses and slipped them into his shirt pocket. 'Not that I can tell you anything anyway,' he added quickly, 'but Kevin said you'd be making the rounds.'

'You were talking to Kevin Taylor?'

'That's right. He phoned me last night to tell me you wanted to talk to everyone who was at the party last Saturday.' Corbett's tone changed to one of anxious concern. 'I couldn't believe it when I heard that someone had tried to burn down the old Grant house, and Claire could have been trapped inside. Terrible business, but I really don't see how I can help you. Kevin told me about your theory that it was someone at the party who did it, but with all due respect, Chief Inspector, I really do think you've got it wrong. I mean it's not as if any of *us* could have had anything to do with what happened to Kevin's father back then, is it?'

He looked to Paget for a response, and when none came, he let out a long breath in a sigh of resignation and said, 'Still, since you're here, I suppose . . .' He waved a hand in the general direction of a chair facing the desk. The words and the gesture hung in the air, a grudging acceptance of the inevitable.

Paget moved in and sat down.

The office was small, with barely enough room between the desk and the wall for Paget to sit comfortably. The desk itself was metal, scuffed and well-used, as wcrc the bookcase and chairs. A tiny fan in one corner of the room was doing its best to move the stale air around, but it was a losing battle.

Not exactly a top-of-the-line estate agent's office, he decided.

As for the man himself, Roger Corbett did not look well. His face was pale, his eyes unnaturally bright, and every so often a nervous tic tugged at the corner of one eye. The fingers of his right hand were nicotine-stained, and there was a half-open packet of cigarettes beside the ashtray. Corbett saw Paget's glance and, as if taking it as a cue, slid a cigarette out, stuck it in his mouth, and lit it. He inhaled deeply, then settled back in his chair and crossed one leg over the other.

'Right,' he said with false heartiness. 'Fire when ready, Chief Inspector.'

But Paget was in no hurry to begin, taking time to loosen his jacket and settle himself more comfortably in his chair while he covertly watched Corbett. The man was doing his best to appear relaxed, but his whole body was tense, and one foot kept tapping the side of the desk as if to make sure it was still there.

'Since you know why I'm here, I'll get straight to the point,' Paget said briskly. 'In the letters Barry Grant left behind, it's clear that he and several friends were involved in the botched

burglary and the killing of George Taylor and Mrs Bergman.
And, since you and some of the others who attended the party
last Saturday were classmates of his at Westonleigh, and were
at university together, I'll be talking to each one of you to
find out which friends he was referring to. So, how well did
you know Barry yourself?'

'Now, wait just a minute!' Corbett's foot hit the floor with
a resounding thump as he uncrossed his legs and sat up
straight. He plucked the cigarette from his mouth and waved
his hand at Paget as if warding him off. 'I think you've got
this all wrong, Chief Inspector. I was never a *friend* of
Barry's. None of us were. In fact we were always trying to
avoid him.'

'Why was that?'

Corbett shrugged uncomfortably. 'He just didn't fit into
our group,' he said evasively. 'It's true we all went to the
same school and then we all went on to Leeds, but I took
Philosophy, and Barry went into Engineering. Kevin was
reading Law, Steph was in Business Admin, and Graham
was taking Accounting, so we were scattered all over the
place. I don't know if you are familiar with the campus? It
covers a lot of ground, but even so, it was hard to avoid
Barry. He was always trying to ingratiate himself; trying to
impress us with wild stories about what he'd done or
intended to do. We couldn't go anywhere without him
popping up and making a nuisance of himself. He was
always there.'

'So tell me, Mr Corbett, if Barry Grant was always *there*,
as you say, when did he have the time to become involved
with another group to the degree that they functioned as a
well organized and disciplined gang who committed several
crimes?'

Corbett shook his head. 'God only knows,' he said. 'But I
can assure you that it was none of our crowd.'

'When you say "our crowd", whom do you mean, exactly?
Was this some sort of exclusive club?'

Corbett shifted uncomfortably in his chair. 'No, of course
not,' he said, 'and I didn't mean it to sound like that. It was
just that we all got on well together, and someone like Barry
just didn't fit in. Apart from myself, the ones from here were
Kevin and Steph, Pete Anderson, Graham Williams and John

Chadwell. There were a couple of others who weren't from around here: Jamie Mac-something-or-other, I forget his last name, and an Australian by the name of Don Wyatt. Don't know where either of them are now. We lost touch once we left uni.'

'And those from here were all old classmates from Westonleigh?'

'That's right. We'd all been to Westonleigh, although not all in the same year, and I didn't get to know some of them well until I got to Leeds. Except Kevin, of course. He was a year ahead of me in Westonleigh, but we ended up as partners on the debating society team in his last year there, and we became good friends.'

A faint smile tugged at the corners of his mouth. 'And then there was Steph, of course,' he said with a meaningful look at Paget. 'Now that *was* a surprise, I can tell you.'

'In what way?'

'Finding out that she and Kevin were living together. I mean I thought I knew Kevin pretty well, but that was a surprise, and one of the first things Kev said to me when I arrived in Leeds was that I wasn't to say a word to anyone back home. I thought he was kidding at first, but he was deadly serious. He said his father was dead set against Steph for some reason, and Kev didn't want him to find out, so he swore me and the others to secrecy.'

'Did he say what his father had against the girl?'

'No. Never did.'

'Do you know if Kevin's father ever found out?'

Corbett butted his cigarette in the ashtray. 'I doubt it,' he said, 'because Kev went back home and worked for his dad the following summer, and from the way he'd spoken about the old man, I doubt if that would have happened if he knew that Kev was still seeing Steph.' He frowned. 'But I don't see what that has to do with your investigation, Chief Inspector.'

Paget ignored the implied question. 'Tell me,' he said, 'where were you between one and three o'clock yesterday morning, Mr Corbett?'

For the first time since Paget had entered the office, Roger Corbett's face creased into a genuine smile as he leaned back and laced his fingers behind his head. 'Ah, yes,' he said with a touch of smugness, 'I was wondering when we would get around to that. And I'm glad you asked, because I do have an alibi for those hours. I'm staying at a friend's house while my wife is away, and she can verify that I was there.'

'The friend's name?'

'Irene Sinclair. She was at the party, too, by the way, but you can take her off your list of suspects because she didn't live in Broadminster back then.'

'And you were in her house overnight?'

'I was,' Corbett confirmed, 'and before you start asking if I could have slipped out without her knowledge, I'm sure she would have noticed if I had, because we shared the same bed.'

'Indeed?'

'Indeed,' Corbett repeated. He seemed to be waiting for Paget to ask another question, and a flicker of irritation crossed his face when Paget remained silent. 'My wife knows all about it, if that's what you're wondering,' he said waspishly. 'In fact we are all good friends; have been for years, so I suggest you look elsewhere.'

He leaned forward to emphasize his next words. 'And believe me, Chief Inspector,' he said earnestly, 'if you are looking for a connection between any of us and Barry Grant, you're wasting your time. He was a complete outsider, and none of us had anything to do with him.'

'Someone did,' said Paget, 'and it seems more than likely that they were people he'd known for some time. People who knew him well enough to trust him to do what he did best, like stealing vans when they needed them. You said yourself he was always looking for ways to ingratiate himself.'

'Could have been anybody, then, couldn't it? I mean who knows what sort of yobs he might have taken up with?'

Paget shook his head. 'I don't think so,' he said quietly, 'because Barry was only interested in being accepted by people like you and your friends; educated people with bright futures, and he was prepared to do anything asked of him to gain that acceptance. And those robberies were not the work of yobs, Mr Corbett. They were carefully planned and executed by intelligent people, such as those attending the party last Saturday, and I think someone at that party felt threatened by what he heard, and decided to do something about it.'

Corbett tapped his cigarette nervously against the rim of the ashtray, but he remained silent.

'I'm told you left university after the first year,' Paget said. 'Mind telling me why?'

Corbett butted the cigarette. 'I was ill,' he said. 'I started the second year, but I was missing more lectures than I attended, so I packed it in.'

'And of course, Barry died that summer, so he didn't go back either, did he?' Paget said. 'I presume this obsession of his with trying to ingratiate himself with you and your friends continued back here during the summer holidays, for example?'

'Oh, yes. It didn't matter where you . . .' Corbett stopped in mid-sentence and looked away.

'So,' Paget continued, 'would it be fair to say that, like it or not, you did see a fair bit of Barry Grant, not only while you were at university, but back here as well during the holidays?'

'But not to the same degree,' Corbett protested. 'I mean we all had summer jobs so we didn't get together as much, but all right, yes, he did sometimes turn up when we were having a drink together, or something like that. Don't ask me how he knew where we were. If it had been nowadays, I'd have said he was tracking us by GPS.'

'You say Barry was always trying to impress people by telling them of his exploits, real or imagined?' He waited for Corbett's confirming nod before going on. 'Which means that you must have learned quite a lot about what he was doing, or claimed to be doing. And given his nature, my guess is that he would find it almost impossible not to at least hint at what he was involved in.'

Paget looked thoughtful as he continued to look at Corbett. 'Unless, of course you knew what he was involved in, because you were involved in the same thing yourself,' he said quietly, then shook his head as if to dismiss the thought. 'But then,' he continued as if talking to himself, 'you've already told me that you went out of your way to avoid Barry, so that hardly seems likely, does it?'

Corbett eyed Paget warily. He wasn't quite sure whether he was expected to respond or not. His hand shook as he lit another cigarette and drew deeply on it. 'Look, Chief Inspector,' he said earnestly, 'I'm not quite sure what you expect of me. I've tried to be honest with you, tried to cooperate, and I resent the implication that I was somehow involved with Barry Grant, when I was not.'

'And yet you are clearly nervous about something,' said Paget mildly. 'And you have certainly gone out of your way to try to make me believe that neither you nor your friends could have had anything to do with Barry Grant. Did you and the others discuss this by any chance after what happened yesterday?'

'Of course not!' Colour flooded into Corbett's face. 'Why would we do that?'

'You tell me.'

Corbett rose to his feet. 'I think you have gone quite far enough with your questions, Chief Inspector,' he said. 'I have told you everything I know about Barry Grant, and I have nothing further to say on the subject. Now, I have work to do, and I would appreciate it if you would leave.'

'Just one thing before I go,' said Paget as he stood up. 'I believe that whoever tried to burn the Grant house down yesterday morning was at the party last Saturday. Had they succeeded, Claire Hammond could have been killed, so, bearing that in mind, tell me this: do you know or do you suspect who that person was, Mr Corbett?'

'No, I do not!' Corbett snapped, then clamped his lips shut and drew a deep breath. 'I'm sorry about what almost happened to Claire,' he said stiffly, 'and I'm glad she escaped without harm. But I've told you all I know, and I'm sorry I can't be more helpful.'

'Oh, but you have been helpful, Mr Corbett,' Paget told him as he made his way to the door. 'Very helpful indeed. Thank you for your time. I shall look forward to talking to you again.'

Corbett watched through the open door as Paget made his way past the secretary, now seated at her desk, and left the building. He closed the door, then returned to his seat. He sat there, eyes screwed up tightly, trying hard to recall what he might have said that had prompted Paget's parting words.

Nothing! He'd given him nothing. The Chief Inspector was bluffing, trying to shake him and make him think he'd given something away. But on the other hand, what if Paget wasn't bluffing?

Roger Corbett opened the bottom drawer of his desk, took out a bottle and glass, and poured himself a drink. He downed it quickly, then poured himself another before reaching for the phone.

There was a message from Fiona waiting for Paget on his return to Charter Lane, asking him to call her as soon as possible. He looked at the time and felt a twinge of guilt. Alcott was right, Fiona could be relied upon to deal with most things that crossed his desk, but it was hardly fair to leave so much to her while the Superintendent was away. He picked up the phone, then put it down again. Better to go up there and find out what she wanted.

What Fiona wanted was a word, and a serious one by the look on her face.

'It's Mr Alcott,' she said with a flick of her head towards the closed door of the Superintendent's office. 'He's in there, and he looks awful. I tried to talk to him; tried to ask him how his wife was, but he just said, "I'll call you if I need you," and almost pushed me out of the door. And that isn't like him, Mr Paget. I know he can be a bit moody at times, but this is something different, and I'm worried about him. Have you heard how his wife is getting on?'

'Nothing beyond what he told us the other day.'

'Could you try to talk to him?'

'I'll see what I can do,' he said. 'Was there anything else?'

'Some expenses that need a signature, but there's no hurry for them. It's Mr Alcott I'm worried about.'

'How long has he been in there?' Paget paused to ask as he made his way towards Alcott's office.

'Half, maybe three quarters of an hour, and not a sound out of him since he went in.'

'Right.' Paget opened the door to Alcott's office and walked in.

The Superintendent sat hunched over his desk. Never a big man, he appeared to have shrunk. His face was drawn, his skin was sallow, and his eyes seemed to have receded into their sockets. His hands moved restlessly back and forth across the surface of the desk, straightening objects and rearranging papers for no apparent reason. He looked as if he hadn't slept for days. Paget had intended to ask about his wife, but looking at the state Alcott was in, he was afraid of what the answer might be.

'Oh! Sorry, sir, I didn't realize you were here,' he said apologetically as he closed the door. 'Just came up to see what had come in this afternoon.'

Alcott lifted his head and stared at the Chief Inspector as if trying to decide whether to acknowledge him or not.

'If there's anything . . .?' Paget began, but was silenced by an impatient wave of Alcott's hand.

'Fiona called you, didn't she?' he said accusingly. 'Fussing about like a mother hen!'

'She's worried about you, sir, and with good reason, I'd say.'

'None of her business,' Alcott growled. 'Nor yours, for that matter.'

'Your wife . . .?' Paget ventured, almost afraid to put the question. 'How is she?'

Alcott lifted his head, then slumped back in his chair and rubbed his face with both hands. 'Emphysema,' he said cryptically. 'Marion has emphysema and now pneumonia. She's on oxygen and they're feeding her antibiotics intravenously. She's dying, Paget, and I'm responsible.'

Paget remained silent. There didn't seem to be anything he could say that wouldn't sound like a platitude in the face of such a statement.

Alcott sat up straight and took a deep breath. 'The damage to her lungs is permanent,' he said. 'Irreversible is what they said, and now, with this pneumonia . . .' He lifted his hands and let them drop in a helpless gesture.

'In that case, sir, shouldn't you be with her, rather than here?'

'Valerie, our youngest, is with her. Taken time off work.' Alcott raised his eyes to meet those of Paget. 'I had to leave,' he said huskily. 'I couldn't take it, watching her, listening to her gasping for air. And I can't stand being in the house on my own. Didn't know what else to do but come here. God knows what I'm going to tell Celeste. She came up from Bristol on the weekend to see her mother, and she all but accused me of killing Marion then. Val hasn't said it, but I'm sure she's thinking it; I can see it in her eyes. And they're right, Paget, it *is my fault!* It should be *me* over there in that bed, not Marion. She's dying and there's not a damned thing I can do about it!'

'Except be with her,' said Paget quietly. 'Let her know you're there. And it won't help matters if you don't look after yourself now. Have you slept at all?'

Alcott shrugged. 'Doctor gave me some tablets, but they don't seem to work.'

'And when did you last eat?'

Alcott glowered. 'You're beginning to sound like the nurses over there,' he said irritably. 'Who wants to eat at a time like this?'

'It's not a matter of wanting to,' Paget said firmly. 'It's a matter of whether or not you want to do what's best for your wife, because if you carry on this way, you're not going to be any good to anyone. Look, sir,' he continued earnestly, 'I know it must be extremely hard for you, but if you don't look after yourself, you'll wind up in hospital as well. Is that what you want?'

Alcott's eyes narrowed and his lips compressed into a thin line. Paget hurried on before he could speak. 'Come with me,' he said, 'and let's get some food into you. I know you may not feel like it, I know you blame yourself for what's happened, but you'll only make matters worse if you fall ill yourself.' He looked at the time. 'That little place on Marlborough Street serves meals all day. It's quiet and it won't be too busy right now. Believe me, sir, you'll feel the better for it.'

Alcott's mouth twitched, and Paget felt sure his offer would be refused. But, slowly, the lines around the Superintendent's mouth softened, and there was less hostility in the eyes as he raised them to meet Paget's own. He heaved himself out of his chair. 'You're right,' he said with weary resignation. 'I suppose it is for the best, although I don't know if I can eat much.'

'We're going out for a bite to eat,' Paget told Fiona as they made their way out. 'I'll be on my mobile if anyone should need me.'

He continued on, but Alcott hung back. 'Sorry I snapped at you,' he said to Fiona. 'It's Marion. She's not doing so well. I just wish . . .' He shrugged in a helpless fashion. 'Sorry,' he said again.

'It's all right . . .' Fiona began, but the words stuck in her throat. She cleared her throat and was about to try again, but Alcott was moving away.

'I hope you realize,' she heard him say as he rejoined Paget, 'that this isn't official business, so don't expect to claim this meal on expenses.'

Fiona stared at the screen in front of her. Her vision was blurred; there were tears in her eyes, but she couldn't help smiling. It seemed no matter how dire the circumstances, some things and some people would never change.

TWELVE

It was too nice an evening to stay inside after dinner, so Paget set up the lawn chairs on the shaded side of the house, while Grace brought out the wine and biscuits and cheese on a tray, and set them on a small table between the two chairs.

Now, sitting there quietly in the hush of the evening, he let his gaze wander over the pastoral scene. In the valley below lay the village of Ashton Prior, half hidden by trees and the shadows of the evening, while beyond, fading into the distance where land and sky melded into one, lay a patchwork of fields and farmhouses and villages whose names he could never remember. He closed his eyes and gave silent thanks to his father for choosing this place as his retreat from the noise and the pressures of life in the city.

It had been Paget's retreat as well when Jill died; not just from the Met and the city, where people and places were constant reminders of memories too painful to bear, but a retreat into himself; a place where he could hide and shut out the world.

His retreat and his salvation as it turned out, thanks in no small measure to his late father's housekeeper, Mrs Wentworth, who had literally bullied him out of his misery, and to Bob McKenzie, his old boss in the Met, who had persuaded him to rejoin the world.

He was grateful to them both, very grateful indeed, but it was Grace who had finally rekindled emotions and feelings he had long thought dead.

He sighed contentedly as he reached for her hand.

'Watch out for the wine,' she warned. 'That table has wobbly legs.'

He groaned. 'There I was in the middle of blissful thoughts and romantic dreams, and you shoot me down with talk of a table with wobbly legs.'

'You poor man,' Grace said with mock sympathy. 'Sorry if I popped your bubble, but you would have been even more upset if the table had gone over and we'd lost the wine. So you see, I was really thinking of you at the time.' She frowned. 'Romantic dreams about who? Or should that be whom?'

'Oh, just some woman I met a while back,' he said, 'but she's gone now. Probably gone to fetch a wedge for the wobbly table. Anyway, you were looking very thoughtful there. What were you thinking about?'

'The Alcotts,' she said softly. 'I haven't been able to get them out of my mind since you told me about the state Mr Alcott was in today. Do you think he did go back to the hospital after you left him?'

'He said he would go, but I don't know if he did. I offered to take him myself, but he insisted on picking up his own car back at Charter Lane, and he went off from there. Honestly, Grace, I have never seen such a change in anyone in such a short time. The man looks as thin as a rail; not that he was ever fat, but his face is gaunt, and he looks as if he hasn't slept since Marion went into hospital. I'm not even sure he's changed his clothes in all that time.'

'Is there anything we can do?'

'I told him he only had to ask. He promised he would let me know if there was anything he needed, but I doubt if he will.'

'No visitors, I suppose?'

'Just family. I'm afraid it doesn't look good.'

'Can I do any shopping for him?' Grace asked. 'It's not too practical to ask him to come all the way out here for a meal, but I could do a meal for him at home if that would help.'

'I think his youngest daughter, Valerie, is taking care of that end of things, but I'll let him know if I find that's not the case.'

Paget's thoughts drifted back to the conversation he'd had
with Alcott at lunchtime. In all the time he'd known the
Superintendent, the man had never had much to say about his
family or his home life, but it had all come pouring out during
the meal. He'd talked about his wife, about his daughters,
even to the point of telling Paget about the scene at the hospital
and again at home.

'I know I'm to blame for Marion's condition,' he'd concluded,
'and I wish to God I could undo what I've done to her, but I
can't. I feel guilty enough about it as it is, so the last thing
I need is Celeste sniping away at me every chance she gets.
Val's been very good, and she tries to tone her sister down,
but she's no match for Celeste.

'As for Marion,' he said, pausing for a moment to draw
breath and steady his voice, 'if she isn't going to recover,
I'd just like her last days to be peaceful and quiet, but
Celeste seems determined to carry on her fight with me at
the bedside. It's as if she wants to make sure that Marion
dies hating me as much as Celeste hates me. I could understand it better if there had been a strong bond between her
and her mother, but Celeste has been as cold and distant
with Marion as she has with me ever since she was a
teenager.'

He'd said no more until they were out in the street, and
then it was just desultory chat to fill the time until they were
back at Charter Lane.

Molly Forsythe looked at the time. She'd arranged to see
Sharon Jessop at nine, so it was time to be going. The sun
was almost down, and there was a faint breeze in the air, a
welcome change from the oppressive heat of the day, and
if she left now she could walk the short distance to Peel
Street.

Sharon Jessop had done her best to put Molly off when
Molly had spoken to her on the phone, but changed her
mind when she was told the alternative would be to take
time off work to come down to Charter Lane for a formal
interview.

'Then you'd better come over,' she'd said, 'but it will have
to be later. I can't put Laura to bed before nine with it being
so light in the evening, and Jimmy will still be up. Still, I

suppose he'll be watching telly, so we can talk in the kitchen.'

Talk, yes, but there had been a distinct lack of enthusiasm in Sharon's voice, and Molly couldn't help wondering if she was wasting her time. And it would be a waste of time if Sharon Jessop proved to be no more forthcoming than Roy Appleyard had been when she and Tregalles had spoken to him earlier in the day, because the man had been in a belligerent mood from the very start.

'I don't know why you expect to find out anything now after thirteen bloody years,' he'd greeted them. 'Waste of time and taxpayers' money if you ask me. Be better if you spent it doing something about the crime on the streets. Had my car done over three months ago. Window smashed, radio pried out, camera stolen. One of your blokes came round and spent God knows how long taking down details and asking damn-fool questions, and I haven't heard a word since, not one bloody word!'

Appleyard had sat back in his chair and eyed them with distaste as they stood in the doorway of his office. He was a big man, heavy-set and fat. Molly remembered thinking his shirt buttons must have been double-sewn, considering the strain they were under. God help anyone standing in the way if one of them ever burst off. His shirtsleeves were rolled up to reveal arms covered in hair, and his trousers were belted tightly beneath a bulging belly.

He waved a grudging hand towards chairs piled high with books and glossy brochures. 'Just shove that stuff on the floor,' he told them, and continued to sit there while they cleared a space to sit down. Tregalles lifted the pile off a chair and set it carefully on the floor, but Molly took Appleyard at his word, and shoved a pile of brochures off her chair and let them spill across the floor. Appleyard had given her a hard look, but she'd ignored it and sat down.

'Get on with it, then,' he said irritably to Tregalles, ignoring Molly completely as he had throughout the rest of the interview. Not that it had lasted long. The man had pretty much repeated what they had read in the thirteen-year-old report, and it soon became clear that he'd been right about one thing – they were wasting their time with him.

'There were four of them, they were covered from head to toe, they kept smacking those metal bars into the palm of their hands as if just waiting for an excuse to use them, and they took my money along with everyone else's. That's what I told the inspector or whatever he was back then, and I told him he needn't come back unless he had my money with him. So, do you have my money, Sergeant? Because if not, you can stop wasting my time and get the hell out of my office, because I have better things to do than answer your idiotic questions.'

Tregalles had tried to go on, but Appleyard had simply continued his harangue against the police, until the Sergeant finally gave up in disgust, and it was left to Molly to 'thank' the man for his cooperation.

Peel Street was bordered on both sides by grim-looking council houses, and yet there was an almost festive air about the place. Small clusters of people stood or squatted around open front doors, smoking, chatting, supping beer from cans, cooling down after the heat of the day. At least a dozen children of all ages were playing football at one end of the short street, while a gang of teenagers on roller blades tested their skills on a rickety ramp made of plywood.

Two women with prams stopped talking to eye Molly suspiciously as she checked the numbers and stopped in front of number 12. They exchanged meaningful glances and continued to watch. *Trouble there again, was there? Haven't seen that one from Social Services before. Must be new.* The door opened and Sharon Jessop stuck her head outside to look around, then almost pulled Molly inside and closed the door. The two women exchanged knowing looks, then went on with their conversation.

'Busybodies!' Sharon muttered as she turned to lead the way down the narrow hall to the kitchen. They passed a closed door behind which could be heard the sound of shooting mixed with the wail of sirens. 'Like I told you on the phone,' said Sharon with a nod as they went past, 'Laura's in bed and Jimmy will be no bother. Hope you don't mind, but I've got to get this ironing done before I go to bed. Seems like there's never enough hours in the day.'

'Funny you should say that, Mrs Jessop,' Molly said, 'because I've only just finished mine from the wash I did last Sunday.'

'Just call me Sharon,' the woman said sharply. 'Jessop might be my name, but it's not one I'm proud of, and I'd just as soon not be reminded of it, thank you. What did you say your name was, again?'

'DC Forsythe, when I'm being formal, but just call me Molly.'

Sharon smiled tiredly. She would be about thirty-one, now, not that much older than Molly herself, but she looked older. Fine-boned and slim, she'd kept her figure, but the wide-set eyes were dull, her chestnut hair looked as if it could do with a trim, and the once-fine lines of her face were beginning to blur. And now that she could see it properly, the shadow beneath Sharon's left eye looked more like a bruise, as did several marks on her bare arms.

'It's the kids, mostly, isn't it?' said Sharon wearily as she folded a well-worn T-shirt. 'Not,' she added hastily, 'that I'd ever want to be without them, but they do make work, don't they? Go through clothes and shoes in no time, and they're so expensive now. You got kids?'

Molly shook her head. 'I'm not married,' she said. 'But I think I know what you mean. I have a couple of nephews and a niece.'

Sharon drew a deep breath, set the iron aside, and said, 'Sod the ironing! I've had enough for one day. Fancy a cup of tea?'

'Thank you. That would be very nice. Anything I can do?'

'No. Just sit yourself down while I put the kettle on and put these clothes away, then I'll sit down and you can ask all the questions you like.'

They chatted in a desultory sort of way while Sharon made the tea and set out a couple of plates. 'They're from Marks and Sparks,' said Sharon a few minutes later as she offered Molly a biscuit, 'and me working at Fairways – at least I am for now, but they're talking about laying off, and I haven't been there all that long compared to some of the others.'

She sat down and took a biscuit herself. 'Don't seem to have time to bake, these days,' she said. 'Besides, they're just as cheap to buy as make them. Tea all right, is it?'

'Just the way I like it,' Molly told her.

'Good. Now, then, what is it you want to know?'

'Tell me about the robbery. I've read the reports, of course, but tell me what you remember.'

Sharon looked past Molly to focus on something in the distance. 'I don't think I can tell you much,' she said slowly. 'It all seems a bit vague, now, as if it happened to someone else rather than to Dad and me. Still, I can go through it again if you think it will help.'

'Please,' said Molly.

'Well, we had the money out on the table, counting it and tallying up, when these four blokes came storming in through the back door. God! I nearly jumped out of my skin. One of them just swept all the crockery off the dresser on to the tiles. Smashed to smithereens, it was; some of Mum's best china. It's a good thing she wasn't there to see it.'

'Were you facing the door when they came in, or did you have your back to them?'

'Facing them. Scared the shit out of me, I can tell you.'

'You were gagged,' Molly prompted. 'Tell me how that was done.'

'They just did it,' Sharon said. 'It all happened so fast. They grabbed Dad from behind and stuck tape over his mouth, then suddenly there was this bloke behind me, with an arm around my throat, pulling me out of my chair. Next thing I know he slaps tape over my mouth, then just held me there. He had this iron bar in his hand, and it felt cold and rough against the side of my face. The others had them as well, and I remember the leader and one of the blokes behind Dad kept slapping them into the palms of their hands. They had leather gloves on, and it was like drums beating. Gave me the shivers, it did. And when Dad tried to struggle, one of them pulled his head back with the bar against his throat like he was going to choke him. I tried to scream at them, but I couldn't because of the tape. Then, suddenly, like there was a signal or something, they slammed those bars on the table so hard that everything jumped around and fell on the floor. I was so scared. It was like a nightmare, except I knew it was real.'

Sharon went on to tell Molly about the leader holding up a card instructing her father to open the safe. 'Dad kept shaking his head, so they pushed his head down on the table and started slamming those bars down so close to his head I really thought they were going to bash it in. I was petrified because I knew that Dad could be stubborn, but he gave in, thank God.'

Even now, after all this time, Molly noted, Sharon's voice

shook as she said, 'I really think they would have done it, too, if he hadn't. I really do.'

'How did he manage to convey that to them, with head down and his mouth taped?' Molly asked. 'Don't misunderstand me, Sharon,' she added quickly, 'it's just that I'm trying to build a picture in my mind.'

'He flapped his hands,' Sharon said, and suddenly giggled. 'I shouldn't laugh,' she said, recovering quickly, 'but it's funny how things like that stick in your mind. I mean they were holding Dad's head down on the table and hammering away with those iron bars, money was jumping around all over the place, and there was Dad flapping his hands like mad, and all I could think of was how they looked like fish flopping about after they're caught.

'Then they let him up and he opened the safe,' she ended soberly.

'Is there anything about these men that stands out in your mind? Size, shape, anything? I know they didn't speak, but is there anything at all you can . . .?' Molly broke off as Sharon's eyes slid away and colour rose in her face. 'What?' Molly demanded. 'What have you remembered, Sharon?'

'Nothing! Honest, it was nothing . . .' She tried to look at Molly, but her eyes quickly slid away.

'Please, Sharon,' said Molly quietly, 'it could be important.'

Sharon tilted her head, and there was an odd little twist to her mouth as she said, 'I don't see how,' and giggled. 'I mean it's not the sort of thing you're looking for.'

Molly was disappointed. For a moment she'd thought that perhaps the young woman had remembered something of importance, but apparently not. On the other hand it was best to make sure.

'I'd still like to know,' she said. 'Sometimes it's the smallest detail that makes all the difference.'

'More tea?' asked Sharon as she picked up the teapot. 'Mine's gone cold.'

'No thank you, Sharon,' said Molly evenly, 'and I think you're avoiding the question. Please, just tell me and let me decide if it is useful or not. We really do need help with this if we're to find the people who committed those robberies and murders.'

Sharon looked thoughtful as she refilled her cup and dropped in two lumps of sugar. 'All right, then,' she said, 'I'll tell you if you promise not to tell my dad. OK?'

Molly eyed her suspiciously. 'Does it involve him directly? Because if it does, we might have to talk to him about it,' she warned.

Sharon, about to take a sip of tea, spluttered. 'That's the *last* thing you'll have to do,' she assured Molly. 'Promise?'

'Promise.'

Sharon set her cup aside. 'I couldn't say anything about it at the time,' she said, 'because Dad would have thrown a fit if he'd known, so I couldn't tell your lot, either. Not that it would have made any difference.'

'Tell us what, Sharon?'

'About them not saying anything during the robbery. That inspector kept going on about it, and we both said they didn't. But the one holding me did talk. Well, he didn't really *speak,* at least not loud enough for anyone else to hear, but he was whispering in my ear while everybody was watching Dad open the safe.'

'Whispering? Why?'

The colour deepened in Sharon's face. 'Because he was feeling me up,' she blurted. 'He had one hand around my neck, and the other one up my blouse. I couldn't say anything, because I had the tape over my mouth, and he was holding that bar in his other hand, and I didn't know what he might do if I struggled. Besides, I thought Dad might do something rash if he saw what was going on.'

Molly eyed Sharon suspiciously. 'You're telling me he was fondling your breasts with *gloves* on?' she said. 'Come on, Sharon, I'm not buying that.'

'He took his glove off. Honest to God. I'm telling you, that's what he did. Took his glove off and slid his hand up under my blouse. I mean why would I say that if he didn't? And I've never told that to anyone till now.'

'All right, Sharon; I believe you,' Molly said. 'You say he was whispering. What was he saying?'

Sharon grimaced. 'Typical man,' she said. 'One-track mind. You know what they're like. He kept saying something like, "You like that, don't you, Sharon? I *know* you do." His mouth was right against my ear, and he kept saying it over and over again, while his hand was, well, you know, under my blouse, and I wasn't wearing a bra.'

'Was there any reason why he said those particular words?' asked Molly.

Sharon looked puzzled. 'I don't know what you mean. I've told you what he said.'

'With the emphasis on "I *know* you do". Why would he say that, Sharon? Why did he say "I *know*"?'

Sharon shrugged, but her eyes were everywhere except on Molly's face.

'Look, Sharon, I'm not here to embarrass you, and whatever you tell me now will remain in confidence, but the man knew your name and it's possible that you knew the man. Did you recognize his voice or something about him?'

Sharon lowered her head and clasped her hands in front of her. She remained in that position for some time before looking up to meet Molly's gaze. 'I didn't *recognize* his voice,' she said, 'but it was like I *should*. Except I couldn't place it, if you know what I mean. Honestly, I didn't know who it was, and I still don't. It was too muffled for that, but it sounded familiar somehow, and I've often wondered about it.'

Sharon glanced furtively from side to side as if she half expected someone else to be listening, then leaned forward across the table and said, 'Look, Molly, I was no angel when I was growing up, and I'd been out with my fair share of lads, so it could have been someone I'd been out with before. But I couldn't say anything, could I? I mean, even if I had, it wasn't as if I could have identified him or anything. Besides, my dad would have killed me.'

Sharon might not have been able to identify the man, but it would have narrowed down the search considerably if she had told the police to start looking at her old boyfriends. 'What about his voice, Sharon? Think. Was there anything distinctive about it? You said he called you by name, so most likely he was young, possibly about your own age. What about the *way* he spoke? Did he sound like a local man? Someone from this part of the country?'

Sharon sighed. 'Honestly, Molly, I don't know,' she said. 'I was scared, and yet it was sort of exciting as well, if you know what I mean. And he was keeping his voice low so the others wouldn't hear; just whispering, that's all.'

She paused, brow furrowed, lips pursed in thought. 'Funny, but I never thought of that before,' she said slowly. 'He sounded local, but a bit more polished, if you know what I mean.' Sharon sat back, shaking her head. 'I just don't know,' she said 'It was a long time ago.'

'And you've never mentioned this to anyone else since that day?'

Sharon snorted. 'Would you?' she challenged. 'I mean it's not exactly something you boast about, is it?' She leaned forward. 'Look, Molly,' she said earnestly, 'I'll be honest with you. My mother died when I was seventeen, and I just went sort of wild after that. I had this girlfriend, Rachel; her parents were evangelicals, and very, very strict, and when they went away on some sort of missionary thing, she was left home alone. She was supposed to be studying for the same sort of work, but she was so sick and tired of being told that she would go straight to hell if she went to a dance or sang anything but hymns, that she *really* kicked over the traces, and it was parties and boys every chance we got. We went out *looking* to get laid. There were so many boys, I don't even remember their names.'

'Could the man behind you have been Barry Grant?'

Sharon looked blank. 'Doesn't ring any bells,' she said, 'but then I never even *knew* the names of some of the boys we went with.'

'But you do remember the robbery of the jeweller's later that year, where two people were killed by the same men who robbed the Rose and Crown?'

Sharon nodded, but looked puzzled by the question.

'Barry Grant committed suicide a few days after that; I'm sure you must have heard about it. He was about your age, and Broadminster isn't *that* big.'

Sharon shook her head slowly from side to side. 'I remember hearing about Mr Taylor being killed along with the woman from the jeweller's, because we used to get our bread and pies from Taylor's bakery, so we knew who he was. But I don't remember anything about a suicide. Sorry, Molly, but I really don't.'

'What about Rachel?' she asked. 'Would she remember some of the names?'

'She might,' Sharon said without conviction. 'Haven't seen

her in years, though. She went off with some bloke a couple of months before we were robbed, but I've no idea where they went. Haven't heard from her since.'

'What was Rachel's last name?'

Sharon frowned in concentration as she looked up at the ceiling. 'It was a funny name,' she said at last. Foreign, like. Could have been German or something like that. Sorry, but I really can't remember.'

Later, as Molly drove home and thought about what she'd heard, she couldn't help wondering about Sharon's memory, or lack of it when it came to names. She'd been clear enough about the details of the robbery, but couldn't seem to remember a single name of the boys she'd been with, or that of her friend. And unless she was a much better actress than Molly gave her credit for, the name of Barry Grant had meant nothing to her.

THIRTEEN

Wednesday, July 15th

L isa Corbett slept in on Wednesday morning. At least it was late for Lisa, who was usually up by six and well into her morning exercises by six-fifteen. But this morning she'd decided this was going to be one of her free days. She did that every so often; giving herself a day off from her normal routine. Oh, she would still do her warm-up stretches and her regular daily run, but she would skip the hour of exercise in what she called her mini-gym that separated her bedroom from Roger's.

She lay there, her naked body covered only by a single sheet, eyes half closed against a shaft of sunlight edging ever closer to her face. She'd get up before it reached her eyes, she told herself, then changed her mind and slid out of bed. She paused to cast a critical eye at the image of herself in the full-length mirror, turning this way and that before moving on. Thirty-five and still looking good, she told herself as she made her way to the shower.

Lisa was proud of her body, and she had every right to be, considering how hard she'd worked to keep it that way for much of her life. Even so, Ramon was probably right; perhaps she did need to shed a couple of pounds. It was surprising how even a pound or two could make a difference to their movements on the dance floor, and she hadn't been watching her diet as closely as she should have during the run-up to the competition.

They'd taken a third at Scarborough, which was good for them, considering the calibre of the competition, but they had both gone up there with high hopes of coming out on top this time, so it was disappointing. Lisa was still convinced that they could have made second if the one judge hadn't been so tight with his marks. But that was all part of the business, and you just had to live with it and try again another day.

Lisa dried herself off, then stepped on to the scales and slowly shook her head. The man was uncanny. Two pounds it was, almost to the ounce. But then, Ramon was rarely wrong about things like that.

She wrapped herself in a bathrobe, brushed out her hair, then wound a towel turban-fashion around her head before going out on to the terrace to stand with her face to the sun. It was going to be hot again today, but right now it was just pleasantly warm, and Lisa was in no hurry to get dressed.

She walked to the edge of the terrace and sat down on the flagstones at the top of the steps leading down to the lawn. Roger should have been up by now if he intended to go to work, but from what she'd seen last night, he would probably come staggering out about ten. Well, that was his problem. As far as she was concerned, Lisa intended to enjoy the morning.

The flagstones were warm. Lisa drew up her knees and wrapped her arms around them and rocked gently back and forth as she took in the familiar scene.

Birds flitted from branch to branch in the trees shading the pond at the bottom of the garden, their twittering and muttering among themselves pierced every so often by the clear, triple trill of a song thrush, barely visible in the shadow of the hedge. A pair of nuthatches worked their way up and down a tree trunk, while from across the fields, in Miller's Copse, came the muted chuck-chuck-chuff sound of a partridge.

Up here on Rutherford Hill, with its tree-lined streets and broad boulevards, it was almost like living in the country. Lisa had spent many happy hours in this house and in this garden as a child, for this had been her grandmother's house, and Lisa's home whenever her parents were out of the country, which had been most of the time until she was ten.

Her house now. And Roger's, of course, but not for very much longer. She was still very fond of him, but until he admitted that he had a problem, there was nothing more that she could do. She'd had enough, and it was time to call it quits.

Lisa pushed the thought to the back of her mind. It was too pleasant out here to be thinking about that. The warmth of the sun, the sound of the birds and the faint smell of hay was seductive, and Lisa could feel herself drifting . . .

But whether she liked it or not, there were things to be done, she reminded herself as she looked at her watch. There wasn't much left in the fridge. The milk was going off – hardly surprising in this weather, which meant there was shopping to do, and she wanted to get it done before it became too hot and muggy in town.

Lisa stood up and stretched. Time to get dressed, but what to wear? Dress or halter and shorts? Dress, she decided as she re-entered the house. She'd spent enough time in the sun with Ramon before coming home; best not to overdo the tan.

She'd call Roger before she went out. He could do what he liked about his own breakfast or lunch, depending on the time.

'Just as well Tregalles wasn't with you,' Paget observed when he read Molly's report. 'I doubt if Mrs Jessop would have been as forthcoming if a man had been there.'

'I'm sure she wouldn't,' Molly agreed, 'but even then, when I asked her to give me the names of former boyfriends, she insisted that she couldn't remember any of them.'

'Did you remind her that by withholding information she could be shielding a murderer?'

'I did, sir, but it made no difference. I got no reaction whatsoever when I mentioned Barry Grant, but I still think she's holding something back. However, I would like to try to find her old girlfriend, Rachel, and see what she remembers. I

don't think it should be too hard to find out who, in the evan-
gelical community, left here some fourteen years ago to do
missionary work, leaving behind a daughter named Rachel.'

Paget nodded approvingly. 'Good idea,' he said. 'Anything
else, Constable?'

Molly wondered if she should mention the bruises on
Sharon's face and arms, but decided against it. It was pure
speculation that the woman was being abused, and she couldn't
see how it could be relevant to the case. She shook her head.
'I believe that's all for now, sir.'

'Right. So, who are you and Tregalles seeing today?'

Molly flipped her notebook open. 'Just the two remaining
people who were at the poker game,' she said. 'Dr Gerald
Warden at the Broadminster Clinic, and Paul Preston, owner
of Preston's Superior Leasing and Rentals – they're the ones
who have all that heavy equipment, like JVCs and such out
on the Clunbridge Road. Unfortunately, Walter Roach, the
solicitor who hosted the card game, left the area several years
ago to join a firm in London, and Alice Nelson died last
year.'

Molly glanced at the time. 'Dr Warden said he could see
us between nine and ten, before the clinic opens, so if there's
nothing else, sir, I'd better be off.' She moved towards the
door, then paused. 'Is there any word on how Mrs Alcott is
doing, sir?' she asked. 'I've only met her once, and only for
a few minutes, but she seemed very nice.'

'You've met Mrs Alcott?' Paget sounded surprised. 'When
was that?'

'A couple of months ago,' Molly told him. 'We happened
to park our cars next to each other in the Village Mall car
park one Saturday. It was just after I received the results from
the Sergeant's exam. I said hello, and was about to carry on,
but Mr Alcott stopped me and introduced me to his wife. It
was a bit embarrassing, really, because she said the
Superintendent had told her about me, and she congratulated
me on my marks. It took me by surprise, because I'd never
thought of the Superintendent as . . .'

Molly stopped speaking. Now she *was* embarrassed. She
hadn't meant to run on like that, especially to DCI Paget.

'Never thought of him as having a softer side?' Paget said
with a smile. 'I doubt if many of us have,' he said.

'Unfortunately, Mrs Alcott's condition is not good, and only time will tell how things will go. But kind of you to ask, Forsythe. Very kind indeed.'

'This is the list of people we've talked to,' Sergeant Ormside told Tregalles, 'and we still have a couple of dozen to go. There may be more, but we've drawn a blank so far. No one, and I mean *no one*, will admit to having been a close friend of Barry Grant. They admit to knowing him, and some have told us stories about him, but that's all.'

'And we're not doing any better with the people who were robbed,' Tregalles told him. 'Anyway, I see Molly's back, and we've got an appointment with Dr Warden at nine, so we'd better get on. I just hope he isn't another pillock like Appleyard.'

In the event, Dr Warden kept them waiting until twenty minutes to ten, and even then he kept glancing at his watch as Tregalles and Molly questioned him. In his late fifties or early sixties, he was short, sharp-featured, and impatient. No, he hadn't thought about the robbery in years, and he certainly couldn't tell them anything more than he'd told the inspector at the time of the first investigation. The one thing he did remember, however, was the amount taken from him.

'Eight hundred and forty-five pounds,' he said heatedly. 'All because of Roach! He's the one who wanted us to settle up each time with cash. But then, that's a solicitor for you.'

'What were you doing before that?' asked Molly. 'I mean, how did you settle up?'

'Originally, we kept a tally of our wins and losses, then settled up at the end of each month, usually by cheque, but Roach decided he didn't like that. He wanted cash. I wasn't much in favour, but no one else objected, so I went along, and look what it got me.'

'How long before the robbery did you make the change to cash?'

Warden frowned in concentration. 'Must have been about six or eight months before,' he said at last. 'I don't remember exactly. I know we'd been doing it for some time, but I can tell you, we never did *that* again. I think, between us, we lost over four thousand pounds that night.'

Tregalles took up the questioning again, but it soon became

obvious that Warden had nothing more to tell them. 'Just one more thing, doctor,' the Sergeant said as they were leaving, 'can you tell us where we can find Mr Roach?'

Warden shook his head. 'Left here four or five years ago,' he said. 'I heard he went with some firm in London, but I'm nor sure about that. Sorry, can't help you.'

'He wasn't a close friend, then?'

'Good lord, no! Insufferable man! But he played one hell of a game of poker.'

They met Paul Preston at his house, a two-storey rambling conversion about a mile past the Broadminster town limits, and within half a mile of his business. The house was on a wooded rise, almost hidden from the road, and Preston himself came out to greet them as Tregalles brought the car to a stop at the top of the circular driveway.

Dressed in an open-necked shirt, shorts and sandals, he was a tall, round-shouldered man, with white hair, white moustache and a kindly face. He shook hands with both of them and then asked if they would mind walking with him through a nature trail behind the house. 'Heart,' he told them cryptically. 'Triple bypass. I walk each day at this time and I like to stick to a routine. Never did much walking before, but I wouldn't miss it now.

'Don't worry,' he said as he saw Tregalles squint at the sun, almost at its zenith, now, 'it's cooler in the woods. Come on, Sergeant, you'll enjoy it.'

The walk was a pleasant one, but they were well along the forest path before Tregalles was finally able to persuade Preston that while they were interested in the events leading up to his heart attack, and the operation itself, they were more interested in what he could recall about the robbery that had taken place thirteen years ago.

Preston apologized, then launched into a rambling account of the robbery and a history of each player and their skills, or lack of them, as poker players, before coming back to his heart attack once more.

Molly and Tregalles walked with Preston for the best part of an hour, and tried hard to keep him focused on the robbery, but in the end they learned nothing they didn't know before – at least about the robbery.

'Well, that was a total waste of time,' Tregalles grumbled as they got into the car.

'Oh, I don't know,' said Molly. 'At least we shouldn't have any trouble recognizing the early warning signs of a heart attack in future, so it was instructive. And I enjoyed the walk. We should do that sort of thing more often.'

FOURTEEN

The timing of Claire Hammond's visit to David Taylor's shop was by no means accidental. She had chosen to arrive fifteen minutes before the shop was due to close quite deliberately, because she knew there was little likelihood of anyone coming in after that. David had been keeping the shop open till six in the hope of catching people coming off work, but as he'd told Claire, only three customers had come in after five in the past month, and only one of those had bought anything, so he had gone back to shutting the shop at five.

In fact, he was startled into wakefulness when the bell over the door jangled harshly as Claire came into the shop. He'd been browsing through an old copy of an art magazine, and had begun to drift.

'Claire!' he said neutrally. 'What brings you here? I left a message for you after Kevin told me what had happened at the house, in fact I left a couple. Are you all right?'

'I'm fine,' she told him, 'and I'm sorry I didn't ring you back, but I've been rather busy, what with the police, the house, and trying to keep up with my business. But I bring good news. My client has agreed to buy the seascape we spoke about last time I was here, so I hope you haven't sold it to someone else in the meantime. Eighteen hundred, wasn't it?' She flashed a smile of mock guilt. 'I hope it was, because that's the price I quoted, and that's the price he's agreed to pay.'

'You're joking, of course?' he said, half believing she might be but hoping she wasn't. 'I told you *maybe* twelve hundred.'

'And I told you it was worth more than that,' Claire countered.

'Then you must have the difference as a commission,' he said. 'And thank, you, Claire. Thank you very much.'

'You're very welcome, David,' she said, 'but no commission. Your seascape fits in beautifully with the motif we are trying to create, which helps me, so there is no way I'm going to accept a commission for that.'

He eyed her for a long moment, but could see from the set of her mouth that there was no point in arguing. 'Then let me buy you dinner,' he said. 'You name the place. Anywhere you want to go. This is fantastic! Are you free tonight?'

'I am and I'd like that,' she said. 'How about Torino's?' It was a small Italian restaurant, tucked away in an alley off Cross Lane, and Claire knew of David's fondness for Italian food. She had been there a number of times herself, and she'd never been disappointed. The pasta was excellent, the cheeses superb, and you could sit there in one of the brick-lined alcoves as long as you liked, sipping wine and enjoying the ambience and the company.

'Great,' he said, glancing at the time. 'I have some cleaning up to do, but I'll give them a ring now and book a table. Would seven be all right for you?'

Later that evening, as they were finishing dinner, David raised his glass and said, 'To you, Claire. Selling that painting couldn't have come at a better time. And as for eighteen hundred? Wow! It really is a lifesaver, because it will give me a bit of breathing room while I decide what to do.'

'Is business really that bad?' Claire asked.

He nodded. 'I'm afraid it is,' he confessed. 'In fact, it's been going downhill for some time now. There are all sorts of reasons I could give you, but it comes down to me in the end. I'm not a businessman, Claire, I'm a painter. My shop is too small, it's in the wrong place, and I can't afford to carry enough really good stock to attract people away from the shopping centres. The Internet doesn't help, either. And to make matters worse, I have almost no time for painting, and the light in my place ...' He spread his hands. 'Well, you've seen it, haven't you?'

She nodded. It wasn't just small, it was *dingy*! How he could even begin to be creative in a place like that she couldn't imagine.

It had never crossed her mind until that moment, but suddenly Claire had a vision of David Taylor in front of an easel in the conservatory in Aunt Jane's house – her house now. There was plenty of light and plenty of room; it would be ideal! For that matter, there was more than enough room in the house for both of them and that would solve his housing problem as well.

On the other hand, she hadn't made up her mind about whether to move in herself, so it would be cruel to raise David's hopes until she was sure. Perhaps she should take a bit more time to think it through.

Claire picked up her glass and gave a sympathetic nod. 'I think you've done very well to have survived at all, considering the odds,' she said. 'Do you have any sort of plan of action in mind?'

He shook his head. 'It's going to be hard to find someone to take over the lease, especially the way things are today. However, with what I've managed to scrape together, and the proceeds from the painting, I can at least get some of my creditors off my back, and that should give me time to work something out with the bank.'

'What would you really *like* to do, David?'

He smiled. 'I'd *like* to go somewhere quiet and peaceful and just spend my time painting and not have to worry about anything else,' he said wistfully, 'but I know that's not going to happen, so my first priority will be to find a job and a place to live.'

'I just wish there was something I could do . . .' Claire began, then stopped, afraid her innermost thoughts might betray her.

'There's not much anyone can do,' he said, 'and I shouldn't be burdening you with my problems, especially after what you've done for me today. We came out to celebrate.' He raised his glass again. 'So, thanks again, Claire. Here's to tomorrow and a brighter future!'

They drank and set their glasses down. 'Now,' he said, 'I'm afraid it's been all about me so far, and I apologize for that.' His voice took on a serious tone as he continued. 'What's happening with the police investigation? It certainly looks as if it stirred someone up if they tried to set fire to the house. Thank God you were able to scare him off. Do you think they knew you were in the house?'

Claire shook her head. 'I'm pretty sure they didn't. They probably assumed the house was empty, because they weren't bothering to be quiet while they were sloshing all that petrol about.'

Impulsively, he reached across the table to cover Claire's hand with his own. 'Do the police have any idea who did it? Kev said they've been talking to everyone who was at the party, and I half expected your Chief Inspector friend to come round again, but I haven't heard from him at all.'

'It's probably only a matter of time,' Claire told him. 'He came to see me yesterday. He was looking for some background on the people who were at the party last Saturday.'

David frowned. 'Background?' he said. 'What sort of background? And why would he come to you? What was he after?'

'Nothing that would incriminate anyone, if that's what you mean,' Claire said lightly. 'And I assume he came to me because I've been involved from the beginning, and I was the one who let it slip that the police were going to search the house. As he said, to him they were just names on a piece of paper, and all he wanted from me was a sort of thumbnail sketch of who they were and how they came to be at the party.'

'Isn't that rather odd? I mean what did you tell him about me, for example?'

'Just that you were there along with everyone else.' Puzzled, Claire withdrew her hand. 'Why? Is there something I *shouldn't* have told him, David? I don't understand. I've said nothing detrimental about you or anyone else, and yet I get the uncomfortable feeling that you think I shouldn't be talking to the police at all. I know it's a long time after the fact, and it won't bring your father back, but I thought you would be pleased to know that they are trying to find the people who killed him.'

Claire sat back in her chair and eyed him quizzically. 'Why are you so nervous about the police talking to me?' she asked quietly. 'There's something you're not telling me, and I'd like to know what it is, because you've been worried about it ever since I came to the flat the other night. Why do I have the feeling that you think I've done something wrong?'

David Taylor sighed heavily. 'You haven't done anything wrong, Claire,' he said. 'It's me. My own guilty conscience about how things were back then. You never knew my father, did you?'

'No, I didn't. Unfortunately, the one clear memory I do have of him is when he shouted at me and told me to get my sticky little fingers off the glass display case. I think I was about five or six at the time, and he scared the daylights out of me.'

'Scared the daylights out of me a good many times as well when I was growing up,' David confessed. 'He could be very sharp, even with his customers. He was a hard worker and a good man in many ways, but everything – and I do mean *everything* – had to be done his way. He had our lives mapped out right from the time Kevin and I were born, and as kids we accepted that. But as we grew older, and developed a few opinions of our own, things became more difficult, especially for me, because I wasn't prepared to follow the plan.'

'The plan . . .?'

'That Kevin and I should have the education he never had, and go on to university with the ultimate goal of going into one of the professions: doctor, dentist, lawyer, whatever, it didn't matter as long as it was a recognized profession, and an arts degree just didn't cut it. He tried everything he could think of to dissuade me. He would remind me that he and my mother had gone without a lot of things so my brother and I could have a good education, and by rejecting what was good for me, I was throwing it back in their faces. There was money in the bank for our education, but it was not going to be frittered away on some fanciful idea that I could earn a living by painting. In short, he did his best to make me feel guilty about the path I'd chosen.'

David took a sip of wine and set the glass down again. 'And he succeeded,' he said quietly. 'Believe me, Claire, I tried to get him to see it would be a sheer waste of time and money for me to follow Kevin, because I had no interest in any of those things, but he wouldn't listen. I just wanted to let the matter drop, but Dad wouldn't let it go. He kept sniping at me every chance he got, and he was doing it again on the morning he died. He was upset to begin with, because something had gone wrong with the first batch of loaves that morning, and we were running behind, so he took it out on me.

'He kept going on about how hard they'd saved to make sure that Kevin and I would make something of our lives, and how ungrateful I was . . .' David looked away as he said, 'I just lost it, Claire. I told him I didn't want his money, and I was quite capable of making it on my own, and I had no intention of spending my life living his dream.'

David picked up his glass and emptied it. 'And that's the last thing I said to him before leaving to do the morning deliveries,' he said. He set the glass down. 'I know I can't change things, but I can't help wishing I hadn't said some of the things I did that day.' He flicked an apologetic glance at Claire. 'So when you told me the other night that the investigation was on again, everything came rushing back, and I'm afraid I overreacted. So between that and Barry's suicide, I . . .'

Claire frowned. 'Barry's suicide?' she said. 'What did that have to do with it?'

But David brushed the question aside. 'Nothing,' he said tersely. 'Just that it happened so soon after, that's all.'

He drew a deep breath. 'But that's enough of that!' he said lightly. 'I'm becoming positively maudlin, and we came out to celebrate. You should have stopped me, Claire.' He picked up the bottle. 'Can't let this go to waste. More wine? Let's have your glass.'

'No need to apologize,' Claire said, allowing him to top up her glass. 'I'm glad you told me because . . . well, I did wonder. I'm just sorry I was the one to stir up old memories. Funny how you and Kevin are so different. Did he ever take sides?'

David laughed. 'As a matter of fact Kevin benefited from my scraps with Dad, because it kept Dad's attention off him and his relationship with Steph.'

Clair looked puzzled. 'Why? What was wrong with that?' she asked. 'I would have thought he would be pleased that Kevin was going to be marrying the daughter of the head of a law firm.'

David made a face. 'He would have been,' he said, 'if it hadn't been for the infamous Cornish pasty case, when Dad was sued by a customer who became ill after eating one of our Cornish pasties.

'You see, Dad and Ed Bradshaw used to be friends. Not close friends, but they'd known each other for a long time. So when he found out that Ed was acting for the customer who was suing Dad over some tainted Cornish pasties that had come from our ovens, he was furious with Ed, and from that time on it was not a good idea to mention Ed Bradshaw's name around our house.

'So, when Dad found out that Kevin was dating Stephanie Bradshaw, that *really* set him off. He told Kevin he could forget any support, financial or otherwise, from him if he continued to see Steph, and told him flat out to drop her.

'Well, you know Kevin; he's nothing if not a realist, and tuition fees, especially for someone reading Law, were pretty steep even back then, so Kevin told Dad he'd dropped her. He hadn't, of course, in fact the two of them were living together on campus, but they had to be very careful whenever they came home between semesters. It was tricky at times, especially after Kevin went to work for Ed Bradshaw, and . . .'

David sucked in his breath and stopped speaking. 'But that is another story,' he said, 'and I've bored you enough for one evening, Claire. Care to go clubbing when we leave here?'

'Thank you, but no,' Claire said. 'Pleasant as this has been, I don't want to be late home tonight, because I have a lot of catching up to do. And don't change the subject. What were you about to say about Kevin going to work for Ed Bradshaw?'

But David refused to be drawn, and when they parted company later that evening, her question still remained unanswered. As did the question David had brushed aside when she'd asked why he had mentioned the suicide of Barry Grant in the same breath as his problems with his father.

FIFTEEN

Thursday, July 16th

It wasn't the sort of venue Molly Forsythe would have chosen for an interview, but Peter Anderson had insisted on it. 'It is the only time I have free, today,' he'd told her on the phone. 'I leave tonight for a conference in Stockholm, so it

is either there this morning or you'll have to wait until after
I come back a week from today.'

'There' was the cafeteria on the first floor of Marks and
Spencer's in Fish Street. It was across the street from
Anderson's office and, as he explained to Molly when they
sat down to face each other across the small table, he had
been coming here almost every morning for years for hot
chocolate and a teacake. 'Best hot chocolate in town,' he told
her as he spooned the whipped cream topping into his mouth.

Molly had her coffee black. She didn't really like it, but
she'd decided she was using too much sugar, so she was trying
to get used to going without.

She glanced around. Mid-morning, and the place was filled
with shoppers, mostly grey-haired couples and women with
babies and small children. The only available table was outside
the baby-change room, and a steady stream of young mothers
paraded past their table. The noise level was high, and Molly
had to listen hard to hear what the man was saying.

Peter Anderson looked as if he'd been carved from rock.
Solid body, square face, deeply chiselled features, hair clipped
short and already turning grey, and pale eyes that never seemed
to blink. A self-important man, Molly decided, because, despite
his insistence that he didn't have much time to spare, it was
becoming clearer by the minute that he was trying to impress
her.

'I am presenting a paper in Stockholm,' he said proudly.
'Representatives from all over the world will be there. My
sphere of interest is in metal fatigue; the stresses and strains
on metals found in everything from the materials used in large
buildings and bridges to such things as hinges and handles
on saucepans and kitchen utensils.'

He paused to sip his hot chocolate, and Molly seized the
opportunity to take control of the conversation. She asked
the standard questions and received the standard answers. Yes,
he had known Barry Grant, and didn't think much of him.
Why? Because he was stupid. He had brains, he could have
been almost anything he wanted, in Anderson's opinion, but
he spent all of his time trying to impress people by doing silly
stunts.

'What sort of stunts?' Molly wanted to know.

Anderson shrugged. 'Like playing truant, then sitting outside the school gates with some older kids in a stolen Porsche or BMW, or whatever, to impress the girls as they came out of class. Absolutely idiotic, of course, because the police would have him before the end of the day. But he never learned. He would do something equally stupid the following week.'

'Are you talking about when he was at Westonleigh?'

'Good God, no! If he'd done that at Westonleigh, he would have been out on his ear, and he knew it. No, this was while he was still at Gordon Street. He would only be about ten or eleven at the time. Police were powerless because of his age, of course, but then that's what happens when we live in a country where no one is responsible for anything any more.'

'But he did do well enough at Westonleigh to go on to university,' Molly pointed out.

'Means to an end,' Anderson said through a mouthful of teacake. 'That's all it was. Means to an end.'

'Meaning what, exactly?'

Anderson stuck a straw into his drink and sucked deeply before sitting back to fix Molly with his pallid eyes. 'Social climbing,' he said. 'That's what Grant was all about. That's all he ever thought about; getting in with the right crowd. Being accepted. But all he succeeded in doing was making a nuisance of himself.'

'Were you in that crowd, Mr Anderson?'

Anderson considered the question. 'I suppose I was,' he conceded. 'I come from, what I suppose Grant would consider to be a wealthy family, although my father worked his way up from an ordinary bricklayer to become the owner of a construction company. As for me, while I was given encouragement at home, I got where I am today through my own merits and hard work. Barry Grant wasn't prepared to do that.'

'You were there last Saturday when Miss Hammond was talking about searching the Grant house, were you not, Mr Anderson?'

The man nodded, popped another piece of teacake in his mouth, and said, 'Yes, and I'm told that someone tried to burn it down on the weekend.' He raised a warning finger. 'I hope you are not suggesting that I had anything to do with that?'

Molly held the man's gaze. 'Did you?' she asked.

'Don't be absurd! Of course not.'

'Where were you from say midnight to three o'clock on Monday morning, Mr Anderson?'

Anderson wiped his mouth with a paper napkin. 'I was asleep in my bed,' he said, 'but I have no wife, no sleeping partner, so you will just have to take my word for it, Miss Forsythe.'

Molly tried another tack. 'Did Barry have a girlfriend when he was in university?'

Another shrug. 'If he did, I don't know who it was. Why would I? I wasn't interested in what he was doing or who his friends were, male or female. In fact I made it a point to avoid him whenever possible.' Anderson looked pointedly at his watch, then pushed his chair away from the table and stood up. 'I'm afraid I have no more time,' he said. 'I'm sorry I couldn't be of more help, but as I said, Grant was no friend of mine, either in school or university.' With a curt nod, Anderson turned and worked his way through the tables to the top of the escalator and disappeared from view.

Molly pushed her mug of cold coffee aside and left her seat to join the queue at the counter, where she ordered a blueberry muffin and a hot chocolate. 'Whipped cream, love?' the woman behind the counter asked.

Molly hesitated. The sugarless coffee had left a foul taste in her mouth. She needed something . . . 'Why not?' she said, and watched as a swirl of cream was added to the foamy chocolate. She had almost an hour to kill before her next appointment, and watching Anderson enjoying his teacake and chocolate had made her hungry.

Paget was in Alcott's office when Ormside rang to tell him that a woman by the name of Irene Sinclair had come in to enquire about Roger Corbett.

'She's with me now,' he said. 'She says Corbett is a friend of hers, and he was in quite a state when he phoned her last Tuesday afternoon and said he had to talk to her. She asked him what it was about, but he wouldn't say. He told her he'd explain when he got there, but he had to talk to someone else first. But he never showed up. He isn't answering his mobile, and nobody seems to have seen him since. He hasn't been to work and he hasn't been home.'

Paget had his notebook out. Ah yes, the woman Corbett

said he was sleeping with on Sunday night. 'Have someone take her to an interview room,' he told the Sergeant. 'And find Tregalles and tell him to meet me there in ten minutes.'

Molly Forsythe was surprised when Stephanie Taylor answered the door herself. Looking at the house and grounds as she drove up the drive, Molly had half expected to be greeted by at least a maid if not a butler. But Stephanie must have seen her coming, because she opened the door before Molly had a chance to touch the bell.

'Detective Constable Forsythe, I presume,' she said, thrusting out a hand. 'I'm Stephanie Taylor. Do come through. I thought we'd be more comfortable on the terrace. It's shaded and quite lovely out there at this time of day. She turned and led Molly through the house, her bare feet slapping softly against the tiles on the floor of a kitchen that was more than half the size of Molly's flat, and out to a paved terrace overlooking a generous expanse of lawn dotted with shade trees. A meandering path led to a summer house on the far side of the property against a backdrop of colourful Japanese maples and a single sturdy oak that looked as if it had been there for a hundred years or more. Molly breathed in deeply; it was a park in miniature.

'I think I could get used to this,' she said softly. 'It's so quiet and peaceful. You must love it here.'

'Oh, yes,' Stephanie said perfunctorily. 'Would you like some iced tea? It's green tea. A special blend. It's very good for you.'

Molly wasn't too sure, but since Stephanie was waiting with jug poised, she said, 'Thank you, I'd like that very much.' She waited until Stephanie filled a glass and handed it to her before settling into what proved to be a very comfortable chair.

Stephanie was taller than Molly by an inch or two, and yet she seemed to fold herself into a neat little package as she sat down and tucked her legs under her. In fact, everything about Stephanie Taylor was neat, thought Molly. From the short blonde hair to the striped shirt and dazzling white shorts, neither of which seemed to be capable of holding anything as untidy as a crease.

She tasted the tea. Ice tinkled softly against the glass. Not bad at all, she decided. In fact much better than she'd expected.

'So, I suppose you want to ask me the same things as the others?' Stephanie said. 'Not,' she added almost as an after-thought, 'that I can add much to what you must know already, but we'll have to see, won't we?'

She flicked a quick glance at the watch on her wrist, perhaps as a gentle reminder to Molly that, while she was prepared to help if she could, she had better things to do.

It was becoming something of a litany by now, but Molly pressed on with the standard questions and, as she had with Anderson, received similar responses until they started to talk about Leeds.

'I always felt rather sorry for Barry,' Stephanie said. 'I suppose I was vaguely aware of him at Westonleigh, but he was a couple of years behind me, and two years between teenagers is a huge gap, so I didn't *really* come into contact with him until later during his first, and last, year at univer-sity. Has anyone told you he had a crush on me?'

'A crush . . .?' Molly said cautiously.

Stephanie laughed, but sobered quickly and became serious. 'I shouldn't laugh,' she said. 'Not after the way he ended his life. I know everyone was down on him, but I thought Barry was rather sweet – at least I did at first.'

Stephanie smiled at Molly's reaction. 'You might well look surprised,' she said. 'In fact I think I surprised myself at the time. Normally I wouldn't have looked at a boy two years younger than myself, and I was already dating Kevin, but Barry was so cheeky. And he was fun at first. He had such an outrageous line you couldn't help but want to find out how far he would go with it.'

'And how far did he go?'

Stephanie hesitated, lips compressed as she looked off into the distance, and when she spoke she sounded almost sad. 'The poor boy claimed he loved me,' she said softly. 'He told me he'd fallen in love with me the very first time he'd set eyes on me when I was at Westonleigh.'

Stephanie turned to face Molly once again. 'It was all a line of course,' she said with a dismissive toss of the head, 'but he was so intensely earnest about it, and I never knew whether to be flattered, amused, or annoyed by his attentions.'

Stephanie sipped her iced tea, then set the glass aside. 'I should have put a stop to it from the very beginning,' she continued, 'but the poor boy seemed so desperately sincere that I halfway believed him.' She smiled. 'It was flattering and rather fun at first, but it wasn't quite so funny when I told him that was all it was.'

The lines around Stephanie's mouth tightened. 'I couldn't get rid of him,' she said. 'He wouldn't leave me alone. He was there every time I turned around, and I finally had to ask Kevin to warn him off, because nothing I said seemed to make any difference.'

'And that put an end to it, did it?' Molly asked.

Stephanie shrugged. 'He still kept popping up, especially when Kevin wasn't around, but he finally got the message.'

'What about the holidays when you were back here in Broadminster? Did you have any trouble with Barry then?'

Stephanie shook her head. 'No, not really,' she said. 'We would run into him the odd time in a pub or on the street, but he didn't bother me. In fact I wondered if he'd found another girl. If he had, I hoped she wouldn't have to go through the same sort of thing that I'd gone through.'

'Did you ever see him with another girl?'

'No. And come to think of it, I can't remember ever seeing Barry with an individual companion, male or female. He was always hovering on the fringes of a group, but he was never a part of it. Sad when you think of it,' Stephanie concluded, 'but Barry Grant couldn't blame anyone but himself for that.'

She grimaced in a self-deprecating way as she picked up her glass and said, 'But here I am going on about myself, and I'm sure that's not what you wanted to hear, is it, detective? I can't see how any of it can be relevant to your investigation. On the other hand, I don't know what I can tell you that would be relevant. Or how it relates to your investigation into Kevin's father's murder back then.'

'We don't know ourselves until we sift through the information,' Molly admitted. 'But there is one thing you can tell me, and that's where you were between midnight and two o'clock last Monday morning?'

Stephanie smiled. 'I wondered when you would get around to that,' she said. 'Kevin told me he'd had to account for his movements, and since you know already that he spent the night in the old house on Oak Street, I have no one to back me up when I tell you I was here all night, alone.'

As Molly drove back into town, she thought about the interview. Interesting, especially the part about Barry Grant's crush on Stephanie, and she wondered why, if they'd all been good friends back then, Peter Anderson hadn't mentioned it when she'd asked him if Barry had a girlfriend. But whatever the answer, Molly couldn't see how it was going to help them with either the attempted arson at the Grant house, or the killing of two people thirteen years ago. In fact, the only glimmer of hope that she could see lay in Sharon Jessop's story about the man who had whispered in her ear. But even that was a long shot, because it depended entirely upon Sharon's memory improving or being able to track down Sharon's friend, Rachel.

SIXTEEN

Paget had the feeling that he had met Irene Sinclair before. Certainly the combination of auburn hair, an oriental cast to her features, and a Scottish accent, was an intriguing mix that, once encountered, would be hard for anyone to forget.

And yet he couldn't place her.

He introduced himself and Tregalles, then sat down facing her across the table. 'Just for the record, is it Miss or Mrs Sinclair?' he asked.

'It's Irene,' she said pleasantly but firmly. 'But if it's necessary for your records, I'm not married.'

The voice. Suddenly he remembered. The theatre. *The Broadminster theatre club. That* was where he'd seen her. His expression must have given him away, because she looked amused as her dark eyes met his own. 'No,' she said, 'we haven't actually met before, Chief Inspector, but I have seen you a number of times at the theatre. I'm the director and sometimes an actor there.'

'And a very good one as I recall,' he said, then turned to business. 'Now, Sergeant Ormside, the man you spoke to earlier, tells me you are afraid that something may have happened to Roger Corbett, and the last time you heard from him was on Tuesday afternoon. Do you remember roughly what time that was?'

'Four o'clock or close to it,' Irene told him. 'He sounded . . . Oh, I don't know, upset, scared, panicky, perhaps? He'd been drinking and it was all a bit jumbled, but the gist of it was that the police had been round asking questions about a boy he used to know, and he was sure they suspected him of something, but he didn't say what. I tried to get him to tell me, but he said he'd tell me later, but he had to talk to someone else first. Then he cut me off.'

'Did he mention the name of the person he was going to talk to?'

'No. He just said, "I've got another call," and then he was gone.'

'He was on a mobile phone?'

'Yes, he was. I have caller ID. He was using his own mobile, and he was calling from the Unicorn in Broad Street.'

'He told you that?'

'No, but that's where he normally goes during the day, and when I didn't hear from him I phoned them to ask if he was there or if he'd been in. The man I spoke to said he'd been in earlier, but had left some time ago.'

'Did he say what time that was?'

He said Roger came in around three-thirty or four and left about half an hour later, but he couldn't be sure of the times. But that sounded about right, because it was around that time when Roger rang me, so he must have left the pub shortly after talking to me.' Irene looked worried. 'I've tried calling at least a dozen times since then, but there's no reply. I've called Lisa, Roger's office, and everyone else I could think of, including the ambulance service and the hospital, but I can't find anyone who has seen Roger or spoken to him since he left the Unicorn on Tuesday.

'Lisa doesn't seem to be very concerned at all,' she continued. 'I'm sure she thinks Roger's gone off drinking with a friend or someone he's met, and he'll turn up in a day or two.'

'Do you know if he's been worried about anything lately?' Paget asked. 'Has he said anything to you? Acted any differently?'

Irene shook her head. 'Not really,' she said. 'He's been

moody these past few days, but then, that's Roger. He does suffer from depression, but he's been quite good lately, and to my knowledge, the only thing that has been at all out of the ordinary lately is the visit from the police he mentioned, but he didn't say what that was about. Do you know anything about that, Chief Inspector?'

Paget said, 'I was the one who spoke to him, on Tuesday in his office. I wanted to know what he could tell me about a lad by the name of Barry Grant, who was involved in a robbery and the killing of George Taylor, Kevin and David Taylor's father. Mr Corbett seemed somewhat nervous, but then a lot of people react that way when questioned by the police, even if they have nothing to hide. But with what you've just told us, I would like to talk to him again. Tell me, Miss Sinclair, did you know Barry Grant back then?'

Irene shook her head. 'We moved to Scotland when I was thirteen, and I lived in Stirling for ten years before returning to Broadminster, so what went on here thirteen years ago was all news to me when Claire mentioned it at the party the other day.'

'Do you recall if Mr Corbett ever mentioned Grant's name before the phone call on Tuesday?'

'If he did, I don't remember.'

'You mentioned Lisa,' Tregalles said. 'That would be his wife, would it?'

'Yes, that's right, Sergeant. Lisa's been away. She came back from Scarborough late Tuesday night, but when I asked her if she'd seen or talked to Roger, she said she hadn't, and she'd assumed that he was with me.'

Tregalles looked puzzled. 'Are you related to Mr Corbett?' he asked.

'No. We're just friends.'

Tregalles scratched his head. 'Then I think I must have missed something,' he said, 'because I don't understand how this works. You said a minute ago that Roger Corbett talked to you about *coming home,* which I took to be to your place. Isn't he living with his wife?'

'Oh, yes, they live together most of the time,' Irene told him, 'but Roger always comes to live with me when Lisa's away – even sometimes when she's not, for that matter. We've all been good friends for years.'

'And he just sort of moves back and forth, does he? Bit odd, that, isn't it?' Tregalles persisted. 'I mean—'

'You say Lisa Corbett didn't appear to be particularly worried by her husband's absence,' Paget broke in. 'Has he disappeared before?'

'Not like this,' Irene said. 'I believe Roger has spent a night or two in your custody for being drunk and disorderly, but the Sergeant I first spoke to told me there's no record of Roger being here now, nor has he been here recently. And that reminds me: Lisa said Roger's car was there at the house. She said she thought that I must have picked him up, because I have done that before. I suppose it's possible that someone else picked him up, but I'd be surprised if that were true, because he didn't like riding with other people. And he didn't take a taxi because I've checked with all of them. The thing is, if he is all right, why doesn't he call or answer his phone?'

Irene Sinclair rose to her feet. 'Look, Chief Inspector,' she said earnestly, 'I know Roger, and I have never heard him sound as scared as he did when he called me last Tuesday, so please take this seriously and help me find him.'

'We will certainly do our best,' Paget told her as he and Tregalles stood up to escort her out. He took out a card and gave it to her as they were approaching the front desk. 'Please ring that number at any time, day or night, if you hear from Mr Corbett,' he said.

'I will,' she told him, 'and thank you for your . . .' Irene stopped speaking, frowning as she looked past Paget. 'Lisa?' she called sharply. 'Lisa! What are you doing here? Have you heard from Roger . . .?'

John Chadwell did not look very happy as Sergeant Ormside led the way to the interview room at the far end of the corridor. He kept glancing around as if fearful of being recognized by someone he knew, and seemed to be relieved when he saw there was to be no one else in the room when Ormside shut the door.

Slightly above average height, Chadwell was a broad-shouldered man with rugged features and dark hair already tinged with grey. Sporting a full moustache beneath a prominent nose, he looked permanently displeased – and probably was, thought Ormside.

'I appreciate your taking the time to come in, sir,' the Sergeant said as they both sat down, 'but as I told you on the phone, we were quite prepared to come to you.'

John Chadwell shook his head impatiently. 'Out of the question,' he said tersely. 'And to be blunt, Sergeant, I'm only here because I didn't want a policeman coming round to the council offices or my house, where everyone would start speculating on the reason. So, let's get on with it, shall we? I have heard from some of the others who were at the party last Saturday, and if what they say is anything to go by, I must say I don't appreciate being cast in the role of a suspect.'

Ormside nodded. 'Fair enough,' he said, 'but since we are being blunt, let me remind you that we are investigating the killing of two people, one of whom was the father of your friend, Mr Taylor. We are talking to everyone who was at the party last Saturday, when Miss Hammond mentioned that the Grant house was to be searched, because someone used that information to try to destroy the place before we could do that.'

Chadwell shrugged impatiently. 'Well, it wasn't me,' he said testily, 'and I'll tell you right now, I hardly even *remember* Barry Grant, and it's ludicrous to even *think* that I had anything to do with what happened at the house. As for the murders, I know nothing about them, so you're wasting your time.' He folded his arms, and glowered at Ormside as if daring him to continue.

'In that case, sir,' Ormside growled, 'the sooner you let me do my job, the better it will be for both of us, and the sooner you'll be out of here. Now, can you tell me where you were between midnight and three o'clock last Monday morning?'

Lisa Corbett was a knockout, Tregalles thought admiringly as he followed the red BMW convertible through the shaded streets of Rutherford Hill. She had to be well into her thirties, but she could pass for mid-to-late twenties without any trouble. But then, she would have to be in good shape, wouldn't she? He'd watched ballroom dancing competitions on TV and marvelled at some of the performances. Fantastic bodies those women had, and Lisa Corbett was no exception. A bit on the thin side, perhaps – Tregalles preferred a bit more meat on the bone, himself – but he wasn't complaining; just watching her move was a pleasure in itself. And those eyes, so dark, so expressive. He could have almost sworn that she was flirting with him even when she was expressing concern about her missing husband back there in Charter Lane.

'Go back to the house with Mrs Corbett, and start from there,' Paget told him as Lisa Corbett was preparing to leave. 'See if there is anything there that might tell us where Corbett has gone. And see if you can make some sense out of this relationship Corbett appears to have with these two women, because I don't understand it. Take Forsythe with you. I saw her come in as Miss Sinclair was leaving, and Mrs Corbett might be a bit more forthcoming with another woman.'

The car ahead slowed to make the turn into a driveway leading to a two-storied house almost completely hidden from the road by beech trees and a dense shrubbery of rhododendrons and hydrangeas. The hydrangeas were in full bloom, and some of them bore flowers the size of dinner plates. The house itself wasn't particularly large, although size was deceptive in this woodland setting. Older than most of its neighbours on the hill, it looked so solid and comfortable that it could almost be taken for part of the natural landscape.

'*Very* nice!' Tregalles observed. 'And worth a bit, even in today's market if she wanted to sell it. I don't think Mrs Corbett is short of a bob or two.'

The BMW stopped in front of the house and Lisa got out. The flared skirt of her white summer dress rode halfway up her perfectly tanned thighs as she slid out of the car and turned to wait for the two detectives as they pulled in behind her.

'There's Roger's car,' Lisa said, as they joined her. She pointed to a three-year-old Volvo parked somewhat haphazardly with one front wheel resting on the edge of a flower bed a short distance away. 'It was there when I came home on Tuesday night. It was very late, close to midnight, actually, so I assumed that Roger was here in the house and asleep in his room.'

'You have separate rooms, Mrs Corbett?'

'That's right, Sergeant.'

'Were there any other signs that might tell us when he was last here?' Molly asked. 'Any indication that he'd had a recent meal, a snack or a drink perhaps?'

'Not unless you can make something out of an empty bag

of crisps, a dirty glass, and half a bottle of whisky on the coffee table in the living room,' Lisa said scornfully.

'I don't suppose they would still be there?'

Lisa shook her head. 'I washed the glass and poured the rest of the whisky down the sink before I went to bed that night,' she said. She turned to Tregalles. 'So, where would you like to start, Sergeant?'

'Do you have the key to the Volvo?'

'I do. It's on my key ring.' Lisa held it out to him.

Tregalles took it from her and walked over to the car. He circled it, looking at the tyres, then tried the driver's door. It was unlocked. He got in, slid the key into the ignition and turned it. The Volvo started immediately. Tregalles ran it for a few seconds, then turned it off and got out.

'As you say, there doesn't seem to be anything wrong with the car,' he said, 'so that wasn't the reason he left without it. Assuming he did leave, of course. But you told us earlier that you've searched the area around the house and found no sign of him.'

'That's right,' Lisa said. 'Not that I really expected to, but there was always the possibility that he'd tripped and fallen and knocked himself unconscious or had a stroke or a heart attack.' She shrugged and spread her hands. 'Not that I really believed that,' she continued, 'but to tell you the truth, I don't know *what* I thought. I think I was more annoyed than worried, which is why I didn't take Irene's concerns very seriously at first.'

Molly looked thoughtful as she eyed the Volvo. 'Tell me, Mrs Corbett,' she said, 'does Mr Corbett always leave his car parked like that?'

Lisa smiled, but it was a tired smile at best. 'Actually, that's probably one of his better efforts,' she said. 'He has been known to end up in the bushes a time or two until I managed to get it through his head that he could kill someone if he continued to drink and drive, and persuaded him to order a taxi when he knows he's had too much.' She sighed and shook her head. 'Obviously, this wasn't one of those times.'

'Do you have a recent picture of your husband?' Tregalles asked.

'I have pictures,' Lisa told him, 'but I think the most recent ones are at least a couple of years old. If you'd like to come inside I'll show you.'

After the glare of the sunlight outside, it took them a minute or two before their eyes became adjusted to the darkened interior of the house, but it was mercifully cool. 'I keep the blinds drawn on the south and west side of the house during the hottest part of the day,' Lisa explained. 'Otherwise it would be unbearable. Now, would you like something to drink? Tea, coffee, lemonade, fruit juice, perhaps?'

'Tea would be nice,' Tregalles said with a questioning glance at Molly, who nodded. 'But perhaps we could take the tour first, because I'm sure I'll have more questions once we're through.'

'Of course. And I'll get those pictures for you. Where would you like to start?'

'Perhaps a quick tour of the house first . . .?' Tregalles suggested.

The house was larger than it looked from the outside. Older, too, as evidenced by such things as parquet flooring and wain-scoting in the hallway, but extensively remodelled by the look of the size of the rooms. Walls had been moved or taken out entirely, doorways had been widened and, as Lisa pointed out, windows had been enlarged and replaced with double glazing. The feeling was one of openness, with each room seeming to flow into the next.

With Lisa Corbett looking on, Tregalles felt a little foolish as they looked under beds, opened cupboards, and checked things like the freezer – in fact anything big enough to hold the body of a man, but it had to be done and recorded.

There were a lot of pictures in the house, almost all of them glossy photographs of Lisa and her dancing partner, Ramon, in various poses, taken at competitions by the look of them, but Lisa had to dig out a photo album in order to produce a picture of her husband.

'I was mistaken,' she said apologetically. 'This has to be at least three years old, but he hasn't changed much since then.'

Tregalles studied the picture. 'How tall is Mr Corbett?' he asked. 'It's hard to tell in this picture.'

'He's about an inch shorter than me,' Lisa told him, 'and I'm five foot six. Why do you want to know?'

'Just general information,' Tregalles said vaguely. 'I'll have copies made and let you have the original back,' he told her as he pocketed the picture.

Downstairs once again, Lisa opened the French doors leading to the terrace. 'We have a gardener who comes in twice a week to keep things tidy,' she explained as she led the way down the steps and across the lawn. 'He does everything except look after the koi pond. That's Roger's domain. He designed and built it; he even did all the stonework himself.' Lisa's tone softened. 'He's very proud of that, and he can spend hours fiddling about with the pump that keeps the water aerated, checking the temperature, dead-heading the water lilies, and experimenting with different underwater plants. Unfortunately, the blooms aren't at their best right now because of the heat, but there are still a few of the hardier ones to be seen. But do come and see the koi.'

'I understand that herons can be a nuisance,' Molly said as they descended the steps to the lawn. 'Have you had a problem with them?'

'Thankfully, no. They don't seem to come our way, which is fortunate, because some people have a lot of trouble with them raiding their ponds.'

The pond was larger than it had looked from the terrace. Irregular in shape, it was about thirty feet long by about twelve or thirteen feet wide. Lily pads and reeds covered almost half of the surface at the far end.

Tregalles caught the glint of white and gold and bent closer to peer into the depths. 'Now, that's a big fish!' he declared, 'but he's hard to see down there. Are they all that big?'

'Most of them are,' Lisa told him, 'and you're right, they are hard to see on a day like today. They stay deep when it's this hot, although they are shaded by the trees during the hottest part of the day. Roger treats them like pets, and he's been quite concerned about them since this heatwave began, so I'm surprised he hasn't . . .' Lisa stopped suddenly in mid-sentence.

'I should have realized,' she said huskily. 'I should have known he wouldn't have gone off and left them during this heatwave. He even talked about building a sort of lattice-work arbour over the far end to give the fish a bit more protection. I do hope nothing has happened to him.'

'There's nothing to be gained by blaming yourself,' Tregalles said soothingly as he stood up. 'But perhaps we should go back to the house. I would like to take a closer look at Mr Corbett's office.'

'Of course. Sorry if I've wasted your time, bringing you out here,' she said, 'but you did say you wanted to have a good look round.'

Molly, who had wandered to the far end of the pond to take a closer look at the few remaining blooms that hadn't wilted beneath the afternoon sun, stayed where she was when Tregalles called to her. 'I don't know about herons,' she called back, 'but it looks to me as if something has been having a go at your fish, Mrs Corbett. Have you seen all these dead plants up here?'

Lisa groaned. 'Oh, no,' she said worriedly as she hurried to join Molly. 'When did that happen, I wonder? Roger will be furious if he's lost any of his fish.'

Tregalles joined them. 'Well, it certainly wasn't a heron that made this mess,' he declared. Something went in from the side by the look of it. Do you have a dog, Mrs Corbett?'

Lisa shook her head vigorously. 'No, we don't,' she said, 'and we're fenced in all the way round, so . . .'

'Maybe we can get a better look if we get rid of this dead stuff,' he said, plucking a long-handled skimming net from its rack at the end of the pond.

'Oh, please, there's no need to do that now,' Lisa told him. 'I can do it later.'

'No trouble,' the Sergeant told her as he scooped out leaves and long, trailing stems. He pushed the net deeper to get beneath more dead leaves. The net caught. He tugged gently, then harder . . .

Lisa stared. Her hand flew to her mouth. 'Oh, my God!' she whispered. 'Oohhh, no!'

SEVENTEEN

'About all I can tell you at this point is that the man has been in the water for something like a couple of days,' said Starkie, the police pathologist. 'Right now the temperature of the water at the surface is seventy-four degrees, but this end of the pool is six feet deep, and the

further down you go, the cooler it gets, so I can't come any
closer than that until I've had him on the table.'

'Two days,' said Paget thoughtfully. 'I saw him myself
Tuesday afternoon, so if he has been in the water for two
days, he must have died sometime late Tuesday afternoon or
that same evening. Now what I need to know is *how* he died?'

'I should think drowning would be one possibility,' Starkie
said, straight-faced, 'but there are one or two bruises on him,
so you will have to wait for the results of the autopsy – which
won't be until tomorrow afternoon at the earliest,' he added
before Paget had a chance to ask.

Paget had been alerted by Tregalles within minutes of the
discovery of the body of Roger Corbett, and he'd driven out
to the house to take charge of the investigation himself.

There was always the possibility that Corbett's death had
been an accident. If, as had been suggested, Corbett had been
drinking heavily, he might have driven home, then gone down
to feed or look at his fish and simply toppled in and drowned.
But considering the timing, Paget preferred to treat it as a
suspicious death.

Inspector Charlie Dobbs, the man in charge of the scenes
of crime investigators, had been notified, and his team was
just now arriving. The house and garden had been declared a
crime scene, and cordoned off by uniformed Constables who
had been called in to assist, and Molly Forsythe was in the
house with Lisa.

'It may not mean anything,' Tregalles said as he and Paget
walked back to the house, 'but I don't think Roger Corbett
was the last person to drive his Volvo. According to his wife,
Corbett is five foot five, yet when I checked the car in the
driveway, I found the seat and rear-view mirror were set for
someone taller.'

'So someone else could have brought him home.'

'That's right. The next question is: how did they get back
to town, assuming that's where they came from in the first
place? Miss Sinclair said she called the cab companies, but
they had no record of being called to this address.'

'Better check with them just the same,' Paget told him,
'because they may not have spent much time looking when
a member of the public called. And have Forensic go over the
car. Then, tomorrow, I want you to start at Corbett's office,

find out when he left, and if he made any phone calls before he left, then find out where he went after that.

'Now, what about Mrs Corbett? How did she react when you first pulled Corbett's body to the surface?'

'She was pretty shaken up,' Tregalles said. 'It wasn't a pleasant sight, with his soggy clothes and him all covered in reeds and muck. Well, you saw him yourself, so you know what I mean. It was enough to put anybody off.'

'Is it possible that her reaction could have been from the shock of having his body discovered when she thought it was safely at the bottom of the pond?'

'*Could* have been, I suppose,' Tregalles said, but he sounded doubtful. 'Although, to tell you the truth, I was concentrating on the body, so I wasn't paying that much attention to Mrs Corbett. Molly may be able to tell you more about that. She helped Mrs Corbett to the bench in the corner, and sat with her for a few minutes.'

'You said it was Mrs Corbett who suggested you look at the pond in the first place?'

'That's right. So why would she do that if she knew Corbett's body was in the pond? Mind you,' he continued slowly, 'now I think about it, she did keep us talking at the shallow end, and we would never have known there was anything wrong if Molly hadn't gone to the deep end to take a closer look at the flowers.'

'So it's possible that Mrs Corbett steered you down here deliberately so you would feel that she was being cooperative in letting you have a good look round, but kept you away from the deep end of the pool?'

Tregalles screwed up his face. 'Possible,' he conceded grudgingly, 'but I don't think so. She certainly didn't show any signs of nervousness while we were there, and she didn't try to stop Molly from going down the other end.'

'Perhaps she didn't think Forsythe would notice anything was amiss,' Paget countered. 'In fact, it probably took those leaves a day or so to turn that colour, so Mrs Corbett may not have been aware that there was any need to be concerned.'

Paget looked at his watch as they reached the steps to the terrace. 'I'm going inside to talk to Mrs Corbett,' he said, 'but I'd like you to stay out here and work with Charlie's

people. They won't be finished here tonight, so get hold of
Ormside and tell him we'll need someone out here on night
watch.'

Inside the house, Paget found Molly and Lisa Corbett in
the kitchen. Lisa was sitting at the table, head lowered, eyes
closed, while Molly stood at the counter pouring boiling water
into an oversized teapot.

'Tea's gone cold, sir, so I'm making a fresh pot,' she told
Paget. 'Would you like a cup?'

'Yes, I would,' he said. 'Thank you, Constable.'

Lisa opened her eyes and acknowledged his presence with
a brief glance before fixing her gaze on her clasped hands
resting on the table in front of her.

'I know this is the worst possible time, Mrs Corbett,' Paget
said apologetically as he drew up a chair, 'but I would like
to ask you a few questions, if you feel up to it?'

Lisa didn't look as if she'd been crying, but her face was
pale and drawn, and she no longer looked as youthful as she
had earlier in the day.

'Of course,' she said in a low voice. 'What would you like
to know?'

'You told us earlier today that it was close to midnight
when you got home after driving back from Scarborough,' he
said. 'Was Mr Corbett's car in the driveway when you arrived?'

'Yes, it was, which is why I assumed he was in the house.'

'Has the car been moved since then?'

'No. But why are you asking questions about the car?'

'Because the seat and rear-view mirror appear to be set to
accommodate a taller driver,' Paget told her. 'Did you have
any reason to move the seat back or adjust the position of the
mirror?'

'No, of course not. Why would I?'

'No reason that I can think of,' Paget said, 'which makes
me wonder if someone else drove your husband home.'

Molly brought a tray to the table and slid a steaming cup
of tea in front of each of them before sitting down at the end
of the table and taking out her notebook.

Lisa's frown deepened as she picked up her cup. 'I suppose
that's possible,' she said, 'but I don't know who would do that
other than Irene, and she says she didn't. Even if she did,
she's no bigger than I am, as you know.'

'You came in by the front door, I take it. Was it locked?'

'No, it wasn't locked, but that wasn't unusual. Roger was inclined to be a bit careless about such things.'

'Mrs Corbett told us that she found a bottle of whisky, a glass, and an empty bag of crisps on the coffee table,' said Molly.

'They were on the coffee table just where Roger had left them,' Lisa explained, 'and I do so hate that, so I cleared up, washed the glass and poured the rest of the whisky down the sink.' Lisa's eyes were moist as she looked at Paget. 'Roger must have gone out to look at his fish before going to bed, and fallen in,' she said huskily.

'When did you first realize that your husband wasn't in the house?'

'When I went to call him just before I left the house to go shopping yesterday morning.'

'Didn't that surprise you?'

'No, not really. I assumed he was with Irene. The fact that the car was there and Roger wasn't didn't have any significance until Irene phoned to ask if he was here, then rang again this morning to say no one had seen him since Tuesday afternoon.'

'Tell me,' he said, 'who feeds the fish when you and your husband are away?'

'The fish?' The question seemed to take Lisa by surprise, but she answered it. 'We're rarely both away at the same time,' she said. 'Even when Roger's staying with Irene, he always comes back up here each day to see to the fish.'

'How often do they have to be fed?'

'In this heat, Roger's been feeding them twice a day.'

'And, since he wasn't here, did you feed them yourself yesterday?'

'Yes, I did,' she said in a low voice.

'And again, today, I presume?'

'That's right.'

'Did you notice any dead leaves on the water at that time?'

Lisa looked uncomfortable as she shook her head. 'They're always fed from the shallow end,' she said, 'so I didn't go to the other end.' She looked troubled as she sat forward to lend emphasis to what she was about to say. 'You must understand, Chief Inspector, I had no idea at that point that anything like

. . .' She broke off to take a deep breath. 'That anything had
happened to Roger. I know how this must sound now, but at
the time I was so annoyed with him for going off without a
word to anyone, that I went down and fed the fish and came
straight back to the house. I *should* have gone down the other
end of the pond to check the temperature of the water and
the filtration system – Roger keeps a running log on everything to do with the fish – but I didn't. That was probably
what Roger was doing when he fell in and couldn't get out,'
she ended huskily.

'If that is what happened,' said Paget neutrally.

Lisa looked at him. 'Just what are you suggesting, Chief
Inspector?' she asked.

'I'm not sure myself,' he said slowly, 'but when I questioned
your husband the other day, I had the distinct impression that
he knew more than he was telling me, and that makes me
suspicious when he is found dead within hours of my talking
to him. I'm not a strong believer in coincidence, Mrs Corbett,
so if there is anything you know; anything you can tell me
that might shed light on the way your husband died, now is
the time to tell me.'

The expression on Lisa Corbett's face hardened, and her
voice was brittle when she said, 'If you're referring to what
you told me this afternoon about this Grant boy and what
happened to Kevin Taylor's father all those years ago, all I
can tell you is that I know nothing about those things because
I didn't live here then, and I'm quite sure that Roger would
never have been involved in any way. So, if you are
suggesting that his drowning in the pond *wasn't* an accident, and he came back here and killed himself, I think the
whole idea is ludicrous. Believe me, Chief Inspector, if
Roger intended to commit suicide, which I don't think for
a single second is true, the koi pond is the last place he
would choose.'

'The last place most people would choose, I should think,'
Paget told her as he stood up and pushed his chair back. 'And
I agree with you, because, like you, I don't think your husband
committed suicide. I can't prove it yet, but I believe he was
murdered.'

EIGHTEEN

Friday, July 17th

Paget came in early the following morning, and went straight upstairs to Alcott's office, where he settled down to tackle the paperwork that had been slowly but steadily mounting in the in tray. Fiona had been a great help, and he was grateful for it, but there were some things he had to deal with himself before he could let them leave the office.

By the time Fiona arrived at her usual time of ten minutes to eight, he'd managed to reduce the pile by roughly a third simply by tackling the easy ones first. 'I have to go down for the morning briefing,' he told her, 'but I should be back within the hour.' He handed her a sheaf of papers. 'I've stuck notes on this lot to say what I'd like done with them, but if you have any questions, just hold them until I return. All right?'

Fiona riffled through the papers, then looked at him over the top of her glasses. She reminded him of a schoolteacher assessing his homework while he waited apprehensively for the verdict.

'I think you're developing a talent for this,' she said approvingly. 'I think we just might make a Superintendent of you yet, Mr Paget.'

He grinned. 'Not if I can help it,' he told her. 'I prefer the job I have, and the sooner I can get back to it full time, the happier I'll be.'

'Let's hope it will be soon, then,' the secretary said. 'Have you heard how Mrs Alcott is doing? I left a message on Mr Alcott's phone yesterday, but he hasn't rung back.'

'Not a word, I'm afraid,' he said. 'But I'll let you know if I hear anything, and perhaps you could do the same for me?'

'I'll call you if I hear anything,' she promised. 'I thought I might send a card or perhaps some flowers? From all of us, you know? What do you think, sir?'

'I think it would be very much appreciated,' he told her, 'so, yes, go ahead and I'll mention it during the briefing as well, and ask Sergeant Ormside to have a whip round down there.'

The briefing itself was short, with most of the time spent bringing everyone up to speed on the events surrounding the death of Roger Corbett.

'We don't yet know the cause of death,' Paget conceded, 'but coming within hours of my speaking to him last Tuesday afternoon, I think we can consider it a suspicious death, and act accordingly. So, Tregalles, I want you to start at Corbett's office and find out where he went and what he did after I left there on Tuesday afternoon.

'And I want you,' he said to Molly, 'to go back out to Rutherford Hill to talk to the Corbetts' neighbours. I want to know if anyone saw Roger Corbett return to the house, and when that was if they did. I want to know if he was with anyone, and if any other vehicles were seen coming or going to or from the house. I would also like to know if anyone saw Lisa Corbett come home when she says she did.'

He turned to Ormside. 'I'd like you to take a close look at the state of the Corbetts' marriage and their finances, and I'm particularly interested in the relationship Corbett had with Irene Sinclair. It's almost as if the man had two wives. The two women appear to be on friendly terms and happy with the situation, but I don't understand it, so see what you can find out.'

But the grizzled Sergeant shook his head. 'No, sir,' he said firmly, 'I'm not tackling that one. That's one for Forsythe. She'd be far better at that sort of thing than I would.'

Paget chuckled. 'Perhaps you're right,' he said. 'All right, Forsythe . . .?'

'Except I have Graham Williams coming in at ten,' she said. 'He's another one who was at school with Barry Grant, and he was at the Taylors' party.'

'Reschedule,' Paget told her, then paused. 'On second thoughts, let Williams come ahead. Sergeant Ormside can talk to him. All right, Len?'

'Sooner him than go poking around in Corbett's love life,' Ormside growled, 'so, yes, I can squeeze him in.'

'Useless!' the fat man behind the desk said baldly. 'Completely bloody useless, and he would have been gone at the end of

the month, anyway. Not that I'm glad he's *dead*, of course,'
he added hastily, 'but he was no good as a salesman.'

The man was Gerry Stone, Roger Corbett's erstwhile boss
and the manager of the Braithwaite Letting Agency.

'Drink,' the man continued. 'That was his problem plain
and simple. He's had one sale in all the time he's been here, and
that was to a friend, if I'm not mistaken. Kept saying he
had prospects, but I never saw any of them if he had. As for
where he went after he left here last Tuesday, I have no idea,
but Joanie might know.'

Joan Hunter, or 'Joanie' as everyone called her, was not,
as Tregalles had thought, Roger Corbett's secretary. Rather
she worked for everyone in the office.

'General dogsbody, that's me,' she said cheerfully when
Tregalles asked. 'I do everything. Typing, filing, make the tea,
run errands, you name it. So if there's anything you want to
know, ask me, because I know more about this office than the
whole lot put together.' She lowered her voice. 'But don't tell
the boss that, 'cause he thinks he's running the show. OK?'

'Agreed,' said Tregalles. 'Now—'

'So what's this all about, then?' Joanie asked before
Tregalles could frame his first question. 'Mr Corbett in trouble,
is he?' She lowered her voice once more. 'Confidentially, I
understand he was going to be given the push at the end of
the month anyway, so I don't suppose we'll be seeing him
around here again. Funny him going off like that, though. I
think he must have got wind of what was going to happen,
and decided to pack it in before he got the chop. Mind you,
I shall miss him, because he could be a real gentleman when
he wasn't what you might call "under the weather".'

'Was he under the weather very often?' Tregalles asked
quickly before Joanie could draw another breath.

'On and off,' she said cautiously.

'He drank,' Tregalles said bluntly.

'Well, yes, he did, but it wasn't his fault, not *really,* if you
see what I mean. He had these headaches and he'd get very
depressed, so he'd have a nip or two to keep him going.
Trouble was, once he'd started he couldn't seem to stop.'

'What about last Tuesday? Tell me what happened after
Chief Inspector Paget left his office?'

Joanie made a face. 'I don't really know,' she said. 'He closed the door then telephoned someone. I could hear him talking, but I don't know who he called. I think he made several calls. I remember his light on my phone going on and off several times before he came out and told me he was going to meet a client, and wouldn't be back that afternoon.'

'A client? Any idea who that might have been?' Tregalles asked.

The secretary shook her head. 'There wasn't any client, at least none that I know of, and I'm sure we would have heard if he did have one, because it would have been his first in a long time. It was just his excuse for skiving off. Besides, he'd been drinking quite a bit in the office. I could smell it on him when he stopped at my desk, and he was not all that steady on his feet when he went out.'

'Was he walking or did he take his car?'

'He went out the back way, so I'm sure he took his car.'

'But client or not, he could have gone to see *someone,*' Tregalles persisted. 'Someone he'd arranged to meet over the phone. Any idea who that might have been or where he might be meeting them?'

'Don't know about who,' Joanie said, 'but if he *was* meeting someone, my bet would be that he'd meet them in a pub somewhere.'

'The Unicorn, perhaps?'

Joanie nodded slowly. 'Could be,' she agreed. 'It's not one that any of us go to, so he might go there. But I'd still like to know what this is all about. What's he done? Some sort of accident was it? Is he all right?'

'I'm sorry to have to tell you this, Joanie,' Tregalles said, 'but Roger Corbett is dead. Drowned in a fish pond at—'

'Not his *koi* pond?' Joanie broke in breathlessly. 'Oh that poor man. He used to talk about those fish all the time. Oh, that poor, poor man!'

Tregalles spent some time in Corbett's office, but there was little to be found. If he'd expected to find a scribbled telephone number on the memo pad of the person Corbett had called prior to leaving the office on Tuesday, he was disappointed. But what he did find in one of the drawers of Corbett's desk was a half empty bottle of Johnny Walker, and an empty bottle of Jameson's in one of the filing cabinets.

As for anything resembling listings, contracts or sales, all the forms were there in pristine condition in the filing cabinet, waiting to be used. Waiting in vain, thought Tregalles as he came out to thank Joanie for her help.

But she was weeping silently, and he felt it best to leave the words unspoken.

The elderly man seated on a stationary ride-on lawnmower in the shade of a huge chestnut tree watched Molly as she made her way up the long driveway. His face was lean and tanned, his eyes deep-set beneath eyebrows turning white. 'You look as if you could do with a drink,' he called. 'Come on over here and rest yourself and I'll get you one.'

The man slid off the seat and walked over to a wooden bench circling the tree. 'I bring my lunch out here on days like this,' he said as Molly walked across the lawn to join him. She'd been working her way around the neighbourhood for the past couple of hours, and the heat was beginning to get to her.

'It's just too hot to carry on with the mowing,' the man said, 'so I'm packing it in for the day. Beer?' he enquired, taking a couple of cans from a cooler. 'No glasses though. Wasn't expecting company.'

'Looks good to me,' said Molly gratefully as she sat down beside him on the bench. 'Thank you very much.'

'Should be wearing a hat,' the man said, pointing to his own well-worn Tilley hat. 'You could get sunstroke on a day like this.' He pulled the tab on both cans and handed one to Molly. 'Bottoms up, but take it slow,' he warned, 'because it's ice-cold.' He took a drink himself and Molly followed suit.

'Oh, that does feel good!' she declared, as she leaned back against the tree. 'Again, thank you very much.'

'Like a sandwich?' he enquired. 'I always make more than I need, then I have to eat them for my tea if I can't manage them for lunch. Name's Fred, Fred Whitfield.' He thrust out a hand.

'Molly Forsythe,' she said in return. 'Detective Constable Forsythe,' she elaborated, 'and thanks, but I have my own lunch in the car.'

The man grunted. 'Didn't think you were selling,' he said. 'Didn't look the type. So what can I do for you?'

'You live here, do you Mr Whitfield?' Molly asked with a nod towards the house.

He smiled. 'Think I was the gardener, did you?' he asked, then laughed. 'Can't say I blame you, looking at these old clothes. Oh, I live here all right, but I don't know for how much longer. The place is too big for me to look after since the wife died, even with help. But that's got nothing to do with why you're here,' he continued, 'so what is it? About that business up the road? The Corbetts? All those police cars coming and going? Is it true he drowned in that pond of his?'

'I'm afraid so. And you're quite right, that is why I'm here. I'm looking for anyone who might have witnessed Mr Corbett, or anyone else for that matter, coming or going last Tuesday afternoon or evening.'

'Why do you want to know that?'

'We're trying to establish exactly when Mr Corbett returned to the house after leaving his office last Tuesday afternoon, and if anyone was with him. Were you out here by any chance last Tuesday?'

Fred Whitfield squinted into the distance. 'Tuesday,' he repeated slowly, then nodded. 'Come to think of it I did see him, well, not Corbett himself, but I saw his car while I was taking Lizzie for a walk.' He nodded towards a hawthorn hedge on the far side of the lawn, where a small dog Molly hadn't noticed till now, lay asleep in the deep shade.

'Half blind and getting old, I'm afraid,' he said sadly, 'but she still likes her walk every day, sometimes twice a day.'

'Do you remember what time that would be?'

'Four thirty, five o'clock, not exactly sure of the time,' Whitfield said. 'Always take Lizzie out then, and we walk up past the Corbetts under the shade trees when it's hot like this. Go up to the fields at the top where Lizzie used to like to run, but she isn't up to it any more, so we have a bit of a rest, then come back. Corbett's car passed me on the way up and turned into his driveway.'

'I don't suppose you saw any activity up at the house as you went by the end of his driveway?' Molly asked hopefully.

But Whitfield shook his head. 'Can't see the house properly this time of year,' he told her. 'Too many trees and shrubs in full leaf. But there was another car in there as well. Saw it come out on the way back.'

'What other car, Mr Whitfield? Have you seen it before? Can you describe it?'

Whitfield thought about that while he took another drink. 'Can't recall seeing that particular one up here before,' he said, 'but it was very much like the Honda CR-V Jack Reynolds drives – he lives just down the road – except his is dark red and the one I saw was silver. It might not have been the same make, but it was similar in size and shape, and quite new by the look of it except for a scratch along the side. It looked like the sort of mindless thing the kids do with a knife or a coin these days, and I remember thinking the owner must have been pretty peeved to have that happen to his car. Oh, yes, and there was a small decal of the Welsh flag just above the back bumper, driver's side. I'm afraid that's about all I can tell you, except there was a man and a woman in it. I only caught a glimpse of them as they came out on to the road.'

'Which one was driving?'

'The man.'

'Can you describe him?'

Whitfield shook his head. 'I wasn't paying that much attention, I'm afraid. Sorry, but it didn't mean anything to me at the time.'

'What about the woman? Can you describe her?'

Whitfield frowned in concentration, replaying the scene in his mind. 'Sorry,' he said again, 'but there was no reason to pay them any attention.'

'Could the woman have been Mrs Corbett?'

'Could have been, but she had a sun hat on and I only caught a very brief glimpse of her, so I really don't know. But why not ask her yourself?'

'I did ask her,' Molly told Ormside later when she phoned in, 'but she said she had no idea whose car it might have been or who would be calling at the house. It certainly wasn't her car Mr Whitfield described, and she reminded me that she didn't arrive home until midnight on Tuesday. So I asked her what time she and her dance partner left Scarborough, and she told me they left there on *Monday*. She spent the night and following day with Ramon – or Ray Short, if you like – before coming home.'

Ormside grunted. 'You mean . . .?'

'I mean she "spent the night",' said Molly, emphasizing the words. 'She was quite open about it.'

'What kind of car does Mr Short drive, I wonder?'

'A ten-year-old Ford Transit,' Molly told him. 'White and rust – genuine rust according to Mrs Corbett. And the driver of the car Whitfield saw was white. Ray Short is black.'

She was about to hang up when Ormside stopped her. 'Did you say the name of the man you spoke to is *Fred* Whitfield?' he asked. 'Tallish, white hair, thin face?'

'That's right. Do you know him?'

'In a way,' said Ormside drily. 'I think you've just been talking to retired High Court judge, the Honourable Mr Justice Fred Whitfield, and you couldn't have a better witness if this ever comes to trial. Nice one, Forsythe.'

NINETEEN

The whey-faced man behind the bar only had to glance at the photograph before he said, 'Yeah, that's him. Corbett. He's a regular. Afternoons, mostly. Why, what's he done?'

Tregalles ignored the question. 'Was he in here last Tuesday afternoon?'

The man scratched his head. His yellow hair was pulled back into a ragged ponytail held in place by a rubber band. It looked more like a wig made of fine straw than the man's natural hair.

'Could have been Tuesday,' he said slowly. 'Yeah, probably was, 'cause I haven't seen him the last couple of days. Came in about half three or quarter to four. Sat over there drinking doubles and making phone calls,' he continued, pointing to a corner seat by the window.

'Did you talk to him? Did he say anything to you?'

The man shook his head. 'Just took his drink and sat down and started making phone calls on his mobile.'

'Was that something he normally did?'

'Not like that. I mean he might make the odd call now and again like everybody else these days, but he must have made at least half-a-dozen of them one after the other when he first came in. Seemed to be working himself up into a bit of a state.'

'Drinking much, was he?'

Instead of answering the question, the barman moved away to serve a middle-aged couple, who had attracted his attention by raising their empty glasses. Tregalles looked around. There weren't many in. Apart from himself and the two at the bar, there were only five other people in the place. Two men with briefcases beside their chairs were enjoying a leisurely drink; a young woman had her nose in a book; and two grey-haired ladies with shopping bags were fanning themselves on a bench seat near the window.

Somewhat reluctantly, the barman drifted back.

'I was asking how much Corbett was drinking,' Tregalles reminded him.

'About the same as usual,' the man said, suddenly cautious.

'The usual? I don't know what that means,' Tregalles said sharply. 'You said he was drinking doubles, so how many of those did he have?'

'Don't remember exactly,' the man hedged. 'A couple maybe.'

'Look,' Tregalles said, 'I'm not after you for serving him drinks when he was probably pissed when he came in, but I do need to know what his condition was when he left. You've already told me he was drinking doubles and he was in a bit of a state, so, how many?'

The man eyed him. 'Could have been four or five,' he admitted, 'but I'll deny it if anyone else asks.'

'Just watch it in future,' Tregalles warned, knowing full well he was wasting his breath. 'So, he made a lot of phone calls. Did you hear any of the conversation?'

The barman shook his head. 'I just took him his drinks when he gave me the sign and left him alone. Anyway, he stopped talking whenever I was close by.'

'What did he do after the phone calls?'

'Just sat there by the window looking out every few minutes as if he was expecting somebody.'

'How long was he here?'

'Dunno, exactly. We got a bit busy and the next time I looked over there he was gone.'

'About what time would that be?'

'Half four. That's when some of the regulars start coming in, so I didn't see him go.'

'Did you see anyone else come in? See anyone talk to Corbett?'

'No. Like I said, we were busy, so they could have done.'

'So he was here for half to three quarters of an hour?'

'Give or take, yeah, something like that.'

'You say he's a regular in here. Does he ever have anyone with him?'

'There's this woman, although she doesn't come in very often. Orange juice, that's all she ever drinks.'

'Are you talking about his wife?'

The man shook his head. 'Don't think so,' he said, 'at least she doesn't wear a ring, and he does.'

'Can you describe her?'

'Good looking woman,' the man said with more animation than he'd previously displayed. 'Looks like she's Chinese or Japanese or something like that, except she has red hair. He told me once she's an actress.'

'Thank you very much, Mrs Draper,' said Molly Forsythe. 'You've been very helpful, and I appreciate your cooperation. I don't think I will need to trouble you again.' She put the phone down and sat back in her chair to think about what she'd been told by Rachel Draper – or Rachel Kiechle as she had been thirteen years ago, when she and Sharon Grady had chummed around together.

Based on what Sharon had told her about Rachel and her parents, it hadn't taken Molly long to discover that there used to be a mission called The Only Way down by the river in an area known as the Flats. It was run by a Reverend Peter Kiechle and his wife, and they had a daughter named Rachel.

Where the Kiechles were now, Molly hadn't been able to find out, but she was able to track Rachel down. Married now, she had two children, and she and her husband ran a bed and breakfast in Brighton.

Rachel had been reluctant to talk about her past at first. 'It's not a period of my life I'm proud of,' she said, 'and I've tried hard to put it behind me. As for Sharon, I haven't been in touch with her since I left Broadminster, so I don't know how I can help you.'

It had taken Molly some time to talk Rachel round; to convince her that her only interest was in the names and background of the young men she and Sharon had dated, and not in anything the two girls had done themselves.

Rachel responded cautiously at first, but once she started talking the floodgates opened, and Molly found herself listening to aspects of Rachel's life that she'd kept bottled up for years.

'It's funny,' Rachel said at last, 'but I don't think Sharon and I hung out together for more than six or maybe eight weeks at the most, and yet it seems much longer than that when I look back.'

Rachel told Molly that she'd been brought up to believe that almost anything even remotely enjoyable was sinful, and any deviation from the 'right path' would lead inevitably to hell and eternal damnation. She said rebellion had been bubbling up inside her throughout her teenage years, but she'd been too afraid of her father to do anything about it. But when her parents left for East Africa, she felt as if she'd been set free, and she was determined to do absolutely everything her parents were against. But she didn't know how to set about it until, by chance, she met Sharon Grady.

'Sharon was going through a rebellious stage herself,' she said. 'Her mother had died suddenly the year before; she'd never been close to her father; and she was mad at the world.' A long sigh drifted over the line, and Rachel sounded incredibly sad when she spoke again. 'We tried everything,' she said. 'We went to parties; we drank ourselves silly; we experimented with drugs; and we had sex with the boys.'

'Who were the boys you went with?' Molly asked. 'Sharon tells me that she had a feeling that one of the men in the robbery I mentioned to you was someone she'd met before. She implied that it could have been someone she'd slept with, so when exactly, did all this partying take place?'

'Let's see, now. You say the pub was robbed at New Year? Then it would have been the July or August before that, because the boys we went with were all from university, and they went back in September, and that's when I moved to Tenborough.'

'They were all university students? Do you remember which university?'

'Leeds, most of them, I think, although some could have been from somewhere else.'

'So what about their names?'

'Ah, yes, the names. Sorry. Didn't mean to run on like that; I must have been boring you to tears with—' She stopped abruptly. 'Oh, God!' she breathed. 'You haven't been recording this, have you?'

'Absolutely not,' Molly told her – which was true in the narrowest sense, but she had been taking shorthand notes. 'The names, Mrs Draper?' she prompted again.

'Yes, of course,' Rachel said. 'Funny, though, Sharon not remembering, because she used to keep a notebook – her scorecard, she called it – and she used to rate each boy according to how good the sex was, with notes on what she thought of him. I remember that well enough, because she always made a point of telling me all about it in lurid detail afterwards. Which reminds me, what's Sharon doing now? Not that I want to get in touch with her or anything like that. I just wondered, you know.'

'She's married now. Her married name is Jessop.'

'Jessop?' Rachel repeated. She sounded surprised. 'Not *Al* Jessop? She didn't marry Albert Jessop, did she?'

'Albert Jessop. Yes, that's his name.'

'Oh, dear. Al Jessop. Poor Sharon. Whatever made her do that, I wonder? He was a nutter back when I was there. I hope he's improved . . .?'

It was an implied question, but Molly refused to be drawn. 'The names, if you don't mind, Mrs Draper?'

'Right. Got a pencil?'

Molly sat looking at the shorthand notes in her notebook. There were eleven names in total – Rachel had a good memory – and four of them were on the list of those who had attended the Taylors' house-warming party.

Molly had just finished relaying the information to Ormside, when Tregalles entered the room, followed almost immediately by Paget.

'Good, you're all here,' the DCI said briskly. 'I've just heard from Starkie, and it is his opinion that Corbett's death was no accident. There are bruises on the back and sides of Corbett's neck, and some of his hair was pulled out, which suggests that someone held him face down and forced his head under water until he drowned. Corbett's blood-alcohol reading was off the scale, but he must have been conscious and struggling, because some of his fingernails are all but torn away from clawing at the side of the pond. And there are bruises and cuts on the back of one of his hands that suggest it was hammered to make him let go. I've passed that information on to Charlie, so we'll see if his people can find any evidence at the pool to support Starkie's theory. He's promised to have his report on my desk first thing Monday morning.'

Paget glanced at the time. 'Now, Tregalles, how far did you get in tracking Corbett's movements after he left the office on Tuesday?'

Tregalles gave a brief account of his talk with Corbett's old boss and Joanie, the secretary, and his subsequent visit to the Unicorn. 'It sounds to me as if Corbett started to panic after you left him,' he said, 'because he started making phone calls as soon as you were out of his office, and he went on making them after he got to the pub, and the barman thinks he was waiting for someone as well. So the next thing I have to do is find out who Corbett was calling and who he was waiting for.'

Tregalles turned to Ormside. 'Can you check that list of things found in Corbett's pockets to see if his mobile phone is on it?' he asked. 'Don't know if we can get anything from it after being under water, but it might save us a bit of time if we can.'

Ormside pulled the folder and opened it. He flipped through the pages until he came to the one he wanted. 'No phone,' he said. 'It could be at the bottom of the pond, assuming he had it with him when he went in.'

Tregalles grimaced. 'Might as well forget it if it's still down there, then,' he said. 'I'll put in a request for his phone records.'

Paget looked thoughtful after hearing Molly's report. 'Do we have anything on Short?' he asked Ormside.

'Not yet,' the Sergeant told him, 'but I'll check with Tenborough and see if they have anything. That's where he lives.'

'Right,' said Paget. 'Anything else?'

'I had Graham Williams in,' Ormside said. 'He's an
accountant. Lives alone and works from his house. He was at
school with Barry, but says he used to be painfully shy, so he
stayed out of Barry's way. And he went to Durham university, when Barry went to Leeds. As for Williams being part
of a gang, I think you can safely scrub him off the list.'

'Well, that's something, at least,' Paget observed as he turned
his attention to Molly. 'What about Irene Sinclair?' he asked.
'Have you had a chance to talk to her about her relationship
with Roger Corbett and his wife?'

'No, sir, not yet,' she said, and went on to explain that Irene
Sinclair was taking part in a pageant in Chester over the
weekend, and wouldn't be back until Monday. 'But I would
like to have another chat with Sharon Jessop. I managed to
track down the girl Sharon used to knock around with the
summer before the pub was robbed, and her memory is much
better than Sharon's. She gave me a list of names of the boys
they went with back then, and I'd like to hear what Sharon
has to say about them, because I think she's been holding out
on me. I thought I might do that tomorrow if . . .'

But Paget was shaking his head. 'No need for that,' he told
her. 'You've all worked too many weekends and unpaid overtime as it is. It's not that often we see fine weather on a
weekend, so enjoy this one while you can. Leave Jessop and
Irene Sinclair till Monday.'

'I had thought about doing salmon on the barbecue this
evening,' Grace said, 'but we would probably have to fight
the wasps for it, so I picked up a barbecued chicken instead.
I'll do a salad to go with it, and have fruit and ice cream afterwards. I could do a jacket potato as well if you like? If you'll
set up the toaster oven on the bench in the garage, we can
keep it cool in here.'

'Good idea,' said Paget. 'I didn't have much time for lunch
today.' He picked up the toaster oven and left the kitchen.

Grace was busy at the sink, scrubbing a couple of potatoes
when he returned.

'So, how was your day?' he asked.

'Quite pleasant, considering the reason we were there,'
Grace said. 'I spent a good part of it messing about in the
Corbett's fish pond. There was a nice bit of shade, and it was

almost cool under the trees, so it was quite enjoyable. And I found Mr Corbett's glasses.'

'You were actually *in* the pond?'

Grace shook her head. 'We were using the submersible probe light and the recovery tools, so we sat on the side with our feet in the pool to do it. It took a long time because we had to be careful not to stir up the mud on the bottom. We shooed the fish out of there and put in a temporary dam first, of course.'

'What did Mrs Corbett have to say about that?'

'She was very helpful, as a matter of fact. She told me that the pond had been her husband's preserve, but she seems to know quite a lot about the feeding and general care of the fish and their habits herself.' Grace dried the potatoes off with a paper towel, then stuck a steel skewer through each one. 'There, they just need a touch of oil on them and they're ready to go once the oven heats up,' she said.

'Find anything else in the pond?' asked Paget. 'Starkie believes that Corbett was held under by someone.'

'So Charlie said. And we did find what appears to be blood and tiny bits of skin on the stonework, which could have been left by Corbett trying to drag himself out of the pond, but we'll have to wait for Forensic to confirm that – or not. But that could have happened just as easily if he had fallen in accidentally. Apparently the man was very drunk, so he could have simply toppled in, and was too drunk to claw his way out.'

'But it wouldn't account for the bruises on either side of his neck, or the fact that someone or something had hammered the back of his right hand.'

'Ah! Charlie didn't mention that bit. So, it does look like murder, then?'

Paget nodded. 'I was pretty sure that Corbett was nervous about something when I spoke to him on Tuesday,' he said. 'Like almost everyone else, he denied knowing anything about Barry Grant, but it didn't ring true to me. I suspect that he knew a lot more about Grant and the robberies and killings than he let on. I have trouble seeing him as a participant, but I think he knew who was, and that's who he was trying to call. You didn't happen to find his mobile, did you?'

'Sorry.'

'Too bad,' he said, 'but if I'm right, chances are that the person or persons who killed Corbett are the same ones who killed George Taylor and Emily Bergman. And speaking of Emily Bergman, love, how would you like to go away for the weekend? This could be the last weekend of sunshine for a while if the forecasters are right about the weather breaking next week.'

Grace eyed him suspiciously. 'Before I answer that,' she said, 'I'd like to know why the name of Emily Bergman triggered the idea of going away for the weekend. Where, exactly, are you suggesting we go?'

'Cambridge.'

'Cambridge . . .?' Grace raised an eyebrow, silently inviting an explanation.

'Tell you in a minute,' he said. 'I'd better get these potatoes started; time's getting on, and you must be hungry.'

Grace chuckled. 'Which is your ever so subtle way of letting me know that *you're* hungry, I suppose,' she said. 'Let's have the potatoes, then, and I'll give them a shot in the microwave first. That will cut the cooking time in half, and the oven should be ready by now. Anyway, why Cambridge?'

He handed the potatoes to Grace. 'Because that's where the Bergmans live now,' he said, 'and after the call I received this afternoon, I'd like to talk to them.'

He moved out of Grace's way to prop himself up in the doorway before going on. 'The phone call was from a Mr Urquhart,' he said. 'He's a vice-president of the company with whom the Bergmans were insured. It seems that Len Ormside rang the local office a couple of days ago to ask for some information regarding the settlement of Bergman's claim for his losses in the robbery. It was a routine enquiry. The amount claimed was in the information we had on file, but as it wasn't settled for several months, the final settlement figure never did get back to us.

'The local man didn't have the information, so he went back to head office for the file, and that's when Mr Urquhart got into the act and phoned me. He wanted to make it very clear that they believe Sam Bergman falsified the records in order to claim far more than he'd actually lost in the robbery. The trouble was, there was such a mixture of cash, jewellery, gold leaf, gold wire and wafers and so on, that it was almost impossible to make a true evaluation. In addition, they said he should have put the alarm on as soon as he and his wife arrived at the shop. In short, they were refusing to settle for the amount he was claiming

'But Sam stood firm, and said if they didn't pay up, he'd take them to court. They were all set to fight it, but their legal people got cold feet at the last minute. They felt they might do the company more harm than good, "relationship wise", as Urquhart put it, by fighting the man in open court so soon after he'd lost his wife in such tragic circumstances. So they held their noses and settled the claim.'

Grace, who had been listening while she stripped the lettuce and washed the leaves, paused to cast Paget a puzzled glance. 'So what did this Mr Urquhart expect you to do about it?' she asked.

Paget shrugged. 'Nothing, directly. The main purpose of the call was to ask if we had considered the possibility that the robbery was a scam, engineered by Bergman, to defraud the insurance company. At first, he said, they thought that was all it was, and Emily had been killed when something went wrong, but when they learned that Sam and his assistant were married within six months of Emily's death, they wondered if that, too, had been part of the deal. Urquhart said it made a lot of sense, considering that Emily had been insured for £300,000.'

Grace frowned. 'Same company?' she asked. 'And they paid up?'

'Different section, but the same company,' Paget told her, 'and since there was no doubt about the way she died, less questions were asked about that claim than were asked about Sam's other claims, so they settled within weeks.'

'That oven should be ready now,' Grace said, 'so pop the potatoes out there for me, will you, love?'

She dried her hands and set the timer for half an hour. 'I wonder where they were married?' she said when Paget reappeared. 'Sam and his assistant, I mean. What was her name?'

'Loretta Thompson. And they were married in Hereford, at least that's what Urquhart told me today. A quiet, civil marriage, he said. Why?'

'Because that means the insurance company must have had their suspicions about both claims if they were keeping that close an eye on them.'

'Good point,' said Paget, 'which means Urquhart may be on to something. And that is why I would like to go to Cambridge tomorrow to have a chat with Sam and his wife.' He picked up a handful of cherry tomatoes. 'These been washed?' he asked.

'No, but if you're offering, go right ahead,' Grace said. 'There's a cucumber in the crisper if you would like to do that as well. But Cambridge in the middle of July? I'm not so sure about that,' she said doubtfully. 'It would take us the best part of the day to get there and even longer to come back; you know what the roads are like on a weekend in midsummer.'

'Three-and-a-half hours,' he countered. 'I checked it on the RAC route planner. If we leave about six thirty in the morning, we can beat the traffic and be there by the time the shops open. And if we stick to the minor roads on the way back, we can do it in four. What do you say, Grace? It would do us both good to get away for a couple of days.'

'Might be hard to get a room at such short notice,' she said, 'or have you checked that out as well, DCI Paget?'

He grimaced guiltily. 'I did just happen to be talking to a Superintendent Hillier in Cambridge,' he admitted, 'and he was kind enough to have someone find a place for us.'

Grace sighed. 'Why does that not surprise me?' she asked rhetorically. 'But it had better be a nice place,' she warned. 'I don't want to end up in the back bedroom of his mother-in-law's flat, or some such thing.'

'Nothing but the best,' he assured her solemnly. 'How does the Crowne Plaza sound? It's one of the best in Cambridge, and it's close to Bergman's shop in the heart of the town.'

'I don't know Cambridge, but it sounds all right,' she said cautiously. 'So I suppose all that's left for me to do is say, yes, and set the alarm clock for five. Mind you, I must say I'm warming to the idea. It really would be nice to get away for a couple of days.'

'Good,' said Paget as he started in on the cucumber. 'So that's settled. And don't worry about the alarm clock. I set it when I went upstairs to wash and change.'

'Your wife has a strong heart,' the specialist had said, 'but the heart needs oxygen, and not enough is getting into the lungs

through the narrowed airways. That means not enough oxygen
is getting into the bloodstream to keep the heart going.'

'Can't you increase the amount? Give her more?'

The specialist had shaken his head. 'We can supply the
oxygen, but the lungs have to do their part, and I'm afraid
your wife's lungs are so far gone that, quite frankly, I don't
know what's keeping her heart going. I'm sorry, Mr Alcott,
but there is nothing more we can do for her.'

The girls had gone, and Alcott was thankful for that. Celeste,
realizing that her mother was fading fast, had decided to stay
overnight rather than return to Bristol. She'd taken up Valerie's
somewhat hesitant offer of a bed for the night after making
it quite clear that she wouldn't even consider staying under
the same roof as her father.

Now, sitting there in the half-dark, listening to Marion
struggle for each and every breath, he cradled his head in his
hands and wept.

TWENTY

Saturday, July 18th

Not only had they made good time, considering they
had made their way across country on secondary
roads, but they had passed through countryside and
any number of picturesque towns and villages they might
otherwise never have seen. Travelling east, facing the sun, had
been hard on the eyes for the first few miles, but from then
on it had been an enjoyable journey.

Even the streets of Cambridge were relatively quiet, but as
Paget pointed out, it was still early; it was a Saturday, and
the colleges were more or less shut down for the summer.

Guided by Grace reading the map of the city she'd taken
off the net the night before, Paget made his way to the police
station on Parkside. 'Just going to let them know I'm here on
their patch,' he told her, 'and thank them for their help
yesterday.'

He emerged some twenty-five minutes later to find Grace

sitting in the car with the doors open to let the breeze through.
'Sorry to take so long,' he apologized, 'but they were giving
me a rundown on Sam Bergman and his business, and as far
as they're concerned, he's a successful businessman with a
clean record.' He handed Grace a sheet of paper. 'That's a
copy of Bergman's listing in the *Yellow Pages*.'

'Impressive,' Grace said as she scanned the page. '"Bespoke
jewellery . . . special commissions . . . gold, silver . . . hand-
made wedding and engagement rings to your design . . .
diamond setting . . ." Sounds as if Samuel Bergman is doing
very well. That insurance settlement must have helped.'

'I imagine it did.' Paget went around and got in the car. 'In
fact he must be doing *very* well, because he moved into a big
new shopping centre called the Grand Arcade at the beginning of this year. I rang Bergman while I was in there to tell
him we'd be visiting him in a few minutes.'

'How did he sound?'

'If you mean, did he sound worried, I'd say no. He sounded
much the same as he did yesterday, when I set up this meeting,
when he told me he'd be pleased to help in any way he could
if it would lead to the capture of the men who killed his wife.'

'Which is probably what I would have said under the circumstances if I'd been complicit in the killing of my wife or
husband . . . or lover,' she added with a smile.

'My, we are being cynical, today, aren't we?' he said as he
handed Grace a second piece of paper. 'Directions on how to
get to the Grand Arcade from here,' he said. 'I'm told it's
impossible to miss, and it's not very far from here.'

The Grand Arcade was hard to miss, and judging by the
number of cars in the multi-storey car park, and the steady
stream of people entering the shopping centre itself, there had
to be a fair bit of money about in Cambridge, thought Paget
as they made their way inside. Sunlight poured through the
domed glass ceiling, giving a light and airy feeling to the
concourse as they followed the directions Paget had been given
in Parkside.

'There it is,' said Grace, pointing. 'Over there on the corner.'

The name, *Samuel Bergman – Jeweller, Gold and
Silversmith,* was written in gold on a black background on
the window.

They entered the shop, where Paget identified himself to a

slim, dark-haired young woman behind the long display counter. 'Ah, yes,' she said, 'Mr Bergman is expecting you, and he will be here in a moment, Chief Inspector.' Even as she was speaking, her hand slid beneath the edge of the counter, and Paget noted the brief tightening of the tendons of her wrist as she pressed a hidden button. He glanced around; there were at least three cameras in the shop, and possibly other safeguards as well, so it seemed that Samuel Bergman had learned something about security since the Broadminster robbery and the killing of his wife.

A door at the far end of the shop opened and a short, heavy-set, balding man advanced towards them, hand extended. 'Chief Inspector Paget,' he said effusively as they shook hands. 'And . . .?' He looked enquiringly at Grace, then back to Paget.

'Ms Lovett is a crime scene investigator,' Paget explained as they both produced their cards for Bergman's inspection. 'She is working with me on the investigation.'

'I see,' said Bergman, but he looked faintly puzzled, and his tone belied his words. 'You had no trouble finding us, then?' he said.

'None at all,' Paget assured him. 'And I must say I'm impressed with the Grand Arcade. I gather it hasn't been open long.'

'Just last year,' Bergman told him. 'In fact we have been here less than six months ourselves.'

'And business . . .?' Paget enquired. 'Has it been affected by the recession?'

'Not as much as you might think,' Bergman said, sounding almost smug. 'People are becoming more conservative in their choice of engagement and wedding rings and jewellery in general, but we also trade in gold and silver; we have done for some years now, and that is where the interest lies today. In fact, I am happy to say, compared to some of my competitors, we are doing very well. But that is not why you're here, is it, Chief Inspector? Please, come this way.'

Bergman led them to the back of the shop, where he ushered them into a small, tastefully furnished room. 'Our viewing and selection room,' he said proudly, directing them to soft leather seats facing an oval, glass-topped, mahogany desk. 'Some of our clients prefer to make their selections in private,' he explained. 'With our assistance, of course,' he added when he saw Paget's eyes flick to the two CCTV cameras monitoring the room.

Bergman moved to the other side of the desk to take his own seat. 'I must apologize for insisting that we meet here, Chief Inspector,' he said, 'but as I explained on the phone yesterday, we are short-handed in our workshop, so my wife and I will be working here throughout the weekend to meet a deadline on a special order. Otherwise, we would have been happy to have you come to our home.'

'This is perfectly fine,' Paget assured him, 'and I'll try not to keep you too long. Is your wife here?'

'She should be here at any moment now,' Bergman told him. 'She is just finishing the repair of a rather fine necklace.'

'Really?' Paget said. 'I didn't realize that Mrs Bergman was involved in that side of the business. According to the notes we have on file, Loretta Thompson was your bookkeeper and part-time assistant in the shop.'

'And that was true at the time,' Bergman said, 'but Loretta was always interested in our work, and Emily began teaching her some of the basics about a year before she died, so Loretta was able to help me afterwards. Later, after moving to Cambridge, Loretta took an art foundation course, then went on to get a degree in jewellery and silversmithing. She has a natural talent for it, and she's been invaluable to me. Ah!' he exclaimed as a door opened and a woman wearing a white smock entered the room. 'Here she is now. Loretta, this is Detective Chief Inspector Paget, and Ms Lovett, who is a . . .' He made an apologetic gesture with his hands. 'I'm sorry, Ms Lovett,' he said, 'but your title is . . .?'

'Crime Scene Investigator,' Grace told him.

'CSI?' the woman said with a smile. 'Is that the same as we see on television?'

'I wish,' Grace said with feeling. 'We do much the same job, but the comparison ends there, I'm afraid, especially when it comes to the equipment and the amount of space they have to work in.'

'Sam said you wanted to talk to both of us about what happened when Emily was killed,' she said, addressing Paget as she sat down, 'but I don't know what I can tell you, because

I wasn't there that day – at least until much later, when the police called me in.'

Loretta Bergman was tall, taller than her husband by several inches. Slim, fine-boned; her shoulder-length fair hair framed a rather plain face, except for the eyes. Calm, restful, yet seductive eyes, thought Grace, and wondered if that was the way Neil would see them as Loretta Bergman looked at him.

'I realize that, Mrs Bergman,' said Paget, 'but I thought it would save time on both sides if we could talk to the two of you together. As I told Mr Bergman on the phone, evidence has come to our attention in the form of a letter of sorts from someone who claims he was the driver for the gang who broke into your shop thirteen years ago. Unfortunately, he did not give us any other names, so we have been talking to everyone who might have been associated with him back then, and with the people who were also robbed by the same gang.

'Their original statements are on file, along with your own, of course, and while I know this may be difficult for you, I would like to talk to you about the events of that day, and anything that might have occurred to you since then.'

Sam Bergman, sitting back in his chair, hands clasped over his stomach, nodded. 'I've thought of little else since you called me yesterday,' he said soberly. 'And you're right, it is hard, but if there's any chance, and I mean *any* chance at all of finding and catching the bastards who killed Emily, I'll help you in any way I can. So, where do you want to start?'

'From the time you entered the shop that Saturday morning,' Paget told him. 'The report I have says you entered by the front door at approximately eight thirty. Was that your usual practise?'

'Yes, it was.'

'Never by the back door?'

'No.'

'Did you, for any reason, open the back door between the time you arrived and when you left again to go down to the cafe on the corner to meet your friends?'

'No. Why would I?' Bergman asked.

'I don't know. Perhaps you heard something going on out there and went to look; perhaps you took some rubbish out to the bin . . .?'

Bergman shook his head. 'Nothing like that,' he said firmly.

'We just got on with the cleaning and getting the shop ready for business. I went over and over this with the inspector at the time. We did nothing different that morning.'

'There seems to have been some question about whether or not you locked the back door when you left. Did you lock it behind you?'

Annoyance flickered in Bergman's eyes as he said, 'No, as I told them at the time, *I* didn't lock the door, but Emily always shot the bolt on the door when I left. And I never left until I heard her do it. The insurance people hammered at that every chance they got, but I know that door was bolted from the inside.'

'And I'm not disputing that,' Paget told him, 'but as you know, there was no indication that the door had been forced, so it must have been your wife who opened the door.'

Bergman nodded agreement. 'I'm sure it was,' he said. 'She probably thought it was me or possibly George.'

'You mean she would open the door if *anyone* knocked?'

Bergman shook his head impatiently. 'Emily wouldn't open the door to just anyone, although, with the benefit of hind-sight, I can see how careless we were. But you have to remember, it was a peaceful town; there had never been so much as a hint of trouble, so I suppose you could say we'd become lax. Emily knew that I always gave three sets of three knocks.' Bergman demonstrated by rapping three times in quick succession on the desk, followed by a pause, doing it again, pause, then a third time. 'Like Morse code,' he explained. '"S" for Sam three times. The only other person who used it was George Taylor from next door.'

Paget turned to Loretta. 'Did you know about that signal at the back door?' he asked.

'Yes, I did,' she said. 'I never had a reason to use it, but I knew about it.'

Paget turned back to Sam. 'If George Taylor knew about it, it seems likely to me that there could have been others who knew it as well,' he said.

Sam bristled. 'Like who?' he demanded. 'I never told anyone else, and I'm sure Emily didn't.'

'And I certainly didn't,' Loretta said.

'What about George Taylor's two boys?' asked Paget. 'They probably knew.'

'I suppose they might,' Sam said, 'but I think you're clutching at straws if you're suggesting that they were involved. They were good lads. Never had any trouble with them.'

'I'm not suggesting anything,' Paget replied, 'except, from what you've told me, it's quite possible that others may have known as well. Tell me, Mr Bergman, did you know a boy by the name of Barry Grant?'

Sam thought for a moment, then shook his head. 'Don't think so,' he said. 'Why?'

'Yes, you did, Sam,' Loretta said. 'Remember? He used to hang around with young David Taylor. The one I warned Tony to stay away from?'

'Grant?' he said with a sharp glance at his wife. 'Was that his name?' He shrugged an apology. 'Sorry, my dear, but I'd forgotten his name.'

Paget was almost afraid to ask. Almost everyone they had spoken to had done their best to distance themselves from Barry Grant. Hardly surprising, perhaps, since no one wanted to be associated with the boy who had confessed to being part of a gang that had killed two people.

'How well did you know Barry?' he asked Loretta.

'Well enough to know he was a bad influence,' she said. 'He was always showing off, talking about things he'd done or was going to do. He was such a cocky kid. I just didn't like him, and I didn't want him anywhere near my son, Tony. Barry was two or three years older than Tony, and Tony thought he was wonderful. Followed him around every chance he got. Fortunately, that ended when Barry went off to university. Although . . .'

Loretta fell silent, leaving the word hanging in the air. Paget was about to ask another question, but held back, sensing there was more to come.

Loretta drew a deep breath, and there was sadness in her eyes as she said, 'Perhaps things would have been different if Barry *hadn't* gone away. At least Tony wouldn't have gone looking for someone to take his place, and he might still be alive.'

Sam Bergman reached out and took his wife's hand in his own. 'You did the best you could, my dear,' he said soothingly. 'Please don't blame yourself.' He looked across at Paget. 'Tony was a good boy,' he said quietly, 'but he was easily led.

After this Grant boy went away, Tony got in with the wrong
crowd; got into drugs, and died of an overdose a couple of
months later. He'd just turned seventeen. Loretta didn't know
anything about it until it was too late.'

Loretta withdrew her hand and looked at Paget. 'Sorry,' she
said. 'It's just that when you mentioned Barry Grant, it all
came back again. Why are you asking about him?'

'Because he is the person I mentioned at the beginning.
The one who drove the van in each of the robberies. He left
some notes behind when he died, but they never came to light
until a week or so ago and, as I said, he didn't name any of
the others, so—'

'He's dead?' Loretta asked sharply.

'That's right. You didn't know? He committed suicide a
couple of days after the robbery.'

Loretta shook her head. 'No, I didn't know,' she said, with
a questioning glance at her husband.

Sam shook his head. 'I don't remember hearing anything
about it,' he said, 'but if I'd known at the time that he was
one of them, I'd have killed the murdering little sod myself!'

It seemed strange that neither of them had known about
Barry's death, but thinking about it now, Paget could see how
that could happen. Sam and Loretta would have been preoccupied with their own problems, and the suicide had not
been given a lot of play in the local media.

Grace looked at Paget, one eyebrow raised in a silent question. He caught the look and nodded for her to go ahead. 'You
mentioned David Taylor, Mrs Bergman,' she said. 'You said
that Barry used to "hang around" with him. Do you remember
any other friends of Barry's . . . or of David's?'

Loretta thought for a moment, then shook her head. 'I
wouldn't have known that much about Barry if it hadn't been
for Tony,' she said. 'I had to keep an eye on him right from
the time he was quite small, because he was far too trusting;
he would go along with anyone and do almost anything they
suggested, so I always tried to make sure I knew who he was
with, but it became almost impossible as he grew older. As
for young David, when I said Barry used to hang around with
him, it always seemed to me that David would like to be rid
of him, but couldn't quite bring himself to see him off. David
always struck me as a nice boy, quiet, always polite, and his

brother was much the same.' She smiled. 'I think that must have come from their mother's side,' she said, 'because they certainly didn't get it from their father.'

'George was all right,' her husband protested. 'I know you thought he was a bit coarse at times, but he was a good friend.'

'I'm not denying that, Sam,' Loretta said softly, 'but you have to admit he was pretty hard on the boys; they could never live up to his expectations, and he was even harder on them after Lydia died.' Loretta saw the question in Grace's eyes. 'Lydia Taylor, George's wife,' she explained. 'She was the buffer between George and the boys, and I think it literally wore her out in the end. She died when they were in their teens. Cervical cancer.'

'You knew the family well, then?' said Grace.

Loretta shook her head. 'I wouldn't say that,' she said, 'but I lived just up the street from the bakery. After my husband died, I sold the house and Tony and I moved into a flat above the tobacconist's on the corner. I first met Lydia at an art course we both attended when the children were small, and we became quite friendly. But then Lydia stopped coming, which was a pity, because she had talent. Apparently George thought it a waste of time and money, so he told her to drop it, and she did. I used to talk to her in the shop quite regularly, but it was never the same after that. It was almost as if she was afraid to spend time talking in case George disapproved. And George was just as hard on the boys after their mother died.'

Sam was shaking his head. 'Be fair, Loretta,' he said. 'It can't have been any picnic trying to raise two teenage boys after their mother died, and run a business as well, especially a bakery. He told me Lydia had always been too soft with them, and they needed discipline.'

'Discipline is one thing, Sam,' Loretta said, 'but those kids worked hard in that bakery, and yet he was never satisfied. You know how he used to yell at them, Sam. We could hear him out there in the lane when they were loading the vans. It didn't seem to matter what they did, he would always find something to grumble about. And the way he went on and on about Kevin when he took up with the Bradshaw girl because of her father . . . I mean it really was ridiculous!'

'What was that about?' asked Paget before Bergman could reply.

Loretta looked to her husband, silently passing the question over to him. Sam shrugged. 'It was just that he felt Ed Bradshaw had betrayed him,' he said.

'Betrayed him in what way?'

'George and Ed had been friends ever since they were kids, so when Ed took on a case for the owner of a café who was taking George to court over some tainted Cornish pasties he'd received from George's bakery, George was furious. And when he lost the case, that was the end of their friendship as far as he was concerned. So, you can imagine how he felt when he found out that Kevin was going with Ed's daughter.'

'But he should never have—' Loretta began heatedly, only to be cut off by Paget.

'Can either of you think of any other friends of David and Kevin Taylor and Barry Grant?'

Sam shook his head. Loretta thought for a moment, then shook her head as well. 'I'm sure there were others,' she said, 'but I can't remember anyone in particular.'

'Right, then,' said Paget, glancing at his watch. 'I know you have a busy day ahead of you, and I do thank you both for your patience, but before we leave, I must ask you, Mrs Bergman, about your hours of work in the shop back then. I know you worked there part-time, but I'm told that you normally worked there on Saturdays, and yet you weren't there on the day the robbery took place. Would you mind telling me why?'

TWENTY-ONE

Sunday, July 19th

They left Cambridge early the following morning, deciding to take the scenic route back to Broadminster.

They stopped for an ice cream and a leisurely stroll down the mile-long High Street in Henley-in-Arden, admiring the timbered houses and shops that lined the street. But the sun was almost at its zenith, and the street was filling rapidly with cars and tourists, so they decided it was time to leave.

'I suppose they *could* have been telling the truth about why Loretta wasn't there that morning,' Paget said as they got in the car. 'But there's no way of checking their story now.'

Grace smiled to herself as she buckled up. 'I wondered how long you could go without talking about the case,' she said. 'For what it's worth, I thought she was telling the truth. She said she'd worked more than the usual number of hours that week, because they were taking inventory, and she'd worked late on Friday, so she was taking Saturday off, and I imagine Rogers would have checked her story at the time. As for the idea that the target could have been Emily, and the robbery was staged to cover the killing, I can't see it, myself. First of all, how would someone like Sam Bergman or Loretta go about finding someone willing to do all that? Secondly, even if they did, they would be laying themselves open to blackmail for the rest of their lives, and I certainly didn't get the impression that they were being bled dry. Did you?'

'You're right,' he said as he started the car and set off. 'But I would like to know what their relationship was before the robbery. I mean for Bergman to marry again so soon after his wife was killed in such a brutal way . . . I just don't understand how anyone could do that.'

Grace remained silent. It had taken Neil a long time to come to terms with the death of his wife, Jill, who had died a violent death herself, and it had taken him even longer to allow himself to love and be loved again without feeling guilty, so she could understand why he felt as he did. But not everyone would react in the same way. Sam had lost his wife and Loretta had lost her husband and her only child. And working together every day in the months following the robbery, it wasn't hard to imagine why they might decide to marry and begin life again in a new place.

Driving back from Leominster that evening, where she had spent the day with her lifelong friend, Jane Thomas, and Jane's five-year-old daughter, Melissa, Molly had all the windows open, but she still felt as if she were burning up. She slid her fingers under the shoulder-straps of her sundress to ease them

away from her skin. She should have known better than to
spend so much time with her god-daughter, Melissa, in the
large inflatable pool in Jane's back garden, and now she was
paying the price. She'd worn a floppy hat to shield her face,
but her neck, shoulders and upper arms were a fiery red by
the end of the day.

Young Melissa, slathered in sunscreen, didn't seem to be
bothered at all. But then, she'd been playing outside all
summer, and neither she nor her mother seemed to be much
affected by the sun.

Molly winced, and tried not to think what her shoulders
and neck would be like when she returned to work in the
morning. Better stop and try to find some soothing cream on
her way home, and get an early night so she would be ready
to tackle Sharon Jessop once again tomorrow.

She hadn't really thought about it before, but it suddenly
occurred to Molly that Sharon would be at work tomorrow,
and it could be awkward trying to talk to her there. Which
meant she would have to wait until tomorrow evening to talk
to Sharon. Or she could get it over and done with tonight by
stopping in Peel Street on her way home.

Twenty minutes later, Molly was knocking on Sharon's door,
conscious that three women two houses down had stopped
talking, and were watching her. Molly knocked again, harder
this time, then stepped back into the street to look for movement at any of the windows.

'She's not there,' one of the women called, then turned to
listen as one of the other women tugged on her arm and said
something. The woman nodded, then left the others to approach
Molly. 'You the one who was here before?' she demanded as
she drew near.

'That's right. You say Sharon's not in? Do you know where
she is or when she might be back?'

The woman sniffed. '*If* she comes back,' she said. 'She
didn't look too good to me when they carried her out this
morning, and I wouldn't give much for her chances. Face all
battered, bones broke. He did a right job on her.'

'Who did a right job on her?' asked Molly sharply.

'That husband of hers. Always has been handy with his
fists, that one. Always coming round for money, but with
Sharon losing her job and all, she wouldn't have none to give,

would she? So he beat her up.' She took cigarettes from her apron pocket and lit one. 'It's a good job the kids weren't in the house at the time, is all I can say. So what do you want?'

'I *did* want to talk to Sharon,' Molly said. 'But tell me more about what happened. You say she was taken to hospital this morning, and the children weren't in the house. Why weren't they there?'

'You're a copper, aren't you?' the woman said, ignoring the question.

'That's right, but . . .'

'So why don't you know about this?' the woman demanded. 'We had the other coppers round.'

'I was away over the weekend,' Molly explained. 'I just got back. Now, about the children?'

Instead of answering, the woman motioned for one of the other woman to come. 'Over here, Vi,' she called. 'She wants to know about the kids and why they weren't at home when their dad beat up their mum. You had 'em; you tell her.'

'That's right,' said the woman called Vi. 'Came round yesterday evening. About nine, it was. Asked me to take the kids. Had 'em with her. Said it would only be for a few hours, but I told her they might as well stay the night.'

'Did she say why she wanted them out of the house?'

'Not really. She was sort of excited and maybe a bit scared, so I knew right away it would be Al coming round to take money off her again. Not that he would get very far this time with her being given her cards on Friday. She was in a right old state then, I can tell you. Crying, and going on about what she and the kids were going to do.'

'So what happened after you took the children?' Molly asked. 'Did you see Al Jessop come to the house?'

Vi shook her head. 'Not when he arrived. Stay out of it is my motto,' she said firmly. 'But I heard his van start up and saw him leave.'

'What time was that?'

Vi pursed her lips and frowned in thought 'Couldn't've been long after I'd put the kids to bed. Half nine, ten o'clock, something like that.'

'Wasn't it dark?'

'There was still a bit of light in the sky, and the street light's just across the road. It was him all right.'

'This is your house?' Molly asked, pointing to the one next door.

'That's right.'

'You saw him through the front window?'

'Bedroom window,' the woman said. 'Slammed the door so hard when he left I went to the window to see what was happening.'

'You didn't go round, then, to see if Sharon was all right?'

'None of my business, was it?' Vi said flatly.

'Who found Sharon this morning?'

'I did when I took the kids round. I mean I'd had 'em all night; I reckoned the least she could do was give 'em breakfast.'

'Where was she in the house? And what state was she in?'

'On the floor in the kitchen, and she was unconscious. She'd been bleeding, but it had stopped and I knew it had been there a while, 'cause it was dry. Face was all beat up and it looked to me like one of her arms was broken, the way it was bent back. The kitchen looked like it had been hit by a bomb, cupboard doors open, stuff dragged out all over the floor. Don't know what the rest of the rooms were like, but they'll probably be the same. I got out of there right quick, I can tell you, and called the ambulance.'

'So who called the police?'

'Wasn't me,' Vi said emphatically. 'Must have been them, 'cause the police didn't come till after the ambulance got there.'

'Where are the children now?'

'Called her dad at the pub, didn't I?' said Vi. 'Came over here right sharp, he did, and took 'em back with him.'

'Did you speak to the police this morning?'

She nodded. 'Told 'em the same as I told you.'

'Have you heard anything since? How Sharon is doing?'

Both women shook their heads.

Molly thanked them and got back in the car. 'Looks like I can say goodbye to an early night,' she muttered beneath her breath as she left the street and headed for the hospital.

TWENTY-TWO

Monday, July 20th

'I think we should be digging deeper into the relationship between Barry Grant and David Taylor,' Paget said after giving a brief summary of his visit to Cambridge on the weekend. 'If George Taylor knew about Sam Bergman's "secret knock", then I'm sure the boys knew about it as well, and there could be others. According to Loretta Bergman, both boys were bullied by their father, so it's possible that it was David who George Taylor recognized when he pulled the mask off, bearing in mind that Barry did mention David by name.

'So, Tregalles,' he said, 'I want you to find out everything you can about David Taylor and any other friends he had back then, and the same goes for Kevin Taylor as well, since he was still seeing his girlfriend after being told by his father that he had to drop her if he wanted his financial support to continue.'

He turned to Ormside. 'Anything on the car or the people Whitfield saw leaving the Corbetts' house?' he asked.

'Nothing yet,' the Sergeant told him.

Paget scanned the whiteboards once again. 'We need to get more people out to canvas the area around the Unicorn to see if anyone remembers seeing Corbett or his car. And since Charlie's people didn't find Corbett's mobile phone in the pond, the sooner we get those phone records, the better.

'Now,' he continued, 'what about this attack on Sharon Jessop?' he asked Molly. 'Do you see it as having anything to do with the Grant investigation?'

Molly shook her head. 'Not if what one of the neighbours told me last night is true. She claims to have seen Al Jessop leaving the house between nine thirty and ten. And Sharon's father told us the other day that Jessop is in the habit of coming round to sub off Sharon whenever she gets paid. Except this time the cupboard was bare because she'd just lost her job.'

'Has Jessop herself said anything about who it was?' Ormside asked.

'No. She was in no condition to talk when I saw her last night, and they're keeping her more or less sedated until they're sure there isn't any pressure on the brain. She has a broken cheekbone, bruises all over her face, head, and upper body, a fractured collarbone, three cracked ribs and possible internal injuries – they're doing more tests today. There are bruises on her throat that suggest her attacker also tried to strangle her. You can see the condition she was in from these pictures.'

Molly produced a large envelope and slid half-a-dozen glossy pictures on to Ormside's desk, where she spread them out for the others to see.

'He really *did* do a job on her,' Tregalles muttered as he bent closer to study one of the pictures. 'What are those marks around her mouth and on her neck?'

Ormside picked up a magnifying glass. 'Looks to me as if he was wearing gloves with a coarse weave,' he said. 'You can see a faint pattern.'

Paget studied the pictures. 'It may be a while before Mrs Jessop can talk to us,' he told Ormside, 'but let's have her husband in for questioning. And we still need to know the name of the man Mrs Jessop claims whispered to her during the robbery at the pub, so, since she knows Forsythe, I want her to monitor Mrs Jessop's condition in hospital, and question her on both counts as soon as possible. Do we have anything on Jessop's husband?'

'Not really,' the Sergeant said. 'He's been involved in a couple of pub brawls, and Uniforms responded to a domestic back in February, but his wife refused to lay charges, and that's about it. He doesn't have a regular job, but he's licensed to drive large goods vehicles, and he sometimes fills in when a driver is off sick or away for any reason. But with yesterday being Sunday, we didn't get very far with our enquiries. We should have better luck today with everyone back at work.'

'You might see if you can find any connection between Jessop and Barry Grant thirteen years ago,' Paget said. 'He sounds like the sort of person who might be up for a robbery.'

He looked at the time. 'In any case, I'd better be on my way,' he said. 'I'll be in Mr Alcott's office for about an hour, but then I'm off to Worcester to talk about the introduction of a series of new courses in next year's training programme. Today is just the preliminary round, but I'll be asking for your input in the next few weeks, so give it some thought.'

'Right,' said Ormside perfunctorily as his gaze swept the office, his mind already focused on what needed to be done, and mentally assigning the individuals who would be best suited for each task. Training was something he could think about later – much later.

The garden appeared to be well tended, but the house in Whitecross Lane was old, small, and in serious need of repair. But that was on the outside; inside, it was clean, airy, and comfortable. Apart from her other talents, it was clear that Irene Sinclair knew how to make the best of small spaces.

'I know the place looks as if it's falling down,' she told Molly as if reading her mind as she ushered her inside, 'but it's rented, you see, and I'm afraid my landlord is a bit slow to respond to my constant reminders. However, the roof doesn't leak, and the windows don't rattle in a storm, so I'm grateful for small mercies. And the rent isn't bad either, so that helps.

'But you didn't come to talk about my house, did you,' she said. 'You want to ask me about Roger and our relationship, don't you? Can I offer you some tea? I should warn you it's Chinese and it's black.'

'Yes, please,' Molly said. 'If it's anything like the tea they serve at the Golden Dragon, I'd like to try it.'

Irene smiled. 'I think you'll like it,' she said. 'Anyway, come through to the kitchen and we can talk while the kettle boils. Is it too early to ask if you know what happened?' She used her foot to hook an old-fashioned bar stool from beneath a high counter, and nudged it towards Molly, then proceeded to fill the kettle and plug it in.

'It is, yes,' said Molly as she sat down. 'Sorry.'

Irene remained standing, arms folded as she leaned with her back against the edge of the counter. 'Is there any way I can help?' she asked.

'As you said when I came in, one of the things we would like to clarify is your relationship with Mr Corbett,' Molly said. 'He was married to Lisa, but he seemed to be equally at home with you, and both you and Mrs Corbett appeared to be quite happy with the arrangement. Would you mind explaining that, Miss Sinclair?'

'Irene, please. And as for our "relationship", it's quite simple: Lisa was Roger's wife and I was Roger's mother. Not literally, of course,' she added quickly, 'but that was the role we played. Although,' she continued thoughtfully, 'I think it would be safe to say that our roles were changing, possibly reversing in fact, because Roger was spending more and more time with me than he was with Lisa.' She shrugged. 'Hardly surprising, I suppose, considering her involvement with her dancing partner, Ramon.'

'Involvement . . .?' Molly queried.

'Lovers, then,' Irene said. 'Have been for years, although Roger didn't twig until fairly recently.' The kettle began to boil, and Irene turned her attention to preparing tea. 'I presume you know she was planning on divorcing Roger?'

'Yes, Mrs Corbett told me herself the other day. How did Mr Corbett feel about that? I understand he found it hard to hold a steady job; in fact it's my impression that he was dependent on his wife for support.'

'Oh, he was. Totally. But what you have to understand is that Roger was a child in many ways. He tried to shut things out. He knew Lisa was going to divorce him, but he wouldn't allow himself to believe it. He abhorred change, so he ignored it.'

'Would you mind elaborating on this role of motherhood? I'm afraid I don't understand it. From what Mr Corbett told DCI Paget, he was sleeping with you the night someone tried to set the Grant house on fire.'

Irene set out two cups and saucers and poured tea. 'That's true,' she said, 'with *sleeping* being the operative word. Roger was impotent; had been for many years. And he had night-mares; terrible nightmares. He would often wake up in tears. We didn't have sex, if that's what you're after.'

'But this back and forth business,' Molly persisted. 'You and Lisa Corbett were both happy with the arrangement? You are actually friends?'

'Good friends,' said Irene firmly. 'In fact, while I know Lisa was very much in love with Roger when she married him, I think as time went on she was grateful for the respite when he came to me.'

'Do you know what his nightmares were about?'

Irene shook her head. 'He would never say. I asked Lisa if she knew, but she said he wouldn't tell her either. But that's why he drank; something happened in his past, but I have no idea what it was.'

'Did he ever talk about the robbery and killings that took place here in Broadminster thirteen years ago? Did he ever mention the name of Barry Grant before it came up at the house-warming party?'

'Chief Inspector Paget asked me that, and the answer is still no,' Irene said. 'And I would tell you if he had. How do you like the tea?'

There was a 'To Let' sign in the corner of the window of the Brush and Palette, and a larger, splashier sign pasted across the window, proclaiming: CLOSING DOWN SALE – 50% OFF! Hardly surprising, Tregalles thought as he switched off the engine. Sheep Lane was off the beaten track, and there were several other more accessible shops in town, where the same art supplies could be bought, probably for less than David Taylor could afford to sell them.

Sitting in his car outside the shop, the Sergeant ran his finger down the list of Roger Corbett's phone calls immediately following Paget's departure from Corbett's office the previous Tuesday.

Top of the list: David Taylor. The conversation had lasted less than a minute, but that would have been long enough to arrange a meeting. The next call was to Irene Sinclair's answering machine. Following that was a call to Kevin Taylor's office. His secretary remembered the call, because the caller had 'muttered an obscenity' when she'd told him that Kevin would be out of the office for the rest of the day. Sixteen minutes later, Corbett rang Irene Sinclair, using his mobile, so presumably he had moved to the Unicorn by then. Four minutes later, he'd tried again and Irene had answered. She'd told Molly that he'd been almost incoherent at first, and he'd only just begun to calm down when he said he had another call coming in, and had cut her off. And that was the last she'd heard from him.

'I was used to Roger's mood swings, and to the way he was when he'd been drinking,' she'd told Molly, 'but it was different this time. Oh, there's no doubt he'd been drinking, but there was something else in his voice. Fear . . .? Desperation . . .? Perhaps a mixture of both. I can't describe it. It worried me.'

The next call Corbett had made was to John Chadwell's office at the town hall. Tregalles still had to check that one out, but it too was brief, followed by a call lasting six minutes to Chadwell's home.

Then nothing.

Tregalles folded the printout and slid it into his jacket pocket. 'So, let's see what you have to say for yourself, Mr Taylor,' he said under his breath as he got out of the car. 'Because I would like to know why you were the first person Corbett rang after Paget rattled his cage.'

'Sharon? Sharon? Remember me? Molly Forsythe?'

The woman in the bed winced as she tried to open her eyes. Bruises covered three-quarters of her face; the flesh surrounding both eyes was swollen and puffy, and there were three stitches in the brow above the right eye. A momentary glint of reflected light appeared through narrows slits of swollen flesh, then disappeared again. Sharon Jessop rolled her head slowly from side to side on the pillow as if to say the effort was too much.

She shivered.

Molly pulled up the blanket, careful to avoid touching the splint immobilizing Sharon's left arm and shoulder. Sharon's eyes remained closed, but a murmur deep inside her throat was taken by Molly as thanks.

'I know you must be in a lot of pain,' she said gently, 'but we do need to know who did this to you, Sharon. Who was it? Please tell me.'

Sharon tried to move her lips, but they, too, were cut and swollen. 'Water,' she managed huskily.

Molly picked up the water bottle on the bedside table and eased the tip of the flexible straw between Sharon's lips. Sharon sucked greedily on the straw, then choked. Molly slipped an arm around her back and eased her into a sitting position. The coughing subsided. Sharon took one more pull on the straw, pushed it out with her tongue, and fell back panting.

Molly withdrew her arm. 'Look, Sharon,' she said, 'I've

been told that they want you downstairs for more tests in a few minutes, so I won't stay long. But you must tell me who did this to you.'

'Don't remember,' Sharon mumbled.

'You don't remember? I'm sorry, Sharon, but I don't believe that. Don't you want that person caught and punished? You could have been killed. Was it your husband, Al? He was seen leaving your house that night.'

Sharon closed her eyes. 'Don't remember,' she said again.

Molly tried another tack. 'I spoke to Rachel. Remember Rachel? The girl you used to party with? She remembers some of the boys you went with back then, and she says you kept a diary of sorts. Do you still have it?'

Sharon turned her head away.

'If it's in your house we'll find it, Sharon,' Molly said. 'It would be better if you tell us where it is.'

'Can't do that. You've no right.'

'You were attacked there,' said Molly. 'It's a crime scene, so yes we can.'

Sharon squinted painfully at her. 'Burned it years ago. Honest to God. I'm telling the truth. Afraid Al would find it.'

'All right, so let's say I believe you,' Molly said. 'What about the man who whispered to you during the robbery. Have you remembered his name? How about one of these?' Molly opened her notebook and read out the names Rachel had given her.

'Don't remember,' said Sharon once again. Tears trickled down her cheeks. 'Don't remember,' she repeated. Her nose started to run; she tried to reach for a tissue from the box on the bedside table, but the effort was too much and she fell back.

Molly handed her a tissue and placed the box beside her on the bed. 'But you do know who beat you up, don't you, Sharon?' she said quietly. 'We know that your husband was seen leaving the house that evening. You could have been killed. Do you really want this to happen to you again?'

Sharon didn't answer. She lay still, eyes closed, her cheeks were damp with tears. Frustrated, Molly rose to leave.

'It was Al.'

The words were spoken so quietly that Molly almost missed them. She bent low over the bed. 'Say that again, please, Sharon,' she said.

'It was Al. He did this. He wanted money; he didn't believe me when I told him I'd lost my job and there wasn't any.'

'Look, I was busy with a customer when Roger called, and I haven't had many of those lately, so I put him off and told him I'd call him back, all right?' said David Taylor heatedly in answer to Tregalles's question. 'I *meant* to call him back when the customer left, but then my landlord came in and we got talking about when I could be out of here, and I'm afraid I forgot about Roger until closing time. I rang him back, but he must have had his mobile shut off, because I couldn't get through. I assumed he would call again if it was very important, but he never did. And that's all there was to it.'

Tregalles eyed him curiously. 'Was it?' he asked softly. 'Because if that's all there was to it, as you say, why go all defensive on me over a simple question? What did Roger Corbett tell you when he rang? What is it you're holding back, Mr Taylor? Because I know there is something you're not telling me, and that could lead to serious consequences if it turns out it has a bearing on how or why Corbett died.'

David shook his head impatiently. 'He didn't tell me anything,' he said tersely. 'In fact the man was drunk and I could barely understand him. All I could make out was that the police had been round to question him about Barry Grant and the killing of my father and Mrs Bergman, and he kept saying he had to talk to me. That's it; that's all I can tell you.'

'But why you?' Tregalles said. 'Corbett made several calls after that, but you were number one, so why did he call you first?'

David shrugged and spread his hands. 'I don't *know,*' he said. 'If I did I would tell you.' He sucked in his breath and let it out again in a sigh of resignation. 'To tell you the truth, I thought he was getting all wound up over nothing. Everyone who was at the house-warming was being questioned; we all knew that, so I couldn't see why Roger was getting so upset? It wasn't as if he could be suspected of anything. Not Roger, for God's sake. The idea's ludicrous. Besides, as I said, he was drunk, so I put him off and told him I'd call him back.'

He shrugged apologetically. 'Look, Sergeant,' he said earnestly, 'I'm sorry, but I'm as much in the dark as you are. I suppose I'm more angry at myself than I am about your questions, because I can't help wondering if it would have made a difference if I hadn't cut him off like that. Would Roger still be alive today?' David's eyes were bleak as they met those of Tregalles. 'Unfortunately, this is the second time it's happened, except last time it was Barry Grant on the other end of the line, and I've never stopped wondering if Barry would be alive today if I hadn't cut him off when he rang me the night he died.'

He fell silent, but Tregalles wasn't going to let him stop there. 'Go on,' he prompted. 'Why did Barry call you in particular, and what did he want?'

'He wanted my help and I failed him,' David said bleakly. 'And I think he called me because he had no one else to call.'

'When was this, exactly?'

'Sunday evening, the day after Dad and Mrs Bergman were killed,' David explained. 'Kevin and I were still in shock. Aunt Edith and Uncle Victor were there. Aunt Edith is Dad's sister, and she and Uncle Victor had come down from Sheffield to help with the arrangements. I mean we were both young; I was twenty-one and Kevin was twenty-two, and we didn't have a clue about what to do. And that inspector whatever-his-name-was kept coming back with questions, so when Barry rang me that night and said he had to talk to me, I brushed him off.'

He sucked in his breath. 'The fact is, Sergeant, I tore a strip off him. I told him I was fed up with him pestering me and my friends, and I didn't give a damn about him or his problems, because I had more than enough of my own. But he kept on and on until, finally, I told him to bloody well grow up, and slammed the phone down. Next thing I heard, he'd killed himself later that night.

'And that's it, Sergeant. Every word of that conversation has been burnt into my brain ever since that night, and when Claire came round to tell me that Barry had left some notes behind, and the investigation was being opened up again, the guilt came rushing back. So how do you think I feel about putting Roger off when he was asking for my help? I failed him in the same way I failed Barry Grant, and now they're both dead, and it's entirely possible that they might be alive if I hadn't turned my back on them when they were looking for help.'

'Which brings me back to my original question,' Tregalles said. 'Why were *you* the first person Corbett called after he was interviewed by DCI Paget? Were you and he particularly close friends?'

David shook his head. 'No more than anyone else,' he said slowly, 'and I've been wondering that myself. I've known Roger for years, and we would run into each other from time to time, but I've no idea why he chose to ring me.'

He sighed, and some of the bitterness went out of his voice as he said, 'God knows Roger didn't have much of a life as it was, and to die like that . . . He was such a nice kid at school, happy, cheerful, full of fun; everyone liked Roger. We lost touch when we left school. I went off to Slade and he and most of the others went off to Leeds. But while Kevin and the others were taking things like law, business administration, and engineering, Roger took philosophical and religious studies, and he was really excited about it that first year, and he was looking forward to going back after the holidays.

'But something changed that second year, and he was only back in uni for a month or so before he dropped out. I remember Kevin and some of the others were quite concerned about him at the time. But then he disappeared, left Broadminster without a word to anyone.

'The next time I saw him was a couple of years later, but he was a changed man. Nervous, uncertain, not at all like the irrepressible chap he used to be. I thought he must be ill, not physically, perhaps, but suffering from depression or something like that, but he always insisted he was all right, even when it was clear to everyone that he was not. He never did say where he'd been, but years later he mentioned something to me about working on his uncle's farm in Dorset, so I assumed that was where he'd gone when he left Broadminster.

'But then he met Lisa, and the two of them hit it off right from the start. They were married within three months, and you could see the change in Roger. He was much more like his old self, and I think the two of them were genuinely happy for a while. But it didn't last. You could see him going down again. He couldn't hold a job; he became moody and argumentative, and I know I wondered at one point if he was on drugs. Until it finally dawned on me that Roger was an alcoholic.

He'd hidden it very well for a number of years, but it reached a point where he couldn't hide it any longer. Lisa did everything she could to help him, but nothing seemed to work, and I think she just gave up in the end. In fact, if it hadn't been for Irene Sinclair, I think the poor chap would have drunk himself to death years ago. I don't know if you were aware of it, but Roger's parents died when he was quite young, and I think Irene became a sort of mother figure to him.'

David made a face. 'It's a damned shame,' he said. 'Basically, Roger was a good man. He didn't deserve to die like that. Are you *quite* sure he was murdered, Sergeant? Isn't it possible that he simply fell into the pond and couldn't get out?'

'Not according to the forensic evidence,' Tregalles told him. 'Which brings me to my next question. Where were you and what were you doing between four o'clock and midnight last Tuesday, Mr Taylor?'

The big box van pulled into the middle of the yard. The driver dropped it into reverse, then backed smoothly into the narrow bay and stopped within inches of the loading platform. He cut the engine, opened the door of the cab and jumped down.

'Very impressive,' said one of the two men in suits who had been watching.

The driver, a tall, fair-haired, skinny man, apart from what appeared to be a good start to a beer belly, acknowledged the words with a wink and a nod. 'Nothing to it,' he said. 'You should see me handle the *really* big rigs.' He made to move on, but the man barred his way.

'Mr Jessop?' he asked. 'Mr Albert Jessop?'

'That's right. Who wants to know?'

'Detective Constable Jones, Broadminster CID,' the man said, holding up his warrant card. 'And this is DC Albright, and we'd like you to come with us down to the station.'

Al Jessop took a step back, eyes narrowed as they flicked from one man to the other. 'Why should I?' he demanded. 'I haven't done anything.'

'Let me see the back of your hands,' Jones said.

'What the hell for?' Jessop flared. 'Like I said, I haven't done anything, and I'm not going anywhere with you.' He made to push past the two men, but they closed on him, backing him against the side of the van. His hands came up, palms facing out in a gesture of surrender. 'All right, all right, no need to get pushy,' he said. 'So what am I supposed to have done, eh? I've been out of town the last couple of days, so what's all this about?'

'Show us the back of your hands,' Jones said again.

Jessop looked mystified, but he held out his hands.

'Scabs,' Jones observed as he looked at the hands. 'Recent by the look of them, wouldn't you say?' he said to his partner.

'Very,' Albright agreed. 'How'd you get them, Mr Jessop?'

Jessop shrugged. 'Get 'em all the time, don't I?' he said. 'Can't avoid it in this job, lifting crates, messing about with tools. Why? What's this all about anyway?'

'We can talk about that down at the station,' Jones said. 'Get in the car.' He nodded to where a car was parked a short distance away.

But Jessop was shaking his head. 'Oh, no,' he said. 'I'm not going anywhere with you. I haven't done anything, so—'

'It's your choice,' Albright said, moving closer. His voice hardened. 'Consider yourself under arrest, Mr Jessop. Now, turn around facing the van and put your hands behind your back and listen carefully while my colleague cautions you.'

Jessop hesitated. He wasn't averse to a scrap, provided the odds were in his favour, but he didn't like the look of them in this case. Both Jones and Albright looked as if they could take very good care of themselves – and him if it came to it. He turned to face the van and put his hands behind his back.

Molly was about to leave for the day when Paget stopped her in the corridor. 'Ah, Forsythe,' he said, 'glad I caught you. Come with me. I'm about to interview Albert Jessop, and since you are familiar with the situation in the Jessop household, I'd like you to sit in.'

Albert Jessop slouching in his seat, arms folded across his chest, stared sullenly at Paget. 'So I was seen by a nosy neighbour,' he sneered. 'I do live there, you know. My wife and kids live there, so why shouldn't I be there, eh? Tell me that.'

'But you haven't been living there for some time, have you?' Paget said. 'According to the people we've been speaking to, you spend more time with a woman by the name of Lucy Gilbert than you do at home. Is that not right, Mr Jessop?'

'So?' Jessop said truculently. 'Sharon's still my wife and they're still my kids, so I have every right to be there. It's not a crime.'

Paget took several large glossy photographs of Sharon Jessop's battered face and upper body from an envelope and placed them in front of Jessop. 'But attempted murder *is* a crime,' he said quietly, 'so I suggest you start taking this interview seriously, because that is what you will be charged with unless you can convince me otherwise.'

'Bloody hell!' Jessop's eyes suddenly widened in shock as he stared at the photographs. 'Christ, no! You're not fitting me up for that! I barely touched her – more of a push, like. She didn't even fall over. Oh, no, you're not having me for that!'

'You were seen,' said Paget flatly. 'People in the street saw you there. You ransacked the house looking for money, but there wasn't any money, was there? No money because your wife had lost her job. So you took it out on her. Beat her unconscious, then just left her there on the floor to die.'

But Jessop was shaking his head violently from side to side. 'I didn't do that!' he burst out. 'I might have slapped her once or twice, but not like *that*, for Christ's sake!' His eyes narrowed as he jabbed a grimy finger at the pictures. 'They're fake!' he said shrilly. 'Have to be, because she was all right when I left. You bastards! You've tarted them up to make it look worse than it is,' he accused. 'Well it won't bloody work, mate, and I'm not saying another word until I see a solicitor.' He sat back in the chair and folded his arms. 'And you can take those fake pictures with you and stuff them, because I know she didn't look like that when I left her.'

'So, what do you think, Forsythe?' Paget asked as they made their way back to what had now become an incident room with the death of Roger Corbett. 'Was that all bluster or do we have the wrong man?'

'I have to admit it was a good performance,' Molly told him. 'He seemed to be genuinely shaken by those pictures, but I don't think Sharon was lying when she told me it was Jessop who beat her up. And, as you said yourself, sir, he admits to being there, even admits to "slapping her", as he put it, and judging by the bruises on Sharon's arms, I'm sure he's done this sort of thing before. I think he just lost it when he realized there was no money and not much chance of getting any since Sharon had lost her job. Thank God the kids weren't there.'

Paget nodded. 'I think you're right,' he said. 'But just to be on the safe side, I'd like you to have another chat with Sharon Jessop to see if she remembers anything else about what happened that night. If she sticks to her story we'll charge him and hold him.'

'The trouble is,' Molly said, 'he'll probably make bail and be out on the street by noon tomorrow. I just hope he doesn't do a runner.'

'Do you think he might?'

Molly shrugged. 'I really don't know that much about him,' she said candidly. 'Everything I've heard comes from Sharon, her father, and her friend, Rachel from years ago, but none of it is good.'

'And yet he doesn't have any form to speak of,' Paget observed, 'so either he is more clever than he appears to be or he's telling the truth.'

'Frankly, sir,' said Molly sceptically, 'I'm not sure I could agree with you on either of those options. Did you see the size of his hands? And the scars on them?'

'I did,' said Paget, 'but you have to bear in mind the kind of work he does.'

Molly remained silent, but it was clear she wasn't convinced.

Marion Alcott died in her sleep ten minutes before midnight. Thomas Alcott, dozing in the chair beside the bed, came awake, only vaguely aware at first that something had changed.

Still only half awake, he listened. Faint, hushed voices came from the nurses' station down the hall, but inside the room . . . The rhythmic, rasping sound he'd become accustomed to was gone. He found himself holding his own breath as he struggled to his feet and leaned over the bed. His wife's hand with the intravenous needle taped to it lay still on top of the covers. He took her hand gently in his own, and only then was he able to bring himself to look at her face.

Perhaps it was the tears in his eyes that distorted his vision, but the face he saw was that of the girl he'd married more than thirty years ago, so young, so vibrant, so full of life and so full of love.

He whispered her name, then, for the first time in many years, he knelt beside the bed and prayed.

TWENTY-THREE

Tuesday, July 21st

'**D**avid Taylor admits to receiving Roger Corbett's phone call,' Tregalles concluded at the morning briefing, 'but he says he was busy and told Corbett he would call him back as soon as he was free. But then he forgot about it until later when he was closing up. He says he tried to call Corbett but couldn't reach him. He claims he spent the rest of the evening either in the shop or upstairs in his flat. He lives alone; he made no phone calls, and he didn't receive any, which means he can't prove he *was* there, and I can't prove he *wasn't*.

'I'm going to talk to Chadwell and Kevin Taylor next. All of the calls Corbett made that day were short, except for the one to Chadwell, so perhaps I can get more out of him.'

Ormside snorted. 'Good luck!' he said, remembering his brief interview with Chadwell. He pulled a bulky file from a drawer. 'But before you go, we'd better have something on record about the call Barry Grant made to David Taylor, because it was never mentioned in the original investigation. Is Taylor coming in to make a statement?'

'I don't think that's really necessary, do you, boss?' Tregalles said with a questioning look in Paget's direction. 'I thought I'd just stick a note in the file.'

Paget agreed. 'Just make sure it's legible,' he warned.

'Better have it typed, then,' Ormside muttered. 'The way Tregalles writes, he should have been a doctor.'

Paget glanced at the time. 'I'll be in Mr Alcott's office for the rest of the morning,' he said, 'and if anyone is looking for me, discourage them, because I do not want to be disturbed.'

Fiona looked strangely subdued as Paget approached her desk outside Alcott's office. Normally, she was on her feet the moment he appeared, ready to bring him up to date on any new developments since she'd seen him last; pass on any messages she hadn't been able to take care of herself, and offer her assistance and/or advice if he asked for it – and sometimes even if he didn't ask for it.

'Something wrong, Fiona?' he asked.

The secretary lifted her head and he could see she'd been crying. 'It's Mrs Alcott,' she said in a low voice. 'She died last night. I tried to ring Mr Alcott this morning to find out how she was, but I couldn't get him, so I phoned the hospital, but they wouldn't tell me anything.'

Fiona took a tissue from her sleeve and blew her nose. 'I knew something was wrong, because they usually say *something* over there when you ask, even though they aren't supposed to unless you're a relative. So I rang his daughter, Valerie. Her phone and mobile number are in Mr Alcott's phone file,' she explained, 'and she told me that her mother had passed away just before midnight last night.'

The phone in Alcott's office rang, and a corresponding light flashed on the secretary's phone. She picked it up and said, 'Superintendent Alcott's office . . . Yes, he's here . . . Yes, yes . . . all right, Sergeant, yes, I'll . . .'

Paget put his hand out for the phone, but instead of giving it to him, Fiona put it down. 'That was Sergeant Tregalles,' she said, 'and he sounded very excited. He said he has something to show you, and he'd like you to go back down there at once to see it for yourself.'

'So much for my instructions that I wasn't to be disturbed,' Paget muttered. He turned to leave, but paused when he saw the question in Fiona's eyes. 'Was there something else?' he asked.

'It's just that Valerie says her father's now gone missing and . . . it's probably silly,' she said, 'but the way he was talking the other day . . . you don't think Mr Alcott would do anything . . . well, you know . . ?' She couldn't bring herself to say the words.

'Paget placed his hand on Fiona's shoulder and held her

eyes with his own. 'No, I don't,' he said firmly. 'I suspect he just needs to be alone for a while. I'm sure he'll turn up when he's ready.'

Tregalles and Ormside were bent over Ormside's desk, each with a magnifying glass in hand, studying a series of black and white photographs when Paget entered the room.

'Take a look at this, boss,' Tregalles said as he straightened up and handed a magnifying glass to Paget. 'These pictures were taken at the scene when Barry Grant is supposed to have killed himself. I just happened to take a look at them when I was putting the file away after adding in the note about Barry's call to David Taylor, and that's when I saw it. Take a look at the one on top, the close-up of the shotgun. Look at the end of the barrels. See the tiny steel fibres left when the barrels were sawn through? There is no way they would have been there if that gun was fired after the barrels were sawn off. They'd have been blown away. Those barrels were sawn off *after* Grant was shot.'

Paget bent over the picture. He didn't see it at first, but suddenly there it was. Tregalles was right; and yet apparently no one had picked it up during the original investigation. Someone had slipped up badly back then. Very badly.

'Well done, Tregalles,' he said as he handed the photograph and magnifying glass back to the Sergeant. 'So, it looks as if someone killed young Grant because he was perceived to be a weak link, and I suspect that Roger Corbett was killed for exactly the same reason.'

The town planning offices were not in the town hall itself, but in the annexe, a cube-like, flat-roofed structure behind the main building, only partly hidden from view by trees and shrubs planted for that very purpose. Built of breeze block and brick cladding – a cost-saving measure at the time – it needed to be hidden, Tregalles thought. He entered the building and approached a counter barring further progress.

'I'm here to see John Chadwell,' he told the girl behind the counter.

'Do you have an appointment?' the girl asked.

'I spoke to him earlier,' Tregalles said, holding up his warrant card.

The girl barely glanced at it before lifting a hinged part of the counter and motioning him through. A telephone rang on a desk behind her. She picked it up and cupped a hand over the mouthpiece. 'Fourth one on the left,' she whispered, pointing to the corridor behind her.

The door to the fourth office on the left was partly open. A burly man with greying hair stood hunched over his desk, head bent as he studied a blueprint. Tregalles pushed the door wider and said, 'Mr Chadwell?'

The man raised his head. 'And who are you?' he demanded.

'I'm the man you told you were too busy to see this morning,' Tregalles said as he entered the office and pushed the door shut behind him. 'Detective Sergeant Tregalles, investigating the murder of a friend of yours, Roger Corbett.'

Chadwell glowered. 'You've got no right to come barging in here like this,' he said. 'How do you think it looks to my colleagues?'

'Like a good citizen helping us with our enquiries,' Tregalles told him. 'Unless, of course, there is some reason why you don't want to help us find the person who killed Roger Corbett, or you have something to hide . . .?'

Chadwell's scowl deepened. 'Of course I don't have anything to hide,' he snapped. 'The reason I put you off when you rang this morning was because I'm busy and it upsets my schedule.'

'I imagine Mr Corbett felt much the same when someone killed him and upset his schedule,' Tregalles observed drily. 'Which brings me to the question I came here to ask you, Mr Chadwell. Why did Roger Corbett ring you, first at the office and then at home, last Tuesday afternoon?' He pulled out a chair and sat down.

Chadwell's face was set as he took his own seat. 'I don't know,' he growled. 'I could barely understand the man. He was drunk and rambling.'

'And yet you stayed on the line for more than six minutes,' Tregalles told him. 'There must have been some sort of exchange between the two of you?' He took out his notebook. 'And I see that you rang Kevin Taylor's number immediately following your conversation with Corbett. What was that about?'

Chadwell sat back in his chair and eyed Tregalles dispas-

sionately. 'All right, then,' he said, glancing at his watch to
emphasize that his time was limited. 'The wife took the call,
but she couldn't make any sense out of what Roger was on
about, so she handed it on to me. As I said, he was drunk,
and it took a few minutes for me to understand what he was
talking about, but I gathered that he was convinced that he
was suspected of having had something to do with that old
case you've been working on, the robbery and killing of Kevin
Taylor's father. I told him that was absurd, but he kept on and
on about it, and it became clear to me that the man was on
the verge of a total breakdown if someone couldn't sort him
out.

'I'll be honest with you, Sergeant, I didn't know what
to do about it. I mean I didn't understand why Roger was
calling me anyway. It's not as if we've ever been close
friends. I know one's not supposed to speak ill of the dead,
but quite frankly, Sergeant, I couldn't stand the man. So I
told him to phone his wife and have her come and take
him home, but he said she was away somewhere. So, finally,
I rang Kevin at his office, but they said he was out, so I
tried his home but he wasn't there either. Tried his mobile,
but he must have had it switched off, because I didn't get
him.'

'Why Kevin Taylor?'

'Because Kevin's always more or less looked out for Roger,
though why he bothered I don't know. As far as I was
concerned, what Corbett needed was a good boot up the backside; sympathy just made him worse. Anyway, I couldn't get
Kevin, so I talked to Steph, and she persuaded me to go down
there and get the man home. I wasn't keen, but the wife was
nagging me to go as well, so I went. Soft as they come, is
Amy.'

'To where, exactly?'

'The Unicorn. That's where he was calling from, but it
turned out to be a waste of time, because Corbett wasn't there
when I got there. They told me he'd been in, but he'd been
gone for some time.'

'What time would that be?' Tregalles asked.

Chadwell shrugged. 'Five thirty or thereabouts,' he said. 'I
can't tell you exactly.'

Tregalles consulted his notebook. 'And yet your call to the

Taylors ended at eighteen minutes past four. That's a gap of an hour or more. Can you explain that?'

Clearly annoyed by the question, Chadwell said, 'I had work to do. Work I had brought home to prepare for a council meeting that evening, and I didn't see why I should just up and leave it and put myself out for a man who was drunk and wallowing in self-pity.'

'I see.' Tregalles closed his notebook and put it in his pocket. 'And then what?' he asked. 'What did you do when you found that Mr Corbett had left the Unicorn?'

'Went back home, of course,' Chadwell told him. 'Barely had time for dinner, such as it was, before I had to be back here in time for the weekly council meeting at seven.'

'And your wife will confirm all this, I suppose?' said Tregalles as he got to his feet.

Chadwell bridled. 'Why do you need to talk to her?' he demanded. 'Isn't my word good enough? It's obvious you have the times of the phone calls, so what is there to verify?'

'Verification is for your benefit as well as ours,' Tregalles told him, 'and I just have a couple of questions before I go. Would you mind telling me how tall you are, sir?'

The man frowned. 'Five eleven,' he said cautiously.

'And what kind of car do you drive?'

'A Jetta diesel, although I don't see—'

'Colour?'

'Oh, for God's sake,' Chadwell snapped, 'it's black! Though God knows what that has to do with anything. Please close the door on your way out.'

'Of course,' Tregalles said amiably as he stood up. 'And thank you for your cooperation, sir.'

Sitting in the car a few minutes later, with his jacket off and the doors open to allow what little breeze there was to flow through, Tregalles consulted his notebook, then punched in Chadwell's home number. It rang five times before the answering machine cut in and a gentle voice with a distinct Welsh flavour asked him to leave a message.

No doubt that would be Amy Chadwell, Tregalles thought, recalling that, according to the information Paget had gleaned from his talk with Claire Hammond, Amy Chadwell hailed from Cardiff.

He didn't leave a message. Instead, he rang the next number on his short list, and Stephanie Taylor answered. He identified himself, and as soon as he told her he would like to talk to her about Roger Corbett, she told him to come ahead. 'Any time,' she said. 'I shall be here until at least three this afternoon. Although I'm not sure how much help I can be; my husband knew Roger much better than I did, but I'll be happy to talk to you if you think it worthwhile.'

'I do,' Tregalles told her, 'and I'll be there shortly.'

Nice voice, Tregalles thought as he put the phone down and started the car. Intriguing and just a little bit sultry. He was looking forward to meeting Stephanie Taylor; even Molly had said she was a good-looking woman, and she'd practically raved about the house and grounds.

Nor was he disappointed with either when Stephanie Taylor greeted him at the door, then led him through the house to the terrace at the back. Molly had described it so well, he almost felt he'd been there before. As for the lady of the house herself, Tregalles found it hard to keep his eyes from lingering on her trim figure and long, suntanned legs.

'I thought you might like some iced tea,' she said as she picked up the jug. 'I can offer you a cold beer if you'd rather, but I suppose that's against the rules, isn't it?'

'Afraid so, Mrs Taylor,' he said regretfully. 'Iced tea will be fine, thank you.' He nodded in the direction of what looked like a small desk, complete with laptop and phone beside Stephanie's chair. 'Do you actually *work* out here?' he asked.

Stephanie smiled. 'Oh, yes – at least on days like this I do. It's on wheels, so we can use it anywhere out here.' She moved the desk back and forth to demonstrate. 'But I'm sure that's not what you came to talk about, is it Sergeant? Something to do with poor Roger's death, you said? I still find it hard to believe that anyone would *murder* Roger. Are you quite sure it wasn't an accident?'

'You're the second one to ask me that question,' he said, 'but, yes, that is what the evidence is telling us.'

Stephanie shrugged as she shook her head. 'I suppose you must be right,' she said, 'but I still find it hard to believe. Roger of all people!'

Tregalles set his glass aside. 'I believe you received a

phone call from John Chadwell after he'd received a call from Mr Corbett last Tuesday afternoon. Is that right, Mrs Taylor?'

'That's right. He wanted to talk to Kevin, but Kevin wasn't here, so he told me that Roger had rung him from a pub in town, saying he was convinced that the police thought he had been involved in the robbery and the killing of Kevin's father.' Stephanie wrinkled her nose. 'True to form, John said he'd told Roger not to be such a damned fool, and to get a taxi and go home and sleep it off. But after hanging up, he began to have second thoughts, so, as I said, he phoned here to talk to Kevin.'

Stephanie sipped her drink, then set it aside. 'I reminded John that Lisa was away, so there would be no one at home, and said I thought someone should go down there and make sure that Roger got home safely. I didn't want to go myself, because Roger could be a bit of a handful and quite belligerent when he was drunk, and I didn't fancy trying to get him home on my own, so I persuaded John to go down there instead. He grumbled a bit, but finally agreed to go.

'But Roger had left by the time he got there, so John assumed that Roger had taken his advice and taken a taxi home. Unfortunately, John was pressed for time himself. He said he had to be at a council meeting that evening, so he went home. At least that's what he told Kevin when he rang later that night.'

'Do you happen to remember what time it was when Mr Chadwell called you that afternoon?' Tregalles asked.

'I do, as a matter of fact,' Stephanie said. 'I'd been working in the garden, and I knew I had to be in by four if I was to get everything done before our guests arrived that evening, and John's phone call came a few minutes after that. Say five to ten past four, Sergeant.' She smiled sweetly. 'But then, I think you knew that already, didn't you, Sergeant?'

'You said your husband wasn't home when Mr Chadwell rang,' Tregalles said, ignoring the question, 'and we know that he wasn't in his office when Mr Corbett tried to reach him there, so can you tell me where he was, Mrs Taylor?'

'In Ludlow,' Stephanie said. 'The firm has an office there, and Kevin spends quite a bit of his time there. And before you ask, I should tell you that he sometimes switches off his mobile if he doesn't want to be disturbed, and he had it off that day.'

'What time did he get home?'

'Shortly after six,' she said, 'but—'

'Did either of you go out again that evening?'

'Not that evening, no, because we were having friends in, but I did go out about five to pick up some wine and one or two other things for our guests. I can give you their names if you wish?'

'No need for that, I'm sure, Mrs Taylor,' Tregalles said as he pushed his chair back and stood up. 'But I will leave you my card, and you might ask your husband to call me at that number to confirm where he was last Tuesday afternoon.'

TWENTY-FOUR

The sign on the door said Closed, but the door opened when Claire turned the handle and pushed hard on it. The old bell above the door rattled asthmatically, sounding as if it were in its death throes as she stepped inside.

'Saw you through the window, standing there looking lost,' she told David Taylor. 'What on earth is going on? It looks as if you've dumped all your stock on the floor. And all these cardboard boxes – are you moving out already? I thought you said the closing down sale would be on till the end of the month. What happened?'

'Trying to decide what to keep out of this lot,' he told her. 'As for the closing down sale, I've made a deal with The Paint Pot in the shopping centre to take the lot. They made me an offer on the weekend – not much of one, but then I've only got a week to get rid of everything, and the way sales have been going I'd never have made it. Anyway, I rang them back yesterday and told them I'd take it. They're getting the best of the bargain by far, but I'm just glad to have it settled. Now, as I said, it's just a matter of picking out a few things I want to keep, then packing up the rest.'

'What about the apartment upstairs?'

'Oh, I'm out of that at the end of the month as well. In fact I wouldn't be surprised if that hasn't been let already.'

'So what are your plans?'

He shrugged. 'Kev said I can stay with them until I sort something out, but meanwhile I have to find somewhere to store my stuff. Kev's got a big garage, but I doubt if either of them would be best pleased to have this sort of stuff cluttering up the place. You know how neat those two are.'

'Then why not bring it over to Aunt Jane's house?' The invitation was out before she realized what she was saying. But in for a penny . . . 'You can stay there as well,' she continued recklessly. 'I'm planning to move there myself when the lease on the flat expires later this year, but it will be sitting vacant until then. I don't fancy the idea of letting it out, so you would be doing me a favour if you'd like to move in – at least until then. In fact, you could set up your studio in the conservatory. What do you say?'

David hesitated. 'It's not that I don't appreciate the offer, Claire,' he said at last, 'but I have to be honest with you. By the time I've cleared all my debts, I'll be left with just about enough to feed and clothe myself, which leaves me virtually nothing for rent, and I couldn't do that to you. There are still things like the rates to pay and the upkeep of the place. It wouldn't be right.'

Claire shook her head. 'You leave the rates and things like that to me,' she said. 'But as I said, I really would like to have someone living there, and I'd rather have someone in there I know I can trust. So let's say I'm hiring you as a live-in care-taker. You look after the place for me, and I'll let you stay there rent free. How does that sound?'

David Taylor picked his way through boxes containing what was left of his business to stand in front of Claire. 'You really are a lifesaver, Claire, and a wonderful friend,' he said with feeling. 'I could kiss you for this.'

Then, why don't you, for heaven's sake? Claire said to herself as he pulled her to him and gave her a hug.

Slumped down in his seat in the van in the hospital car park, Al Jessop looked at his watch for perhaps the tenth time in the past five minutes. Still another ten minutes to go before visiting hours began. He was anxious to get going, but was forcing himself to wait so he could mingle with the rest of the visitors going in at two o'clock, because the last thing he wanted to do was attract attention.

By five minutes to two, people were beginning to leave their cars and make their way into the hospital. Jessop waited a couple of minutes more, then joined them. Up the steps to the main door, into the rotunda, left down the corridor to the lifts. Head down, hands stuffed in his pockets, he stood at the back of the group waiting for one of the lifts to arrive.

The white light went on and the bell sounded softly as the doors opened. The people in front of Jessop pressed forward, barely allowing those in the lift enough room to get out. Jessop started to move with them, then slid to one side as two uniformed policemen pushed their way through. They passed within inches of him, but were too intent on their conversation to pay any attention to him. Even so, he had left it too late, and the doors closed.

He joined the throng at the next door and managed to get in without any trouble. 'Four,' he muttered when a woman closest to the door asked who wanted which floor. Fourth floor. That would be the one Sharon was on, he was quite sure. He'd been in and out of this hospital a few times himself, so he knew the structure of the wards. The next question was one that had dogged him ever since yesterday, and that was, would she be guarded?

Chances were she wouldn't be, he told himself. He couldn't see the cops spending time and money guarding someone like Sharon. One of the conditions of bail was that he stay away from his wife or bail would be revoked. That's what the magistrate had said. He snickered to himself as he got out of the lift. Silly old fart. Did he really think that was going to stop him?

They were too busy at the nursing station to be paying any attention to the visitors streaming to the various rooms. Jessop looked right and left. The hall to the left was the shortest, so he tried that first. The doors to the rooms were open, so all it took was a quick look inside as he made his way to the end. No luck there, so he made his way back and tried the other end.

And there she was; fifth room down on the right-hand side. Room 428. Single room, no sign of any security. That was handy – but it wasn't like the NHS to give a private room to someone like Sharon, *so how the hell had she wangled that?* He carried on walking, turned at the end and made his way back

She was lying on her side, eyes closed. He looked up and down the hallway, then stepped into the room.

He wasn't really worried about Alcott, Paget told himself, but he remembered all too vividly how hard it had been to cope with Jill's untimely death, and he felt the need to satisfy himself that the Superintendent was all right.

'Just going to pop round to Mr Alcott's house to see if there is anything we can do,' he'd told Fiona, and knew he'd done the right thing when he saw both relief and gratitude in the secretary's eyes.

'Tell him we're thinking of him,' Fiona called after him as he'd headed for the stairs.

Now, as he neared the house, he was relieved to see that the door to the garage was up, and Alcott's five-year-old Volvo was inside. Paget parked the car on the street and walked up to the front door and rang the bell. He waited. No answer. He rang again. Still no answer. Perhaps Alcott simply didn't want to be disturbed, but Paget was reluctant to go away without seeing the man himself to make sure he was all right. Perhaps, if there was a door leading directly from the garage to the house, he could get in that way.

He crossed a narrow strip of lawn and entered the garage. Coming out of the bright sun, it was hard to see anything clearly at first, so he had moved almost the full length of the car before realizing that Alcott was inside. Sitting behind the wheel, head slumped forward, the Superintendent appeared to be fast asleep.

Paget opened the door and shook him gently. Alcott grunted and stirred. Paget shook him again. Alcott lifted his head, opened his eyes to squint at Paget, then shut them again. 'What do you want?' he demanded gruffly. 'Leave me alone and let me sleep.'

'I will as soon as I get you inside,' Paget promised. 'Come on, sir. Give me a hand.'

Alcott breathed a sigh of resignation. 'Never could leave well enough alone, could you, Paget?' he grumbled as he allowed the DCI to help him out of the car. 'And I haven't been drinking, if that's why you're sniffing. I'm just tired, that's all. So *bloody* tired I just want to go to sleep and never wake up again.'

Paget got him into the house, then rang Valerie, who thanked him profusely when he told her he was with her father. 'He must have just come home,' she said, 'because I've been round there twice myself and he wasn't in. I can be there in fifteen minutes, if you wouldn't mind waiting until I get there.' She paused to draw breath. 'How is he, Chief Inspector?'

'Exhausted,' he told her. 'He just wants to sleep, so he could be in bed by the time you get here.'

But Alcott was shaking his head. 'Tell her I'm all right and I'll be awake when she gets here,' he said, then headed for the kitchen.

Paget put the phone down and followed him. 'Have you eaten anything today?' he asked.

'Don't want anything,' Alcott said, 'and I don't want another one of your lectures, either. I'm not hungry – but since you ask, a hot cup of tea wouldn't go amiss. Mouth tastes like a Sumo wrestler's armpit on a hot day.'

'Can't say I've ever been that closely acquainted with a Sumo wrestler or his armpit,' Paget said as he filled the kettle and plugged it in, 'so I'll take your word for it, sir. Where do you keep the tea?'

'Excuse me, but what do you think you're doing?' The speaker's tone was sharp and challenging.

Caught bending over the bed, Al Jessop swung round to face a heavy-set man in a white coat. The man was drying his hands on a paper towel after washing them at the dispenser behind the open door.

'Came to see the wife,' Jessop said belligerently. 'Something wrong with that, is there? And who the hell are you?'

Before the doctor could reply, Sharon stirred and opened her eyes. She opened them wider and screamed. 'No, Al, no!' she gasped as she tried to scramble away from him. 'Get him away from me. Please, please get him away from me,' she pleaded hysterically.

The doctor took a phone from his pocket as he moved

swiftly between Jessop and the bed. 'I'm calling Security,' he said as he flipped it open, 'and—'

Jessop drove a fist into the doctor's stomach, then bolted through the door and made for the stairs at the end of the corridor. He crashed through the door and leapt down the stairs, two, three, four at a time. He had to get to the ground floor and out of the building before the doctor recovered and alerted Security. Once clear, he would have to put as much distance as possible between himself and the hospital, because, after assaulting a doctor, every cop in town would be looking for him.

'It's not your fault, Molly,' Ormside told her. 'If it's anyone's fault it was mine. You put your case to have her guarded, and I discussed it with Mr Paget, but I must admit I didn't press all that hard what with our people spread as thin as they are. Obviously I was wrong, so I'm setting up a twenty-four hour watch on Mrs Jessop. I haven't had a chance to speak to the boss yet, but I'm sure he will back me up after what's happened this afternoon. Meanwhile, I want you to get over to the hospital and get statements from Sharon and the doctor her husband assaulted.' He looked at the clock. 'I'm afraid you'll have to stay there until I can set up a rota and get someone else to take over, but I don't have any other choice. All right?'

Molly sighed heavily as she picked up her handbag and slung it over her shoulder. 'There goes another exciting evening at home,' she said. 'Mind if I take the file on Sharon with me? I don't know if it will do any good, but I'd like to review what she told me before and after she was attacked. There might be something in there that will give me a clue about where we might find Jessop. Funny thing is, I still think she's holding something back, and I don't know why.'

Ormside hesitated. 'Go on, then' he said. 'But don't let her see you with it. Keep it in your case until you get home, and I want to see it back here first thing tomorrow morning.'

TWENTY-FIVE

Wednesday, July 22nd

W hen Molly Forsythe arrived at work the following morning, the first thing she did was seek out PC Gordon Fry. She found him filling his mug with coffee from the machine in the hall.

'Want some?' he offered, reaching for a styrofoam cup.

Molly shook her head. 'No, thanks, Gordon,' she said, 'but I do want to talk to you about the statement you took from Sharon Jessop's neighbour, a Mrs Martin. When, exactly, did you take that statement? It has yesterday's date on it.'

PC Fry moved away from the machine to let others in. 'That's right,' he said. 'Took it yesterday lunchtime. First time I've been able to catch her in. Been back there several times, but she was always out. Likes her bingo games does Mrs Martin.'

'I thought everyone played bingo on line these days.'

'A lot do, but the old church hall in Portland Road runs games six days a week, and it's well attended. Mostly seniors, but there are some younger ones as well.'

'And when did you put her statement in the file?'

'Yesterday afternoon,' he told her. 'You weren't there, so Sergeant Ormside took it and put it in the file. Why? Something wrong?'

'There could be,' said Molly slowly. 'Oh, not with what you did, but I'm having trouble with what Mrs Martin told you. You say she saw Al Jessop come "storming out of the house" with Sharon screaming after him before she went back in the house and slammed the door. Were those her words or yours?'

Fry grinned sheepishly. 'Her actual words, as I recall, were: "Al came flying out of the house with young Sharon chewing on his arse and screaming at him." I thought "storming out of the house" was a reasonable interpretation, but I can change it if you want.'

'No, no, that's not what I'm after,' Molly told him. 'And this would be between nine thirty and ten on Saturday night?'

'That's right. She said she was standing in the open doorway taking in a last breath of fresh air before locking up for the night.'

'And it was definitely Sharon who slammed the door?'

'That's right.' PC Fry looked puzzled. 'I don't understand,' he said. 'Why all the questions? I'm sorry it took so long to get Mrs Martin's statement to you, but as I said, I called back several times before . . .'

'No, no, you did nothing wrong,' Molly assured him. 'But if what this woman told you is right, then it wasn't Al Jessop who beat up his wife as she said. I suppose he could have come back later, but knowing there was no money in the house, why would he?'

Molly reached for a styrofoam cup. 'I think I will have that coffee now,' she said. 'I think I'm going to need it.'

Sharon Jessop was propped up in bed trying to drink orange juice through a straw. Her lips were less swollen than they'd been the day before, but the skin around the eyes was still puffy, and the bruises were even more colourful than they'd been on Sunday night.

A very bored looking PC put down the morning paper and got to his feet and stretched. 'Nothing to report,' he said, and yawned. 'Mind if I go and get myself a coffee while you're here?'

'No, go ahead, but don't be too long,' said Molly. 'I don't expect what I have to do will take very long.' She turned to the woman in the bed. 'Did you get much sleep last night, Sharon?' she asked solicitously. 'No nightmares about being attacked by your husband?'

'No, thank God! They gave me something to help me sleep.' Sharon shivered. 'Have you caught him yet?' Her words were slurred, but clearer than they had been.

'Not yet,' said Molly. 'But we will.'

'So . . . why are you here?'

'I need to ask you again about what happened last Saturday night, when Al came looking for money. Take me through it again from the time Al arrived at the house.'

Sharon winced as if she were in pain. 'I don't even want

to *think* about it, let alone talk about it,' she said. 'Besides, I told you that already and you wrote it down, so why do you want me to go through it again?'

'Just bear with me, Sharon. We can't be too careful if we want to put Al away for a long time for what he did to you. Assault and battery, maybe even attempted murder – they both carry a stiff sentence, but the way things go in court, it will be your word against his, so let's just go over it once again. You do want him put away, don't you, Sharon?'

''Course I do.' Sharon eased herself down in the bed and pulled the covers up under her chin.

'Good,' said Molly briskly. 'I don't want to tire you out, so let's get on with it, shall we? You say Al came round somewhere between nine thirty and ten o'clock that night, right?' Sharon nodded. 'So tell me, how did you know he was coming? Did he phone you ahead of time?'

Sharon frowned. 'No. Why would he? He never phones. He just comes when he feels like it.'

'But you were expecting him, weren't you? I mean you did send the children next door so they would be out of harm's way.'

'I just knew he would be round, that's all. He knows when I normally get paid. But they paid me in lieu of two week's notice on Friday, so I kept thirty quid and took the rest round for Dad to keep for me, because I knew if Al got wind of it he'd be after it.'

'But why were you so sure he would be coming on that particular night?' Molly persisted.

'Oh, God, does it matter?' Sharon asked wearily. She buried her face in the crook of her arm as if to blot out the sight of her questioner. 'I knew he'd be round,' she continued with exaggerated emphasis on each word, 'because he didn't come round on the Friday like he usually does, OK? Maybe he was doing a run out of town or something on Friday, I don't know, but I *did* know he'd be round the minute he got back. That's why I sent the kids next door.'

'All right, let's leave that for now,' said Molly soothingly. 'So he came round and you let him in. Why did you do that if you knew there'd be trouble?'

Sharon uncovered her face. 'Easier than having him kick

the door in and have half the street out watching,' she said wearily. 'Look, Molly, I'm tired. Can't we just let it alone?'

'I wish we could,' Molly said, 'but it is necessary, so I'll try to be brief. Now,' she continued quickly before Sharon could object, 'according to your statement, Al came in, you told him you'd lost your job and there was no money in the house, but he didn't believe you. He searched the place, didn't find anything, and that was when he came back and really went to work on you. Is that right?'

Sharon nodded, touching the bruises on her face as if to make sure that Molly got the picture.

'So you didn't see him leave?'

Sharon rolled her eyes. 'How could I, for Christ's sake?' she snapped, and winced. 'I was unconscious, wasn't I?'

'Were you, Sharon . . .?'

Sharon's eyes slid away. ''Course I was,' she said truculently. 'It's a wonder I'm not dead.'

'True,' Molly agreed quietly, 'but, you see, Sharon, I have a problem with that. Because if you were lying on the floor after being beaten unconscious by your husband, how do you account for the fact that someone saw you at the door, screaming at him as he left?'

'She's lying, of course,' Molly told Ormside later, 'but she wouldn't admit it. And she's scared. First she said whoever had said they saw her at the door must have been talking about another time, and then she said her head was hurting, and she'd been having trouble remembering things, and if it had happened that way, then Al must have come back a second time, and so on and so on. Then she rang for the nurse and complained that I was upsetting her and she had these awful pains in her head . . .' Molly shook her head. 'I didn't have any choice; I had to leave.'

'But she still insists it was Al who beat her up?'

'Oh, yes, she's sticking to that, no matter what anyone says, but I don't think it was Al at all. Oh, he was there all right; the neighbours saw him, and he probably slapped Sharon around, but I think she was expecting someone else that night. The woman next door said that Sharon had acted as if she were scared but excited at the same time when she brought the children round.'

Ormside sighed. 'So it's back to square one,' he said. 'Which means we'll have to canvas the street again to find out if anyone saw any activity around the Jessop house later on that night or early Sunday morning. When do you think Sharon can be questioned again?'

'Depends on how long she's able to convince her doctor that she's having memory problems. I doubt if she'll be able to keep it up for long, but it could be a few days.'

'Any thoughts on who this second person might be? Assuming there was a second person.'

'I was thinking about that on my way in,' said Molly. 'Remember I said I had the feeling that Sharon was holding out on me? Well, I can't help wondering if she remembered who the man was who held her during the robbery of the Rose and Crown, and tried to contact him.'

'Go on,' said Ormside neutrally.

'Well, Sharon is desperate for money. She's just lost her job, and if she *had* remembered who it was, and that person is still living here in Broadminster, she may have attempted to blackmail him.'

Ormside looked sceptical. 'And invited him to her house?' he said. 'The woman may not be very bright, but I can't see her doing that, can you?'

'I don't know,' said Molly slowly. 'There has to be a reason she sent her children out of the house, so it seems reasonable to me that she was expecting someone, or she was going out to meet someone, and I don't think it was Al Jessop. Jessop did seem to be genuinely surprised when he saw the pictures of her injuries. I thought it was an act at the time, but now I'm not so sure.'

'Assuming for a moment that you're right, why didn't he finish the job and simply kill her?'

'Perhaps he thought he had.'

'Maybe,' Ormside conceded sceptically. 'Still, I suppose it's a theory, and God knows we've got nothing else to work with, so write up your report and put it up on the boards as a line of enquiry. And take a look at her phone records,' he called after her as Molly moved away.

'Oh, God, not you again?' David Taylor groaned as the bell clattered and Tregalles stepped into the shop and closed the door behind him. 'So what do you want this time, Sergeant?'

'I thought you might like to know that Barry Grant didn't commit suicide after all,' Tregalles said. 'He was murdered, and the killer set it up to look like suicide. But perhaps you knew that already, Mr Taylor?'

David's face darkened. 'If you're suggesting that I had something to do with it, you are very much mistaken,' he said heatedly. 'If Barry was murdered, this is the first I've heard of it, so why accuse me?'

'I don't believe I did,' Tregalles said, 'but as you told me yourself, you were the person he called only a few hours before he was killed, and yours is the only name Barry mentions in the notes he left behind. And you knew the code Sam Bergman used when he wanted his wife to open the back door.'

David bristled. 'Everyone knew that code,' he shot back. 'Dad knew it, Kevin knew it, we all did, and I'm sure every one of Sam's cronies knew it, so don't try to make it look as if I was the only one.'

'Tell me again about that call you received from Barry that Sunday evening following the death of your father. What *exactly* did he say?'

'Oh, for God's sake, Sergeant!' said David irritably. 'You can't expect me to remember something like that after all these years. I told you—'

'You told me the other day,' Tregalles cut in sharply, 'that every word of that conversation was burnt into your brain, so don't give me that. Tell me.'

David sucked in his breath. 'You're right,' he conceded, 'I must have gone over that conversation a thousand times since that night, and when Claire came by to tell me that you'd reopened the investigation, suddenly that was all I could think about.'

He pushed a couple of cardboard boxes aside and wiped his hand on a cloth. 'Care for a coffee, Sergeant?' he asked. 'It is made. I've probably had more than I should today, but I could still use another one.'

A few minutes later, with a large mug of coffee beside him, Taylor sat on the counter, legs dangling. Tregalles, seated on an upturned wooden crate and holding an equally large mug of coffee, waited for Taylor to begin.

'As I told you,' David began quietly, 'it was the Sunday night after Dad was killed. We were all there in the living room, and Aunt Edith was trying to discuss funeral arrangement with us, but the trouble was neither Kevin nor I had a clue about what Dad would have wanted, and to be honest, I don't think either of us wanted to talk about it at all. Dad had never said anything about what sort of funeral he'd like – he always shied away from things like that – so we weren't much help, and tempers were getting a bit frayed on both sides.

'Then Barry rang.' David sipped his coffee and stared off into the distance as if recreating the scene in his mind. 'I think his first words were, "David, you've got to help me. You're the only one I can trust." Then he said, "Please, David, I'm in trouble and I *really* need to talk to you. Please come."'

David grimaced guiltily. 'And I said something like, For Christ's sake, Barry, get lost. I haven't got time for you and your games. Don't you know my father was killed yesterday? I'm sitting here trying to sort out funeral arrangements, and the last thing I need right now is you and your problems, so call someone else, because I don't want to hear from you again!'

David Taylor set his half-empty mug on the counter beside him, and his voice was husky as he said, 'Barry didn't say anything for a moment or two, and then he said, "You probably won't, David, because there is no one else who can help me. Goodbye."'

He picked up his mug again, but sat holding it in his hands. 'I told him not to be such an idiot, and slammed the phone down,' he said softly, 'and twelve hours later I heard he had shot himself.' He paused to look quizzically at Tregalles. 'But now you're saying he *didn't* shoot himself. That he was murdered? How do you know?'

'Not at liberty to say,' Tregalles told him. 'But since we're talking about that, I'd like you to take me back to the morning your father and Mrs Bergman were killed. You and your brother were on your morning rounds at the time, as I recall. Did each of you have a particular area you covered?'

'That's right. I did the shops, pubs, and cafes on the south side of town, plus the villages, Ardlington, Clapton Cross, and some of the others out that way, and Kev covered the north end, Little Stoneford, Winset, and Shebbington, although I did his in-town ones that morning, which is why I was a bit later than usual getting back and found the lane blocked off and police everywhere.'

'Why did you do your brother's rounds that day?'

David looked at him blankly. 'Oh, that,' he said. 'Sorry, I . . .' He waved his hands as if trying to erase something in the air. 'That was because Kevin was in *l-o-o-v-e*,' he said, drawing the word out. 'He had it so bad it was painful – more so for me, because I was living under the same roof with him and Dad, and I was always afraid I would say something that would set Dad off. Believe me, it was hard going that summer.'

'You lost me,' Tregalles confessed. He had an inkling about where the conversation was heading, because Paget had mentioned something of the sort on his return from Cambridge, but now that David Taylor seemed to be in a talkative mood, he wanted to know more. 'What was so bad about your brother being in love?'

'It was *who* he was in love with,' David said, and went on to tell Tregalles what he had told Claire the week before. 'And believe me, it was tricky with us all living under the same roof, because despite our differences, Dad was still prepared to hire us during the summer, because Kev and I would work for less than anyone else. But it included bed and board, and that was a plus as far as we were concerned.

'But as I said, it was tricky, more so for Kevin than for me because not only was he still dating Steph, he was working for Ed Bradshaw as well. You see, our work at the bakery and the deliveries took place in the morning, so we were free in the afternoon. Ed Bradshaw was quite taken with Kevin as a potential son-in-law, and he wanted him to join the firm once he was through in Leeds. So he offered Kev a job in the afternoons at the Ludlow office, where there was little likelihood of Dad finding out. It was mostly researching material for other solicitors in the firm, but it was valuable experience for Kevin, and it gave him and Steph a chance to be together.'

'Pretty dangerous, though, wasn't it?' Tregalles observed. 'I mean Kevin could have been up the creek if your father had found out.'

'Oh, yes,' David said seriously, 'and I didn't want to be the one to blurt something out and wreck everything, so there were times when I was more than a little annoyed with Kev for taking so many chances.'

'Let's get back to why your brother asked you to do part of his rounds for him that Saturday,' Tregalles said. 'Are you saying that was something to do with Stephanie Bradshaw as well?'

David set his coffee to one side and sat frowning as if at some unpleasant memory. 'Steph and her father were leaving that afternoon for Amsterdam,' he said slowly, 'and Kevin just had to see Steph before they went. Ed's family came from there originally, and Steph had a grandmother and a couple of aunts in Amsterdam, and she and Ed used to pop over to see them on a weekend every now and again. I mean Steph was only going to be gone for a couple of days, but even that was too long for Kev. But it was no good arguing with him, so I agreed to do some of his rounds for him while he went skiving off to see Steph.'

Tregalles stood up and set his empty mug on the counter. 'Thanks for the coffee,' he said, 'and thanks for filling me in on what happened that day.' He walked to the door, then paused. 'You said your father didn't have a lot of money, but he still had the business, so it must have brought in quite a bit when it was sold. You and your brother share it, did you?'

The muscles around David Taylor's mouth tightened as he said, 'That's right, Sergeant. Kevin and I shared it with the building society. You see, the money we thought Dad had been saving for our education, actually came from a mortgage on the house and business, and all Dad had been paying off for years was little more than the interest, so by the time everything was settled and taxes paid, we ended up with less than eight thousand pounds apiece. Hardly what you would call a motive for killing our father, wouldn't you say?'

'True,' Tregalles conceded, 'but on the other hand, you said yourself you didn't know the place was mortgaged to the hilt until he died, did you? Have a nice day, Mr Taylor. I'm sure we'll be talking again soon.'

David Taylor remained where he was, eyes closed, mouth clamped shut as he silently chastised himself for the slip of the tongue that had forced him to lie about Kevin's absence that fateful Saturday morning. At least he'd had the good sense

not to mention Kevin's unexplained disappearance on the
Sunday, and the fact that Kevin had lied about that as well.

It was only by chance that David had discovered the lie his
brother had told him about where he was on Saturday morning,
and he suspected that Kevin had also lied about where he'd
gone on the Sunday night after receiving a call on his newly
acquired mobile phone.

He wrinkled his nose. Even now, it was impossible to forget
the smell on Kevin's clothes. The smell had filled his nose,
his mouth, and his lungs as he'd come out of a sound sleep
to find Kevin standing between the two beds.

He remembered peering at the figures on the digital clock,
and saying, 'For God's sake, Kev, it's four o'clock in the
morning. Where the hell have you been? Aunt Edith wanted
to know where you'd gone, and I didn't know what to tell
her. And what *is* that bloody awful stink?'

'Steph and I were trying to get Ed's barbecue going and I
spilt fluid on my trousers,' his brother whispered as he stripped
off his clothes and sat down on his own bed. 'Go back to
sleep. I'll open the widow and the smell will be gone by
morning.'

'I thought Steph was in Amsterdam with her father?'

'She was, but they had to come back early. Something to
do with a case Ed's working on.'

David hadn't believed it then and he didn't believe it now.

He smiled grimly to himself. Kev had never been a very
good liar, and David had often teased him about it being a
serious handicap if he hoped to become a successful lawyer.
But the fact remained that if Kevin didn't tell the police about
where he'd been before they discovered it for themselves, they
would wonder what else he had lied about, and who could
blame them?

He glanced at the time. He'd have to talk to Kevin. It
wasn't something he wanted to discuss over the phone, and
if Steph didn't know about what Kevin had been up to back
then, he didn't want her learning about it from him. Best thing
to do, he decided, would be to ask Kevin to come to the shop
to give him a hand and help him with the packing.

TWENTY-SIX

Kevin Taylor parked the car in the garage, picked up his briefcase and got out. His footsteps sounded hollow as he crossed the floor and entered the house.

'I'm home,' he called as he walked down the hall. 'Where are you, Steph?'

The greeting had started off as a joke the first few times he'd come home to the new house, because it was so much bigger than their old house on Oak Street, but it was fast becoming a standard greeting.

'Right behind you in the kitchen,' Stephanie called loudly. 'Come and tell me what you think of this. It's a new recipe I'm trying out, and I need a guinea pig. How was your day?'

'A bit dull, actually,' he said as he reversed course and entered the kitchen. 'How about yours?'

'About the same, except for a visit I had from a very nice gentleman caller, who couldn't quite make up his mind which he liked best, my iced tea or my legs.'

Kevin set the briefcase on the floor and gave his wife a quick peck on the cheek. 'No contest,' he said perfunctorily. 'Anyone I know?'

'Detective Sergeant Tregalles. Funny little chap with a sort of wrinkly face. Well, not exactly little, I suppose, but very pleasant. Have you met him?'

'Yes I have,' Kevin said cautiously. 'He was with Chief Inspector Paget when they came to the office the other week. What did he want?'

The liquid in the large pot on the stove began to bubble. Stephanie turned quickly to stir it with a long wooden spoon. 'Got to keep this stuff moving or it sticks to the bottom and burns,' she said. 'He wanted to know where you and I were when Roger was killed, and he'd like you to call him to confirm what I told him about where you were that evening. He left me his card.'

Kevin frowned. 'Why does he want to know where we were?'

Stephanie shrugged. 'I didn't get the impression that we
are at the top of his list, but he did ask a lot of questions
about Roger's call to John Chadwell, and John's call to me
that afternoon. I suppose it's more or less standard pro-
cedure to talk to anyone and everyone who either saw or
spoke to Roger that day. They seem to think he was killed
sometime around five or six o'clock, so when the Sergeant
asked where you were, I told him I thought you were either
in the Ludlow office or on your way home. That is right,
isn't it?'

'That's right,' Kevin said absently as he peered over his
wife's shoulder. 'What is that stuff, anyway?' he asked.

'It's a sort of stew,' Stephanie told him. 'It sounded good
so I decided to try it out. Here, taste it.' She handed him a
large spoon.

He dipped the spoon in, blew on it, then took a tentative
sip. 'Tastes all right,' he said, 'but isn't it a bit much in this
heat, Steph?'

'Oh, this isn't for now. It freezes – at least that's what it
says in the article, so I hope they're right.'

'Glad to hear it,' Kevin said, sounding relieved, 'because I
was trying to work out how to say I didn't want any for supper
without hurting the cook's feelings.'

'Chef, darling,' Stephanie corrected, 'so be careful. They're
known to be temperamental. Oh, yes, and before I forget,
David rang to ask if you could spare him an hour or so this
evening. It seems he's running behind schedule, and he could
use an extra hand to help pack his stuff.'

'I suppose I could,' he said. 'I don't think we have anything
on, tonight, do we, Steph?' His wife continued to stir as she
shook her head. 'Did he mention a time?'

'Just said whenever it was convenient. He's still living above
the shop, so he'll be there all evening. Did you know he's
moving into Claire's house? Well, the old Grant house, I
suppose it is, really. Just until he can get sorted out.'

'No, I didn't know,' said Kevin. 'But I wonder if he ever
will? Get sorted out, I mean?'

'Not much to show for almost nine years of your life, is it?'
David said wistfully as he poked at a box with his toe.
'Compared to how far you've come, Kev. Partner in the firm

when old Mortimer retires. And then what? Onward and upward, eh? Head of the firm when Ed retires?'

'Who knows,' Kevin said. 'And you've not done so badly. I've seen some of the work you've done locally, and I think you're on your way. And now, with this offer of Claire's, you'll have more time to devote to your painting. Are you and Claire . . .?'

David shook his head. 'It's simply a business arrangement,' he said. 'Claire would like someone in the house, and I need a place to stay and store my stuff. We're just good friends.'

'Are you sure about that?' Kevin asked archly. 'It seems to me that she's inviting you to move in with her.'

David laughed. 'You always did have a good imagination, Kevin,' he said, 'but it's not like that at all. She has her own place in town, so we won't be living in the same house.'

'Still, it could be the first move,' his brother said, 'and you could do a lot worse, so think about it. Anyway, now we've got your love life out of the way, what needs packing next?'

'Actually, that's not why I asked you to come,' David said, 'I told Steph I needed your help with the packing because I wanted to talk to you in private. I had a visit from that detective chap, Tregalles, today, and he told me that Barry Grant didn't kill himself. They now believe he was murdered, so they're going back to square one to look at the statements everyone made at the time, and I have the distinct feeling that he thinks you and I had something to do with the robberies and Dad's death.'

'A *feeling* . . .?' Kevin said sharply. 'Why? What did he say?'

'Nothing specific. But he did mention that we probably both knew about the way Sam used to knock on the back door to be let in, which we did, of course, and that we and Dad didn't always get on, and we benefited financially from his death, things like that.'

He paused to take a deep breath, 'Unfortunately, I happened to mention that I covered your rounds for you that morning, and he picked up on it. I'm sorry, Kev, but it just slipped out, so I had to explain it was because you wanted to see Steph before she and her father left for Amsterdam to visit her grandmother.

'The trouble is, that wasn't true, was it? Because when I

asked Steph a couple of weeks later how her grandmother
was, she said she hadn't seen her for several months, and
when I said I thought she'd been to see her the weekend Dad
was killed, she said no, she'd been in Birmingham that day
to do some shopping. So you lied to me about where you
were going, didn't you?'

Kevin stared at his brother. 'So it just slipped out, did it?'
he said coldly. 'Just what the hell were you thinking of? You
know what they're like, for God's sake.'

'But it's not too late to set things straight,' David protested.
'I think I know *why* you lied, and I don't blame you because
it would have looked bad at the time, but times have changed,
and I think you should tell the police the truth before they
find out for themselves.'

Kevin started to speak, but David hurried on. 'Look,
Kev,' he said, 'I don't want to see you in trouble with the
police, but if you tell them the truth, and I don't mean that
load of codswallop you gave me that night, I'm sure they'll
understand.'

He chuckled. 'I mean you have to admit that the story you
gave me about the barbecue when you came in at four in the
morning was bullshit. That wasn't lighter fluid on you, was
it? That smelt like petrol to me. Besides, Ed's barbecue is
gas-fired anyway, and Steph was supposed to be in Amsterdam,
but you made up some story about Ed having to return early,
remember?'

Kevin stared warily at his brother for a long moment before
turning away. Head down, hands behind his back, he paced
the length of the shop before turning to face David once again.
'All right,' he said, 'you say you think you know what I was
up to, so tell me, what do you think it was?'

'Drugs,' said David. 'I think you were messing about with
drugs. All the signs were there. You were tense, jumpy, you
weren't sleeping well, and you would disappear at odd times,
and snap at me if I asked where you were going. That in itself
was a dead giveaway that you were up to something, because
we used to tell each other everything, yet suddenly you were
very secretive. It was almost as if your whole personality had
changed, and that was what tipped me off, because I'd run
into it before.

'The lad I shared digs with at Slade got into drugs the

second year I was there, and the same thing happened to him, so it wasn't hard to work out. In fact I was getting so worried about you that I'd decided to tackle you about it when Dad died. But that seemed to bring you to your senses, and you settled down after that, so I decided not to say anything. So what the hell were you doing that Sunday night to get yourself covered in petrol?'

Kevin grinned sheepishly. 'I should have known I wasn't fooling my little brother,' he said. 'And you're quite right, that was petrol you could smell; petrol and smoke from the fire. But that bit about the barbecue was partly right, except it was down by the rock pools on the other side of the river. We were all pretty high, so when we couldn't get the thing going, someone had the bright idea of throwing petrol on it. Next thing we knew the tall grass was on fire, and we were in the middle of it trying to stamp it out before someone raised the alarm and called the cops.

'It's a wonder we weren't all killed,' he said. 'In fact, I think that was the moment when I realized what a fool I'd been, and decided to quit the drugs. Not that I'd ever been into them as heavily as some of the others, but it still took one hell of an effort on my part. I don't know if you noticed, but I wasn't exactly myself for weeks after that. I couldn't seem to make even the simplest decisions.'

'I was never sure if that was because of the drugs or because of the way Dad died,' David said quietly. His brow furrowed as he shot a questioning glance at Kevin and said, 'Steph wasn't at that party, was she?'

'Good God, no! If Steph had known I was playing around with that stuff, it would have been all over. She was death on that sort of thing. And that is why, little brother, noble as your intentions may be, I shall *not* be telling the police about what I was doing that weekend, because it's bound to get back to her. And nor will you.'

Kevin Taylor got out of the car and pressed the remote control, then waited until the double-width garage door rolled down and locked itself in place before he entered the house and locked that door behind him.

'I'm out here,' Stephanie called from the terrace. 'Come and look at the stars. They're quite magnificent tonight.'

He found her lying almost flat on her back on the chaise longue, looking at the stars through binoculars. 'There's something moving across the sky up there,' she said as he joined her, 'and I'm not sure if it is some sort of shooting star or one of those bits of space junk that falls out of the sky from time to time. At least it's not coming this way, if that's what it is. Here, take a look.' She handed the binoculars to Kevin and pointed.

'Can't see it,' Kevin said, sweeping back and forth across the area his wife was pointing to. He handed the binoculars back to Stephanie. 'Are you sure it's still there?'

Stephanie took the binoculars, but instead of using them again, she set them down beside her. 'So what did David *really* want?' she asked quietly.

'Just some help in packing up his stuff,' he said. 'Would you like a drink?' He crossed the patio to the drinks cabinet and opened it, then stood there frowning. 'What happened to the ice?' he asked.

'I forgot to refill the ice maker,' Stephanie told him, 'but there's some in the fridge in the kitchen if you really need it. Anyway, stop trying to change the subject. David never could lie convincingly, and I knew straightaway he wasn't telling the truth when he rang this afternoon. Any more than you can, darling.' She grinned. 'Except when you're in court, of course. So get your drink, then come and sit down and tell me the real reason he wanted to get you over there alone.'

TWENTY-SEVEN

Thursday, July 23rd

When Molly walked into the room, Sharon Jessop was sitting on the side of her bed, talking animatedly to her guardian for the day, a very solid-looking WPC by the name of Brenda Borden. Sharon stopped speaking when she saw Molly, then slid her legs back under the covers, and eased herself back on to the raised pillows.

'Feeling a bit better, then, are we, Sharon?' Molly asked

brightly. 'Good,' she continued without waiting for an answer, 'because I have some news for you. But first, I'd like to have a word with Constable Borden. In private,' she added, with a nod to Borden. The Constable rose to her feet and followed Molly out of the room. At the door, Molly turned to flash Sharon an encouraging smile, then closed the door behind her.

Two minutes later, Molly re-entered the room and sat down in the chair beside the bed. 'Sorry to deprive you of your company,' she said, 'but since there's no need for her to be here now, I told her she could go. We had a tip around three o'clock this morning, and found Al in bed with his girlfriend at her place in Potters Lane. Her mother tipped us off, so he's back in custody now, and you won't have to worry about him coming to attack you. I'm sure you'll be relieved to hear that.'

But Sharon Jessop looked anything but relieved as she slid further down under the covers, her eyes fixed on Molly. 'They could let him out,' she said huskily. 'They did the last time and they could again. I mean I wouldn't have a chance the way I am stuck here in this bed.'

Molly shook her head. 'There's no way,' she said firmly. 'His bail has been revoked and he's behind bars, Sharon, so there's nothing to worry about now, except getting better. I had a word with the doctor before I came in, and he tells me your tests for internal injuries turned out better than he'd hoped, so you might not be in here for as long as you thought.'

She pushed her chair back and stood up as if to leave, but Sharon's hand shot out from beneath the covers to grab Molly's arm. 'You can't just leave me like this,' she said plaintively. 'I mean in here, all by myself. If Al could get in here, then ...' She clamped her lips together and looked away, but it was too late.

'Then what, Sharon?' Molly asked. The friendly tone was gone. 'What are you afraid of? Or perhaps I should say, *who* are you afraid of, Sharon? Could it be this person?' She took a mobile phone from her handbag and held it up for Sharon to see. 'The person you rang last Saturday morning, using this phone?'

'That's my phone! You've no right. That's got nothing to do with this.'

'Then explain it to me, Sharon. Tell me why you rang this number. Is this the man you told me about? The one you say was fondling you during the robbery? What do you think he will say when I ask him?'

'No!' Colour drained from Sharon's face. 'Oh, God, Molly, you mustn't. He'll . . .' Her voice broke and tears spilled down her face as she began to sob.

'He'll what, Sharon? Come back and finish the job? Is that what you want? Because if you don't tell me the truth, that's what could happen. You tried to blackmail him, didn't you? But why in heaven's name did you tell him where you lived?'

'I didn't,' Sharon wailed, wincing at the word 'blackmail'. 'And it wasn't like that. I just asked him to help me out; tide me over like until I could get another job.'

'Tell me exactly what you said to him,' Molly said. 'From the beginning. What did you say when he answered the phone?'

Sharon blew her nose and brushed away the tears with the back of her hand. 'I told him who I was and asked him if he remembered me, and I started to ask if he could help me out, but he cut me off sharp like, and said he didn't know what I was talking about. I was afraid he was going to hang up, so I reminded him about the robbery and him whispering to me. He said he didn't know anything about any robbery, but he remembered me from the parties me and Rachel used to go to, and he said he was sorry to hear I'd lost my job, and he'd like to help me for old times' sake. To tell the truth, Molly, he was so nice about it I began to wonder if I *had* got it wrong after all these years, and he wasn't the one. He sounded like he really cared and wanted to help.'

'And he suggested that you meet?'

'That's right. So I told him I'd meet him that night at eleven o'clock in the Green Man in Box Lane, because they stay open late. I thought it would be all right, because there would be lots of people around, but he must have found out where I lived somehow, because he came to the back door. I thought it was Vi or one of the neighbours, so I opened it, and the next thing I knew he was inside and beating the shit out of me.'

'But you got a good look at him?'

Sharon snorted. 'Didn't have much chance, did I?' she said. 'He punched me in the face as soon as I opened the door. Besides, he was wearing this stocking mask thing over his face so his nose was sort of squashed and you couldn't really tell who it was, but I'm sure it was him.' Sharon winced at the memory. 'He kept hitting me, punching me, and kicking me when I went down, and he had his hands around my neck and I couldn't breathe, and that's all I remember until I found myself in here, and that's God's truth.'

'When was the last time you saw this man face to face? Before the other night, I mean.'

Sharon pushed out her lower lip. 'Don't know as I've seen him since before the pub was robbed.'

'And you didn't actually see him the night the pub was robbed, did you? So what you are telling me is that you couldn't possibly identify this man in court, right?'

Sharon seemed to shrink beneath the covers as she shook her head. 'Suppose not if you put it that way,' she said in a small voice. 'But it had to be him, didn't it?'

Molly sighed. 'That may be true,' she said, 'but that argument isn't going to fly in court. What about his voice? Did he say anything? Could you identify him by his voice or by what he said?'

Sharon shook her head. 'Never said a word. Just sort of grunted every time he hit me, but who else could it be, for Christ's sake? It had to be him, Molly. It had to be.' Tears welled up again and spilled over.

'I'm sorry, Sharon, but from what you've told me, there isn't a shred of hard evidence to connect this man to the one who beat you up. But tell me, how did you pick on him in the first place? Have you always known or suspected? Or did it trigger a memory when I first came to the house to question you last week?'

'I kept thinking about it after you'd gone and suddenly it just came to me, clear as anything. I was going to tell you, honestly, but when I lost my job I thought maybe I could get some money from him. Like I said, I wasn't asking for much; just a couple of hundred to tide me over.'

'Oh, Sharon,' Molly said sadly, 'did it not occur to you that you were dealing with a man who may have been responsible for at least two brutal murders, and possibly more than that?'

Shock widened Sharon's eyes. 'Oh, God!' she breathed. 'I never thought of that. I was just thinking of the night when they robbed the pub.'

'Seems to me there was a lot you didn't think about,' said Molly grimly, 'but it's too late to do anything about that now.'

Sharon struggled to sit upright in bed. 'But you have to arrest him' she said earnestly. 'I know it was him. For Christ's sake, Molly, I need protection; he could come after me again. I mean if Al could get in here past everyone, so can he. For God's sake, Molly, help me. Please, please help me . . . You can't leave me here like this.'

'All right, all right,' said Molly wearily. The pretence had gone on long enough. 'You aren't alone, Sharon. Constable Borden is outside. I told her to stay out there until I was finished here. She'll be staying with you, so you can settle down. But you are not out of the woods yourself, you know. You've withheld vital evidence, you lied about who attacked you, you had us arrest your husband for something you knew he didn't do, and you attempted to blackmail someone, and that's an offence regardless of what that person may or may not have done.'

Molly moved towards the door. 'So think about that,' she said quietly, 'and if you remember *anything* that might help us put this man away, for heaven's sake tell us at once.'

Outside in the hallway, WPC Borden quickly snuffed out the cigarette cupped in her hand. 'I heard that,' she said quietly. 'Do you really know who this bloke is?'

Molly nodded. 'But proving it is something else. Sharon may be sure she knows who attacked her, and I'm sure she's right, but unless Forensic comes up with something more than they have so far, we have no case.'

On her return to Charter Lane, Molly sought out Tregalles, and the two of them sat down to compare notes. 'It had to be Chadwell who attacked her,' Molly concluded. 'I mean she told the man who she was, and it wouldn't be all that hard for him to find out where she lived. And since Chadwell was also one of the people Roger Corbett rang not long before he was killed, it suggests to me that Sharon is right, and he was one of the gang responsible for the robberies and the killing of George Taylor and Emily Bergman.'

Tregalles agreed. 'And I think Roger Corbett was also part of that gang,' he said. 'David Taylor told me that Corbett had been going great guns in university until shortly after he went back in September that year, and then he suddenly dropped out and left Broadminster. Taylor said Corbett had changed when he returned a couple of years later. So much so that he'd wondered if Corbett might be seriously ill.

'I think Corbett was there when the killings took place. He may not have done the actual killing himself, but I think it affected him, and the guilt was so great he couldn't handle it. Then, when the case came up again, and Paget questioned him, he came close to cracking. He panicked, and started calling for help. Unfortunately, instead of help, someone decided they couldn't take the risk of him folding under pressure, so they killed him.

'And right now, it looks to me as if that someone could be John Chadwell, except he couldn't have killed Corbett himself, because he was only gone from home for roughly half an hour. Chadwell told me he didn't leave home until half past five, and the barman at the Unicorn remembers Chadwell coming in to look for Corbett about an hour after the man had left, so it looks as if Chadwell can be ruled out. But that's not to say he didn't have someone else do it.

'The trouble is,' the Sergeant continued as he pocketed his notebook and stood up, 'all we really have against the man is Mrs Jessop's word, and after having her husband charged with beating her up, then changing her story and saying it was Chadwell, her word is worthless, so let's have another go at Chadwell and see what he was to say for himself.'

'Mr Chadwell?' The girl at the desk looked at the clock then back at Tregalles. 'Sorry,' she said, 'but you've just missed him. He always goes for his lunch at half twelve. But he'll be back at half past one. Very punctual is Mr Chadwell.'

'Do you know where he has his lunch?'

'Probably feeding the ducks by the pond in the park,' the girl said with a nod in the direction of Mortimer Park on the far side of the building. 'But he doesn't like to be disturbed while he's having his lunch,' she added hastily when Tregalles thanked her and began to move away.

'Wouldn't dream of it,' Tregalles assured her solemnly as he and Molly made for the door.

They found Chadwell sitting on a bench under the trees at

the edge of the pond, surrounded by squabbling ducks vying
for position as he tossed out chunks of bread. He had the
bench to himself, and he was clearly annoyed when the two
detectives shooed away some of the birds and sat down beside
him.

'Very pleasant out here,' Tregalles said amiably as he sat
back and took in the scene. 'Enjoy feeding the ducks, do you?'

'I did,' Chadwell said pointedly, 'and I prefer their company
to yours, if you don't mind.'

'Oh, but we do mind, Mr Chadwell,' Tregalles told him. 'I
don't think you've met my colleague, Detective Constable
Forsythe, have you?' he continued as Molly held up her warrant
card for inspection. 'But she has a few questions for you.'

'Then I suggest she make an appointment and let me get
on with my lunch,' Chadwell said roughly without so much
as turning his head to look at Molly or the proffered card.
Hunched forward, he reached into a paper bag and tossed out
a handful of bread to the impatient birds.

'On the other hand,' Tregalles said, 'if you don't wish to
cooperate with us here, we could do this down at Charter
Lane. It's your choice, Mr Chadwell, but I can assure you it
will be one or the other.'

Chadwell grunted. 'So what is it this time?' he demanded.
'More silly questions about how tall I am or what sort of car
I drive?'

With a nod from Tregalles, it was Molly who answered.
'You received a phone call at nine forty-two last Saturday
morning,' she said. 'A call from a woman who identified herself
as an old acquaintance of yours, and she asked you for money.
Isn't that right, Mr Chadwell?'

The man sat back on the bench and turned to look at Molly
for the first time. 'Monitoring my phone calls, now, are you?'
he asked, then turned to Tregalles. 'Isn't that illegal, Sergeant?'

'Mobile phone calls are recorded, as I'm sure you know,'
said Molly. 'What exactly did the woman say, and what did
she want?'

Chadwell snorted. 'You just said it yourself,' he said. 'She
wanted money. In fact it is she you should be talking to,
because she tried to blackmail me with some outlandish story
about a robbery. Claimed she knew I was one of a gang, and
if I didn't pay up she was going to go to the police with the

information. Never heard such a load of rubbish in my life.'

'I take it you're telling us that you were *not* a member of the gang who robbed the pub back then?' said Molly.

'Of course I wasn't,' Chadwell snapped impatiently.

'So why do you think she picked on you? She must have had a reason.'

'Oh, for God's sake, how the hell should I know?' Chadwell said irritably. 'Why don't you go and ask her?' He shook the last of the bread out of the bag and tossed it to the birds. 'It was such a pitiful attempt at blackmail,' he continued in a slightly less belligerent tone, 'because I recognized who she was almost from the start. I couldn't remember her name, but she gave herself away almost immediately, and I remembered she was the daughter of the landlord of the Rose and Crown, and a girl I knew briefly back in my university days. Saucy little thing she was then; turned up at just about every party we ever had. Feed her a few drinks and she was yours for the night. Used to come with another girl; can't remember her name, but she was a nice kid, completely out of her depth. Never did know what happened to either of them.'

'What was your reaction to her demands?'

Chadwell looked surprised. 'Same as yours would be, I expect, if someone phoned you out of the blue and accused you of something like that,' he said. 'I was mad as hell! At least I was until I realized who she was, and that she had to be pretty desperate to try a stupid stunt like that. I mean it was such a pitiful attempt that I couldn't take her seriously. She never was particularly bright when I knew her, but then we weren't exactly looking for brains in those days. So I was curious to find out how desperate she was for money, and see what she was prepared to do for me if I did decide to help her out. So I said I would meet her in the Green Man Saturday night at eleven o'clock, but she never came. Got cold feet, I expect. I waited half an hour past the time, then went home. Haven't heard from her since.'

'Was that your suggestion or hers? The Green Man, I mean.'

'It was hers.'

'And what would you have done if she had shown up?'

'I honestly don't know. As I said, I was curious. I suppose it would have depended on what she had to say when she got there. Anyway, how did you get on to this? Get caught trying it on someone else, did she?'

'Do you remember what time it was when you got to the Green Man?' asked Molly.

'Ten thirty, give or take five minutes,' Chadwell said. 'Why? Is it important?'

'So you were there about an hour. Can anyone verify that?'

'One of the barmaids certainly can,' Chadwell, said smugly. 'Chatty little blonde by the name of Linda.'

'So you won't mind if we ask her if she remembers you?'

Chadwell shrugged. 'Be my guest,' he said.

Molly eyed Chadwell speculatively. 'I wonder,' she said hesitantly, 'if I might take your picture? It's just that it would make it so much simpler than trying to describe you to this Linda, or having you come down to the Green Man yourself.'

The look on Chadwell's face was a mixture of surprise and perplexity. He stared at Molly for a long moment, and she was almost sure he was about to refuse. She'd made the suggestion on the spur of the moment, and by the look on Tregalles's face, she had taken the Sergeant by surprise as well.

'Why not?' Chadwell said with an airy wave of the hand. 'I've got nothing to hide.'

Molly delved into the bottom of her voluminous handbag to produce a tiny digital camera. She rose and shuffled her way through the ducks, then turned to face Chadwell to take two head-and-shoulder shots in quick succession. 'You say you left the Green Man at eleven thirty and went home,' she said as she put the camera away and returned to her seat. 'Can your wife confirm the time you got home?'

Chadwell's brows came together in a scowl. 'She could,' he said, 'but I want her left out of this. All she can tell you is that I went out to have a drink with an old friend, who was in town for a few hours. I mean I was hardly going to tell her I was going to meet a woman I'd slept with a few times in my youth, and who was now trying to blackmail me, was I? So I'd just as soon leave her out of this, *if* you don't mind.'

He began to flatten and fold the paper bag that had contained the bread. 'Anyway, I presume you have this woman in custody, so what does she have to say for herself?'

'She says you beat the shit out of her and left her on her

kitchen floor to die,' Tregalles said baldly. 'What do you say to that, Mr Chadwell?'

Chadwell's eyes narrowed. 'I don't believe you,' he said flatly. 'All I know is that the woman who phoned me never showed up. Maybe she tried the same scheme on someone else and they decided to teach her a lesson. When was this anyway?'

'Last Saturday night,' Molly told him. 'About the time you say you were in the Green Man, which is only a couple of streets over from where she was attacked.'

'Then it couldn't have been me, could it?' Chadwell said contemptuously. 'So stop wasting my time and yours and go and look for whoever really did it.'

'You say you knew this woman years ago, but you don't remember her name. Does Sharon Grady ring a bell?'

Chadwell nodded slowly. 'That's right,' he said. 'She still at the pub, is she? I haven't been in the Crown for years.'

'Probably not since the night of the robbery,' Molly said, goading him.

Chadwell picked up the bag that had contained his own lunch and stood up. 'Come back and talk to me when you have evidence of that,' he told her. 'Meanwhile I have work to do, and it seems to me that you have some to do as well if you are to find this person you're looking for. And if you want to talk to me again, I suggest you call my solicitor first. I'm sure he knows how to deal with false allegations and police harassment.'

'That wouldn't happen to be Kevin Taylor, would it?' Tregalles asked.

'Why? Is that supposed to be significant?'

'No. Just curious, that's all, Mr Chadwell. And thank you for your time. I'm sure we'll be talking to you again.'

'Not if I have anything to do with it,' Chadwell called over his shoulders as he walked away.

'Fancy an ice cream?' Tregalles asked as they started back towards the car. 'There's an ice cream van over there, and I think you deserve some sort of reward for sheer bloody cheek, asking for his photograph like that. I couldn't believe it when he said yes.'

Molly grinned. 'I think he thought we might draw the wrong conclusions if he refused,' she said. 'Plus the fact that he probably thought he'd humour me because I'm a woman. It might not have worked if you had asked him.'

Tregalles wrinkled his nose. 'Don't see what that's got to do with it,' he said. 'Unless you think he fancies you.'

'I think the only one he fancies is himself,' Molly said. 'Did you hear what he said about how he might help Sharon out "depending on what she was prepared to do for him"? I think that man has a very low opinion of women. He didn't see me as a threat, so he humoured me. And I don't believe his professed concern for his wife's feelings either. Anyway, now we have his picture, we can use it to see if anyone remembers seeing him near Sharon's house or around the Unicorn the day Corbett was killed.'

'He is a slippery bastard,' Tregalles agreed once they'd sat down to enjoy their ice creams, 'and he was ready for us. He was even smart enough to volunteer the information that Jessop was trying to blackmail him, so he must have been aware that she was still alive and talking.

'But I don't believe that stuff about him waiting in the Green Man for Sharron Jessop because he wanted to see her again. The minute Sharon told him she remembered him as the man who had held her during the robbery at the Rose and Crown, he would see her as a threat that had to be dealt with. There's no way that man would stand for an attempt to blackmail him, especially if what the blackmailer said was true.'

Tregalles shook his head in a bewildered sort of way. 'Didn't Sharon see that?' he asked rhetorically. 'I can't believe the woman could be so stupid.'

'I think it was more a case of desperation than stupidity,' Molly said. 'Sharon's been beaten down over the years, trying to make ends meet, while her husband robs her of what little she has every chance he gets, and on top of that she loses her job. She simply wasn't thinking, and when Chadwell realized how naive she was, he pretended to want to help her and she fell for it.'

'I suppose,' Tregalles said without conviction. 'But I still don't understand why he didn't kill her outright when he had the chance.'

'Perhaps he thought he had. The problem we have now is, how are we going to *prove* it was Chadwell who beat her up?'

'I don't know,' Tregalles said, 'but your mentioning his attitude towards women reminds me I never did get round to talking to his wife after I saw him in his office the other day. He tried to put me off talking to her then, much the same as he did today, so let's see if she's in.'

The Sergeant consulted his notebook, then dialled a number on his mobile phone and waited. 'Oh, sorry,' he mumbled gruffly, when a woman answered. 'Must have dialled the wrong number. Sorry to have troubled you.'

'She's home,' he told Molly as he closed the phone, 'but I didn't want to tell her we were coming in case she decided to alert Chadwell, and I don't want him around when we talk to her.'

TWENTY-EIGHT

Molly's first impression of Amy Chadwell was of someone who had just got out of bed. She wore no make-up, her hair was frizzy, and her slim body was draped in a shapeless short-sleeved dress that could almost be mistaken for a nightgown.

'Sorry to call on you at lunchtime,' Tregalles said, 'but we happened to be in the area and thought we'd take a chance. Do you mind? Just a few questions. It won't take long.'

'No . . . no, it's all right,' Amy said hesitantly. Her slender fingers fluttered to her neck, touched her face, touched her hair as if to assure herself that she looked all right before opening the door wider for them to enter. 'In fact I don't have a set time for meals during the holidays,' she explained. She lowered her voice as if afraid of being overheard. 'Except for dinner, of course,' she confided. 'John is such a creature of habit, and he does like his dinner on time.'

'You're a teacher?' Molly said as Amy Chadwell led the way into the front room and turned to face them. 'Primary school, is it? What ages do you teach?' Molly knew the answers to her questions, because she'd read the background material on John Chadwell and his wife, but felt a few non-threatening questions might help put the woman at ease.

'That's right.' The lines around Amy's mouth softened. 'I

get them when they're first starting school,' she said. 'Four-
and five-year-olds. They're such a delight at that age, and
so eager to learn. Do you have children, Miss . . . er . . . I'm
sorry, Detective Constable . . .?'

Molly smiled. 'Constable Forsythe,' she said, 'and, no, I
don't have children.'

Amy looked away. 'Nor do we,' she said wistfully. 'But
then, as John says, with both of us working full time it would
hardly be fair, and he's right, of course.'

Tregalles cleared his throat. 'If I may . . .?' he began.

He was interrupted by Amy saying, 'Would you like tea?'

'That's very kind of you, Mrs Chadwell,' Molly said
quickly before Tregalles could speak, 'but we won't be here
long, so thank you, but no. May we sit down?'

'Oh! Oh dear, yes, of course. I'm sorry . . . I should have
. . . Yes, please do sit down.' Amy indicated well-worn
armchairs on either side of the bay window that overlooked
the street. She waited until they were settled, then sat down
facing them, hands clasped tightly around her knees.

'This is about poor Roger, isn't it?' she said. 'Yes, yes,
of course, it must be. John told me a detective had been to
see him in his office, but I never expected anyone to . . . I
mean all I did was answer the phone; John was the one Roger
wanted to talk to, and I could barely make out what Roger was
saying anyway. John went down to the Unicorn to try to
help Roger, but he was gone by the time John got there. He
did try to get hold of Kevin, but he couldn't, so he went
down there himself, and that's about all I can tell you,' she
ended breathlessly.

'Why, exactly, was Mr Chadwell trying to contact Kevin
Taylor?' Tregalles asked.

Amy shifted uncomfortably in her chair. 'Perhaps I shouldn't
be telling you this,' she said guiltily, 'but, to be honest, John
never cared much for Roger.' She laughed nervously. 'Couldn't
stand the man if truth be told – with good reason,' she added
hastily, 'because Roger could be quite . . . quite difficult at
times. But Kevin has always looked out for Roger, so John
thought it would be best to have Kevin talk to him.'

Molly said, 'Do you happen to remember what time the
call came in, Mrs Chadwell?'

'When Roger called? Oh, yes. It was a few minutes after

four. Five past, perhaps? John came home early that day. He had some work to do before the council meeting that night, and he'd said he would be home by four, and he'd just come in when Roger phoned. John is always punctual.'

'I know you said it was hard to understand Mr Corbett, but did he say *why* he was in such a state?'

Amy frowned in concentration. 'It sounded to me as if he was saying something like "everything is coming apart",' she said slowly. 'But John said I must have been mistaken; he said it was nothing like that, so I was probably mistaken. Roger was slurring his words quite badly.'

'Anything else you remember?'

'No. I turned the phone over to John at that point.'

'You say your husband had a council meeting that evening,' Tregalles said.

Amy grimaced. 'That's what made him so annoyed,' she said. 'He'd brought work home to prepare for the meeting, and it upset him to have to leave it to go into town. And he really did try hard to find Roger, because he was gone a long time, and barely had time to eat his dinner when he got back before he had to go back into town for the meeting. Upsetting for both of us, actually, because he went off in such a hurry that he took my car instead of his own, since it was already in the street and his was in the garage, and I was beginning to think he wouldn't be back in time for me to go to the end-of-term party at the school, and I didn't want to miss that. The teachers and staff usually get together for a bit of a do to celebrate the end of the school year,' she explained.

Tregalles looked puzzled. 'I don't understand,' he said. 'You say Mr Chadwell's car was in the garage, and yet you told us he'd just come home?'

'Oh, he always does that,' Amy said. 'John doesn't like to leave it out in the hot sun because it does something to the finish, so he puts it in the garage as soon as he gets home.'

While yours sits out in the blazing sun, thought Molly as she and Tregalles exchanged glances. 'Just to make sure I have the times right,' she said, making a show of writing something in her notebook, 'would it be fair to say that Mr Chadwell left within ten or fifteen minutes of taking the call from Mr Corbett?'

Amy frowned into the distance. 'Oh, yes,' she said firmly.
'As I said, he had hoped to get Kevin to go, but since Kevin
wasn't around, Stephanie talked John into going himself.'
For the first time since they'd arrived, Amy smiled. It was
a secretive sort of smile, and she sounded almost pleased as
she said, 'John tried to persuade Stephanie to go instead,
but she wasn't having any, and I don't blame her. Roger
could be quite a handful when he was drunk.'

'I'd like to ask you about another phone call your husband
received,' Tregalles said. 'Last Saturday morning.'

Amy Chadwell's eyes underwent a subtle change. 'Last
Saturday?' she repeated vaguely. 'What does that have to do
with poor Roger?'

'Perhaps nothing,' Tregalles told her, 'but it is of interest
to us. Mr Chadwell received a call from an old friend, I
believe . . .?'

'But why do you want to know about that?' Amy persisted.

'Perhaps we can deal with that later,' said Tregalles. 'Do
you remember the call?'

'Not the call itself, but John told me he'd had a call from
an old friend who was in town for a short time, and he was
going to meet him for a drink later that night.' Amy
Chadwell's voice was strangely flat.

'Did he tell you the friend's name?' Tregalles persisted.

'No, he just said a friend had called.'

'You say your husband said he was going to meet *him* for
a drink. Is that right, Mrs Chadwell?'

She nodded, but remained silent.

'Which wasn't true, was it?' Tregalles said gently, 'because
it was a woman who rang him that morning. But then, I
think you knew that, didn't you, Mrs Chadwell? Did you
know, or at least suspect, who the caller was?'

Amy looked down at her hands and shook her head. 'As
you say,' she said in a voice barely above a whisper, 'I thought
it might be a woman, but I had no idea who she was.'

'So this sort of thing has happened before?'

Amy raised her head. 'Yes, if you must know,' she said
defiantly, 'but I don't know why it is any of your business.
Why are you asking all these questions?'

'I'm asking these questions because the woman who made
that call and arranged to meet your husband was severely

beaten shortly before she was to have met him in a local pub. She was left unconscious on her kitchen floor, and wasn't found until the following morning. She was rushed to hospital, but it's only by the grace of God she's still alive.'

What little colour there had been in Amy Chadwell's face drained away. 'You're surely not suggesting that John had anything to do with that?' she said. Her voice was strained and she had trouble getting the words out.

'I'm not suggesting anything,' Tregalles told her. 'But I am trying to piece together the movements of anyone who might have been in contact with this woman. Do you happen to remember what time your husband left the house that night?'

'Just before ten,' she said quickly. 'I remember that distinctly because I go to bed at ten, but John usually stays up and watches television till midnight, but that night I switched it off before going to bed, because John had left by then. And he was back here again before midnight.' Amy looked pleased with herself. No doubt she thought she was proving their suspicions false, thought Molly, while in fact she might have just tightened the noose around her husband's neck.

'And he was extremely annoyed,' Amy continued, 'because the person he'd gone to meet hadn't turned up, and they hadn't so much as sent a message to say they couldn't be there, so the whole thing was a wasted journey. So, if this woman was attacked in her home, I don't see how you can think John had anything to do with it or why she's saying that he did. Who is this woman anyway?'

'Sorry, but we're not at liberty to tell you that,' Tregalles said. 'Although I can tell you that she was someone your husband knew quite well some years ago.'

'Well, I'm sure she's wrong, and there's been some terrible mistake. What possible reason would John have for doing such a thing anyway?'

'Perhaps because the woman was attempting to blackmail him,' Tregalles said. 'Threatening to expose him.' The words were spoken quietly, but their impact on Amy Chadwell was clearly visible.

'Blackmail?' she said with an effort. 'Oh, no. No, you

must be mistaken. I can't believe that. John of all people would never stand for anything like that. He would have gone straight to the police and have them deal with it.'

'Unless the blackmailer's allegations were true.'

'Allegations . . .?' Amy drew a deep breath to steady herself before attempting to speak again. 'What allegations?' she asked faintly.

'That your husband belonged to a gang that took part in several robberies and a double murder thirteen years ago,' Tregalles said bluntly.

Amy swallowed noisily several times before she was able to speak. 'I can't believe you're saying this,' she said faintly. 'I don't know where you are getting your information from, but it's completely—'

'From the woman herself,' Tregalles cut in, 'and your husband confirmed that she did ask him for money when we spoke to him earlier today. He denied attacking her, of course, but it seems more than a coincidence to me that the woman, who had asked him for money in the morning, was beaten and left for dead later that same evening.'

He leaned forward. 'So tell me, Mrs Chadwell,' he said, 'does this *really* come as a surprise to you? You knew, or at least suspected, that your husband was lying when he referred to his "old friend" as a man, and this wasn't the first time he had done this sort of thing, was it? Yet you didn't challenge him? You didn't object?'

Tregalles settled back in his chair. 'So what did you do, Mrs Chadwell?' he asked softly. 'Go quietly off to bed while your husband went off to see this woman? Or did you follow him to the house where this woman lived, and watch from a distance while he went in and—'

'No!' Amy Chadwell was shaking her head violently from side to side. 'That's not true! None of it is true. I never left the house, and John wouldn't . . . He couldn't . . . He didn't even meet her because she didn't turn up. He told me she didn't turn up when he came home. He said—'

'She . . . ?' Tregalles broke in quickly. 'He *told* you at that point it was a woman he'd gone to meet?'

'No, no, you're confusing me,' Amy said desperately. 'He didn't *say* it was a woman. He said his *friend* hadn't turned up, and he was annoyed because he hadn't so much as tried to contact him at the pub to let John know he wouldn't be coming.'

'And you weren't even curious enough to challenge the fiction that the friend was a man? I must say I find that hard to believe.'

'Well, it's true. As I said, John was annoyed and he was tired . . .'

'And it doesn't pay to ask questions when John's annoyed,' Tregalles said quietly. 'Isn't that right, Mrs Chadwell?'

Amy refused to look at him. 'I want you to leave,' she said shakily. 'I don't have to listen to this, so please go and leave me alone.'

The two detectives got to their feet, but Molly paused to look out of the window. 'Is that your car out there in the street, Mrs Chadwell?' she asked.

Amy eyed her suspiciously, clearly puzzled by the question. 'The silver Hyundai,' Molly elaborated. 'Is it yours?'

Amy nodded. 'Yes, that's mine,' she said cautiously. 'Why do you want to know?'

'Just curious,' Molly said as she followed Tregalles to the door. 'And thank you, Mrs Chadwell. No, please don't get up,' she said quickly as Amy started to rise. 'We can see ourselves out.'

'So what was that all about?' Tregalles wanted to know as they got in the car. 'Looking for a new car, yourself, are you, Molly? Spending that Sergeant's pay ahead of time, are you?'

'Take a look at the back of her car as we go by,' said Molly. 'See there? Just above the bumper, driver's side. Isn't that a Welsh flag? And I think you'll find there's a scratch along the side just as Mr Whitfield described.'

The knife slipped out of Amy's nervous fingers and clattered to the floor. She bent swiftly to retrieve it, and found her husband's eyes focused on her when she straightened up.

'First you burn the potatoes, though God knows how even you can manage to do that,' he said softly. 'Then you slop the tea, and now you can't even handle a knife? So what's going on, Amy. Tell me, what have you been up to?'

'Nothing. Honestly, John, it's just the heat. You know how

it disorients me, and the kitchen gets so hot with the sun coming in, and with the oven on . . .' She stopped. It was no use. He would sit there staring at her in that way that made her feel so utterly useless and inadequate until she told him. Amy closed her eyes and took a deep breath. Better to get it over with now, because it would only be worse if she tried to lie.

TWENTY-NINE

Friday, July 24th

They were gathered in front of the whiteboards for the morning briefing: Paget, Ormside, and Molly Forsythe, waiting for Tregalles to finish writing.

He turned to face them. 'I think that's everything,' he said with a quick look at Molly for confirmation.

'So,' he continued, 'if his wife is to be believed, Chadwell lied about the time he left the house after Corbett rang him, which means he had more than enough time to drive Corbett home and drown him in the fish pond. He must have gone back to the Unicorn *after* killing Corbett to ask if anyone had seen him so it would be assumed that he had only just got there from home.'

'And,' Molly added quickly, 'he used his wife's car, a Silver Hyundai Santa Fe with a decal of the Welsh flag on the back and a scratch down the side, which matches the description of the vehicle Judge Whitfield saw coming out of the Corbetts' driveway shortly after five o'clock the day Corbett was killed.'

Paget said, 'Didn't the judge say there was a woman in the car as well? Could that have been Mrs Chadwell?'

Tregalles and Molly looked at each other. 'I suppose it could have been,' Molly said doubtfully, 'but she told us her husband had taken her car when he went to see Corbett, and she was afraid he wouldn't have it back before she had to go out. I suppose she could have said that to throw us off, but that wasn't my impression at the time.'

'It's a possibility,' Tregalles conceded, 'but I'm with Forsythe on this one. I think Mrs Chadwell was pretty shaken when we told her about the blackmail, and I also think she's afraid of her husband.'

He turned to scan the boards to refresh his memory. 'We spoke to Linda Drake, the barmaid at the Green Man,' he continued, 'and she remembers Chadwell, because he kept trying to chat her up even though he could see she was busy. And she's quite sure it was closer to eleven when she first saw him at the bar. She said she thought there was something odd about him when he first appeared and pushed an empty glass across the bar and asked for the "same again". She told us she'd been working that end of the bar most of the evening, and she would have remembered if she had served him earlier. But when she asked what he'd been drinking, he said something like, "I suppose it's hard remembering everyone's drinks when it's late and you're rushed off your feet, but never mind, I'll have a whisky instead."'

Tregalles grinned. 'That was a big mistake on Chadwell's part,' he explained, 'because Linda's been in that job a long time and she's proud of her memory for faces and what people drink. She said she would have remembered him if for no other reason than he was new to the pub. She wondered why he'd done that, but she was busy, so she didn't think much more of it. When I asked her if she remembered anything else about him, she said he kept looking at his watch, and he volunteered the information that he was waiting for a friend, then complained about the thoughtlessness of "some people" when his friend failed to show up. He also made a point of mentioning the time when he left.'

'Sounds like he's a bit heavy-footed,' Ormside observed.

Tregalles nodded. 'Arrogant with it, too,' he said.

'So how did he find out where Jessop lived?' Ormside asked. 'The woman may not be all that bright, but surely to God she didn't tell him where she lived?'

'She swears she didn't,' Molly said, 'but she did identify herself, so we thought one way he could have found out was by talking to someone at the Rose and Crown.'

'So,' Tregalles cut in, 'we showed Chadwell's picture to Grady and Bridgette, Grady's current live-in girlfriend and barmaid, and Bridgette said she was almost certain it was the same man who had come in around noon that Saturday. She said there was quite a crush at the bar, and they were very busy, but she remembered him saying he hadn't been in the Crown for years, and the last time he was there he'd been served by a very pretty girl, and he wondered what she was doing now. So she told him.

'He was wearing a jacket and a baseball cap, which she thought a bit odd, because it was like an oven in the bar, and no one else was wearing a jacket.'

Ormside grunted. 'A bad actor and overdressed for the part,' he said.

'Maybe,' said Paget,' but *almost* certain isn't good enough, is it? Do we have any confirmation at all? Anyone else hear what was said? Any CCTV cameras in the area?'

'Sorry, boss, but no,' Tregalles told him. 'We checked.'

'Do either of you have anything to add?' Paget looked from Tregalles to Molly and back again.

Tregalles moved away from the boards. 'I think we should have Chadwell in for further questioning,' he said. 'In fact I think we should have both him and his wife in, and I think we have enough to get a warrant to examine Mrs Chadwell's car and search the house.'

'I agree,' said Paget, 'except we don't have enough evidence to justify a search of the house, so the warrant will be limited to the car.' He held up his hand as Tregalles opened his mouth to object, to say, 'I'll need a lot more than you've given me to justify a warrant for the house. If Forensic can find evidence that links the car to the Corbett killing in some way, then perhaps we can talk about searching Chadwell's house. Meanwhile, I'll need the details on the car.'

'I have them,' Molly told him, flipping through the pages of her notebook until she found what she was looking for. She handed the book to Paget, who jotted down the information and handed the notebook back.

'I don't want them to have a chance to talk to each other before we question them,' he said as he put his own notebook away, 'so I want Mrs Chadwell brought in first, and let's have some Forensic people there to take her car away at the same time. Her husband can be brought in later, but I don't want either one to know that the other is in the building, nor is Chadwell to be told we're examining his wife's car.'

He paused to scan the whiteboards one last time. 'I'll talk to Mrs Chadwell myself,' he said, 'so, Forsythe, you'll be with me for the interview, and you and Len can deal with Chadwell,' he told Tregalles.

Tregalles groaned. 'Chadwell's a pillock,' he said. 'Besides, Forsythe is better with him than I am. Can't we swop?'

'Afraid not, Tregalles,' Paget said. 'With the way things have been going, I don't want anything to go wrong, so I need another female in the room when I interview Mrs Chadwell.'

When Chadwell was brought in, he'd refused to say anything without his lawyer being present. Now, with Kevin Taylor sitting beside him in the interview room, he continued to deny having anything to do with the attack on Sharon Jessop, and he insisted that his wife was mistaken about the time he'd left the house.

'She never did have much of a concept of time,' he said with a dismissive shrug. 'Always late for things. You can't put any faith in anything she tells you when it comes to time. I'm telling you, I didn't leave the house until something like twenty past ten, and I was in the Green Man by twenty to eleven at the latest.'

'She told us you usually watch television between ten and midnight, but she remembers turning the set off before going to bed that night, because you had left the house by then.'

'Oh, God, that woman,' Chadwell said with a sigh of long-suffering. 'She fell asleep watching television while I was getting ready to go out, and she only woke up when I told her I was leaving and I wouldn't be late home. That's when she turned it off.'

'So what about the woman who served you at the Green Man? She says it was close to eleven when she first served you,' said Tregalles.

Chadwell shook his head impatiently. 'That was the *second* time,' he insisted. 'She served me when I first went in. Granted she was busy, so I suppose it's not surprising she didn't remember when I asked for the same again.'

'Except she claims to have a very good memory for people and the drinks they order, especially when they come in for the first time. Which was what made her suspicious when you tried to suggest that she'd served you earlier.'

'That's nonsense,' Chadwell said contemptuously. 'The woman just doesn't want to admit she's wrong.'

Ormside stirred. 'Funny, but it seems odd to me that no one other than you has a good memory,' he observed drily. 'What about the woman behind the bar in the Rose and Crown? Is she mistaken as well?'

Chadwell was quick to mask the shock that flared in his eyes, but it was clear to both detectives that he had been shaken. He cast a furtive sidelong glance at Kevin Taylor, but there was no visible response from the lawyer.

He moistened his lips. 'I told him,' he said with a nod in Tregalles's direction, 'that I hadn't been in the Rose and Crown for years, and I haven't, so I don't know what you're talking about.'

'Strange, but we have a witness who says otherwise,' Tregalles told him. 'Last Saturday around noon? Does that jog your memory, Mr Chadwell?'

'It isn't *my* memory that needs jogging,' Chadwell snarled. 'I'm telling you, I was nowhere near the Rose and Crown last Saturday or any other time in recent years for that matter.'

'So everyone is lying except you, is that it, Mr Chadwell?'

Chadwell sat back in his chair and folded his arms, but he didn't reply.

Tregalles tried another tack. 'You used your wife's car when you went to meet Roger Corbett at the Unicorn, didn't you?' he said.

'So? What if I did? Is there some law against that, too?' Chadwell asked sarcastically.

'No, but there are laws against murder, Mr Chadwell, and we have a witness who saw you in that car when you left Corbett's house *very* close to the time he was killed, and I'm wondering if you intend to claim that this witness was mistaken as well?'

Chadwell's eyes narrowed, his face a mask as he tried to hold Tregalles's gaze. 'I don't know what you're talking about,' he said as he turned to Kevin Taylor. 'Look,' he said, 'I don't know what they're talking about. I went down to the Unicorn to look for him, but he wasn't there. I went outside, searched the car park and immediate area for any sign of him or his car, and when I couldn't find him or his car, I went home.

End of story. And if they did have a witness to any of this, they'd have charged me by now.

'As for this crazy woman and her wild stories, the one who tried to blackmail me, I have no idea why she picked me as her target. The only reason I agreed to meet her at the pub was because I remembered her from our university days, and she was making such a balls up of trying to blackmail me, that I was curious. But as I told them before, she didn't turn up, so I went home.' Chadwell shoved his chair back. 'And I don't intend to sit here and be called a liar,' he concluded with a malevolent glance at Tregalles.

'Nor should you have to,' Taylor agreed. 'So, Sergeant, unless you are prepared to back your accusations by charging my client, I'm advising him to answer no more questions, and we are finished here.'

Tregalles would have dearly loved to charge Chadwell, but he had already stretched the truth when he'd said they had a witness who had seen Chadwell outside Corbett's house. 'Be that as it may,' he said, 'but we still need a formal statement from Mr Chadwell.'

'And you shall have it, Sergeant,' Taylor said blandly. 'But not now when Mr Chadwell is clearly being subjected to pressure. Perhaps tomorrow. I'm sure it can wait till then. So, unless there is anything else, I take it we can go . . .?'

'Cocky bugger,' Ormside observed laconically a few minutes later as he and Tregalles watched Chadwell and Taylor cross the car park, deep in conversation. The two detectives stood at the top of the main entrance steps, grateful for a breath of fresh air after the stale dead air of the interview room.

'Not quite as cocky as when he came in,' Tregalles muttered, still chafing at having to let Chadwell go. 'God! I'd really like to nail the slimy sod.'

'I meant his friend, Taylor,' Ormside said. 'Although they don't look all that friendly at the moment, do they?'

Ormside was right. Chadwell and Taylor had stopped to face each other as they reached Taylor's car, and Chadwell was clearly upset about something. He was waving his arms about and talking loudly – unfortunately not loud enough for the two detectives to hear what he was saying – but if Taylor's body language was anything to go by, he didn't like what he was hearing. He started to turn away, but Chadwell grabbed his arm and spun him round to face him. That was a mistake, because Chadwell suddenly found himself face down across the bonnet of the car, with his arm twisted behind his back.

'Reckon we could arrest them for brawling in a public place?' Ormside asked.

It was almost as if Taylor had heard him, because he glanced in their direction, then, still keeping Chadwell pinned down, he bent and said something to the struggling man before releasing him. He stepped back, straightened his tie, then got into the car. Slowly, Chadwell pushed himself upright and flexed his arm as if to make sure it was still working. Then he walked around to the other side of the car and got in.

'So, what's the next move?' Ormside asked as they went back into the building. 'Forensic says they won't have time to do anything with Mrs Chadwell's car until after the weekend, and we've had no success in finding anyone who saw Corbett and Chadwell together in the vicinity of the Unicorn, so let's hope the boss fares better with Mrs Chadwell than we did with her husband.'

'Not much chance of that,' Tregalles said glumly. 'I don't think she knows much more than we do. Even if she does and agrees to testify against him, she's not the sort who would do well in a witness box. She wouldn't last five minutes under cross examination.'

THIRTY

Behind the closed door of interview room number one, Paget and Molly Forsythe were still talking to Amy Chadwell. From the very beginning, Paget had done everything he could to put her at ease and assure her that she was only there to clarify some of the information she had already given before signing a formal statement.

But Amy sat stiffly in her chair, hands folded in her lap, fingers plucking nervously at the mother-of-pearl buttons on the cuffs of her long-sleeved blouse. Her eyes were watchful, and her face was even paler than it had been the day before, and her answers were far more hesitant and circumspect.

At first, Molly thought it was nothing more than nervousness. After all, it wasn't every day the police came knocking on your door, take possession of your car, and insist that you accompany them to the station. But it was becoming clear that something more was bothering Amy Chadwell.

Molly was still thinking about that when Paget asked Amy about her husband leaving the house to meet his 'friend' on Saturday evening. 'You told Sergeant Tregalles that your husband left the house just before ten—' he said, only to be cut off by Amy in mid-sentence.

'No, no, that's not right,' she said quickly. 'Sorry.' She flicked an apologetic glance at Molly. 'I was going to tell you. I remembered after you left; I was wrong about the time. I forgot I fell asleep watching television, and it was half *past* ten when I woke up, and John was just going out. I made a mistake. It was half past ten, not ten o'clock when he left the house.'

'You seemed to be quite certain yesterday that Mr Chadwell left the house before ten,' said Molly.

Amy looked away. 'Yes, I know,' she said huskily, 'but as I said, I forgot. It wasn't until John reminded me . . . I'm sorry if I misled you. It wasn't intentional.'

'Are you quite sure you aren't misleading us now, Mrs Chadwell?' asked Paget.

Amy shook her head, but she avoided his eyes.

'So you would be prepared to swear to that in a court of law if it comes to it?' he asked gently.

Amy Chadwell drew a deep breath. 'Yes,' she said. 'Yes, of course. It's the truth.'

'Very well then, Mrs Chadwell, let's leave that for the moment and talk about the other phone call, the one you received on Tuesday, July fourteenth, from Roger Corbett at approximately four o'clock in the afternoon.'

'I took the call but Roger wanted to speak to John,' she said quickly. 'As I said yesterday, I could barely make out what he was saying, so you would have to talk to John about that.'

'But I believe you were on there long enough to hear Mr Corbett say something like "Everything is coming apart". Isn't that right, Mrs Chadwell?'

'Did I?' she said vaguely. 'I'm sorry,' she said, looking at

Molly, 'but I was so surprised and shocked by what you were suggesting that I really don't remember what I said.'

'But I'm sure you do remember telling Sergeant Tregalles and DC Forsythe that your husband responded quickly to Corbett's plea for help, and he left the house within fifteen minutes of receiving the call. Is that not right, Mrs Chadwell?'

Amy looked down at her hands, frowning. 'I'm sorry,' she said again, 'but I really don't remember. Thinking about it now, I seem to remember John having to finish some work for the council before he left.' She spread her hands apologetically. 'John will tell you I have a terrible memory for things like that.'

'And a selective one as well,' said Paget thinly. 'Tell me about your car. Why did Mr Chadwell take it rather than his own?'

'He was in a hurry. His car was in the garage and mine was on the street, and he wanted to get back in time to finish his work for the—' Amy stopped, mouth half open, eyes wide as she realized what she was saying, and colour flooded into her face.

'He was in a hurry,' Paget said deliberately, 'because he knew he had to get to Corbett before the man did something foolish and started talking to us about what happened thirteen years ago. That is why he left right away, isn't it, Mrs Chadwell? He met Corbett at the Unicorn, then drove him to his house in your car, which was seen by a neighbour, and he drowned Corbett in the fish pond. We know a woman was with him, Mrs Chadwell, and I think that woman was you!'

'No!' Amy jerked backwards in her chair as if she'd been struck. 'I'm not listening to this,' she said shrilly. She started to rise, then clutched at her shoulder and sat down hard on the chair, face distorted with pain. She sat gasping for air as both Molly and Paget rounded the table to help her. Molly reached out to her, but Amy shook her head violently from side to side and tried to pull away.

'No, no, I'm all right,' she gasped, shrinking back in her chair. 'Really, it's just –' she closed her eyes – 'cramp,' she said breathlessly. 'It happens sometimes.'

Molly and Paget exchanged glances. 'I think it's a bit more than cramp, Mrs Chadwell,' said Molly. 'Please, let me look.'

'No, really, that's all it is. It took me by surprise, that's all,'

Amy insisted. 'I'll be all right in a minute. I just need to go home.'

'I'm afraid we can't let you do that until we've had a doctor examine you,' Paget told her. 'Our regulations won't permit it. Anyone who becomes ill or is injured during an interview or while in police custody must be examined by our doctor or taken immediately to hospital.'

'But I'm all right. It's passing. Honestly. Please, just let me go home.'

Molly, who had been watching closely, said, 'It's not just your shoulder, is it, Mrs Chadwell? It's your ribs as well. And your arm. Would you mind rolling up your sleeve?' She reached out to undo the buttons on the cuff.

Panic flared in Amy's eyes. 'You can't do this,' she panted. She jerked her arm away, but the sudden movement brought a sharp cry of pain, and tears spilled down her cheeks. The sleeve came loose and Molly pushed it gently up her arm.

Amy moaned softly and turned her head away. 'Don't,' she whispered. 'Please don't do this . . .' She said something else as well, but neither Molly nor Paget could make out the words.

'These bruises weren't there yesterday,' Molly said quietly, 'and I'm sure the other injuries weren't there either.'

Paget already had his phone out. He punched in a number. 'Paget,' he said when someone answered. 'We need a doctor immediately. Room number one.'

'And now,' he said, not unkindly, as he pocketed the phone, 'while we're waiting for the doctor, I think it's time you told us the truth, Mrs Chadwell, and the first thing I want to know is, who did this to you? And please don't try to tell us you got those bruises falling down the stairs.'

The ambulance had come and gone. Still trying to insist that she was all right, Amy had been overruled by the medical examiner and sent off to hospital, accompanied by a WPC.

'I believe that woman has been used as a punching bag long before this,' the doctor told Paget as he closed his bag. 'As for her most recent injuries, I'm surprised she was able to walk in here under her own steam. She must have been in a lot of pain, although from the smell of her breath and the feel of her hair and skin, I suspect she's been taking painkillers by the handful. I assume you'll be charging the husband?'

'Only if we can persuade Mrs Chadwell to testify that it was her husband who inflicted the injuries,' said Paget, 'but so far she's refused to do so, and I think it's unlikely she will.'

'It never ceases to amaze me what some women will put up with,' the doctor said, shaking his head sadly. 'It's at times like these I wonder if we did the right thing when we abolished public flogging. Anyway, let me know if he is charged. I'd be only too happy to testify in this case.'

THIRTY-ONE

Kevin Taylor sat drink in hand, watching the shadows lengthen as the fiery disk of the sun slid lower and finally disappeared behind the trees. It was a beautiful evening, but he was aware of none of it, because his inner eye refused to see beyond the scene that had taken place outside the police station in Charter Lane earlier in the day. Nor could he stop the seemingly endless tape that kept playing Chadwell's words over and over again inside his head until he thought it would explode.

He heard a sound, the light slapping sound of bare feet on tiles as Stephanie came up behind him and placed her hands on his shoulders. 'Problems?' she asked as she began to massage the muscles at the base of his neck.

He could smell the chlorine, and her hands were cool and damp. 'Did you enjoy your swim?' he asked.

'It was lovely,' she said. 'The water was just right.' She reached over his shoulder and took the drink from his hand. 'You should go for a swim before bed,' she said lightly. 'It would do you more good than sitting here brooding and drinking. You're very tense, and you've hardly said a word since you came home. Is John being difficult?'

'In a way,' Kevin said evasively.

'Would you like to talk about it? It might help.' Stephanie, still in her swimsuit, came around to stand in front of him.

His eyes swept over her body. If anything she was even more beautiful than when he'd first met her. Small wonder that detective Sergeant hadn't been able to take his eyes off her.

He shook his head and held out his hand for his drink. Stephanie hesitated. She was puzzled. This wasn't like Kevin; he rarely had more than one or two drinks in an evening, even at parties, but something was clearly troubling him. She handed him the glass.

Kevin drained it and reached for the half-empty bottle. He started to pour, then stopped. 'Perhaps it would be best to talk about it now,' he said. He put the bottle back on the table and set his empty glass beside it. 'Sit down, Steph, and I'll tell you what John Chadwell told me this afternoon.'

He didn't know how long he had been sitting there, but dusk was fading to black, and stars had been visible for some time. Steph was somewhere in the house; he could hear her moving about.

The sound didn't register at first, although he'd heard it often enough. It was the sound of the garage door going up, followed by the sound of a car being started.

'Where the hell . . .?' He sucked in his breath. 'Oh, God, no!' he whispered as he pushed himself out of the chair. 'Steph?' he bellowed as he ran through the house. 'Steph, no! For God's sake, stop!'

He reached the front door and flung it open in time to see the rear lights of his wife's car disappearing into the night.

John Chadwell sat in semi-darkness. The television was on, but he had long ago lost interest in the programme. He was still trying to work out what he should do about Amy.

The atmosphere inside the car as he and Kevin had driven from the police station to Chadwell's place of work at the town hall had been, to say the least, extremely tense, and when Chadwell had tried to say something before alighting from the car, Kevin had cut him off. 'You're a liar,' he'd snapped, 'and I don't believe you. So just shut up and get out!' He'd barely given Chadwell a chance to get clear of the door before slamming the car into gear and driving off, spraying gravel behind him.

Chadwell wanted some time to himself to think about what had happened that morning in Charter Lane, so instead of

returning to his office, he got in his car and drove straight
home.

Still chafing about the way the interview had gone – it had
really knocked the wind out of him when they said they knew
about his visit to the Rose and Crown – to say nothing of
Kevin Taylor's attitude afterwards, it hadn't helped his temper
when he'd found Amy wasn't there when he got home. He
tried to call her mobile, but she'd either switched it off or let
the battery die. Either way it was typical of the woman.
Scatterbrain, no thought for anyone but herself. Fuming, he'd
slammed the phone down and marched into the kitchen. He
was hungry, but thanks to the police, his lunch was still sitting
in the fridge at the office.

He'd made a sandwich and taken it and a cold beer into
the garden to sit in the shade of the apple tree and try to calm
down. But he'd barely settled himself in the wicker chair
before the woman from next door came out and pretended to
fuss with her flowers before she noticed him.

'Oh, hello, Mr Chadwell,' she said, feigning surprise. 'Is
your wife all right, then? Accident was it? The car didn't look
damaged when they took it away, but then, you can't always
tell, can you? Was she hurt? I mean she looked all right when
she got into the police car, but then, you never know, do you?'

Now, sitting here in the gloom, he felt once again the chill
that had gone through him when his neighbour explained what
had happened that morning: Amy's car loaded on to a trailer,
and Amy being taken away in a police car. He couldn't
remember what he'd said to the woman, but whatever it was
it had got rid of the nosy old cow, because she'd scuttled back
indoors and slammed the door behind her.

And then there had been the phone call from that surly
Detective Sergeant Ormside, telling him that Amy had been
helping them with their enquiries when she'd been taken ill.
He'd gone on to say that she was now in the hospital, where
it had been determined that she was haemorrhaging internally
due to multiple injuries to the body, and she was now in
surgery.

'Mrs Chadwell was unable to tell us how she came by her
injuries,' the Sergeant continued, 'and we were hoping that
you might be able to help us. Was she in an accident, do you
know, sir?'

His first thought had been to tell Ormside that any injuries Amy might have must have been caused by the police themselves, but instinct warned him to tread carefully until he knew more. After all, Amy couldn't have been hurt *that* badly, and the Sergeant had said she hadn't told them anything, so what were they up to?

'If she was, it must have happened while I was there at the station myself this morning,' he said, sounding concerned, 'so I don't know any more than you do, but I'll go down to the hospital immediately. And thank you for letting me know.'

'Just one thing, sir. We are concerned about how your wife came by those injuries, and we are hoping you can help us in this regard. So, if you wouldn't mind, sir, we'd like you to come by the station – after you've seen to your wife, of course, sir. Perhaps tomorrow . . .?'

'Yes, of course, Sergeant. And thanks again.'

Now, eyes closed, Chadwell recalled how his hands had shaken so much that he'd had trouble replacing the phone. *Had* Amy talked, he wondered? He pushed the thought away. No, she couldn't have or they would have been at the door by now. Besides, she wouldn't dare!

He hadn't wanted to go to the hospital, but he didn't see any way around it.

They'd had to remove one kidney, but he was assured that she'd make a full recovery. After having done his duty, he'd come home and spent much of the evening wandering about the house, or trying to watch television, and going to the window every few minutes to see if he could spot any vehicles he didn't recognize in the street.

Chadwell stood up and stretched and rubbed his eyes. It was getting late, but he knew he wouldn't sleep if he went to bed. He went to the window again. There were more cars in the street now, but then there always were late at night with residents returning after an evening out. He didn't really have anything to worry about, he kept telling himself, but on the other hand he wouldn't be able to feel completely safe until he could talk to Amy and find out what she had or hadn't said.

But then, there was her car. He'd almost forgotten that. Not that the police could learn much from it, but then there was always the chance that . . .

The doorbell rang. He pressed his face against the window, but all he could see by the light from the street was the blurred outline of a single person standing close to the door. If it was the police, and they had come for him, there would have been at least two of them, and there was no car standing by in the street. Frowning, he went to the door. 'Who is it?' he demanded.

'John, it's me, Steph. Open the door. Please. It's important.'

Still cautious, Chadwell put his face close to the opening as he slipped the latch and opened the door about an inch.

'Why . . .?' he started to say, but the words died in his throat as the edge of the door slammed into his face. He staggered back against the wall as Stephanie Taylor stepped over the sill. Dazed, he clutched at the wall for support. Blood ran from his mouth; one side of his face felt numb, and he could feel a loose tooth in his mouth. He tried to speak, but his tongue wouldn't work.

'You bastard!' she said softly. 'You just had to do it, didn't you? You couldn't keep your mouth shut, could you? I should never have trusted you. You're a coward at heart, John, always have been. A bully and a coward.' She shook her head as if in sadness. 'I should have done this a long time ago, but it's not too late. Say goodbye, John.'

He made a grab for the knife as it arced upward, aimed at the belly, and felt it slice through his flesh. Blood poured from the gash in his hand. He lashed out with his foot, missed and felt himself falling. He went down hard on one shoulder, shrieking with pain as his arm was torn from its socket. Writhing in agony, he could feel the warmth of his lifeblood draining away; watching in horror as it inched its way outward across the tiled floor.

Steph stood over him, then dropped to one knee, her eyes fixed on his own as if she wanted to make sure he knew what was coming.

The bitch is enjoying this! he thought tiredly. He squeezed his eyes shut, waiting for the blow that would finish it.

He screamed when something heavy hit his chest, smothering him, crushing him into the floor. He couldn't move. He opened his eyes to see Steph sprawled across his body, her face mere inches from his own. Her eyes were open, vacant, staring as rivulets of blood trickled from her battered head.

His vision blurred. Someone else was there, a dark figure holding the cast-iron umbrella stand that normally stood behind the front door. He tried to speak, but the effort was too much, and somehow nothing seemed to matter any more as darkness closed around him.

The young Constable taking calls in the Control Room looked startled. He hit the mute switch on his set and gestured to his Sergeant. 'I think you'd better hear this for yourself, Sarge,' he said. 'It could be a hoax, but I don't think so. I've got a man here who says he's just killed his wife.'

THIRTY-TWO

Saturday, July 25th

Kevin Taylor was formally charged with the killing of his wife. John Chadwell was fighting for his life in hospital, not so much from the loss of blood from his hand, but from a wound he'd suffered when the knife in Stephanie Taylor's hand had pierced his abdomen when she fell across his body. Kevin had made a tourniquet to regulate the flow of blood from Chadwell's hand, and called for an ambulance, but with Chadwell unconscious, the wound to the abdomen had gone unnoticed until the paramedics arrived. The damage was extensive, and the prognosis was not good.

Kevin Taylor had been remarkably calm, even relieved when he was taken into custody and the charge was read, but Paget, well aware of the man's reputation as a lawyer, insisted on him being cautioned once again for the record at the beginning of the formal interview conducted by him and Tregalles.

Taylor had smiled. 'There's no need,' he said wearily. 'I've been living with fear and guilt for thirteen years and I'm glad it's over. I killed my wife and I am well aware of the consequences, so go ahead and ask your questions and let's be done with it.'

The interview began just after nine o'clock on Saturday morning and went on for two-and-a-half hours. Taylor was given every opportunity to avail himself of legal representation, but he'd declined the offer. 'I don't need anyone,' he said, deliberately raising his voice for the benefit of the recorder. 'Besides, who in this town would want to represent me? Certainly not Ed Bradshaw after what I did to his daughter, and no one else would dare take on my defence.'

'In that case, let's get started,' Paget said, 'and tell me if I'm right. We're pretty sure that Roger Corbett and John Chadwell were members of the gang who robbed Bergman's jewellery store and killed two people, but were you also a member of that gang?'

Taylor nodded. 'And so was Steph,' he said, and went on to explain that the whole bizarre series of events that year had begun as a student prank. 'We were down from university for the Christmas holidays, having a few drinks in a pub one night, when someone mentioned a recent robbery where the man was caught within hours, because of some idiotic mistake, and we decided that any one of us could do much better. So we had another round of drinks and started talking about "the perfect robbery".'

Taylor fell silent, frowning slightly as if trying to recall the scene. 'Steph didn't say much at first,' he said. 'She just listened to us babbling on for a while, then proceeded to pick our plans apart, bit by bit, and said she could do better than the rest of us put together. So we challenged her to prove it – and she did.'

Tregalles eyed Taylor sceptically. 'Are you trying to tell us that the robberies were all your *wife's* idea?' he said. 'The baggy clothes, the flash cards, and remaining silent?'

'It's true,' said Taylor, 'and whether you choose to believe me or not, it was also her idea to use the iron bars as a means of intimidation.

'We thought it was brilliant,' he continued, 'but Steph wasn't finished. She said it was all very well for us to sit there in a pub, pissed to the ears, and talk about it, but we would never know if it would really work unless we tried it out. She said that she was prepared to put it to the test, and, to put it plainly, asked the rest of us if we had the guts to follow her.'

Taylor made a face. 'I make no excuses for my part in all

this,' he said. 'Even pissed as I was at the time, I could hear warning bells going off in my head, but I was very much in love with Steph, and there was no way I was going to appear to be a coward in her eyes. I suspect the others had misgivings as well, but in the end we all agreed.

'But the one thing we lacked was transport, a getaway van and driver, and once again it was Steph who came up with the answer. Barry Grant. The kid was a whizz with cars, and we all knew he'd stolen cars as a youngster. He'd always fancied his chances with Steph and he'd do just about anything she asked of him.'

Taylor stopped to massage his temples with his fingers. 'Any chance of a cup of tea?' he asked. 'I'm getting a bit of a headache, and my Paracetamol tablets were taken away with the rest of my things last night.'

Paget nodded to the uniformed Constable seated by the door. 'See what you can do,' he told him. Then he said, 'Interview suspended at nine twenty-eight for a short break,' and shut off the tape. He sat back and studied Taylor, who had his eyes closed. He was puzzled by the lawyer's apparent willingness to tell them everything. He must realize better than most that he was facing a life sentence, yet it didn't seem to bother him.

'*Is* it just a headache?' he asked Taylor. 'Or is it something more serious?'

Taylor opened his eyes and shook his head. 'It's stress,' he said. 'I'm finding this harder than I thought it would be, but I'll be fine once it's over. Will it take much longer?'

'That very much depends on you, but there will be questions.'

Taylor nodded. 'I understand that,' he said. 'And thanks for the break.'

Tregalles sat fiddling with a pencil, brows furrowed as he tried to work out what was going on. Taylor was no fool; he must understand that he was digging his own grave, and yet he didn't seem to care. Paget seemed to be taking it at face value, but there had to be something behind it. After all, the man was a lawyer, and as far as Tregalles was concerned, you couldn't trust any of them.

The tea came, together with a couple of tablets, and the interview resumed.

'The Rose and Crown was chosen,' said Taylor in answer

to Paget's question, 'because John Chadwell had been out a
few times the previous summer with the landlord's daughter,
and he knew how they cashed up each night. The night of
New Year's day was chosen simply because there would be
three nights' takings on the table.

'We all went back to university, feeling very smug and
proud of ourselves for having pulled it off, and I thought that
was the end of it, but when we were all back home again
during the summer holidays, Steph started prodding us to do
at least two more robberies to prove that our success with the
first one wasn't just a fluke. She even had the next target
picked out: the weekly poker game at the home of Walter
Roach, which she knew about because her father had been a
regular player there at one time.'

Taylor sipped his tea. 'The second robbery went like clock-
work as well. Barry hid the van in the shed behind the Grant
house until it was time to get rid of it, and we divided the
money between us, equal shares.' He wrinkled his nose as if
in distaste for what he was about to say. 'I should tell you
that when the plans were first discussed, the proceeds of the
robberies were to be returned anonymously to the victims, but
because we all had very large student loans, greed raised its
ugly head and that idea soon went by the board.'

'Is that why you decided to rob the jewellers next door to
the bakery?' asked Paget. 'The lure of all that money, the
jewellery, the gold, the silver, which I'm sure you must have
known about, either from your father or Sam Bergman
himself?'

Taylor nodded. 'I knew about it, of course,' he said, 'but
once again it was Steph who took that knowledge and put it
all together, and it became the next target. To tell the truth,
the idea of doing something like that so close to home scared
the hell out of me, but Steph talked me round as she always
did.' He sucked in his breath. 'I know I should have shown
more backbone, but I couldn't back out without appearing to
be chicken, and I wasn't prepared to take the chance of losing
Steph, so I went along with it, and so did John and Roger.'

'And Barry Grant,' said Paget. 'We know from the notes
he left behind, that he was on lookout in the lane. But he must
have been facing away from the bakery, because he didn't see
your father come out and go next door. He said there was a

struggle and someone's ski mask came off. You were inside, so tell us what happened.'

Taylor looked away. 'It was Steph's,' he said. 'Suddenly Dad was there right next to Steph and it stunned us all. I don't think any of us could believe it, and it wasn't until he grabbed Steph and ripped her ski mask off that any of us moved.

'Of course he recognized her straightaway,' Taylor continued. 'He had her by the throat, and I can still remember what he said to this day. He said, "You thieving little bitch! You're just like your father. And you thought you were going to marry my son?" Then he slapped her across the face so hard it knocked her down.'

Taylor took a deep breath and looked straight at Paget. 'I didn't stop to think,' he said. 'I had the bar in my hand and I simply lashed out blindly. He fell forward, hit his head on the corner of the counter, and went down next to Steph. There was blood all over his head. Emily Bergman started to scream and John hit her to make her stop, then kept on hitting her until she was dead. Then Roger was sick all over the floor. It was sheer pandemonium in there.

'Steph scrambled to her knees and felt for a pulse on Dad's neck, then she looked at me and shook her head and said, "I'm sorry, Kevin, but he's dead."'

Taylor picked up the mug of tea and drained it, then held it with both hands as if to warm them. 'It was a nightmare,' he said. 'I couldn't think, I couldn't speak; I couldn't move, and Steph finally had to scream at me to take Roger out, while she and Chadwell stayed behind to "take care of things".

'I don't remember much of the next twenty-four hours. We changed clothes in the van, then they dropped me off where I'd left the delivery van, and I just sat there, trying to calm down and pluck up the courage to go back to the bakery.

'I remember the police being there in the lane when I got there; I remember my brother telling me that Dad was dead, and I remember I was scared to death for fear David would figure out the real reason I'd asked him to cover my rounds for me that morning.'

Taylor set the mug aside. 'As I said, I don't remember very much about the rest of the weekend, but it was late Sunday evening when I received a call from Steph. She said she was parked a short distance down the street, and we had to talk, so I went out to meet her there. She said Barry was panicking, and something had to be done to persuade him not to do anything foolish. She'd arranged to meet him in the big shed behind the Grant house, where the van and the proceeds from the robbery were stored, and she wanted me to come with her.

'Shortly before we got there, Steph said perhaps it would be better if she talked to Barry alone. She said she thought she might have a better chance or reasoning with him; that he might feel intimidated if both of us were there, and I was only too happy to agree with her.

'We stopped some distance away from the house, and Steph went the rest of the way on foot. I don't remember how long she was gone, but when she returned, she was driving the getaway van, and she looked pretty shaken up. She said that Barry had confronted her with a loaded shotgun. He said he'd made up his mind; he intended to go to the police in the morning and tell them everything. Steph said she tried to talk him out of it, but the more she talked, the angrier he became. She made a grab for the gun. They struggled and it went off, killing Barry.'

'Are you sure it wasn't the other way round?' Tregalles said. 'It seems to me that your wife – sorry, your girlfriend as she was then – is being blamed for just about everything now she's dead. It seems more likely to me that it was you who went to meet Barry Grant and it was you who killed him, then set it up to look like a suicide. I've met your wife, and I can't see her doing anything like that on her own, especially back then. She couldn't have been much more than a kid herself. What was she? Nineteen . . . twenty, maybe . . .?'

Taylor smiled tiredly. 'Twenty-one,' he said, 'and I don't blame you for wanting to believe the best of her. Steph is . . . *was* very persuasive, and I should know. God knows I made myself believe everything she told me for years. And I believed her then, because I *wanted* to believe her, and—'

'You said Stephanie returned with the van?' Paget cut in firmly. 'Please carry on, Mr Taylor.'

'That's right. She drove the van and I followed in her car to the old strip-mine in Collier's Wood, where we set fire to the van, then drove back to town.'

'What happened to the money, the jewellery, and the rest of the proceeds from the robbery?'

A dry, mirthless chuckle rumbled in Taylor's throat. 'Good question,' he said. 'Steph told me that Barry must have hidden it somewhere else, because she'd searched the shed and there was no sign of it. I believed her at the time, in fact I believed it right up until last night. But perhaps I can come to that later, because everything changed after John Chadwell and I left here yesterday afternoon.

'We were walking to the car when I told John he would have to get someone else to defend him if he was charged with the murder of Roger Corbett and the beating of Sharon Jessop, because I believed he was guilty in both cases. He became angry, denied it and tried to bluster his way out, but when he saw that wasn't working, he admitted I was right about Mrs Jessop, but not about Roger, and his only regret was that he hadn't made sure that Sharon Jessop was dead.'

Taylor looked away. 'And that was when he said if I didn't defend him, he would make sure that Steph would go down with him, not only for the death of Roger Corbett, but for killing my father as well. He also threatened to take me down as well, saying that he would swear that I had known what Steph was doing from the beginning.

'I refused to believe him,' Taylor said. 'At least, I didn't *want* to believe him, and yet I knew I couldn't leave it there; I had to talk to Steph and find out if what he'd said was true.'

He fell silent for a long moment, reliving once again a painful memory. 'You see,' he said at last, 'John told me that Steph had lied to me from the very beginning. He said my father was stunned but alive when Steph told me he was dead. He said she lied deliberately to make me believe that I had killed my father, then told me to get Roger out of there to get me out of the way so she could "finish the job properly", as she told me yesterday.

'And there was more. John said he was sure it was Steph who reacted to the reopening of the investigation by attempting to burn down the Grant house in case there was something to be found there. I didn't think to ask Steph about that last night, but I'm sure he was right. It would be one of those things that "had to be done".'

Kevin looked up at the ceiling, more to avoid looking at

either of the two detectives than for any other reason. Then he continued. 'John then went on to tell me about Roger,' he said quietly. 'John said when Roger phoned him after you talked to him in his office, he phoned Steph immediately to warn her that Roger might break down and start talking. He said she never even hesitated. She told him to meet her in the car park behind the Unicorn in fifteen minutes. Once there, he said Steph phoned Roger and told him to come out to his car, where she would be waiting to take him home.

'He said Roger was barely able to walk by then, so the two of them bundled him into the passenger's seat of his own car, and Steph drove him home, while John followed close behind. When they got there, Steph told John to stay in his car and be ready to drive her back to town once she'd dealt with Corbett. He said she was gone about twenty minutes, and when she came back she was dripping wet, and spent most of the time on the way back drying herself off. He said she didn't tell him what she'd done, except to say they wouldn't have to worry about Roger any more. Back in town, he said Steph picked up her own car and went home, while he went into the Unicorn to ask if anyone had seen Roger. He stayed just long enough to make sure everyone would remember the time, then went home himself.'

Taylor fought hard to control his voice as he went on. 'I tackled Steph about it last night. I told her everything that John had said, hoping against hope that he had made it all up and she would deny it, but I had to know.'

He ran his tongue over his lips and there were tears in his eyes as he said, 'She admitted it. Never batted an eye. She said, "It was necessary, Kevin. It had to be done, so I took care of it. If your father had left there alive, we would have both been finished. Careers and future down the drain. I knew you didn't have the balls for it, so I took care of it." As for the killing of Roger, she said the same thing. It had to be done.

'She was very calm, very matter-of-fact. She told me she had killed Barry for the same reason, to protect us both, and she took the proceeds from the robbery and hid them until she could recover them later.'

'So how did she dispose of the jewellery and the gold?' asked Paget.

'Bit by bit in Amsterdam when she went to visit her relatives over there. She said they ripped her off over there, because all she got was eight thousand for the lot when it was worth at least twice that much.'

Paget and Tregalles exchanged glances. So much for the claim the Bergman's had made.

'What prompted her to go after Chadwell?' asked Paget.

'I suppose I did, when I told her he'd threatened to take us both down,' said Taylor. 'She reacted as she'd always done. John posed a threat, so he had to go. Unfortunately, I was still sitting there trying to understand how Steph could be so matter-of-fact about what she'd done, and trying to understand how I could have been so blind for so many years.' He shook his head sadly. 'Wilfully blind,' he ended huskily.

'It wasn't until I heard the garage door go up that I realized where she was going and what she was going to do. I followed, but got there just a bit too late.'

'But how did she think *you* would react to another killing, especially after admitting to killing your father and allowing you to think that you had done it?'

'I think Steph believed that I would never betray her, no matter what she did. And with good reason, because I have always been so afraid of losing her that I have gone along with virtually everything she ever asked of me.'

'But why kill her?' Tregalles asked. 'Why didn't you just pull her off Chadwell instead of bashing her skull in with that iron stand?'

Taylor turned to look at him. His cheeks were moist, his face was pale, and his eyes were like chips of ice. 'She had to be stopped,' he said, 'no matter what the consequences. The killing had to end. Besides,' he added with a wry twist of the mouth, 'I knew that sooner or later she would see me as a potential threat, and Steph was nothing if not practical, so I would have to go. This way, for once in my life, it was *my* choice, not Steph's.'

THIRTY-THREE

Monday, July 27th

The breakfast tray sat untouched beside the bed. Amy didn't feel like eating after being told that John had died during the night. It wasn't that she was in shock, or anything like that; in fact she wasn't conscious of feeling anything at all, except, perhaps, relief.

It was just that there was so much to think about now that he was gone; so much to do; so many decisions to make. Thank goodness it had happened at the beginning of the holidays, because it meant she would have at least a month to deal with things before she returned to school.

If she returned to school . . .

The thought surprised her. It seemed to have come from nowhere. She started to dismiss it, then paused. After all, the house would be hers. John had a good life insurance policy; there would be something coming from work, and she could sell his car, so chances were there would be enough to pay off the mortgage on the house, or at least reduce it by a considerable amount.

And it was big enough.

Amy pursed her lips as she thought about it. She'd always dreamed of running a play school. Parents, especially working parents, were always looking for somewhere to leave their younger children, and there were never enough facilities to meet demand, so why not? She was a qualified teacher; she'd taught small children for years, and her last review at school had commended her for her after-hours work with the little ones as well, so there should be no problem there.

Amy winced as she put her hands behind her head and closed her eyes, but she barely noticed the pain. Her mind was racing. If she knocked out the wall between the living and dining room . . .

*   *   *

'Never did get a chance to question Chadwell before he died,' Tregalles told Ormside. 'He never regained consciousness. I went to the hospital again last night, hoping he'd come round, but he never did, so I packed it in at eleven, and I'm told he died around three this morning.'

'Still, what Kevin Taylor said about what Chadwell told him about the killing of Roger Corbett seems to be checking out,' said Ormside. 'Forensic found wads of tissue and pond residue under the passenger's seat of Mrs Chadwell's car, and they found a pair of stained trainers belonging to Mrs Taylor in the laundry room of Taylor's house. They think there's a good chance that they were soaked when she was drowning Corbett, so they're testing for a match.

'They also found a pair of heavy gardening gloves in Chadwell's garden shed. The weave matches the pattern on some of Sharon Jessop's bruises when she was first taken into hospital.'

Tregalles pulled up a chair and sat down. 'I'm not sorry to see Chadwell gone,' he said, 'but I still can't make up my mind about Taylor. If what he told us about his wife is true, then I can almost feel sorry for him. But he must have known, or at least suspected, that some of the things she told him weren't true, and yet he let himself believe her.

'Mind you,' he continued, 'I can see it in a way. You never met her, did you, Len?' Tregalles rolled his eyes. 'Well, I did, and I can tell you, she was one *really* good-looking woman, and she must have been something to see thirteen years ago. I think I'd have been ready to believe anything she told me back then.'

'You still would,' Ormside said bluntly. 'Is it true Taylor could have made bail, but refused it?'

Tregalles nodded. 'That's right. And unless he decides to change his plea to not guilty, he'll be going away for a very long time.'

David Taylor staggered along the hallway, under the weight of a large cardboard box, to the sun room at the back of the house. He set the box next to the others then sat down on it and mopped his brow. 'That's the last one,' he gasped. He glanced around. 'Sorry about the mess, Claire. I'll have it sorted in a couple of days. What is the temperature anyway?'

'In the shade, about thirty-one,' Claire told him, 'but it must be twice that in that old van of yours. I hope your paints will be all right.' She popped the tab on a can of beer and handed it to him. 'That should help,' she said, and opened a can for herself.

He raised the can in a gesture of thanks and drank. 'I packed them in the cooler, so they'll be fine,' he assured her as he wiped his mouth. 'And thanks for everything, Claire. I really don't know where I would have gone if you hadn't offered me this. And the light in here is fantastic.'

David took another drink. 'They let me see Kevin this morning,' he said abruptly. 'Ten minutes, that's all they'd allow us. I still don't understand what happened. I can't believe that he was a member of that gang, although it does explain why he wanted me to cover for him that morning, and the way he was acting before and after Dad was killed. I wanted to ask him so much, but as I said, we only had ten minutes. But Stephanie . . .?' He shook his head. 'It doesn't seem possible that she could have done the things the police are saying she did, yet Kevin says it's true.

'Funny,' he went on, 'she was always nice to me, pleasant and all that, and she and Kevin seemed to be so right for each other, and yet I could never quite take to her; never felt completely comfortable in her company. Don't know why; it was just a feeling. What did you think of her, Claire?'

'Oddly enough, my feelings towards her were very much the same as yours,' she said. 'As you say, she was always pleasant, but I couldn't escape the feeling that she had control of the strings, and the rest of us were puppets. Silly, I suppose, but that is how I felt.'

'I don't think it's silly at all,' David said seriously. He took a long pull at his beer, then set the can aside. 'But this isn't getting me unpacked and settled in, is it? Do you think this is going to work, Claire? My living here I mean?'

'We'll just have to see, won't we?' Claire said lightly. 'But right now I'd better get the dinner started. You must be famished after what you have done today.' She left the room and went into the kitchen, with the question still rattling around in her head. Would things work out for both of them? Only time would tell, but she was going to do everything she could to make sure that they did.

* * *

'Hard day?' asked Grace as she greeted Paget at the door. 'You look tired. I was hoping that things would ease up a bit now that Kevin Taylor is behind bars, and the case is all but closed.'

He kissed her. 'Oh, they will,' he said. 'There are still the usual loose ends to be sorted out. You know what it's like, but Tregalles and Ormside will take care of most of those. As for me, I have something else to think about.'

'Such as . . .?'

'Such as the future,' he said. 'I had a call from Chief Superintendent Brock just before I left. He told me that Alcott is in hospital, the psychiatric ward. It seems he's had a breakdown, and there's no telling when he'll be back – or if he'll be back for that matter. Brock didn't give any details, but he seemed to think it unlikely, and he's asked me if I want to continue on as Acting Superintendent until we know for certain.'

'Which you're doing now,' said Grace, 'so what's the problem?'

'The way Brock sees it, whoever takes on the acting position will be the most likely candidate for the permanent job if Alcott doesn't return. So, if I accept, I would have to be willing to take on the job permanently in that event. If I'm not prepared to take it, then he would move someone else in who would be.'

Grace frowned. 'But wouldn't they have to post it when it comes to filling the position permanently?'

'Technically, yes, but you know how it works, Grace. Unless the person who's been acting makes a complete mess of things, he's got a head start on everyone else, so it would be a commitment.'

Grace stepped back to search his face. 'So what did you tell him?' she asked.

'Nothing yet. He told me to think about it and let him know.'

'It's a good step up,' Grace said cautiously.

'It is,' he said, 'but it would mean I would have to spend a lot more time behind a desk and leave the street-level stuff to others, and I'm not sure I'm ready for that. I like what I do, and I like the people I work with.'

'So, when do you have to give him an answer?'

His mouth twitched. Grace couldn't tell if it was meant to be a grin or a grimace. 'Tomorrow,' he said. 'First thing. So guess what we're going to be talking about over dinner tonight?'